Stopping Power

An Agent Carrie Harris
Undead
Thriller

GJ Stevens

A note from the author

It all started with my first novel, *Fate's Ambition*, a speculative work about an average guy who could make people believe anything he wanted with just a touch.

Whilst using his ability to track down a friend who disappeared, he soon drew the attention of a powerful but secretive group seeking to keep the world's powers in balance. In walks Agent Carrie Harris, and I soon fell in love with the borderline sociopath crowned with strawberry blonde hair. She's an intelligent and ruthless killer, with a complete inability to know who not to fall for.

Then the undead arrived in a page-turning series as our heroes rushed to get away from the stinking hoards ready to eat your flesh. A fun romp to write and devoured by the fans.

It was a fan who first planted the seed. Rosanne is her name. What would happen if the two worlds collide? How would Carrie deal with everything turned on its head? If you read on, you're going to find out.

GJ Stevens

BRASS PIKE

1

"They're all dead. That's what she said."

Dressed only in a hospital gown, Agent Fletcher sat on the edge of a low camp bed and stared through sheets of thin plastic hanging from the tent's white canopy. He'd long given up trying to make out the features of the man he knew only as major and who wore a yellow hazmat suit with a bulbous head covering as he sat on a chair beyond.

"Major. She was… she was… covered in so much blood and holding a mangled length of steel pipe with blood dripping from the end."

The major leaned forward on the canvas chair, his breath condensing on the clear plastic in front of his face.

"Was Agent Harris injured?"

Fletcher shook his head. "She shrugged when I asked, but there was so much blood, it was inconceivable that none of it was hers."

The major nodded. "Other than her appearance, how did she seem?"

Straightening the gown around his legs, Fletcher lowered his brow as he thought back, even though barely a couple of hours had passed since he'd found her. Eventually, he shook his head. "Spaced out, I guess. Where is she?"

"In another room getting checked out. Then what happened?"

"She stepped toward the car. I got out and I told her help was on its way. She looked around as if searching for who I'd brought with me, then she asked for my weapon." His voice quavered, and he stopped talking, coughing into his fist.

The major sat up a little straighter. "Take a minute, Agent Fletcher. Do you mind if I call you Colin?"

"Sure," Colin replied as he looked up from the canvas groundsheet.

"How long were you with her before we arrived?"

"About half an hour," Colin said, wiping his mouth on the back of his hand.

"Did she say anything else?"

He nodded slowly then clenched his eyes shut. "She told me everything."

The major leaned forward, the plastic suit rustling as he did. "It's very important you tell me what she said from the very beginning."

After a pause, Colin opened his eyes and nodded.

2

I'd just come off a forward air control training exercise at RAF Lossiemouth, marvelling at Tornados flying low over the mountains. Anyway, I got the call from the Ops Centre, and after apologising for the tasking just as I was due to head home and put my feet up in the Beacons, the desk officer told me about a secure research station which had lost all comms. Protocol meant they needed someone to knock on the door and check everything was okay before they sent the engineers in.

I was the closest asset with sufficient clearance and I'd be on site only for a few minutes, not that I'd ever turn down an assignment.

With what I had left of my compact field kit, and a Range Rover borrowed from the base, I decided it might be nice to take a trip through the beautiful countryside. The shuteye on the plane could wait until later.

Having been told not to hurry, I took my time, welcoming the warmth inside the car. It must have been a couple of hours before I arrived at the unmanned outer gates, and after using the combinations they'd provided on the locks, I drove around the dirt track beneath the tree canopy, looking for signs or anything that would give me a clue as to where I should head.

With no obvious buildings, I must have driven for half an hour at least until I saw the house.

It was a pretty standard place, much like you'd find on any average street, and if it wasn't for the earlier locked gates, I would have put money on being in the wrong place.

I checked my phone for bars again, knowing of course if there was signal, those at the facility would have used it to check in.

With no other choice, I stopped at the house. There was no path leading up to the front door, just unkempt grass with no sign of recent footsteps. After glancing to a CCTV camera peering out from the eaves, I waved, expecting the locks to click, or for someone to open the door with a greeting.

When nothing happened, I peered in through the window, a little taken aback to find what looked like a show home from the eighties, as if no one had touched it in years.

Despite being sure it was just some forgotten building on a massive government estate, I went to the boot of my car, opened the field kit and pulled out the compact Glock 26. Adding a spare magazine into my jean's pocket and a short pry-bar, I would have taken the small torch but the batteries died on the last day of the exercise.

Deciding against grabbing a second magazine, I pulled the boot shut, and turning back to the house, I realised it wasn't beyond the sadistic bastards back at the Ops Centre to set me up on a training exercise, even after the week I'd just had.

Either way, I wasn't going to hang around. If the doors weren't open, I was putting a window in.

Giving them a little more time to see me on the CCTV, I lingered outside, peering through the window at the brown carpet and magnolia wood chip walls throughout. In the open plan living room, a deep TV sat in the corner above a bulky VHS player. With a line of thick video cases, I couldn't help but notice how much it looked like the pictures of my parent's quarters when they married.

The double-glazed windows were the only sign the place hadn't been left to rot for the last twenty years.

Walking around the outside of the house, I checked both the front and back doors. Finding them locked, I pried the glass from the pane beside the front door without a fuss.

Dust hung heavy in the stale air as I climbed in, noticing there were no photos, or ornaments, or trinkets. Nothing told me anyone had ever lived there.

The kitchen was much the same, and able to see most of the ground floor from where I stood, guilt tugged at my insides at what I'd done to the window. About to climb out and tour the forest in search of where I was supposed to be, I spotted a slight pathway depressed into the carpet pile.

Leaning to the side to get a better angle, I peered along its path which ran from the front door, snaking around the kitchen units before heading to what I guessed was the hallway.

With growing intrigue, I stepped along the route and through the kitchen door, stopping as it ended at a doorway underneath the stairs.

With my ear close to the wood, I listened.

Hearing nothing, I pulled it open to find, other than a gas and electricity meter on the left wall, it was an empty cupboard, but the track in the carpet continued as if heading straight through the opposite wall.

With a gentle push, the wall pivoted open, springing back at my touch, the hinges squeaking as I pulled it wide. I stepped toward the darkness beyond.

Finding a pull cord hanging from the ceiling, I tugged, freezing on the spot when the light disappeared past the missing floor only a step ahead.

3

Leaning forward, I frowned at a rusted steel ladder clinging to the discoloured concrete wall of a snug round shaft heading into the darkness.

With no sign of another switch or cord to light up the rungs heading into the void, I thought back to what I'd brought with me, and what I'd left in the car. I had no batteries for the torch, and the matches were long burnt from so many campfires in the mountains.

Back in the kitchen, I found the drawer and cupboards empty, their insides not even lined with dust, as if never used.

Shaking my head, ideas came and went, dismissing each until I had only one left.

I glanced around the living room, searching for anything the size of my hand, but with no clutter, the only things I saw were the VHS cases underneath the TV.

I pulled one from its home.

Back in the cupboard, I held the tape over the opening, and for the first time I took notice of the cover. Stephen King's Pet Sematary, a film I'd never seen, and for a moment I wondered what it was about until I let it fall down the hole.

The plastic shattered almost before I started counting. Two stories, or thereabouts, I guessed. Then, sitting on the floor of the cupboard, I shuffled across the carpet, dangling my legs into the darkness.

After climbing down the first few rungs, finding it easy enough to place my feet with some accuracy, I tried to figure out how far remained, realising I'd guessed one step too many when my foot couldn't find where next to place.

Holding on with just my hands, my legs dangling in the air, I listened whilst I lowered until I reached the last hand hold.

With no other choice but to drop, despite only having a vague idea of how close I was to the ground, I bent my legs and let go.

My boots crunched the shattered cassette, and pushing my hands out for balance, I stood staring into the darkness with only a single red LED shining ahead of me.

Tracing circles with my hands out in front, I stepped forward and felt a tacky pull against the sole of my boot, the other the same as it followed. I imagined the floor covered in a layer of treacle, until my foot slipped in places.

Waving my hands in front of me, I edged toward the pin prick light as I fought the floor's pull. When my hand touched the LED, I traced its contours with my index finger, feeling the outer dimensions of a box and soon found the raised edge of a switch.

The lights flickered on as I pressed, covering my eyes with my hands. But as my vision adjusted, I turned around, not able to look anywhere but at the chaos of footsteps in the blood covering the concrete floor.

4

Pulling my gun from the holster and pushing my arms out at forty-five degrees, I turned, looking around the small room where my gaze fell to the bloody plastic shards of the VHS case and the black tape strewn by the wall. A broken chair lay as a pile of wood on the floor, with blood-soaked papers scattered everywhere, their writing just visible. With no immediate threats, I turned on the spot to take a second look.

Formed of raw concrete, the room was no great surprise, nor was the heavy bulkhead door standing wide beside the light switch. To my left, a floor-to-ceiling cage partitioned off a third of the space, its wire bulky and uneven with so many years of paint. A door of the same construction stood open in its middle and inside was just a simple, rugged case with the top hinged open.

Bloody fingerprints smeared its green surface, and the four empty foam inserts confirmed my suspicions, even before I spotted the discarded cardboard of a cartridge box torn along one edge.

Looking back to where I'd dropped from the house, I realised I'd lowered myself a little further than one and a half times my height. On the wall beside the hole, a bright yellow stepladder lay flat, strapped to the concrete with a yellow and black sign at its side.

IN CASE OF EMERGENCY.

Turning back to the heavy door, I raised the gun level, lifting my chin whilst taking a slow breath through my nose, but found nothing lingering in the air except for the tang of blood and stale dust.

A camera peered out from the high left corner beside the door, but I was more interested in tracing the footprints in the blood heading through the opening and beyond, out of sight along the illuminated corridor. With no other choice besides leaving the way I'd arrived, I followed the prints running parallel to tracks that looked like someone had dragged something through the mess.

With the soles of my feet sticking with every other step, and slipping in between, I reminded myself how much blood there was in men.

Beyond the door with my Glock taking the lead, I didn't linger or stare at the green over-painted doors, which without windows, would look at home in a Victorian prison, if it weren't for the bloody smeared handprints.

Each door had a number stencilled in white paint on the top third, but with no words printed to describe what waited beyond, I moved on. It was more important to find who'd caused this chaos, or a comms station and survivors, in that order.

Stepping through the bend, a door at the end stood open, almost blocking the corridor.

Whilst staring at the white number ten on the green paint, and taking another step, my foot slipped, sending something pinging against the wall. Despite already guessing what I'd kicked, I bent down but didn't pick up the blood-caked nine-millimetre shell casing.

Looking up, more brass littered the floor ahead, and I had to pick my way through the mess, testing each step before I put my weight down.

Arriving at the open door, I eased my way through the gap between the door and the wall, and with only a quick glance to my right as the corridor opened out further along, I squinted into the room with just the light cast from the corridor. Glass-fronted fridges hummed along the back wall, the room much the same size as the one I'd dropped into.

I leaned in to the room, finding a light switch to the right, and I used the nose of the Glock to press against the blood-smeared plastic.

After wiping the gun along my jeans, I stepped back. Amongst the bent steel pipes scattered on the floor and cracked computer screens, glass carpeted the concrete, all sitting in a rainbow slick of liquid beside crumbled yellow and black biohazard signs.

The fridges were empty, and I guessed it was their former contents that formed the slick by my feet. Despite the signs, I didn't cover my mouth, figuring it was already too late.

About to step back into the corridor, keen to get away from the room, my gaze fell on a rugged red container much like the one I'd seen in the cage, apart from the bright colour. Yellow and black hazard warning triangles clung to each of the sides, along with a white sticker the size of an envelope covered with writing I couldn't make out.

I looked away, then around the room whilst shaking my head. Despite the box having nothing to do with my objective, I couldn't leave without seeing what the label said.

I peered at the writing again, squinting as I stepped right up to the edge of the sticky, colourful liquor, but it was no good. Pushing my mouth and nose into the crook of my elbow, I edged forward, crunching glass under my weight.

As I leaned in as far as I dared, the bold black letters MAO told me the package had passed through a Brazilian airport, but much of the rest of the writing was too small. The numbers told me it was the second of three boxes, each with a different destination based on what I thought might be addresses on the rest of the page, but there was no way I was getting any closer to check.

Eventually I stepped back and out of the room, turning toward the end of the corridor and taking in the much larger room further along with another open bulkhead standing opposite.

The room was about double the size of the other two I'd seen; the floor soaked with blood and scattered with broken furniture and debris I couldn't identify. Across the wall to my right, a bank of six monitors hung in two rows, each screen busy with black and white static, dashing my hopes of checking the place out with the cameras. My mood climbed when below the monitors was a digital radio base station, beside which was a laminated red A4 sign displaying just two words.

Brass Pike.

To its side, another sign showed an aerial plan of the complex, with numbered locations for each of the fifteen cameras.

The building was the shape of a tee, and where I stood, the three arms met. Each of the two corridors I hadn't yet been down had the same kink. The drawing showed the other corridors were much the same size but with different configurations of rooms. The one to the right was labelled as an exit in bold letters.

Behind me stood another wide-open door with a similar, but wider corridor beyond, heading off in the same fashion.

A red light on the radio confirmed it had power, and I picked up the handset. Watching as the LED turned to green, I pressed the talk button, speaking with as little volume as I dared.

"This is Brass Pike, urgent. Is anyone receiving?"

5

When a deep, male voice boomed from the tiny speaker, I scrabbled with the volume knob, silencing the noise to a whisper. Twisting around, I pointed the Glock at each of the corridor entrances. Whilst trying to ignore the voice, I kept as still as I could, listening.

With a shake of my head when I'd heard nothing of concern, I turned back to the radio, edging the volume a little higher and spoke in a whisper.

"This is Brass Pike. Please repeat."

After a moment of silence, the voice came back.

"Brass Pike, this is Iron Temple. Who am I addressing?"

"Iron Temple, this is Red Unicorn."

There was a short pause before the voice came back. "Received Red Unicorn. Pass your message."

"Brass Pike is not secure. Alphas unaccounted for, but it looks like they're a loss. Suspect blue x-ray or x-rays, but I have not confirmed this. Biohazard protocols breached. Send urgent assistance with hazmat capabilities."

"That's all received Red Unicorn. Are you safe?"

"Negative. Sweep incomplete…"

Hearing movement in the corridor at my back, I turned, lingering with the pistol outstretched.

When the sound didn't repeat within a few breaths, I pushed the microphone back to my mouth. "Will return asap to update."

"Received Red Unicorn. Help is on the way. Eta twenty minutes to your location."

Twisting the volume to the left, I turned around, peering along the pistol's sight to the corridor forming the long edge of the tee.

After a moment, I relaxed my aim, lowering the gun as I spotted distinct pairs of footsteps mixed with the jumble of prints in the mess. The tracks didn't follow the streaks of blood along the corridor, instead veering off to a short door to the left and up to what looked like a cupboard.

Taking care to be silent, I stepped up to the door, gripping the handle whilst doing my best not to touch the smeared blood.

With a twist and a sharp pull, the door opened, but the sight of a gun's muzzle rushing out from the darkness sent me slipping on the mess just as rounds exploded out and I fell backwards to the floor.

6

As the third bullet showered me with concrete dust from behind, the pistol, a Glock 17 from what I'd seen, clicked empty, the slide locking back. I jumped to my feet, surging forward and grabbing the hot barrel in my left palm, snatching it from the hold of a wide-eyed man, his face smeared with blood. For a second, he kept his arm outstretched as if he still held the gun.

Dropping his weapon to the floor, I grabbed him around the scruff of his polo shirt, pushing the muzzle of my 26 to his cheek.

Shaking so violently, I thought he might fit. When he tried to speak, he couldn't get the words out.

"I'm so sorry… I thought…"

Shaking my head, I pushed the barrel harder, enough to stop his noise, then yanked him into the light. He pushed his pale hands out, screaming as he tried to get free from my grip whilst attempting to move back into the shallow cupboard.

With his feet slipping in the mess, I jabbed my fist into his throat to shut him up, pushing him to the ground face first and keeping him there with a foot on the small of his back.

As he gasped for breath, I dropped my 27 into my pocket and looked across the contents of the cupboard, peering at pipes and wires and shelves stacked with so much.

Spotting a ball of string, I had his wrists and ankles bound within a few moments, then quickly turned my attention to wiping the blood from the floor off my hands, but having dried, it clung like glue.

Looking behind me, I raised a brow at the three small craters in the concrete above where I'd been standing, then looked down to the scared little man.

Despite how he'd reacted, I couldn't imagine him being responsible for what I'd seen and a clang of metal down the corridor was enough for me to know I was right.

Seeing the guy still struggling for breath, I had him up and pushed back in the cupboard within a moment. With his face and white lab coat covered in blood, he looked such a sorry sight as I gripped him by his upper arms and spoke quietly right up in his face.

"What happened?"

He didn't reply, other than to shake his head, his eyes widening when a scream echoed from somewhere behind me. I shoved him backward, pushing the door closed as a single gunshot shocked my ears, the sound seeming to be everywhere at once.

After drawing my gun and running as fast as my slipping feet would let me, I tried to slow as the break in the corridor approached.

Stumbling forward, my feet on cubes of glass all over the floor, I leaned to the left, looking partway along the corridor and to a space where a glass door should have been.

Halted by my shoulder slamming into the kink in the corridor, the jolt sending the Glock clattering to the floor, I was about to bend down to sweep it up when I peered around the corner to bays with beds beyond the half glass walls.

With medical equipment and a wide dark monitor at each head, my attention left the inside of the room when toward the far end of the corridor I saw a naked man standing hunched over, his torso covered in blood as he pulled his hand from a convulsing body leaning up against the wall.

For a moment I squinted, unsure what he held, then somehow stopped myself from gasping when I saw the cavity in the victim's chest and whatever he held dripping a dark liquid.

7

Unable to look away, my mouth gaped open as my gaze followed thick black veins tracing his body whilst he stared back, his expression hanging slack as if unsure at what, or whom, he was looking at.

I blinked, my lids heavy as the body he'd crouched over fell out of sight.

Despite knowing survival almost always came to those who reacted first, I felt helpless to move. Only as the man's mouth widened, his eyes narrowing and teeth slamming together, could I bend over, reaching for my weapon.

After gathering up the gun in one swift movement, the composite slick with blood and mottled with clinging glass cubes, I raised my aim, watching as the heart dropped from the man's grip, slopping to the mess at his feet as he bounded towards me.

The hours on the range, the months in the field, and my confidence in my weapon kept my breath steady and my aim level at his centre mass as I pulled the trigger three times in quick succession.

When he didn't even flinch, despite knowing I'd made perfect shots, I fired again, watching the hole punch into his shoulder.

Still he kept coming. Knowing I only had four rounds left, I turned and with my feet wheeling along the bloody concrete floor as I tried to run, I reminded myself I'd read about this kind of thing before in a handful of after-action reports.

Those people were jacked up on drugs, so high they felt no pain, the body's signals blocked from getting the reports of catastrophic damage to the brain. All I needed to do was give his physiology the time it needed to react, and he'd drop dead before I'd left the corridor.

Navigating the crook, I pushed myself the short distance to the middle room, but when I heard something heavy thud against a wall, I pulled up, slowing to turn to where I'd expected him to have collapsed. Instead, he was still upright, pushing off the wall as he came around the corridor with his mouth wide as if with a silent roar.

Raising the gun, I fired again, aiming the shot to the left of where I'd already mangled his chest, hoping he was one of the few whose heart wasn't in the normal place.

Making another perfect shot, he didn't falter. Instead, his speed built and I shot again, the slide locking back too soon.

I didn't wait for any delayed reaction, and with my feet still slipping in the bloody debris, I ejected the magazine and pushed home the spare as my options raced through my head.

I could head back the way I'd arrived in hope I could jump high enough to catch the bottom rung and pull myself up before he gripped my legs, whilst assuming he couldn't climb in his state. But I knew that wasn't a real choice and so I slipped and slid towards the right-hand corridor where I hadn't yet been.

Slapping at the wall with my free hand for extra traction, I was through the doorway just as a high scream cut short in its prime.

Using the kink in the corridor ahead to stop myself, I glanced back, raising the gun, ready to empty the magazine.

He hadn't followed and the sickening crunch of bone told me what had slowed him down.

I bounded back, retracing my steps, not hesitating when I saw the bloody man facing me in silence, his mouth open as he held the guy from the cupboard so high off his feet, his neck at an angle that shouldn't have been possible.

The wet tearing of flesh and the fabric of the white lab coat broke the silence as, with a single jerk, both arms came free from the body, the wrists still tied together as the rest of the man fell to the floor.

I fired, aiming right at the abhorrence's head, not knowing how many shots I'd taken until the empty click echoed.

8

Its foul body fell to the floor, the head unrecognisable, leaving behind a mess of blood, most of which splattered against the wall behind.

I stared for a long moment with the empty Glock pointed at the remains, panting as I waited for it to move.

There was no chance I could refer to it as human after what I'd seen. How could any person take that much punishment and still keep rushing forward?

When it hadn't risen for a long while, I turned, searching out the radio, desperate to know how long it would be for backup to arrive.

As I stepped to the console, my stomach knotting, I remembered how long it had taken me to find this place. If they were to get to me quickly, then I'd better call and give directions, making sure they brought shotguns, flamethrowers and high-powered assault rifles.

About to pick up the handset, I span on the spot, steadying myself when I almost slipped in the drying blood, recalling the earlier sound of gunfire; a reminder I wasn't the only one left alive in this place.

Peering down the only corridor I'd yet to explore, the same kink as in the others hid where I'd need to head, both to get to the exit marked on the plan, and to find who'd taken the shot.

With a step in that direction, I once again fought the need to rush to where I'd entered this damned place. But I was a professional with a job to do, and despite my fear, I couldn't leave someone alone. Not again.

Realising the gun in my hand was empty, and with no spare magazines, I dropped it into my pocket and looked around the room, hoping to find something I could use as a weapon.

When nothing presented itself, I remembered the broken steel pipes in the room behind the green door and retraced my route. Holding my breath as I arrived, I pulled a pipe from the sticky mess, giving only a passing thought of what it was covered in.

After heading back to the start of the corridor, gripping the pipe two-handed, I closed my eyes, listening for any sound.

The place was silent, apart from the gentle hum of the lights, and I stepped into the corridor, soon reaching the kink, looking up when it seemed darker than the rest of the space.

Unable to control a shiver, dried blood covered the strip light's diffuser, a splatter of red across the surface.

I turned around the kink, finding the corridor much like the first one I'd seen. With green doors on either side, light streamed from the furthest away which stood ajar.

The corridor ended in a room much like where I'd dropped into, only with a bright yellow bulkhead door and a wheel handle in its centre. The yellow paint had faded at the edges, the rest battered and bruised, exposing the light primer in several places, but I was more interested in the green sign above.

EXIT.

I sped forward whilst taking care with my steps, slowing just as I got to the ajar door. Moving against the opposite side of the corridor as far as I could, my knees almost gave way when I pulled it wide and looked in, quickly turning from the floor piled two or three high with naked bodies, only looking back when in the corner of my vision I saw a man close to the threshold holding a revolver, a Colt Python, next to what remained of his head.

With his finger tight on the trigger, propellent filled the air, mixing with the stench of blood and bodily fluids.

About to reach down and grab the gun, I spotted movement towards the back of the room. It took me a moment, but after seeing the chewing motion of their mouth, the black veins spidering across their face, I realised I wasn't looking at a victim.

Before it turned to me, I swooped my hand down, at the same time dropping the pipe. Just as it clattered to the floor, the sound echoing across the room, I had the Colt wrenched from the dead hand and pointed right between the eyes of the creature, my finger already pulling the trigger.

The hammer clicked against the metal, and I saw the empty chambers as I felt the blood drain from my face.

9

Dropping the gun, I turned, sweeping up the steel pipe by my feet as I ran, my legs like a cartoon character's wheeling for traction whilst glaring at the exit I had to open before that thing untangled itself from the bodies.

Despite arriving at the door within a few moments, as soon as my hand tugged at the curved metal handle and it wouldn't budge, I knew I needed more time.

Hearing movement in the corridor, I dropped the pipe to get a two-handed grip on the wheel, but even after straining with all I could give, it moved only the smallest amount.

Feeling a presence behind me, and before I could grab the pipe from the floor, I turned around, pulling back at the blood running from its mouth as it reached out, swiping at the side of my head and sending me to the floor.

With stars across my view as I lifted my head from the concrete, I swept my arms either side in search of the pipe. When my hand curled around its length, I felt a sharp stab of fingers digging into my side, pinching so hard as if at any moment it would rip flesh from my bones.

I jabbed out with the pipe one handed, hitting the bloodied knuckles which held me in its grip, then again when the creature didn't flinch. Relenting, it snatched its hand away and I fell back, only then realising it had me off the ground.

With no time to think, its hands were back out and coming towards me.

Scrabbling backward along the floor, I rushed out of its reach, hitting out, swinging the pipe as it strode towards me. Jumping to my feet, I swung again left and right, batting at its hands despite its steps. I couldn't help feeling it was playing games and at any moment it would lunge, and I'd be powerless to protect myself.

But I didn't give up. Spotting the pipe's end battered flat, I jabbed it out, watching as it drew blood when I struck the thing's hand.

After pulling away, I hit harder this time and it stopped its advance when the pipe slipped into the flesh between its thumb and forefinger, the weapon still embedded.

Jumping away unarmed, my back hit the wall. I had nowhere to go.

With a contorted expression, it glared at me, raising its hands as if to lunge, but mustering every ounce of reserve, I charged forward, my shoulder hitting in the centre of its chest.

It didn't budge, its arms wrapping around my upper body, but I bent at the knees, turning just as the hand with the embedded pipe swept in from the side, rushing at my face.

Before it made contact, I pushed out my hands, grabbing at the pipe and yanking it free. Then, turning and standing in one fluid motion, I pivoted with all my weight and plunged the end into its eye socket.

I felt barely any resistance as it slipped in, the metal halting only as it hit the back of its skull. The remaining eye shot wide, and the creature fell to its knees where it held for a moment as I stepped out of from its limp grasp and yanked the pipe from its socket.

Shoving at its shoulder, it fell backward.

With the echo of my breath the only sound, I stared at what lay on the floor, only stepping away when I remembered the door.

I didn't rush, taking considered steps, then heaving the wheel with everything I had left, letting go when daylight broke through the opening.

10

"And you saw Agent Fletcher when you came outside?" the man in the hazmat suit replied through the plastic hanging down between them.

Carrie nodded, her face impassive as the plastic-suited nurse ran the wet gauze across her cheek.

"Were there any survivors?" he said, lifting his chin.

Carrie shook her head.

"Did you get them all…" he added, but stopped.

Before she could answer, a scream tore through the background noise, followed by a rapid volley of gunshots.

"I guess not," she said slowly, shaking her head. "Now you better tell me how many other sites got the same delivery?"

CONTACT

11

His hair was longer, more ragged and a little lighter, but with so many years off the radar, it wasn't a surprise. Still, the man who slipped through the train station's turnstile was the right height, just under six feet, and clearly hadn't been scoffing down on cake since the final photos in his file, a condensed version of which I'd reviewed on my phone.

His face was a little more tanned, the lines a little deeper, but he was still every bit the grey man whose success littered the pages.

Cold coffee touched my bottom lip as I drew up the cup, but it was the gesture I was interested in and not the taste. Lifting the newspaper I hadn't read a single word of, I glanced at the mobile phone on the table in front of me and sent a message to Clark.

Contact.

The word conveyed my congratulations and celebrated that he'd been right. The target had indeed come out of hiding that very day, risking everything he'd worked for since going dark just because his daughter was getting married the day after.

Within a second, the phone rang, sounding off only in my hidden earpiece. Sliding my finger across the screen, I didn't speak.

"I have him on CCTV," Clark said. Despite his rolling Welsh accent, I heard no sense of excitement as his words reminded me this wasn't the place to move to the next phase.

Letting my inner smile settle, I watched the target glance to the line of three minicabs waiting at the nearby rank, and then along the street leading to the centre of town, before looking at his watch and changing direction, taking the few short steps to a phone box.

Clark soon confirmed the target had not dialled a number, despite the motion of his fingers, his mouth opening and closing as he leant against the glass, glancing at the line of passengers filing in and out of the station entrance.

I couldn't help but wonder if it was just the legacy of our shared occupation, or if he knew someone would be coming for him.

Only after he replaced the receiver as the bustle from the station died, leaving the phone box to stroll along the road towards the town, did I down the remains of the cold coffee. Folding the paper and leaving it on the table, I headed through the door and out into the air, the temperature suiting my thin dark jacket.

With Clark narrating the journey from screens almost two hundred miles away, I kept the target at the edge of my vision, only increasing my pace as I lost him from view, leaving me just with the commentary. After hearing he'd stepped into a florist, I drifted to a stop outside a Post Office.

Staring at the travel advice in the window, at first I concentrated on the words, knowing I couldn't let my thoughts drift, needing to be ready at any moment. Despite my efforts, the stark reds and yellows of the ad soon sent me back to the figure riddled with my bullets as I gripped the empty Glock, watching the thing lift one foot across the bloodied floor, followed by the other.

Desperate to run, my feet stuck to the tacky floor as my pounding heart sent adrenaline sparking through every nerve.

Still, in the back of my head I knew I'd survived, but despite the three days that had passed, I couldn't help but scream with terror on the inside.

Clark's voice shattered the vision, and with a deep breath I glanced down at the pavement, feeling more than a little regret I hadn't told Devlin I wasn't over what happened in Scotland.

But that's what I'd said, knowing my place was on the street, not alone with my thoughts and an arsenal of weapons at my disposal.

What good could he have done when Franklin left me in no doubt I wasn't to discuss the details of what happened with anyone, not even Clark?

Clark's friendly voice repeated his words and this time I took note, but glancing at the poster, I wondered, perhaps for the first time, if I was the kind of person who could bask in the Spanish sun beside a pool all day.

The target was on the move and easy to spot in the window's reflection, where I watched him heading down the street carrying an enormous bunch of flowers.

I didn't turn and soon I congratulated myself for my decision when, without warning, he stepped through the door of a café, only to peer out from the tall window.

Within a moment, he was back on the street, playing out the last steps of a surveillance detection route filled with double backs and needless course changes he'd started many hours before; none of which mattered because I knew where he was headed to.

I turned, following along the long row of terraced houses whose doors opened out onto the street. I stayed well back, watching as he walked past the address of a daughter he probably didn't think we knew about. An illegitimate child conceived whilst in service, the bond strong enough to risk all he'd achieved in the last few years.

After rounding the corner, he was soon back in sight and heading towards me. If I hadn't stayed away, I'd be right in his path, and not in the background with the rest of those going about their business.

With his knock at her door, I knew I'd stayed hidden, and as I stopped beside a tall white van, bending over to tie my shoelace, I watched his caution vanish as, after a slight hesitation, he pressed into his daughter's embrace.

Slipping in through the passenger door of the Mercedes Sprinter van, I pulled it closed behind me, heading between the thick curtain covering the gap where the middle seat should be and felt the thick carpet pile beneath my trainers.

With a single press of a switch, the screens lining the interior lit up the darkness.

12

With a clear view of the daughter's front door filling the far left monitor, and in the light of the screens alone, I slipped off my blue trainers with great care, not wanting the van to rock even though the active suspension set itself hard when stationary.

Leaving my phone on the desk, gone was the thin black jacket and the short blonde wig as I let my strawberry blonde hair fall past my shoulders before shaking it out to give it some air.

Keeping one eye on the far left screen, I uncoiled myself from the holster under my arm and stripped off the blue jeans and white t-shirt, taking my time to fold and place everything in one of three kit bags in cubby holes held in place with cargo webbing.

In my white bra and knickers, I looked way from the screen and bent over, pulling at the two Velcro straps securing the combat blade. Holding the knife, which was only just shorter than my hand, its length warm from my heat, I stared at the blotched, yellowing bruises covering most of my upper arms then traced its route across my ribs and legs before it stopped just above my knees.

Feeling a weight in my eyelids, I pulled a sharp breath, turning to another bag before grabbing black leggings and sliding them on. The pain in my muscles reminded me things could have ended so differently as I rolled the leg of my leggings high above the dress's hem.

Taking a blue vest top, I soon pushed it back, realising it could be weeks before my skin didn't draw attention. Instead, I tugged on a long sleeve pink t-shirt.

Slipping on a floral summer dress, the kind I would never wear except at gunpoint or when I wanted to look like anyone but myself, I buckled a thin belt around my middle, topping it off with a reversible denim jacket before tying my hair up. A jet black wig which came to just above my shoulders completed the transformation.

With the press of my thumb and the turn of the numbered dials, I raised the lid of an attaché case, not bothering to hold back my smile. Placing the Glock in its empty foam mould, I took the much smaller Ruger LCP from beside it, pulling back the chamber just enough to make sure the brass sat where it should.

After savouring its weight in my grip, I slipped it into a pouch sown into the dress at the small of my back.

With a flick knife from the second level of the case in my jacket pocket, I released the webbing of the next cubby hole along, pulling out the container and placing it at my feet as I peered over the collection of handbags, clutches and rucksacks. Taking a bag about the size of a wash kit I'd previously packed tight with everything I might need, I stuffed it into a cream clutch, followed by the bag's straps, still wondering how women got things done when they carried these things around.

With the clutch inside a pink rucksack with dainty straps, I placed it on the desk next to the controller for the camera system. Reaching for the chair from towards the rear doors, I dragged it along the rail in the middle of the floor it fixed to.

Sitting, I grabbed my trainer, but rather than slipping it on, with care I picked at the outer edge of the material where the fabric wall met the sole and when I was sure I'd loosened only what I needed, I pulled away the thin blue covering, like peeling off sunburnt skin, and discarded the sheet to the rubbish bin, repeating the process on the other before slipping on the newly white trainers.

Pushing back in my seat and shuffling to stop the pistol jabbing into my back, I lifted my legs, resting them on the desk as I drew a deep breath.

Staring at the daughter's front door, I couldn't help but wonder how safe my target felt whilst drinking tea, listening to all her news as she filled him in on the many years they'd lost.

It didn't take long for my eyes to close, but they snapped open within a few seconds and I stood holding my breath, trying to feel if the van had moved.

After convincing myself all was okay, I knew I had to find something to keep me awake, knowing that despite not being able to sleep for more than a few hours since Scotland, now would be just the time for my body to want to shut down.

Rifling in a drawer under the desk, I found a wireless earpiece. After turning it on and off several times to get it to connect, and blowing away the dust, I pushed it into my ear. With a few commands tapped into the computer, I glared at the screen, willing a passer-by to cross in front of the house so I could test the system.

It took half an hour before they did, but with the old couple making their way along the path, and a tone ringing in my ear, I knew I could relax. With a smile, I watched them doddering across the view, stepping into the field of three of the other cameras as they chatted and laughed whilst holding each other's hands.

When they were out of view, I glanced at my phone sitting on the side and felt an almost overwhelming need to dial Clark's personal number. He'd be home from the centre, or in the accommodation, depending how late he'd finished, but either way he'd be off official channels and out of the earshot of those around him.

We'd been through so much together in the decade we'd worked side by side. He saved my skin every day with his diligence and insight. He knew everything about what I'd had to do over most of the years of my career; everything that is, except for what happened in Scotland.

If I picked up the phone, no one would know, but I just couldn't bring myself to deliver the burden. If telling him everything made him understand what I'd gone through, he'd never be the same person again.

Closing my eyes, I thought about sleeping, but knew my body would deny me if I tried, instead sending me back to Brass Pike. I went to the drawer where I'd found the earpiece, plucking out a book before leaning back in the seat and thumbing with care through the pages of the Jane's

Guns Recognition Handbook, two editions out of date.

I let the words push away the fear that I'd never be able to close my eyes again without being transported back to that place.

Darkness had fallen before I'd turned the hundredth page. With barely a chime in my ear in that time to disturb me, I absorbed myself in the detail of each weapon system.

It was another hundred pages or thereabouts before my eyelids grew heavy again.

Placing the book on my lap, I let myself relax, but I knew it was a mistake even before I drifted back to where I sat on the bed with the man in the hazmat suit staring at me as he dismissed the screams coming from outside. He ignored the gunshots, and apparently didn't agree with my concern about which other sites received the same mysterious delivery from Brazil.

I knew he was lying, but if they didn't want my help then I was glad to get away from that place as soon as they let me.

My eyelids flew wide and I stood, placing the book on the desk as I stretched out each of my limbs, savouring the pain that softened each day.

After taking a sip of water from a bottle I'd opened at some point in the night, I was about to sit and reach out for the book when something caught my eye.

Looking up at the left-hand screen, at first I saw nothing but the daughter's front door. But then movement came from the next few screens as a figure stood at the passenger door, peering into the cab.

Still standing, I tapped the side of my jacket pocket for the reassuring weight of the knife and watched as the figure with a dark scarf around the lower part of their face moved to the next screen and around to the back of the van.

At first I assumed it was a young man, but I knew not to presume and the thought fell away when I saw they carried a battered crowbar as they halted to stare at the rear lock surrounded by a stainless steel plate.

Not able to stop myself smiling, the figure lifted the

crowbar toward the lock as I carefully stepped along the length of the van, slipping out of the passenger door and out into the chill of the night air.

Hearing the scrape of metal and with my hand curling around the knife in my pocket, I walked along the side of the van, watching as the man's head snapped up, his eyes wide. But, rather than running, his feet seemed fixed to the spot.

About to stage whisper for him to clear off, the tone ringing in my ear changed everything and forced my wide smile to drop.

13

Gripping the body of the flick knife in my fist, I drew my hand from my jacket pocket, keeping the blade in its home as my knuckles connected just behind the masked stranger's cheek sending his feet from under him.

I lurched forward, dropping to a knee and grabbing the crowbar from his loosening grip just before it clattered to the road as he collapsed.

Holding my breath, I pushed the knife back into my jacket, my eyes closing for a split second as I thought about my options.

The chime couldn't tell me who'd set off the alert. It could be the target leaving under the cover of darkness, or just revellers heading home from a late night.

With the silence of the early morning still unbroken, I had to assume it was my light-footed quarry. Looking down at the figure, I knew that despite his dark clothes and being well in the shadow, even a group of drunk guys would probably notice the body.

After placing the crowbar behind the wheel under the van, I grabbed an arm and heaved his weight over my shoulder. Thankfully he seemed to be mostly skin and bones, and with the tone going off a second time, I moved along the side of the van, making the most of its cover whilst trying not to grunt with the effort.

Thinking several stages ahead and knowing I might soon be on my target's tail again, I glanced down at the floral dress and denim jacket, kicking myself that they weren't the clothes you'd expect someone to wear out for a stroll at four in the morning.

Hearing faint footsteps for the first time, and despite still straining under the weight, I glared forward, trying to think what I'd do if they decided to cross over the road. I might have no choice but to execute my orders sooner than I'd chosen.

With the footsteps growing louder and the body still

limp over my shoulder, I edged further along the van, peering at the target address in search of any sign, perhaps movement or lights, a twitch of the curtain or anything that should change what I'd planned.

Seeing no cause for concern, and with the steps receding the other way, I crept forward, laying the figure between the next two cars, placing him on his side with care and moving his head, arms and legs into the recovery position.

Feeling breath on my hand, I pulled down the scarf and found a face covered in acne and thin wisps of a first beard.

Not lingering on what I'd found, I peered along the pavement and past the van, nodding to myself when I confirmed a figure in the distance looked like my target walking toward the town.

With a glance down either side of the dark street, I opened the van door with care. Inside I rewound the images, confirming what I'd suspected. Then, taking my phone from the desk, the screen blank as I'd expected, I tapped in the code, my thumb hovering over Clark's number.

Knowing he'd be asleep and not wanting to deal with the night cover, I sent him a message for when he woke.

Target on the move. Get rid of the van.

Still taking care to keep my movements precise, I pulled the nested bags from the desk and hooked the straps onto my back before grabbing a puffer coat from a rack and a black cap at its side, tucking the skirt of my dress into the belt, then rolling down the leggings.

After pushing my hair into the cap and killing the monitors with a press of a switch, I set the auto-lock on the van and closed the door, only moving away when I heard the near-silent click.

Peering along the street whilst staying as close to the van as I dared, only just able to see him against the darkness, I crossed the road before jogging in my target's direction.

Despite the boiling heat under the coat, the bag hitting my back and ribs, and the gun slapping against the small of my back with each stride, I stared ahead on my side of the road whilst keeping track of the target in my peripheral vision, not speeding when he slipped out of view at the edge of town, turning a corner in the opposite direction of the railway station.

Knowing the first train wouldn't leave for at least another hour, the buses the same, and the cabs almost impossible to get hold of so early, I was confident he was executing another detection route, which I had to avoid being drawn into.

The thoughts shuffled backwards in my head when around the opposite corner a group of young men walked toward me, their mouths soon opening with calls I could have predicted.

"Oi, Oi."

They each held a white paper wrapper in an open palm and picked at food, pushing it to their mouths between the calls. One guy walked a couple of paces ahead of the rest, his face round with thinning hair on his head, and rather than leering at me, he could have done with paying more attention to stopping himself from stumbling.

Those behind him looked my way, each appearing to be just a slight variation on the man at the front.

As we grew nearer, they collectively ditched the remains of their wrappers as if they needed their full concentration.

Looking away as the guy in the front grabbed his crotch and thrust himself forward at the hips, I shook my head before stepping to the side and between the cars to cross the road. As I arrived on the other side I soon saw it hadn't taken long for three of the group to change course to intercept me.

I kept my pace steady, reminding myself they were probably stand up members of the community when they weren't tanked up and in a pack, and wouldn't normally revert to the Stone Age when they saw a woman who'd taken no interest in them.

But I didn't have time to be nice.

Stifling a smile as one of the closest three stumbled down the kerb, bashing into a car before righting himself, they were soon about three car lengths away. I pushed my hand into my coat, feeling a flash of adrenaline when I remembered the knife was in the jacket underneath.

Locking eyes with the lead man for a second as they drew so close, I looked over his shoulder and along the road to make sure the target hadn't reappeared before I slowed to a stop.

"Hey, lady, you ever had a treat from six bulls at once?" the lead guy said.

Without replying, I touched at my coat's zip, dragging it down as each pair of eyes followed the journey.

Opening the coat, I slipped a hand under to the denim jacket, watching as each of their eyebrows twitched as if with confusion, but by the time my hand was in and out of the pocket, the blade sang free from the handle and I shot forward, lifting it up for all to see.

The front guy smiled, but the corners of his lips drooped as I closed the last of the space between us, putting my face to his and the blade at his crotch.

"Hey, gentlemen, have you ever had your dicks cut off?"

14

Unsure how each of the three men standing directly in front of me would react, I poised to turn and defend myself from both sides, knowing I could leap away, vault over the car at my side and run off.

When the lead guy I held the knife to didn't say a word and only the flickering of his eyelids telling me he hadn't turned to a statue, the others gawked on as if not knowing what to make of it all.

With a raise of my brow, I stepped back, but not without flicking the knife up as I withdrew, slicing through the guy's thin leather belt and sending his trousers falling to his ankles.

A chorus of laughter rose as his friends pointed and stared, two of them doubling over with hysterics as the other three soon joined them, barely noticing me as I forced my way to the left of the group before jogging at a steady pace with the knife back in my pocket.

Only their laughter followed as I rushed away, but when blue lights strobed across the night minutes later, I stepped into an alley, hoping the police had been called by someone who'd watched with concern at a window, rather than raising the alarm because of what I'd done to the young lad who'd tried to break into the van.

I hoped perhaps by the time the cops arrived on the scene, the drunken men would have wandered off with their tails between their legs. The last thing I wanted was for the police to search for a victim.

The flashing lights passed by at speed and I reminded myself why I was there. Pulling off the coat and unfurling the dress from around my waist, I took the bag from my shoulders and held it in my hands.

With the creases already falling out of the Teflon injected dress material and ditching the coat, I stepped from the alley's shadows and pulled off the cap to let my hair fall down my back as I walked toward the train station, knowing the target should still be doing his best to make sure he wasn't being followed.

Each of the shops forming an archway around the entrance were closed and with no-one about, I couldn't see anywhere for someone to hide.

Keeping my pace casual and trying not to take any interest on any point in particular, I headed straight for the ticket machine, paying with a card for what I guessed I might need, even though all I wanted to do was get through the barrier without arousing the suspicion of someone watching the cameras.

With the sun already lightening the sky, I found the platform empty and walked to the furthest point from the entrance before tucking myself behind a metal roof support.

Leaning against the beam, I slowed my breathing and closed my eyes, forcing them wide as the image in my mind reddened and I smelt a metallic hint in the air.

The day was much brighter than I'd expected, as if I'd slept as I stood, but I shuffled away the thought of what could have happened if I'd dozed when I heard footsteps joining me on the platform.

Peering around the side of the support, I saw men and women in suits and more following in quick order. Then a couple of men in paint stained overalls joined the thin crowd with their chatter adding to the birds singing for the new morning.

I imagined the target doing the same thing, secreting himself in some unseen place. It was only as the second announcement rang out from the speakers, joined by the low vibration of the tracks and the six cars of the train heading towards me, that I saw him come through the entrance.

With the carriage doors opening with a chime, I waited, glancing at the driver in his cab as he looked through his rearview mirrors.

I left my safe space and crossed the small gap as the guard stepped up, readying to lift his paddle and blow the whistle, listening as the doors chimed and closed behind me.

With a glance out of the window, I confirmed we'd left no one on the platform.

Facing against the direction of travel, I sat, tapping at Clark's number as we moved off.

"He's on the five thirty three to Oxford. For now, at least. I'll get as close as possible."

To the sound of his incessant typing, Clark gave a simple "Received."

I hung up.

Standing after a few moments, I searched around the seats, but the cleaners from the night before had been too efficient, leaving no discarded newspapers to hide behind. The last thing I wanted was for my target to get a good look at my face, knowing he'd make a mental note of some distinguishing feature on everyone he saw.

Still, I continued along the aisle, keeping my expression relaxed and reminding myself he could have taken a seat anywhere on the train.

Peering through the window between the cars, it was empty and I pushed through, soon spotting him in the next carriage before I'd stepped across the threshold. He was looking down at something in his lap and I stayed put, ducking to the side.

Leaning against the wall, and after checking my carriage was still clear, I opened my bag, diving between the zips of the other two nested inside and sliding out a thin leather pouch. Pulling it open, I looked past the lock picks and found a rounded mirror the size of my thumbnail.

Taking a small wad of tack from its side, I warmed it up in my fingers as I put everything back in its place.

Using the tack on the back of the mirror, I pressed it against the handrail rising from the floor, adjusting the angle with fine movements until I got a vague image of the target still in his seat. Leaning in closer, I recognised him well enough and watched as another man stood, the target studying him before the stranger headed away and out of the carriage.

Three stations passed by and the target made no move,

the doors right by me opening and closing each time. Even as we slowed for Reading, he stayed fixed to the spot. His only movement was to brush his hand to his left ear as if with an itch.

The doors opened again, filling the cabin with fresh air, and I glanced at the platform beyond as people piled in, most of whom were commuters in suits heading toward Oxford.

Turning back to the mirror, I tensed when I found my target's seat empty.

With no time to think, I pulled the tiny mirror from the pole, not worried if the tack stayed behind as I stepped onto the platform, looking high as if searching for a sign.

I glanced down at my thin watch, but still not able to see him anywhere in my peripheral vision, and with no other choice, I turned my head for a better look. Most people rushed in a group toward the escalator rising halfway along the platform, but I couldn't see him and feared he'd stayed on the train, perhaps just moving to another carriage.

With barely enough time to get back on board, and knowing how obvious it would look, my instincts told me to move. Just as I took my first step to follow the crowd, the target slipped between the train's closing doors and walked alongside me.

15

Without altering my speed and hoping I hadn't otherwise reacted, I stared straight ahead at the last of those heading up the escalator whilst trying my best to see what the target was doing out of the corner of my eye.

I half expected him to stare back as if trying to figure out if he'd seen me too many times already, but other than glancing at his watch, he seemed to look in the same direction.

Only as we neared the escalator did I drop my pace, slowing to let him go first, and he did, leaving me silently thanking him for not being a gentleman and offering to let me go in front, therefore making my next task so much more difficult.

I knew the station well, a bustling interchange for the west of the country with so many destinations he could choose from, even at such an early hour.

At the top of the escalator, he dived to the left, heading further into the station and not toward the exit, his choice narrowing the number of destinations in my favour. I diverted in the opposite direction and the ladies toilet a short walk away, I pushed at the wood but didn't go through. Instead, I glanced over my shoulder then turned back when I saw which platform he headed to.

After checking out the train times on a suspended screen, I headed in. Finding a stall, whilst ignoring the lingering smell, I pulled off the denim jacket, turning it inside out and hanging it on the back of the door. Then after taking out the Ruger and placing it on top of the toilet, the dress came off to hang on the hook before rolling down the leggings to cover my ankles. With the t-shirt off next, I turned it to the white side before placing it back on.

He'd seen my hair and it was striking enough to be recognisable no matter what I did with it, so opening the rucksack I pulled out the clutch. Opening the bag within, I quickly unfolded a thin dark cap with a bright red logo

42

across the front and black hair hanging around the edge. Before I put it on, I tied up my natural hair with a band. With the addition of a pair of black-rimmed glasses and the jacket now turned to a pastel shade of pink, I pushed the gun into my pocket and slid the lock on the stall door across.

After a quick check in the mirror to make sure my hair stayed hidden, and with the dress stuffed in the bag I no longer needed, I glanced at my watch, nodding to myself when I saw it had taken less than a minute to become a new person.

With the bag and dress discarded into the washroom's bin, I opened the main door and moved to the centre of the space as I glanced again to the screen.

The next train to arrive on the platform he'd headed to was due in five minutes before making its way to Guildford. I wandered over to the edge of the bridge which formed the bulk of the station, but despite the clear view of half of each of the platforms stretching out, I couldn't see the target anywhere.

Knowing he was likely to be on the other side of the platform I couldn't see, I waited in case he was watching or moving around in another phase of his detection route.

With two minutes to go before the train arrived, I glanced at the board, spotting that another train for Basingstoke was due on the next platform only a minute after the Guildford should be departing.

Not wanting to take the chance, I moved away from the edge, ambling toward the escalators heading down, knowing I would have to make a choice at some point and stick to it.

Seeing the Guildford train on the tracks in the distance, I'd made my mind up, but veered to the other platform when the target peaked on the opposite escalator on my left before heading right toward me.

I didn't look away, and he soon turned his fleeting attention to the other faces rushing from elsewhere as we all funnelled down to the platform with the long Basingstoke train pulling into the station.

Having already seen me, I followed him in, settling

down in a seat a couple of rows away in the same carriage. With the perfect view, I poised myself for action as every station approached.

When he made no move at any of them, even at the last minute, he seemed as if he was there to stay as the train slid into the penultimate station of Bramley, until, watching on with delight, he brushed his ear with his left hand.

I stood even though he hadn't, and walked to the doors, arriving as we came to a halt and the chimes rang out. My self-congratulation subsided when he still hadn't moved and I had no choice but to step off as the doors opened, putting all my trust that I'd correctly spotted his tell and that it wasn't a red herring he was using to play me.

16

Much to my relief the target eventually stepped from the train, his action confirming I'd isolated his tell, which meant I was already on the platform and in turn he'd have to discount me as I hurried towards the stairs, following the exit signs as if I had an appointment to keep.

When I didn't hear his footsteps following on the wooden steps behind me, and knowing he was the only other person to leave the train, I could do nothing but continue to climb.

Glancing back whilst maintaining my speed, I confirmed he hadn't followed, but knowing he might look over at any moment, I carried along the short bridge before stepping down towards the exit, not indicating that I would change my mind.

Unknowingly or not, he'd forced me to commit, reminding me his experiences weren't just written in his file.

A brief look to the screens confirmed the next train, an express to Weymouth, would arrive in fifteen minutes.

I had no other choice but to slip through the exit barriers and scoured either side of the small station for somewhere I could switch to my final change of clothes, despite knowing I would need some extra distraction if I stood a chance of being the only other person on the platform.

With a stuttered flow of new passengers arriving, before I could decide where to change, diving either between the bushes on the other side of the road or a gap between the parked cars, my saviour came in the form of a coach pulling in a few steps away.

Out of sight of the target still back in the station, I watched as the coach door opened with two women rushing down the steps before the air brakes had barely stopped hissing. Both were a little younger than myself and busied themselves beckoning bleary-eyed teenagers in school uniform from behind, whilst corralling them to stay in some sort of line.

The taller of the two women, and the first to have stepped out, had dark hair tied in a ponytail and wore a skirt down to her knees with a raincoat over a blouse as she hurried towards the station entrance. The other rushed behind with the children in tow whilst fishing for something in her pocket.

The last from the coach were another two women who followed the end of the line of kids and joined in, motioning with their hands to guide them to follow the other teachers and head through the barrier opened by an attendant.

With a glance away from the end of the line and without making a sound, I ripped off the red logo from the front of the cap and tucked the fabric into my pocket in hope the vibrant patch had been prominent enough for the target to latch on to.

Tucking in behind the last of the rabble, I got in amongst their chatter, and despite the odd sideways look, they seemed to take little notice of a stranger in their group as I tramped up the wooden steps.

The target was plain to see as after heading across the bridge we descended to the platform, and I looked away as if talking to the kids, but before I did, I saw he'd turned away, discounting every one of the group before I slipped further down the platform and out of sight. Within five minutes the platform emptied onto the express train.

As the doors shut behind me, I headed to the rear-most carriage to give myself a chance of seeing along the length of the train when we pulled into the next station.

He was off at Basingstoke and it was busy enough I could stay hidden, following him to another train which headed to Woking, and then another to Guildford, where I pushed the cap back into the bag and left the coat under the seat on the train, which forced me to put the Ruger out of easy reach.

With each new leg of the journey, I got a little closer in the carriage and with every mile away from where his daughter lived, he seemed to relax further, almost to the stage where he was getting sloppy. He barely looked around, but gave his tell as we arrived at Aldershot. I couldn't help but feel we were nearing the end of the journey and that perhaps executing the last phase of the operation wouldn't be as difficult as I'd first feared.

From Aldershot there was only one stop left, and I was confident Alton would be the last, even though he could just stay on the train as it headed back in the opposite direction.

With a call to Clark, I gave him a clipped update and made sure those above hadn't changed their mind.

The tension in Clark's tone was easy to hear. The target was, after all, one of us, in another lifetime anyway.

Clark confirmed my objective hadn't altered.

"Then what?" I asked, but only silence replied, as if he was seeking confirmation.

"Get the hell out of there," he eventually said, and I ended the call.

As we pulled into Alton, I followed the target off the train. With the four remaining passengers, we headed in the same direction until they each dispersed as we stepped into a large car park.

I fell back, watching as he sauntered along as if with all the time in the world. Going so slowly along the path, he forced me to speed up or otherwise show my hand.

Passing him, I arrived at the bus stop and peered at the timetable and then at my watch, but paid no attention to either, instead glancing over as he went by.

Seeming to speed up, it wasn't going to be long before he moved out of sight, and with the bus turning into the station's entrance, I grabbed my phone and pulled up a map before staring at the huge expanse of trees just outside the village.

My mouth nearly fell open when I realised this was the kind of place *I'd* make my home if I wanted to hide from the world.

17

In so many ways, he wasn't me, but in many others, he was the same. Our training, and what we'd seen over the years, ignoring the past few days, would round a person in a certain way.

It all made sense. How else had he defeated the vast net of CCTV and other detection systems embedded into society for all this time if he wasn't living like a wild man in the woods?

I waited at the bus stop as the target turned left and out of my sight, a sickness rising in my stomach at the thought I might not have been right, the feeling exasperated when the bus took an age before it turned around in the station forecourt and the door lined up with the bus stop.

Climbing on board, I paid the lowest fare, shrugging when the driver asked for the destination, instead pointing along the road. After a moment, he gave in and nodded along the aisle and I took a seat midway down the bus, just as it pulled off before turning left to follow the route the target had taken.

I soon spotted him a little way off down a country road lined with the trees either side I'd seen on the map from above. I leaned out of sight as we passed, despite knowing he had no reason to pay the bus any attention.

As the bus rounded the next sweeping corner, I sauntered to the front, pressing the button and asking the driver to stop in clipped English.

Despite his protests, and unable to understand my Latvian follow up, I made it clear he'd be the one to clean up the floor if he didn't stop immediately.

The doors opened moments later and I stepped out onto the road and then into the darkness between the trees as the vehicle disappeared from view.

With a glance back and not yet able to see the target, I unzipped the bag, placing the Ruger on the ground, then took the inner bag out, discarding the outer and covering it with leaves. From the last bag, I unfolded a thin black waterproof coat and put it on. After peeling the last layer from my trainers to black them out, I smeared dark camo paint across my face and around my ankles so that before long the whites of my eyes would be the only thing that could betray where I stood.

With straps I'd tucked inside, the bag became a small backpack, and with the pistol back in my pocket, I watched, barely blinking as I stared back along the length of the road.

I didn't have to wait long before he came into view and I stepped further into the darkness with care as he slowly headed toward me.

He was easy to follow in parallel with the cover of the trees; the birds and other animals and the wind rustling the leaves were enough to obscure my journey. Only as we arrived at a dirt track across my path did I hang back, watching as he left the road and headed into the woods.

I couldn't help but smile when his move confirmed I was probably right about where he'd been all this time.

Keeping as far back as I dared whilst still able to see him moving along the path, he halted and turned around as if he'd heard something, but the sound hadn't come from me. At one point, it was as if he was looking in my direction, but I was sure it was just a coincidence.

Eventually, he turned away, stepping from the dirt path and in between the trees.

I didn't move, instead counting the passage of five minutes before I took another step.

Despite losing sight of him during the wait, his tracks were still clear, the grass and bushes only just recovering. With my senses on alert for any sign of where he'd gone, I held back when I saw, after a while, the tracks disappeared in front of a thicket of brambles as if he'd walked through without leaving a trace.

Just as an idea formed as to what might have happened, the phone ringing in my ear cut through my thoughts.

Answering the call with a brush of my finger against the phone in my jacket pocket, I stayed silent, knowing Clark would understand why I couldn't speak.

"Abort mission," he said.

The words were enough to catch me off guard. After looking left and then right, I almost contemplated speaking, but having still not figured out where the target had gone, I instead stepped up to the brambles.

"You've been reassigned. It's a priority one," Clark added.

The words caught in my head. A priority one meant drop everything. It meant someone was so close to making terrible things happen.

Shuffling my feet as I contemplated how to respond, the bushes just in front swept away to either side, revealing a patch of hard-packed dirt.

Beyond was a steel door, but before I could react, the cocking of a pump-action shotgun sounded from right behind me.

OVERKILL

18

"Raise your arms slowly and turn around," said the unfamiliar deep voice from behind me.

I looked up from the hard-packed mud where the bushes had swept to either side and stared into the thick foliage beyond before I did as I was told, pushing my arms high and turning on the spot. My gaze fell on the man I'd been following for the last few hours.

He peered down the sight of an all-black Armsan pump-action shotgun with the butt pushed into his shoulder and the business end aimed in my direction.

"Say something," he said with urgency.

My eyes narrowed at the odd command, as he jolted the weapon with impatience. "Is that an RS-X1?"

His shoulders relaxed at my words, but his face remained tense, his gaze fixed down the sight.

Pushing away my intrigue as to why he was so desperate to hear my voice, I laughed and lowered my arms a little.

"Of course it is, Dylan," I said, my brow raising along with a thin smile. "I was just being polite."

His head twitched to the side, as if a stranger hadn't spoken that name in his presence for such a long time. He showed no sign of lowering his aim.

"Who sent you? Why are you here?" he said, his voice gruff as if he'd worn it out having spoken more in the last day than he had in all the years he'd hidden himself away.

"Is it okay if I use that name?" I said raising a brow, hoping he appreciated the respect I was showing by not using the name he gave up when he joined the service.

His eyes narrowed, but when he didn't say no, I nodded, letting my smile rise a little more. "And you should know why I'm here," I replied. "This was always going to happen after you disappeared off the face of the earth."

When Clark's voice sounded in my ear, I only just managed to keep my voice even. "You've got ten minutes to wrap things up and get to the coordinates I've sent to your phone."

Dylan's eyes narrowed as if he'd seen a reaction in my face and the line in my ear went dead just as the phone vibrated in my jacket.

"Turn out your pockets," Dylan said, raising the shotgun just a little higher.

I nodded, but didn't lower my hands.

"I have a pistol and a knife. Both are in my jacket pocket," I said, his eyes widening just a little. "But that's where they're staying."

Dylan shuffled his feet as if to get a more comfortable position. "I'm calling the shots. Now keep your hands up and take a step forward."

With a glance at the ground in front of me, I did as he said and listened to the brambles as I pictured them sweeping back in from the side to cover the metal door.

"That's pretty neat," I said. "But listen. I haven't got much time. I'm just here to find out why you went dark. You knew they'd want to keep tabs on you, for a little while at least. It's protocol. You must have realised someone would come looking for you."

"What do you want from me?" he said, still eyeing me with suspicion.

"All I need to know is that you're just living out your years in isolation, keeping to yourself. That kind of thing."

"And not working for another firm," he said turning his head to the side.

I nodded, letting my hands down a little more.

"Where are the rest of the team?" he said with a quick glance to the left, then the right.

I shook my head. "There's no one else," I said, watching him frown in disbelief as he looked me up and down.

"How did you find me?"

"Your daughter. We found her first and thought you couldn't resist a visit on her special day."

His eyes flashed wide, but only for a moment and watched his realisation that he'd lost some of his craft in the years he'd been out.

"How did you track me?"

"I'm sorry to say that despite your record, it was pretty easy," I said, lowering my left hand before touching at my ear.

Dylan's shoulders fell and he let the gun drop. "Shit," he said, looking at the ground.

"Don't beat yourself up. I'm like you," I said. "But not as old," I added, watching as a smirk crossed his face and he let the shotgun lower further to point at the grass.

"Do you mind?" I said, glancing up at my raised arms.

He contemplated me for a moment and then nodded, watching with interest as I lowered my limbs whilst being careful to keep my hands away from my pockets.

With slow movements, I shrugged the bag from my back whilst keeping eye contact to make sure he was okay with everything I did.

Eventually, I pulled out a packet of wet wipes and after placing the bag on the floor, wiped my face, cleaning the camo paint from my skin as he watched.

"So you've been living with nature?" I said, as I wiped each area until the damp cloth came back clean and I swapped to another.

He nodded toward the bushes behind me. "It started out as an old bomb shelter, but it's much more now."

"Neat," I said. "It's a shame I haven't got time for you to show me around."

He narrowed his eyes.

"I've been reassigned. Just as we were chatting, in fact. It's a priority one."

His brow raised, and I ignored the inference as he looked me up and down again.

"Why'd you leave?" I said, as I knelt and ran the cloth over each of my ankles.

"Let's just say our interests diverged."

"So much so you moved to a bunker?" I replied as I stood up.

After taking a long but controlled deep breath, he spoke. "There's only so much a person can take before it hangs around inside your head. Some things just can't be unseen. Some things can't be forgiven."

Despite my best effort, my smile dropped and I thought back to Brass Pike. If he'd have said the same thing just a week ago, it wouldn't have meant anything to me.

At the thought of not being able to leave the terror behind, I knew the colour had drained from my face, just as the energy had fled from my muscles.

"It looks like you've seen plenty already," he said, his voice quiet.

After a pause, I lifted myself tall and forced a smile, but let it drop, raising my chin as I tried to defy my thoughts.

"Let's get this done. Are you here to kill me?" he said, the words reversing my downward mood.

I looked up and shook my head. "Perhaps it sounds cliché, but if I was, you'd be dead already."

He let go of the shotgun with his left hand as he smiled. His eyes told me he didn't believe a word I'd said, and despite knowing I had nothing to prove, I bent over and picked up the bag, throwing it across the gap between us and hitting him in the face, sending him off balance.

With his eyes closed and his left hand at his face, I stepped forward and grabbed the shotgun, snatching from his grip. I took a step back, pumping the slide so one by one the cartridges flew out of the ejection port.

"Nice weapon," I said, watching as his expression relaxed before laughter took over and he raised his hands into the air.

With the last of the rounds falling to the ground, I handed the empty shotgun over.

He shook his head and I thought perhaps I saw a glimmer of respect as he took the gun by the barrel.

"A bit overkill, don't you think?" I said.

He glanced down at the gun and his smile fell. "It depends what you're up against," he said.

As he looked up, he was smiling again, then his eyes narrowed as if studying my face now clean of the black paint.

"Have we met before?"

I shook my head, confident I'd never seen him until I'd read his file.

He nodded, but his raised brow told me he still wasn't quite sure. "What now?"

"I've got to go. The priority one," I said, the faint drumming of rotors carrying in the air. "Maybe I'll come back one day for a cup of tea and a tour."

He laughed as I gathered up my things and headed between the trees, not slowing as he shouted after me.

"Know when you're done. You can have that advice for free."

19

Clark's briefing over the headset in the RAF Merlin was vague. A tasking to find a thirty-year-old male only from information in a forty-page personnel file, much of which was redacted with bold marker pen. I was left with just a name, Isaac Brown, and an address for his next of kin, plus a head shot and a greyed out night vision image captured from CCTV of him running amongst trees.

After a short walk to a hotel from the field where we landed, I took a few minutes to grab a quick shower and get rid of the last of the camo paint, then changed into fresh jeans and a t-shirt waiting for me in the room, before securing a holster across my shoulders, then stripping, inspecting and cleaning the Ruger, then pushing it home under my arm.

As I sat in the cafe forecourt under the ornate roof of the picturesque station in Windsor with a small paper cup of coffee, I tapped at Clark's number and took in the detail of my surroundings.

"How is he a priority one exactly?" I said, holding the phone up to my ear so it didn't look as if I was talking to myself.

"You know as much as I do," he said, pausing. "But…" he added, leaving the sentence unfinished.

"What?" I said, looking away from a man who'd just stepped from a high end cookware shop nestled between two art galleries. His height didn't fit the description.

"There's a lot more we're not being told," Clark said in a lowered voice. "I've got to go," he added, and cut the call.

His words reminded me of my secret. Not allowed to speak of the recent events, I couldn't help but wonder what Clark thought I'd been doing in the days I went dark after heading into the Scottish forest. Extended R&R was just not me, but he said nothing when I offered the explanation early this morning.

I pushed away the thought and turned my attention to

the thin crowd of shoppers, tourists and patrons of a bar just beyond, whilst picturing the target in my mind. With light mousey brown hair, a lean build and standing just over six feet tall, I knew nothing of Brown's occupation, but from the thickness of his personnel file he held civil service positions which required the highest level of ongoing vetting, recording the details of his various postings over the years, none of which were hinted at in the file I'd seen.

The Operations Centre had spotted him on CCTV earlier in the day, whilst I was with Dylan. The details of that location weren't repeated but the team back in the Brecon Beacons must have thought there was a certainty he'd head my way, passing through the station at least. With his parent's house not far away, I imagined he had many connections to the town.

I also knew I was the only egg in their basket, with no other agents on the tasking. I alone had to cover the whole place. With no mobile phone to track, I pretended to drink cold coffee whilst I waited for him to pass me by. A visit to his parents would be the next resort where I hoped I'd find a minefield of information compared to what they'd already shared.

On the flight over, I'd taken time to concentrate on his photo, staring at the straightness of his nose, the flatness of his cheeks and the distance between his eyes. His eyebrows were darker than his hair. This was his standout feature, but he could defeat me with just a thick pair of glasses. Likewise, the faint acne scars on his chin were easy to cover after a few days without a shave.

A couple caught my eye at the edge of my vision and I looked towards them as the target's image evaporated from my mind. The woman held a baby as she walked beside a man pushing a stroller and they looked the picture of happiness, sauntering across the concourse with seemingly nothing more to do than enjoy the afternoon.

I could never tell a young child's age with any accuracy. A lack of exposure, and need, I guessed, but this time I didn't even try. Instead, I couldn't help but think that out of all the sights and experiences of my career, if people knew of what I'd gone through in Scotland, would they be so keen to bring new life into this world?

I'd seen the worst of people, of governments, and many times I'd made a difference, but what had it all been for if experiments like what I'd witnessed were going on around the world? How many more were waiting to go wrong in such a bad way?

Right on cue a pair of armed police officers crossed my view, and with their bulky stab vests, side arms at the hip, bright yellow tasers holstered on their chests and the MP5 assault rifle held in one hand across their fronts, along with the many other pockets and items hanging off them, I knew the outcome if they came across what I'd seen in that confined space.

The sight reminded me of the castle less than a minute's walk away and I couldn't help wondering if, with a priority one threat wandering around, had they shipped the Queen back to London, or somewhere further afield?

Sitting back in the metal-framed seat, I blinked my dry eyes and rubbed my left with the tip of my finger. Feeling my lids sting with tiredness, I moved my hand away, forcing my eyes wide as I tried to focus on each of the faces passing in front of me.

I pulled the cup to my lips and took a sip, but could already feel my mind drifting when I saw the family standing by the steam engine trapped in the encircling iron fence at the entrance to the platform as the father pointed out features as if the baby took interest.

On the brink of ringing Clark to tell him I needed to leave, and that I was no good to anyone in this state and should volunteer for the first time to meet with Devlin, the first few people at the head of a crowd came from behind the old relic.

Sitting up straight, my subconscious took over, waking me from a sleep I didn't know I'd slipped into. With the cup at my lips, I glanced at each of the faces, most of which were tourists of many ethnicities already regaled with their union flags and bags covered in soldiers in the dress uniform of the royal guards.

Not discounting any of them until I'd got a good look, my gaze moved towards the back of the messy line until the hair on my neck stood to attention. With goosebumps rushing across my arms and over my shoulders, I realised the man I stared at was the perfect match. Wearing a black NYC cap pulled low, it wasn't enough to hide his dark brow as he raised his head to navigate through the crowd.

Still sitting, I looked away, knowing I'd lingered long enough already, even though he hadn't turned toward me.

Stealing another look after a moment, I watched as he filtered through the crowd, soon passing between the barriers of the cafe's outdoor seating area and those for the bar opposite. Wearing a creased white t-shirt and blue jeans, he peered ahead as he rubbed his hand across a couple of days of stubble.

For the first time I noticed there was something a little different compared his photo. He was a little older, but as I pushed the side button on the phone in my pocket to fast dial Clark's number, I couldn't put my finger on what else nagged in my head.

"I have him," I said, but Clark didn't give me a chance to follow up.

"How does he look?" he said, his voice urgent.

"What do you mean?" I added, as I stood to make my way around the chairs and out into the station proper, following the target as he veered to the left and away from the crowd before heading between the shops and towards the high street and the castle.

When Clark didn't answer, I took a closer look at Brown.

"He's sweaty. Perhaps a little pale. Come to think of it, he doesn't look that well.

20

"Shit," Clark said, then apologised before the line went silent, as if he'd put me on mute. After a moment, he was back, his words much more even.

"Follow him, but keep your distance."

"What's going on, Clark?" I replied, trying my best not to raise my voice.

"Which exit is he heading toward?" he said, not answering my question.

"The castle," I replied, but there was only silence on the other end of the line.

"Give me commentary when you can," he eventually said.

It was my turn not to reply. Instead, I hung back as Isaac's pace slowed a little, and I watched as he veered to the left as if trying to avoid a small group of school children, then repeated the deviation to his right as others headed towards him past the cafes and restaurants and tourist shops selling overpriced sweets along with everything you could think of printed with the Union Jack.

As our spacing increased, the clearer it was he walked with a slight limp. Clark didn't reply as I commented on Isaac's gait and I couldn't help feeling that despite what Clark had said earlier, he was the one who was holding back, not those above him.

"That's a right out of the station," I said as I turned the corner, watching as Brown stepped between the cars, walking down the road rather than along the pavement and against the trickle of sauntering pedestrians as they peered up at the stone walls of the castle.

"What's your spacing?" Clark said, causing more than a little surprise because he'd never questioned my field craft before.

"Three cars," I said, trying to keep the question out of my voice.

"Drop back a little, if possible," he replied.

"Okay," I said, unable to stop myself from extending the word. Still, I did as he said, dropping back to double the distance between us, whilst knowing there must have been so many cameras focused this way, I didn't need to let him know what I'd done.

As we worked our way from the bustling centre of the town, Brown rejoined the path with the limp becoming more pronounced as time went on. Not once had he looked over his shoulder or performed any sort of counter-surveillance measure and I concluded we didn't share an employer, and he didn't work for any of the other better known agencies in a similar line of business.

"It's a right down Sheet Street, towards Victoria barracks," I said in a whisper with only a few other people in sight. "He's looking around as if he's lost. Hold," I added, watching as he slowed and reached inside his pocket, soon pulling out a piece of paper which he glanced at, then pushed back.

Increasing his speed, he turned right again, walking in front of houses, some of which were homes, whilst others were converted into offices.

I relayed the information but got nothing back, and I couldn't help but wonder what had happened on the other end of the line. In the many years I'd worked with the team, even in the tensest of moments when perhaps the mission, lives, my life even, were on the line, whoever was on the phone in the Operations Centre would stay calm and collected, the consummate professional able to feedback and assist however they could. But this time it felt as if they were scrabbling around and had no time for what I was doing, despite knowing more about the importance of what I'd been tasked with.

Pushing the thoughts away, I concentrated on his journey and watched as he glanced with what looked like purpose to either side of the road. I mirrored the swing of his head and scanned the occasional signs and banners out in front of the buildings, discounting each as he passed by.

Soon he slowed, and it felt as if he was getting close to

what he was looking for.

"He's searching for somewhere down Victoria Street," I said. "Is there any connection in the file I've missed?"

"Wait one," was the only reply, but it wasn't Clark's voice.

There were still only a few other people on the street, plus the odd car passing by, and every so often I'd cross paths with someone walking the other way on either side of the road.

Eventually, sensing Brown would stop at any moment, I crossed over the road, searching for some excuse to hold station.

When we passed a multi-storey car park, signalling we were again getting closer to the busy town centre, the unfamiliar voice spoke in my ear.

"There's nothing we can see."

I saw the moment Brown found his destination, his neck craning to look up the two floors above as he drifted from the main path and headed towards a door sandwiched between an office building and the edge of the tall car park.

"He's heading to 57A, Victoria Street. Do I intercept or observe?"

"Observe only." The man's words were instant, as if he'd been poised all along. "Acknowledge."

"Acknowledged," I said and slowed. Despite being confident Brown wouldn't turn around and check before entering, I tucked down a street to the right and stopped before peering back, my mouth almost falling open when I heard the wooden door splitting as he pushed his hand to the outer part of the frame and forced it open without slowing his step. The fragments of the door hanging wide were the only thing that told me his apparent super-human strength wasn't a figment of my sleep deprived mind.

"He just pushed through the locked door like it was made of putty," I said, the words slow and ringing in my ears.

When no one replied, I checked my phone, making sure the comms were still working. They were, the man's voice soon coming across the line, but a scream from inside the building Brown had just broken into swallowed the words up.

I had a split second to choose, but I needed less and stepped into the road when I saw a shadow rush past the windows on the top floor.

21

"Agent Harris? What the hell?" the frantic male voice said in my ear.

"Screams from inside. I'm going in," I replied, looking left, then right as I crossed the road.

"No," another distinct voice said in my earpiece.

Before I could consider if I would listen to the order, a third unfamiliar voice spoke into my ear.

"Wait," the man added, and I knew from the tone the message wasn't for me.

As the line went quiet, I was already at the remains of the door and pushing past the threshold. Glaring at a closed door directly to the right, I dismissed it, instead heading up a set of steps straight in front of me as I listened to heavy feet thumping on the floor above, the crashing and banging mixing with frantic, muffled calls.

Gripping the Ruger in both hands, I kept it pointed to the steps as I took each as fast as I could.

Looking up at the window with the sun beaming through from the first floor, I glanced where the corridor led to the left and right at the top.

Amongst the dust and stale air was another scent, the sweet and sour odour reminding me of an infected wound.

At the top of the steps, I kept the gun pointing low. With my back against the wall, I peered left then right in quick succession, but long enough to spot three doors either way along the corridor and one at each far end.

With the sounds of a commotion still carrying from the right and the chaos of movement vibrating through the floor, I rushed in the sound's direction, soon pushing my ear to the first door whilst taking only casual notice of the company name on the rectangular label fixed to the wood.

Realising the sounds were from further along, I spotted the fire exit sign on the door at the end of the corridor with its long push bar, and took a long step before listening at the next door.

Just as I leaned in, the commotion stopped.

Letting go of the Ruger with my left hand, I pushed down the handle and opened the door a crack, finding only a small office with two women staring wide eyed at each other with their hands to their mouths.

I pushed the door a little further, using my body to cover the Ruger as they turned toward me.

"Stay here and lock the door," I said, stepping away and giving no pause for questions as I pulled it closed behind me.

With sounds of the struggle just a memory, I could only hear the footsteps from the room I'd just left as one of the women ran across the room. With a click of the lock, I knew she'd done as I'd asked.

This time I paid attention to the final label on the wood, *Jones Corporate Travel*. The door was closed and with nothing to listen to, I stepped up and pressed my hand on the handle.

"I think I'm too late," I said in a whisper, pushing at the side of my phone in my pocket to let the message send. "He's on the other side of the door and it's all gone quiet."

"Hold station." Again, the voice wasn't Clark's, and I did as they said.

"What now?" I whispered.

"Wait one whilst we get a decision," the voice replied, and I couldn't help but shake my head. This wasn't what I wanted to hear.

With steps on the other side of the door, and a heavy footed movement somewhere beyond, I pushed down the door handle, twisting my shoulder to lean against the wood as I inched it open.

There were desks to the left of the room beside a window, and my breath caught in my throat when I spotted the target sat behind a desk in front of me, his fingers tapping at an unseen keyboard.

I couldn't help but gawk at the dark red mess around his mouth as he looked up from the keyboard and stared right at me over the computer monitor.

"Holy shit. Not again," I said, as Brown leapt up, jumping onto the desk and baring his teeth.

Splashes of blood across the room came into focus as I raised the pistol, but my finger wouldn't drop from the guard.

I was helpless again, just like in Scotland.

22

I'd frozen and couldn't even move when I saw the front of his t-shirt soaked with blood like a teenager's poor attempt to tie-dye their clothes. I did nothing as it stared at me, not able to pull the trigger or even turn and run. Instead I was back at Brass Pike in the moments after I'd emptied the magazine into the creature's chest, reliving the utter helplessness once again.

This time there was a desk between us, but not for long as it bounded over the monitors in a single leap with the wood creaking as it landed on the other side.

With the creature who'd once been Brown still glaring at me, I could do nothing but watch as if in a bad dream I couldn't wake myself from. All the while, my head swam with the realisation that to see what I had seen in the isolation of Brass Pike was one thing, but to experience the same in the midst of the community was another level, and I could do nothing to stop it.

Despite feeling like a lifetime had passed, the moment went by in a flash and the fear soon displaced with anger at knowing that I'd done so much good in my time, but when it came to the real crunch, I was letting everyone down.

With that thought I felt my finger touch the trigger, my muscles coming alive with energy. I retrained my sights on the creature, watching as it jumped to the floor, but rather than rushing towards me as I came to my senses, it ran to its right, leaping at the window.

It didn't stop, instead dipping its right shoulder toward the large double glazed pane and I knew it wouldn't feel a thing as the glass disintegrated and he disappeared from view, leaving me with guilt welling in my chest at the relief it was gone, whilst knowing I was powerless to stop the pain and suffering it would cause.

Staring at the space where the glass had been, I flinched at the sound of flesh thumping as it hit the ground below. I couldn't bring myself to move to the window and peer out, already knowing it would get to its feet as if nothing had happened.

"Agent Harris?" the voice said in my ear, the tone telling me it wasn't the first time they'd tried to raise me.

I ignored another command to report and soon Clark's familiar voice sounded, the high pitch not hiding his concern.

"Carrie. What's going on? Are you okay? Acknowledge... Say something, Carrie."

"I froze," I said, as blood running down the walls held my focus. Eventually, I turned away and stared across the desks and the backs of computers. There were four desks in all, each arranged around the corners of the room, and despite still feeling as if I wasn't in full control of my body, I stepped across the threshold, slowing my breathing as my nostrils filled with the tang of metallic blood.

"It got away. There was nothing I could do." My words were slow and empty of energy.

"They just told me what's going on," Clark said. "I'm sorry, Carrie, I didn't know what happened the other day."

The line clicked and another man's voice sounded in my ear.

"Where is the target now?"

I couldn't remember if I'd heard him before.

I looked back at the space in the window frame, feeling a breeze on my face.

"Out through a window," I replied, shaking my head.

"Agent Harris, report. Pull yourself together," the raised voice said.

As if a veil covering my senses lifted, control of my muscles flooded back as I looked around the room, the images snapping to focus.

"Shit. Sorry. The struggle had died down, and I opened the door. The target was sitting at a computer and tapping at the keyboard, but when it saw me it jumped onto the desk and then bolted, smashing through the window like the glass wasn't there."

"What's your exact position?" the voice said.

"Office six. First floor. There's so much…" I added as I looked around, noting another set of desks in the right hand corners of room. Taking a step forward, I stopped when I reached the first of the blood soaked into the carpet. With it came the first realisation that the life-giving fluid must have come from someone.

I looked to the right, peering between the desks, and trained the aim of the Ruger on the body I'd expected. A man lay on the floor between the two, his legs broken below the knees, bent in places they shouldn't be. With his shirt ripped open, coils of intestine were on show and the carpet looked as if it had a mirror finish from what had once been running in his veins.

As I picked out another patch of clean carpet to step to for a better look, I wished I hadn't when I saw his face lined with deep scratches, the end of his nose missing. Staring at his head for a long moment, eventually I took solace at the mercy he wasn't still breathing.

"One body confirmed."

A barrage of questions exploded in my ear, so many voices all talking at once.

About to dig the earpiece out for some relief, the voice of my chief, Franklin, cut through the chaos with a single word.

"Stop."

Lowering my aim, I looked at the floor and tried to make sense of the mass of prints in the blood.

I turned to the desk where I'd found Brown sitting. About to take another tentative step to see what was on the screen before the saver kicked in, I pulled my foot back, lifting the gun toward to the desk in the far corner of the room and the sound of whimpering.

23

"Show yourself," I screamed in my best drill instructor's voice as I lifted the aim of my weapon to the noise. "Get up. I'm armed."

"Report," came the voice in my ear, but I didn't reply, instead watching as a brown head of hair slowly rose from behind the desk to reveal a man, his eyes and cheeks red with streaming tears.

"Hands in the air," I shouted, not lowering the volume.

He wore a short sleeve white shirt and did as he was told, raising his arms high as he came to full height.

"Contact," I said. "Possible victim."

No one replied as the guy in front of me stared back, his whole body shaking as his gaze fixed on the end of my gun.

"Are they injured?" a voice came back in my ear.

"Are you injured?" I asked, but when the guy didn't respond, I shouted the question again and he shook his head.

"He says no."

"Make sure," came the reply.

"Keep your hands up and turn around," I said.

After a moment's delay, he pivoted on the spot, but all I could see, other than the white of his shirt, were the wet patches under his arms.

"Make really sure," the voice said.

"Step out from around the desk," I said, motioning with the gun for him to come to the right because a printer blocked the way to his left, realising with dismay that he'd have to move around the body.

"Don't look down," I added, as he gingerly came around the side of the desk, his eyes going wide at the sight.

"Look at me," I snapped, and he turned his head up high, then I made him twist around on the spot again, confirming he had no signs of injury.

"He's fine. Nothing a couple of years inside an

institution won't fix," I said, and motioned for him to walk past the body and come towards me.

Realising I was still pointing the gun at him, I dropped my aim, watching as he swallowed hard then stepped into the puddle of blood encircling the body.

It took all my self-control not to look away, watching as he took a second step, but not able to stop himself from glancing down.

I softened my voice this time.

"What's your name?" I said. "I'm Clare."

He stared back without speaking.

"Look at me, not down there."

"Christian," he eventually said, then a voice cut into my thoughts.

"Police are on the way, Agent Harris. Secure the scene. We have another team a few minutes behind. Don't let the cops into the room."

I was about to ask what I should do with the guy when movement on the floor caught my eye. Barely able to understand what I saw, the man who I'd believed couldn't be anything but dead rose his hand from his side, grabbing at Christian's trousers.

With a yelp, Christian looked down, tugging with all he could at his leg, but then lost his footing and slipped in the blood, sending him crashing to the floor.

I stepped forward, no longer concerned about the mess, and raised my gun, pointing it at the dead man.

My eyes went wide at its raised head, jerking forward and biting down on Christian's exposed ankle.

BLOODSHOT

24

The first shot was perfect, slitting the creature's eye, but I'd learnt my lesson from Brass Pike and didn't stop pulling the trigger this time. Three rounds crashed through its skull until its jaw relaxed, its head falling back just as Christian pulled away.

I didn't stop there.

Three more rounds slammed into its head, and only as the skull collapsed in on itself did I relax my finger. Still, I held the gun out whilst I panted for breath, ready to unload the last in the magazine.

"It's happened again," I said over the phone. "It wasn't dead."

"Is the threat neutralised?" said the voice in my ear.

I didn't reply.

"Agent Harris, what is your status?"

I looked up from the body and stood tall, peering around.

"Threat neutralised, but it bit Christian."

"Who's Christian?" the voice said.

"The survivor."

"Where is he?" the voice replied, not hiding his concern.

A dread rose inside my gut when I realised he wasn't in the room as I looked around. Only the hammering of his footsteps, followed by the slamming of a door in the corridor gave any indication of where he'd gone.

"He's running," I said. "I'm on it," I added, as I rushed from the room, following the red blotched footsteps out into the corridor and toward the fire escape.

I pushed the wide bar, only just missing the sticky mess

of blood on the brushed metal, but I put the thought of what I'd almost touched behind me as the door opened to a metal platform the other side with the same metal grid forming steps down to the lower floor where Christian had already arrived.

With my feet clattering on the grid, I watched as Christian tried to rush down the alley between the buildings, but could barely manage more than a jog as he limped on his left foot.

Thankful he'd run out of sight of the road, I glanced toward the front of the building where my gaze fell to a bloody imprint on the path. The impression of Brown's body sent a renewed rush of adrenaline as I scanned the scene for the expected destruction he'd left behind.

Shaking my head, I picked up the pace, soon rounding the halfway point of the stairs where I pushed the Ruger into its holster for fear of anyone who might pass by. Landing on the tarmac with a leap down the last couple of steps, I rushed alongside the trail of bloody footprints Christian had left behind.

He'd been surprisingly quick despite the injury, but I'd seen so many times before what fear could do, sometimes helping whilst other times forcing poor decisions.

Closing my eyes for a split second, I did my best to ignore the rising guilt at how I'd coped with my first real dose of terror. I'd frozen, but my fear wasn't due to what it could do to me, but that it might be a sign my skills were dulling. Had I lost my edge? If I lived, would I have to retire to behind a desk?

Never.

Determined not to let the thought gain strength, I pushed myself to run faster.

With Christian in the alley's shade ahead, I called out, "I can help. Just wait."

When he didn't turn or even slow, I shouted again. "A doctor is on his way," I said, watching as his pace stuttered then slowed, before he turned his head, almost tripping as he looked over his shoulder. He came to a stop, and I slowed, raising my palms towards him with the first calls of sirens in the background.

"Please," I said, the background noise growing louder each moment. "It's gone and I need your help."

Heaving, he bent over double, glancing up every other moment, both at me and behind my back as I approached.

Eventually, I stood beside him with much of the day's light blocked by the high walls on either side of us.

"I'm with Christian now," I said, as I ran my hand up and down his back whilst glancing along each end of the deserted alleyway which ran behind the row of buildings. With the coast clear of immediate threats, I focused on the blood soaking his trainers red and darkening the ankle of his blue trousers.

"I can't breathe," he said as he tried to stand.

"It's okay. Take your time," I said, still rubbing up and down his sweat-soaked back. "There's no hurry."

"Is he bitten?" said the voice in my ear.

"Affirmative. How long until the doctor gets here?" I replied, smiling back as he caught my eye.

"No doctors. You need to terminate immediately."

25

"What happened?" Christian said standing up straight then shaking his head as if he'd blocked out the last ten minutes. I withdrew my hand from his back, my thoughts turning to the almost empty peashooter in my pocket.

"Acknowledge, Agent Harris," the voice in my ear insisted, but I did my best to pretend I hadn't heard.

"Did you know that man?" I asked.

Christian moved his open hand to his chest and shook his head.

"That was no man." His voice slowed more with each word.

Expecting a repeat of the order in my ear, I was a little surprised when there was nothing but silence.

"Tell me what happened before I arrived," I asked, keeping my voice as soft as I could as I reached out and placed my hand on his back again.

Bursting into tears, Christian doubled over as if in pain, but soon looked up, quickly glancing left and right, his gaze seeming to flit in every direction.

"You're safe now," I said, leaning closer. "Tell me what happened." He looked at me sideways with tears dripping from his nose. "The ambulance is on its way. It's important you tell me everything you saw."

"Where is it now?" he said, shifting to look behind me, then turning his head the other way.

"Don't worry," I said, speeding my hand up and down his back. "They're searching for him and I'm here to look after you."

Christian seemed to calm at my words and stood up a little taller, wiping snot and tears away with the back of his hand.

I pulled my palm away.

"I've never seen him before. He just burst in and looked around as if he was searching for someone. When he saw Pete behind his desk, he bounded over and grabbed him right out of his seat. I dropped to the floor, but could still hear him attacking Pete. He tried to fight back, but that didn't last long. The guy was going crazy. Eventually I stopped hearing the fight but I could still hear him pounding on him. It was like Pete was being ripped apart by a wild…"

The words caught in his throat and he looked away, but then turned back to me with a sudden calm.

"He was like a wild animal, then the noises just stopped. I waited behind the desk and didn't help. What could I have done?"

I shook my head, closing my eyes for a short moment as he continued.

"For a long while I thought he might have left, and I was so relieved, but terrified at the same time. Then I heard tapping. Pete has this old, noisy keyboard which he refused to replace. For a moment, I thought it was all in my head, and perhaps I was having some sort of episode. Maybe Pete was still at his desk, but then you burst in."

"Agent Harris. Report. Is the target still secure?" the voice said in my ear.

"Yes, around the back of the alley," I replied, and Christian's eyes screwed up until I pointed to my ear as the voice spoke again.

"You know more than any of us about what you have to do. Neutralise him, and do it quietly. Acknowledge."

The voice was right, of course. What had been Isaac Brown had bitten Pete, who'd then taken a chunk out of Christian, and if he was anything like what I'd come up against in Brass Pike, I had to take action before the worst happened.

Still, I couldn't shake the guilt that if I hadn't been so spaced out, so locked in the terror of what I'd seen, he might not have been bitten, and I wouldn't have to deal with him.

I'd taken many lives before, more than I could count, but each was for a good reason, without exception. They were wrapped up in something so bad, guilty by anyone's measure. This guy had done nothing wrong. He'd been in the wrong place at the wrong time, but still there was no other choice than for him to die. It would be a mercy for him and for everyone.

I would do it, but I made a promise to myself that he would be the first and last innocent to die at my hand. There was no other choice but to put right what I'd done. I would be the one to find and deal with Isaac Brown, no matter what the voices in my ear had planned.

"Acknowledged," I said.

Holding Christian's shoulder, I turned him around, drawing back a little when I saw his eyes were bloodshot, the whites bathed red.

There was no decision to be made and I didn't have long.

"I don't feel well. There's something very wrong," he said. His shoulder felt cold to the touch.

"I'm going to help you," I said, nodding. "Let me look at your ankle. I'd turn away if I were you."

I watched as he looked away down the alley, then I bent over, pulling up my trouser leg before sliding the knife from the sheath at my ankle.

With the blade behind my back, I straightened up.

"It looks pretty nasty, but you're going to be fine," I said, pressing my left hand on his breastbone as I jabbed the knife into his back with the other.

When he couldn't catch his breath, I knew I'd hit the lung and pulled the knife out, slipping it in the opposite side.

He stared at me, his expression blank, his mouth moving as he tried to talk.

I didn't have to fane the sympathy on my cheeks as I gently lowered him to the ground and onto his back.

"It's going to be okay," I said, then pushed the knife into his heart, only pulling it out as his eyes closed. "You're okay now," I added, as I wiped the knife on his shirt, then stood.

"It's done," I said, turning and walking away.

"Are you sure?" the voice replied, and I halted my steps before twisting around to stare at the limp body.

26

After wiping the knife on Christian's shirt, I thought better of pushing it back into the holster, dropping it beside the body instead. With hope that not even in the worst of my nightmares could the spinal cord reconnect, I headed back along the side of the building, ducking my head as the police officer raised the blue and white tape.

I didn't glance at the bustle of activity at the front of the building as I walked down the street. Instead, I pulled out my phone and made a call, speaking before they had a chance to answer.

"Get everyone in a room together pronto and tell me all you know, or you can clean up this fucking mess by yourself." I hung up before anyone could reply.

With a text message vibrating my pocket, I nodded to myself as I read the instructions. To avoid going past the building I'd just left, I headed down the next street, back toward the town centre, all whilst transporting my thoughts to the Jane's handbook from last night to keep everything else from crashing in.

It wasn't long before I took the next left and soon found myself walking along the outside of the high, almost prison-like walls of the barracks.

A corporal in desert DPMs and a Glock holstered at his side stepped forward as I arrived at the looming black gates across the main entrance.

I nodded away his salute.

"Welcome to Victoria Barracks," he said, his tone clipped as he offered his hand toward the much smaller pedestrian gate he stood beside.

Stepping through, I waited to the side as the corporal followed before a sentry armed with an SA80 rifle shut us in.

"This way, ma'am," he said, striding around me in an arc, then leading me along the road between two towering three-storey buildings. The place seemed deserted as we hurried along and I followed in step with the NCO, as if the old habits from Sandhurst had never quite faded from my subconscious.

After a few minutes the route took us through a right turn, heading between the buildings and deeper into the warren, only pausing to move to the side as a wide low-loader lorry, its trailer empty, passed us by. Rounding another corner, the space opened out and everywhere I looked was a hive of activity.

Half the area had a tarmac finish, with half of it marked with white lines and a scattering of parked cars. The other part must have been the parade ground, and they'd need plenty of space to practice; this was after all where they walked from in uniform up to the castle all dressed up in their finest ceremonial black and red.

In the corner, and right by the building, stood an olive green shipping container adapted with openings as several soldiers in fatigues and bright yellow vests busied themselves lifting panels and pressing buttons, or retrieving equipment from one end and connecting a long blue pipe which came from a standpipe rising through the ground.

To the left, the other half of the wide space was covered in grass and I guessed it was where they played cricket or otherwise burnt off their spare energy, but today was different. Instead, it was filled with olive green trucks with two forklifts of the same colour, buzzing around unloading wooden crates and stacking them in a neat line to the side.

"Ma'am," the corporal said, his voice a little distant.

I turned to find he'd stood at an open door in the side of the container I'd spotted earlier.

Just as I arrived the hum of a generator close by started up with bright light pouring out through the doorway.

"Please step inside."

With a nod to the corporal, who took a step back, my eyes narrowed with the sting of antiseptic as I climbed the short steps. No sooner than I'd cleared the doorway, the metal slammed behind me, the catches clicking into place and sending the clash echoing across the room.

Squinting into the brightness, I didn't wait for my eyes to adjust, instead straining to take in the sparse detail of the square, whose space took up the entire width of the container. There were no other doors, but to the left, a wide shower head protruded from the ceiling with no sign of any control on the wall.

My gaze moved down to the middle of the floor, where a metal drain cover sat in the middle.

A dark panel covered the top half of the right-hand wall, which looked like it could be a mirror, or glass, perhaps. A shallow countertop protruded beneath it, with panels further down below.

After a moment, the dark glass lit up to reveal a smiling young blonde woman standing in a room just as bare as the one I was in. She wore a white nurse's smock and on top of her ponytail sat a sand-coloured beret, with the badge showing the cross of the Queen Alexandra Royal Army Nursing core.

When her cheeks bunched instead of offering a salute, I knew this was going to be a little easier than I'd first thought. Without the nurse moving, a panel to my right slid out to reveal a yellow contaminated rubbish bag fixed to a thin metal frame and I tried not to smile when the pretty young woman whose cheeks glowed with a rose hue asked me to take off my clothes and dispose of them in the bin.

If surprised I did so without question, she didn't show it, nodding when I removed the magazine from the Ruger and the remaining round from the chamber, before placing it all on the counter.

My gaze locked with hers as I pulled down my knickers and unclipped my bra, throwing them into the bin like I was chucking a basketball. I watched her because she was comforting to look at; an island of calm in the sea of carnage it felt like I was floundering in.

She spoke softly again for me to raise my arms and slowly turn around, and I did as I was told, not totally hating that she was probably more uncomfortable than I was at having to check me out.

It all made sense, of course. They had to make sure I hadn't been bitten. I didn't protest when she asked me to lift each of my breasts and open my legs, then tip my head forward, standing close to the glass as I moved my hair out of the way so she could check every part of my scalp.

I couldn't help but put myself in her place, wondering how I would feel as she asked me to stand under the shower head, but the thoughts vanished as scolding hot water washed down my skin, then I followed her instructions to keep my eyes closed as the water was replaced with an unpleasant disinfectant. The heat was soon back, but then turned ice cold before eventually warming to something more pleasant just as it came to a halt.

Dripping wet with my skin coloured like a cooked lobster, at least I felt wide awake as a new drawer slid open to reveal a towel. The light on the other side went off and I couldn't help but imagine the woman still standing there watching me, to make sure I was doing everything right, of course.

Dry, but still bright red, another compartment opened, but rather than a fresh change of clothes, it instead presented a long swab in a sterile packet beside a sample bottle.

The light came on again and with relief, it was the same woman.

"You want me to pee into that?" I said, the words echoing across the small room as I dropped the wet towel onto the floor.

The nurse laughed but soon forced away the smile, instead directing me to rub the cotton end along my arms and legs and across my stomach. I did as I was told, before sealing it away into the bottle and placing it back in the drawer.

As the drawer closed, she looked up and smiled, her cheeks bunching as she reached out just as the light went off again, leaving me naked and feeling a little self-conscious on my own.

I didn't have to wait for long before the last drawer slid

out to reveal a fresh packet of knickers, a bra still on the hanger and an olive green t-shirt alongside desert DPM trousers, with socks and boots underneath.

It felt like a lifetime since I'd dressed this way.

Lacing up the final boot, the door catches released, and I pushed my way out, this time squinting at the natural light as my gaze settled on the corporal.

"This way," he said, and I followed him across the car park, leading me to a door of the main building, which already stood open. The windows were blacked-out and through the doorway I spotted a row of monitors hanging on the nearest wall.

The corporal didn't follow as I stepped in, and my initial look around the room confirmed it was as I'd first thought. The door closed behind me again. With its window covered in a dark film, I didn't know if he waited on the other side, and, if he did, whether he was keeping me in or others out.

A long table filled most of the space and with around sixteen chairs gathered along its length, only the one at the far end stood halfway out with a bottle of water and an upturned glass waiting for me.

Sitting at the head of the table, the first of four monitors hanging on the opposite wall blinked to life as I poured a glass of water. I smiled, but the gesture fell when Clark's expression was missing his perpetual optimism, his skin so much paler than I'd ever seen.

Before I could ask, the head of an older guy I didn't recognise appeared on the screen to the right, along with his hand retreating from adjusting the camera. His background was lighter than the dark of the conference room where Clark sat. Instead, his walls were an anonymous magnolia.

"Hello," I said, but Clark acknowledged me only with a nod, the stranger taking no notice.

With mousey brown hair receding halfway up his head and a grey beard and thin glasses, I guessed him at around mid-fifties, perhaps an analyst or academic of sorts, with his stare betraying no experience in the field.

He looked as if he was about to speak, but kept quiet as

the monitor to his right came to life with Franklin's face rough like tree bark, his hair glinting silver from the overhead lights. In front of a matching background, he was probably in the same place as Clark and I was about to speak, dispensing with the formalities when the next monitor lit up.

"Oh fuck," I said, realising I must be heading for a tough few days when Devlin's round face appeared on the screen as he sat in his office in the Brecon bunker.

27

"Good to see you too," Dr Devlin said, the only one of the four to bear a smile.

Regretting how much I'd given away with my reaction, I curled my lips in a brief smile.

I liked the service's psychologist, but the only times I ever met with him were to debrief emotionally from a highly charged mission, perhaps coming in from being someone else for months on end and inevitably coming down from intense action to deal with some threat. Then after debriefing with the operational teams for hours, I'd have something to eat before being forced to unpack whatever emotional baggage I'd stored up, often spending longer with him than with the case agents.

At first I'd fought against his insistence to open up, but I'd quickly realised the time was better spent actually getting out all that I'd kept hidden for so long. But I didn't have to enjoy it.

The other circumstance was rarer, but sometimes he'd advise on how to set my perspective, perhaps to understand how I could protect my mental wellbeing. That he was in an operational discussion was unusual enough, but for a case with such a high level of priority was unheard of.

Franklin looked off camera as if distracted by an unheard question. He'd muted himself and his mouth moved as if talking to someone else in the room. A moment later, he looked into the camera.

"How bad is it?" I asked. When none of them reacted, I said, "I won't let you send me in blind anymore. If you hold back, you've lost me for good."

Clark shuffled in his seat as I forced myself to calm, willing myself not to show the shock of what I'd just said to the most senior member of the service I knew. Never in my career had I been so blunt, despite the many times I'd felt like saying so much. I wasn't a 'Yes' type of person, but I'd never demanded from the leadership team in such a way.

Franklin drew a deep breath, and I readied myself for the legendary father-like reply I'd witnessed him dole out to so many others.

Unsure how I'd feel, like a let-down perhaps, I lifted my chin, reminding myself I'd done nothing wrong.

"I'm sorry," Franklin said, the words taking me by surprise and sweeping away my hardened expression.

I snapped my mouth closed from where it had fallen open, chastising myself from not hiding my reaction, which was, after all, a major part of my career. Almost every day of my service, it was my job to hide my intent from those I interacted with.

Not knowing what to say, I kept quiet, letting his voice fill the void.

"It was my decision to keep you out of the loop and for that I apologise."

I nodded, stopping myself from over-correcting and shrugging.

"But you're right. It was the wrong thing to do," he added.

"Is it us?" I said, watching Franklin's eyes widen before his brow lowered with his head turning to the side. "Was Brass Pike us?"

The raise of his brow was the recognition I waited for, and he shook his head. "No. It was a…" he said, choosing his words with care. "A sister organisation, and I have to say, this was *all* news to me two days ago."

I knew there was no chance of any more detail. He'd already said more than I'd ever expected, so I didn't ask him to elaborate. It was enough to know my people hadn't caused what I'd been through.

"Professor McBride is here to explain what he can, but I think most of it you've already guessed. For operational security, he can't see or hear you."

That explained the professor's lack of reaction and for the first time I looked away from Franklin, my gaze flitting back to Clark, who was still so pale. It was then I remembered that he'd only just been told what was going on.

"Go ahead, Professor," Franklin said.

"Thank you," he said, his accent Scottish, then covered his mouth with his fist and cleared his throat. "I'll be as direct as I can. What you saw at the facility was a five year experiment gone wrong. The facility was much like that we have at Portland Down, but its existence was well hidden. Higher than Top Secret. We've recovered a large amount of data which our teams are pouring over, but we don't have access to everything yet," he said, then swallowed hard, coughing into his fist.

"It appears they have been investigating an organic discovery made in the Amazon rainforest in Brazil. British troops working with the local government on a joint operation disrupted an illegal logging camp. Biologists attached to the group to assess the logging impact on the local ecology discovered a rare plant which locals said had anti-ageing properties. That information was enough to have it sent back here for tests. Initial examinations were very promising, and they gave the project over to…" He paused and seemed to stare into the camera for a long moment. "The sister organisation."

"But I'm pretty sure…" I said, and Franklin raised his palm to stop the professor as I spoke. "The crate inside Brass Pike had a date that was within the last couple of months."

Franklin repeated my words, and I watched as the professor nodded.

"Yes. It would seem they were getting regular samples of the source material. There is a permanent team searching for more examples of the flora. Apparently, the experiments demanded a constant supply of the rare plant.

"After a year, testing began on animals, but stepped up last month when experimentation on humans started."

Franklin chipped in. "They'd been dark for three days before protocols called for a safety check. We didn't know that's what we were sending you to."

I nodded. "Despite what I've seen, I need you to tell me

what happened to those people."

Franklin paused, then relayed the message, and I watched the professor nod, his eyes blinking as if he had something in them. Eventually he drew a deep breath, looking at the table as if reading from his notes before staring right down the camera.

"The dose they gave was deadly."

28

"Just a single injection was enough," the professor continued. "Where it had revealed almost magical results on primates, slowing the ageing process and improving healing times fivefold, it killed the first human test subject as if it were the deadliest poison."

I didn't speak, knowing there was so much more for him to say.

"But then they came back to life." Even before he'd finished speaking, he shook his head as I tried to take in the words. "No. That's not quite right. I'm sorry, it just sounds unbelievable, even after reading your account and watching the recovered CCTV footage." He drew a deep breath and slowly let it out.

"They reanimated, came back from the dead. But," he said, raising a finger in the air, "were different from the people they were before. They were like wild animals."

There was nothing else I could do but nod along. Nothing I'd experienced contradicted what he'd said.

"You killed… disabled…" he continued, then shrugged before bunching his cheeks and rubbing his chin as if unable to find a word that fit. "You disrupted their biological processes, but only because of the massive amount of damage you inflicted to key areas." He raised an eyebrow and spoke again. "Unfortunately, the damage was so total, you left us nothing to study."

Silence took over the room as I tried to reason the information, to normalise it. With no one speaking, I could only relate what he'd said to the past, and I kept coming back to a word from popular culture which waited on the tip of my tongue. I couldn't bring myself to say it.

"Where does Isaac Brown come into this?" I said, relieved when the moment passed.

"There were two other facilities," Franklin said, and I nodded. I'd guessed as much from the label on the package. "After what happened at Brass Pike, they took action to shut down the other locations, but their efforts were not successful. They entered Tin Spear and took control with ease and found they were still testing on animals. We shut it down. However, Copper Flail, although using a different protocol, testing had gone the same way as Brass Pike.

"During the operation, Isaac Brown fled the scene and was only found missing after we tapped into the CCTV and counted the remains."

Franklin looked down at the desk.

"Many operatives died in the operation to take the facility." He looked up and back down the camera. "It's secure, but they're not in control by any stretch of the imagination. What you did single-handed in thirty minutes, a crack team failed to do in four hours."

"When did you realise Brown was infected?" I said, not giving time for what Franklin was inferring.

"We had our suspicions when you reported he looked unwell, and of course knew for sure at the same time as you."

"There's something not right here," I said, shaking my head. "It's clear he's infected. What I saw in that office was just like I'd witnessed at Brass Pike, but before then he was walking around like everyone else. The professor said it was lethal, and they came back different."

Franklin squinted and I spoke again.

"What I saw in Brass Pike were animals. They were insatiable and would do anything to tear me apart, but something in Brown is still in control, to some degree at least. It was like he has a purpose. He left Christian, the guy in the corner, but obliterated the other man until he was barely recognisable as a human, whilst moments before he'd been walking down the street.

"At any point, he could have ripped me to shreds, but he jumped from the second floor to get away. He was using the computer when I came into the room. I mean really using it. So what have you not told me?"

Franklin looked sideways, and when Clark turned the opposite way, I knew they were looking at each other.

"He was a scientist active in the research programme," Franklin said, "and knew its potential to prolong life or kill as a weapon. He knows everything and we think perhaps he took a sample of material. Perhaps he's hidden it somewhere. We think he might try to sell it, and we can guarantee there will be plenty of interest when news gets out."

I nodded. "If it hasn't already," I added. "You should have told me to take him out when I had the chance."

"Yes. I should," Franklin replied. "But hindsight is a wonderful thing."

I shook my head. I'd met some terrible people in the past. Those who gave no consideration to the people they might hurt in pursuing money or power, but the danger Brown was putting people in was the worst I'd ever come across.

"He must have seen what happened to his colleagues, but still he's out there putting so many people at risk," I said.

"Perhaps he doesn't realise what he's become," Dr Devlin chipped in.

Franklin nodded slowly, then looked right down the camera.

"Plus, I think he's searching for the antidote."

29

"Roll back the tapes," I said, shaking my head. "There's an antidote already?"

Franklin nodded and asked the professor to explain.

"From what we can gather, Tin Spear's primary objective was to develop countermeasures for the potential applications of the compound. Like a vaccine or antidote."

"So they *were* developing a weapon?" I asked, but stopped as the professor continued to talk, only halting when Franklin raised his hand and relayed the question.

"There's no indication they'd started work to refine the substance or any delivery mechanism. These investigations were still in the initial stages and focused on discovering the effect on mammalian biology."

Franklin took over. "The very least we know is that they developed a rudimentary antidote. It's untested as far as we're aware, but either way, Isaac Brown is working to some aim, perhaps to find someone, or something, and we need to stop him."

Despite the questions firing across my brain, Franklin was right. For the moment, nothing else mattered. Taking Brown down was the priority.

"And we don't know where he's gone?" I said.

Both Clark and Franklin shook their heads.

"And you want me to go back out there and hunt him down?"

Franklin was the only one to nod. "I need to show you something," he said, and I watched as the professor's screen went dark before it was replaced with an unsteady, low-resolution image showing the end of an assault rifle in the bottom half of the view. I'd seen these types of images many times before and, based on the height of the camera and its drifting movement, I guessed it was mounted to someone's head, on a combat helmet.

With no audio, I watched as the soldier looked at a huge round metal door I recognised. It was the door I'd walked the other way through at Brass Pike. The door I'd glanced back to so many times to make sure it wasn't opening of its own accord.

After a moment, the soldier turned their head, looking along a line of at least ten men gathered behind at their back in full black assault gear, their faces smeared in camo paint. I saw the focus in their eyes, the controlled adrenaline in their expressions as they steeled themselves for the command.

As the guy with the camera turned back to the door, another pair of arms came into the shot and wound the circular handle to the left, and then with a nod of the camera, the hands pulled the door open.

Without pause, they moved forward, and feeling as if I were with them looking over their shoulder, I felt a sudden need to hold a weapon as my body tensed for action. I had a good idea what was coming.

Beyond the door was a darkened space with a dull red light emanating out and I already knew the reason for the colour. The view jerked up towards the blood-splashed ceiling, then just as quickly the bearer of the camera looked down at the dark slick covering the concrete floor. He didn't linger on the sight, instead lifting his head and looking left and then right as he moved forward.

With another few steps, I realised they weren't at Brass Pike. Despite having been in such a hurry to escape, I could tell many details were different, things out of place and equipment I just hadn't seen.

I tried to keep my breath steady as the view rushed forward, and I hoped Devlin couldn't see the fear on my expression. I tried thinking of something else, zoning out, but that all fell away when the bullets started flying.

30

The assault rifle, an MP5, burst into life, emptying its nine millimetre rounds into the body of the half-naked man charging toward them. In a blur of the camera's movement, I couldn't help but shake my head, willing them to lift their aims and ignore their training.

As the volley of shots silenced, following their drills, the soldier stepped to the side with another moving in from the right to take over the attack, whilst the guy with the camera glanced down to change the magazine.

The video feed soon tilted up, showing another figure covered in blood rushing in from behind the first dead man who'd grown so close in the brief space of time. He was still standing despite the damage to his chest.

Before I could take much more in, a fist flew from the side and across the camera before the screen went black.

Not able to find the words, I closed my eyes, but I couldn't hide from the memories flooding into my head.

"Four men lost before they pulled back," Franklin said, and I was about to stand, unable to take the thought of what might come next.

"That was Copper Flail," Clark said, his voice a comfort, despite the flatness of his tone. "The same place Brown worked.

Settling back in the seat, I took a gulp of water, watching as the professor's image reappeared on the monitor.

"What's its status now?" I said, despite being afraid of the answer.

"Sealed," Franklin said. "They're preparing for alternative actions."

Guessing what that meant, I sat up straight. "They're going to blow the place up."

"It's one consideration I'm led to believe," he replied with a nod.

"But if all they do is break open the containment…" I added, watching as Franklin raised his chin. "Tactical nukes would be the only thing sure to get the job done."

Franklin didn't flinch.

"How did Brown get out?" I continued.

"There's an emergency escape shaft," Clark replied.

"That's how I got in," I added, my gaze flitting between the pair.

"But that's also secure now," Clark said, as if that mattered.

Glancing down at the desk, I shook my head, then looked up to see Franklin nodding as if agreeing with my sentiment.

A silence followed, but I couldn't bear it for long.

"Okay. So what here singles me out for the job?"

Franklin drew a slow breath. "I won't flatter you, but even before you took on what you found at Brass Pike, you were always our first choice. Plus, you've gone through the initial shock of what you've seen and come out the other side. We don't know how anyone else will react."

I didn't care for the answer; it wasn't what I wanted. I'd have preferred him to say I was expendable and was just the first in a long line of those waiting in the wings to take over, not the only one they trusted with doing the job. All this knowing that I'd frozen when I'd come across Brown for the first time. But what choice did I have?

"Tell me what we're up against. The biology, not the man."

"Professor, over to you," Franklin said. "She needs to know everything."

The professor launched into a long dialogue, explaining the science, most of which I didn't even try to get my head around. Instead, I picked out words like mutation and losing control, resetting the host's brain to run on its instinct alone. The dry words helped to calm the energy coursing through my bloodstream, and after five minutes I was nodding along.

"Transmission is through the exchange of bodily fluids," he said.

I raised my eyebrows and looked right at Clark.

"With primary transmission through a break in the skin."

"Thank goodness for that," I said, and watched as a small smile rose on Clark's pale lips, but then fell as Franklin's eyes narrowed. The professor raised his chin as if he'd guessed at the exchange.

"So why is Brown so different from what you're telling me?" I said, tapping the desk with a finger while Franklin relayed the message.

"The infection appears to take minutes to race through the initial stages, as I think you've seen, therefore our only conclusion was that Brown was conducting an undocumented experiment with the antidote on himself."

My brow raised. It made sense, after all, and it gave me hope he wasn't quite the monster I'd see in the underground bunker.

"Assuming Brown targeted the man I witnessed," I said, with Franklin and Clark nodding along, "how long do we expect him to keep that level of control?"

Seeing Devlin's eyes narrow on the screen, I stopped tapping on the desk and flattened my hand as Franklin repeated my question.

The professor nodded along. "We don't know, I'm afraid."

As he spoke, I heard the unmistakable twin rotors of a Chinook transport helicopter growing closer.

I already knew that would be the answer, but the question bought me a moment inside my head. I'd always been decisive, able to make the right decision almost on impulse. But this time, I needed something I didn't have.

Time.

"I have a few conditions," I said, leaving out that I'd accepted the assignment.

"Go ahead," Franklin said, raising his chin.

"Hide anything critical from me again, then I'm out. For good. I mean it."

Franklin nodded.

"I deal with Clark on this, if you're up to it?" I said,

looking his way.

He glanced over to Franklin, then back to the camera and nodded.

"Good. So no unknown voices in my ear. I decide what happens on the ground with the information you relay to me."

"Clark didn't know," Franklin said.

I nodded, staring at Clark's image, knowing all too well that what he'd been told and what he'd seen could change someone forever.

With that thought, my mind flashed back to standing in front of Dylan as he held the shotgun pointed toward my chest, his words echoing in my head and my heart palpitating at the sudden understanding of their meaning.

Some things just can't be unseen. Some things just can't be forgiven.

RAMPAGE

31

The double glazing did nothing to hide the pounding of the helicopter landing just outside.

"I want Dylan O'Connor's full file with no redactions asap," I said as I watched the screen for Franklin's reaction.

His eyebrows twitched before he looked across to Clark, who sat near to him somewhere in the conference room hundreds of miles away. The professor and Devlin remained impassive on their screens.

"The assignment we broke Agent Harris from this morning," Clark replied, and I watched Franklin about to speak. Seeming to change his mind, he turned to the camera with a thoughtful nod.

"Plus, I need access to whatever hardware I see fit," I quickly added, before he could think of any objection to my last question. "Nine millimetre rounds just don't cut it, but I know I can't very well sling a machine gun under my arm walking around Windsor," I said, raising a brow.

When Franklin held my gaze, ignoring my unspoken question, I thought back to O'Connor standing in front of me in the woods.

"Get me shotguns. Automatics if possible. The HKCAWS would be a good choice, but you might struggle to find them."

"I'll send a request to all special forces units to see if they've got anything similar under their beds," Clark cut in, his eyes wide with enthusiasm "You know what they're like."

I nodded. "Perhaps the Americans have some in country?"

"Or at worst we can get them on a flight from the US,"

Clark added, just as my thoughts flashed back to the handful of operations where I'd worked alongside Delta units who always brought along an eclectic array of firepower.

Clark nodded, scribbling out of the shot.

"I want FRAG-12 explosive shells for the shotguns," I added, and watched as Clark continued to nod, but he then broke off, looking toward Franklin's scowl. "They're made in London, but will need downgrading. They're too powerful on spec."

Clark continued to write at speed as Franklin moved away from the microphone, speaking then gesturing off screen before leaning back in.

"We'll get you what you need. I don't know how long it will take and this is a covert operation, so no squad level weapons amongst the tourists."

I nodded, knowing he was right, but there was no getting away from the inevitable upset on the streets.

"How about we tell people there's a film in production?" I said, watching as Clark's brow lowered then raised with what seemed like understanding. "We could put out a few well-placed rumours?"

Clark nodded. "Perhaps hints of a Bond film might take the edge off any slipups."

Franklin's only reaction was a slight nod before he said, "that doesn't mean we don't have to be sensitive to the theatre."

I nodded as Clark made another note, but I couldn't shake the thought of members of the public cruising the streets on the lookout for stars who, despite their million dollar bank accounts, wouldn't know what to do if confronted by the horror of what I sought.

"One more thing," I added as the feeling fell away. I took a deep breath, hoping to ready myself for their reaction. "I need back up. I need a team."

Franklin lifted his head, his brow raising. It was the first time I'd ever asked for help. I avoided Devlin's reaction altogether, but hoped he was professional enough not to slip in any hint of the conversations we'd had in our sessions.

We all knew team play was not my strong point.

Clark continued his default nod, keen to talk. "We've already secured a detachment from the Regiment. Six troopers and a liaison."

"We thought perhaps you'd be resistant," Devlin said, unable to hold back.

I raised a brow, choosing it as my only reply.

"Is that enough?" Franklin said, but continued speaking before I could answer. "We have to keep our footprint small. The last thing we want is mass panic."

We all agreed with a nod.

"But remember, they're the muscle, you're the brains. Stay at a safe distance. Do you understand?"

"What's the safe distance?" I said, not missing a beat.

Listening to the drum of the helicopter's twin rotors as it lifted, I didn't press him for an answer.

"We've got more we can do to support you," Clark said as the noise subsided. "Including something we've retrieved from Tin Spear."

A knock sounded at the door to the left of the screens and he fell silent as the corporal walked in with a green equipment case carried at his side, which he placed on the table in front of me before walking from the room.

"The condition," Clark said as the door closed, "for want of a better word, is caused by a microbe, a trace of which is left behind from an infected person's touch. What you have there," he said, nodding forward, "is a system for detecting those traces. Open it up."

I stood, pulling at the catches and lifting the lid to reveal two small pouches set in a dark foam. Hinging the lid to rest on the table behind, the pouch to the left was a little larger than the other, but both were about the size of a pencil case.

"The left pouch," Clark said as I pulled open the Velcro flap at the top of the bag, "contains swabs impregnated with a reactant. Apply it to the test area, then rub it against the reader, included in the pouch, for no less than five seconds. Within ten seconds, the digital display will show the microbe's count in parts per million."

I nodded, flicking through the clear zip lock plastic bags which each contained a moistened square of gauze about half the length of my finger.

"What numbers am I interested in?" I said, looking over the small black rectangle of plastic with a blank two digit LED segment at the top.

Clark nodded. "With a reading of thirty or more, there's a high risk of infection if in contact with broken skin or otherwise ingested. Professor?"

"The microbe decays rapidly on surfaces and even more quickly in the air," the professor took over. "I would expect the same sample analysed ten minutes later to be around twenty, then ten minutes after, perhaps fifteen or lower still."

I nodded.

"We swabbed your clothes," Franklin said, and I watched Clark raise his chin.

"Go on," I said with anticipation.

"The maximum reading was ten," he replied.

"And that was just from being in the room with him?" I said as I pushed back in my seat.

Clark and Franklin both nodded.

Not wanting to ponder on the thought, I looked back to the case and the second cut out.

"In the second pouch is what we believe to be the antidote," Clark said.

I raised my eyebrows. "I have so many questions," I said, not knowing where to start.

"Let me explain," Franklin said. "From what we can gather, Tin Spear had some success with their objective."

"Then isn't this the answer to all of our problems?" I said, tilting my head to the side.

Clark shook his head as the professor stared into the camera.

"With Tin Spear shut down, we don't know how long it will be before we can produce more. Plus…" Clark said before glancing over to Franklin and then back to the camera. "There's only one way of confirming that it works—"

"I don't have to say this," Franklin cut him off, "but if you're bitten, or otherwise exposed at a high level, then that's the time to use it."

"Why don't I just use it on Brown when I find him?" I said.

Franklin shook his head. "He's too far gone."

"Even in our best projections," Clark took over, "it won't reverse the effects, but if used immediately on a new infection, signs are it will stand some chance of reversing the damage."

"And to be clear," Franklin butted in. "This is for you alone. Do you understand?"

Something didn't seem right, but still I nodded. I was sure Clark at least believed what he was saying, but to have just a single dose available made little sense. I couldn't stop the thought creeping in that perhaps it was nothing more than saline, something Devlin had come up with to make me think it wasn't just a suicide mission.

"Thank you, Professor," Franklin said.

Just as the academic leaned in as if to close his connection, I said, "Wait," then paused as Franklin asked the professor to stay on the line. "How can we be sure those places weren't developing something on the side that you're not aware of?"

Franklin nodded and relayed the question before the professor spoke.

"The programme had meticulous protocols for recording how they used the samples and a third party regularly audited the results. There wouldn't be sufficient material for any other areas of research."

I thought for a moment, knowing there were many ways they could get around the controls, but I'd met many scientists before, and it was very rare for them to be so sure about anything.

I nodded to the camera and the academic's screen went blank just as I stood, then I pushed the two pouches into the pockets of my trousers.

"Agent Harris," Franklin said. "There's one last thing you should know."

I raised my eyebrows "I get it. If I fail, they'll blow the town off the map rather than risk the rest of the country."

Franklin nodded slowly.

"Then I better go do my job," I said and pulled the door open, hurrying when I heard him ask if Devlin had anything to add.

32

The corporal led me in silence to a nearby room, where I changed into a waiting pair of jeans and t-shirt before strapping a new holster under my arm. A moment later, a gentle knock at the door gave me pause for thought as I slid the packed magazine into a replacement Glock.

Slipping the pistol into the leather, I felt all too aware it might be the young blonde from earlier standing on the other side of the plain wooden door. After a brief delay figuring out what I might say, I called out, hiding my pang of disappointment as a male nurse carrying a small plastic tray stepped through the doorway. His business-like smile was enough to remind me now wasn't the time for distractions.

With an arm full of broad-spectrum anti-viral drugs, I pulled on the black jacket, which was bulky enough to hide the pouches secured in each inside pocket, but not too thick for the fading season's weather.

Walking through the gate, I headed toward the Brown's place, knowing Clark and his team would be busy with my list of requests.

The last I'd heard, the support team was on route by road. Coming from the Welsh borders, they'd be with me in a couple of hours. In the meantime, I wouldn't wait for the scent to go cold, but with no idea how long it would be for the weapons to arrive, I'd have to make do with the pea shooter under my arm.

I'd barely stepped out of the shadow of the tall walls when Clark called to confirm there'd been no reports of a man running around in a blood-drenched shirt, and as I walked each street spotted with the early afternoon traffic, I couldn't help wondering how the people I saw would react to what I'd witnessed.

Then again, if I did my job right, they'd never need to find out.

Only three streets away from the base, Clark was back

on the line to confirm they'd tracked down the parents through the network of ANPR cameras protecting the Queen's neighbourhood. A pair of plain clothed cops were on their tail and followed on foot out of sight between the aisles of a supermarket, whilst uniformed colleagues waited close by.

The parents lived in a pretty little terrace whose front door opened right onto the street, forcing me to walk the entire length of the row to find the deserted alley behind. With door numbers on many of the rear gates, their place was easy to find again. The slatted wood bolted on the inside wasn't difficult to climb without being spotted.

With no picks to tackle the mortice lock in the wooden back door, the dilapidated shed drew my attention and, after pulling off sections of dry, curled wooden panels that had seen better days, I had my run of the treasure trove inside.

All I needed was the long flat-blade screwdriver waiting with such obedience in a jam jar on a paint-stained workbench, and I had the putty from the back door's glass scraped free within a few minutes.

Placing my feet on the kitchen floor, I felt an impulse to wash my hands, but I looked away from the sink, sniffing the air for any sign of a rotten wound. With nothing of the kind peaking my fears, I pulled out the larger of the two pouches, taking a swab from the baggie before stuffing the rest away as I moved around the house, scouring the conventional detail of the home. The ornaments and dated wallpaper confirmed those from an older generation lived here.

Swabbing the kitchen counter first, I ran the damp gauze across the handle of the fridge, then over each door handle as I searched for anything that might hint at a recent visit by Brown.

Dabbing the swab over the TV remote, I reasoned he might have checked the news for signs of our chase. But, on the ground floor at least, I found nothing to hint that someone other than the older couple were living in the space.

Taking care to move up the steps, I pushed my feet either side of the wood, running the swab along the banister as I rose to the first floor landing, where six doors stood, three of them wide. The first open door gave a view of a toilet and a sink ahead, then a bathroom to the left, before further around I found a master with a double bed in the centre dressed in a yellow floral print.

Creeping along, I swabbed the handles of three closed doors as I listened, but despite hearing nothing, I rested the gauze on the carpet and slipped the Glock from its home as I glared at the door to the right of the toilet.

Discarding my normal drills, the ones I'd followed for over ten years, I raised the gun as I snapped down the handle and pushed. It wouldn't budge and I pulled it open instead, closing it after finding rows of towels in a cupboard.

Moving to the next room, I repeated the same, stepping into a small bedroom as I swept my aim through the forty-five degrees it took to know it was uninhabited.

Not delaying, I opened the next door. With posters on the wall and a boxy stereo and speakers in the corner, other than the made bed and the lack of clothes scattered across the floor, it looked more like a teenager's room than that of a scientist who should have left home almost a decade ago.

About to call Clark to find if they had another child, the name on the graduation certificates from UCL confirmed I had the right place.

Collecting the swab from the hallway, I ran it over the handles of a chest of drawers along the far edge of the room, the single drawer handle of a bedside unit, then down the length of the shallow wooden TV stand to my right, along with the remote control before I took the square reader from the bag. After sliding the switch on the side, I rubbed the swab across the face several times.

Resting it in front of the TV as the digits flashed, telling me to wait, I peered down, scanning past the single drawer below the TV and the shelves filled with DVDs and CDs, before looking over the room for a second time.

Taking care, I opened the bedside drawer, pausing at

the sight of a small leather-bound address book nestled amongst other detritus. About to reach out to take the book, behind me the reader beeped, and I turned, glancing at the twenty one displayed in red.

Brown had been here.

Kicking myself that I'd not brought gloves, the thought fell away at the sound of the lock on the front door clicking at the bottom of the stairs.

33

"What's the status of the Browns?" I whispered, peering around the wall as I stared at the dark shadow through the frosted glass in the front door.

"Wait one," Clark replied a second after he answered the call.

I moved out of sight just as the front door swung open, giving me no time to see anything more than a bulky figure crossing the threshold.

The door clicked closed, and I dared not move, listening instead to the creak of the wood as feet climbed the stairs.

Whoever it was, they'd not spoken or made any other sound, hinting that it wasn't the parents who'd arrived, having unwittingly lost their surveillance. The lack of voices also didn't rule out that Brown hadn't come back.

It would have been a foolish move, but he'd so far shown no field craft or any operational awareness and there was no way of telling if it was how he'd always been or if the infection had affected his mind.

The silence also didn't point away from some unknown party coming to search the place. The initial racket at the door hinted this might be the case.

"We have visual confirmed. They're still secure in the shop," Clark said in my earpiece. "What's your situation?"

When I didn't reply, he would have known straight away, but without the panic code, a double tap at the side of the phone, he wouldn't call for whatever cavalry they could muster to my location. I wouldn't use that option unless it was life or death. The last thing we needed was a load of cops covering themselves in what the swabs had detected.

Waiting around the side of the wall, I held the pistol up high and with the sound of footsteps just the other side, I imagined someone looking into each of the rooms just as I had.

With care, I took a step further into the bedroom, extending my arms to set my aim on where I hoped their head would be when they came around the corner, even though the last thing I wanted to do was raise the alarm by firing.

Listening out to the occasional creak, I snapped the gun higher as a man in a black shirt, dark jeans and a black jacket rounded the corner. He was unarmed, jerking back when he saw the muzzle aimed his way, then froze, having enough awareness that to run could be his last decision.

At just under six feet tall and with a crew cut, his skin a little tanned, his eyes narrowed as his gaze looked past the weapon for the first time.

Still not knowing how many people had followed him into the house, or waited outside, I kept quiet, not barking a command for him to get to the floor. Instead, stepping back, I motioned with the gun for him to follow me further into the room.

He lifted his chin, still looking me in the eye, his expression relaxing, then with a raise of his brow and a slight smile forming on his lips, I knew he'd underestimated what I was capable of.

Confirmation came within a blink of an eye as his shoulders relaxed, then dropped forward, falling below my aim as he rushed toward me.

Taking a step back, I bought myself a moment, then as his shoulder connected to my stomach, his hands wrapping around my hips, I left only my right hand to grip the Glock, bringing down the butt on his occipital, the part of the skull at the back where it curved inward.

With the air forced from my lungs, and falling backwards against his dead weight, I did my best to push my shoulders forward to protect my head from hitting the chest of drawers behind, but I didn't have time to tuck my hands in and the knuckles of my left hand smashed on the edge of the TV unit.

Coming to rest with my lower half smothered by the stranger and pain flaring in my hand, somehow I kept a tight hold on the gun. At first I thought my blow had done the job, but it only took a second before I felt his body tense, his arms gripping around my torso, giving me no time to wrestle from under his weight.

I raised the gun, but with his head to the side of mine, I couldn't bring down its full weight. Instead, I grabbed at the narrow TV unit on my left but it wouldn't move. Thinking as fast as I could, I planted my right elbow into his spine, burying it with all the force I could muster. He cried out, but his grip around my chest tightened so much I couldn't pull a breath.

Feeling light-headed, but somehow able to keep the panic at bay, I kept my elbow buried deep. Guessing he wasn't alone, I knew my options were diminishing.

Listening to his grunt of relief as I pulled back my elbow, I swapped the gun between my hands and brought the muzzle to the base of his neck, pushing as hard as I could. Despite knowing he couldn't have missed what I was doing, with a low rumbling growl he squeezed tighter still.

With no breath to call out a warning, the energy draining from my muscles as every second passed and my vision narrowing to a point, I still wasn't ready to concede and blow his brains out. Hearing nothing but the rush of blood in my ears for a long moment, a woman's high voice called out from downstairs, telling me I had no time left.

"Got anything?"

Reaching across myself, I grabbed at the drawer handle under the TV unit, then yanked as hard as I could. The drawer came free, scattering the contents across his back, but I saw nothing amongst the clutter that would save me.

34

With my vision just a pinpoint of light, I closed my eyes, forgetting I held the gun limp in my hand and that with only a little more effort, I could have finished it all.

All I could think of was taking one more breath and that I'd gone through so much and survived with so many people wanting me dead. The faces of people I'd defeated over the years rattled through my mind like a high speed picture show. There were murderers, traitors, and right down evil people, and none of them had bested me, despite how close some of them got.

No. I couldn't let this be how it all ended.

A sudden clarity took control and, using everything I could muster, I opened my eyes, my gaze catching on a glint of metal on the carpet in amongst the debris from the drawer I'd pulled on top of us.

Sellotape. Paper. A stapler and a pair of scissors.

Blinking, my circle of vision expanded and the man's grunts became crisp in my ears, as did the rush of footsteps up the stairs . I leaned forward as far as I could despite the pain in my ribs, but it was enough for me to hook my finger through a single eye of the metal and slip it in my hand.

Almost dropping the two joined blades before I could lift them up, I doubled down on my grip and slammed the sharp end into his back, pulling out then jabbing again, plunging the metal into his meat as he cried out in pain. His grip released a little more with each plunge of the shears until I took what felt like my first ever breath.

As his cries halted and his fight fell to nothing, and with my vision expanding with each inhale, I saw my hand covered in blood, but gripping the scissors tight, and using all my growing strength, I lifted the dead weight enough to roll away to the left.

Barely able to stop myself from blacking out from the pain across my front, I gave one last shove to push him away. He woke, cursing as he turned to look at me, but his eyes closed as I jabbed the scissors in the side of his neck as far as they would go, then repeated as he reached for the wound.

Heavy footsteps turned my attention to the corridor, where a woman appeared wearing a smaller version of his outfit. She'd drawn an unimaginative Browning Hi Power, but her startled gaze lingered too long at her colleague's ineffective wrangling with the scissors in his neck and I was up on my feet with the TV wrenched from the unit, the plugs and cables pulled clean out of the sockets as I sent it flying before she looked toward me, and long before she could raise the pistol.

The TV hit her square in the face and she fell backwards, her head hitting with a thump against the wall before she slumped with the appliance on top of her, the gun strewn to the side as she lay motionless.

Rather than revelling in the ease of how she'd gone down, I turned around, knowing if the guy on the ground had anything left, he'd be drawing his weapon.

I felt no sorrow when I saw his eyes closed, not stirring as blood gulped from his neck, its motion slowing with each pulse.

With a deep breath and wincing with the pain that I hoped would ease soon, I inspected my left hand covered in blood, then looked down at my jacket, equally drenched. Stepping over to the bed, I wiped my hand on the cover, feeling a little pain as I scraped the grazed knuckles, whilst trying not to think of the wounds as it left a trail of red.

After reaching inside the guy's jacket and finding another Hi Power, with his surge of blood slowing to a trickle, I didn't need to check for a pulse to know it wouldn't be long before he'd never pose a threat again.

I kicked the woman's pistol well out of her reach, then gripped the TV, pulling its weight from on top of her, not able to stop myself from wincing at the graze on her forehead surrounded by a growing bruise already the size of my fist.

The drum against my fingers as I touched at her throat

told me all I needed to know and I rolled her on to her face, listening as she moaned and then stepped back into the room to get the tape before picking at the end.

Eventually I had her hands taped together, then wound it around her feet until the roll ran out and she started to rouse. Just as I leaned over to turn her onto her back, I saw the plastic transmitter in her ear and froze, holding my breath.

Removing the earpiece, which looked much like the compact model I wore, the woman moaned, but her eyes remained closed as I listened to the end of a message.

"…eet still clear."

The voice was that of a young man with an edge of gravel in his tone and, by the sound of it, neither of the two had raised the alarm. From what I'd caught of the transmission, the guy was outside or had tapped into CCTV cameras I hadn't spotted on my approach.

Either way, it wouldn't be long before they were missed.

35

Creeping back to the window, I stood at the side, spotting the silver Mercedes Vito van parked five spaces along with a driver in the seat glancing up at the house through the wing mirror.

Carefully placing the earpiece on the carpet and then leaning down the stairwell before gripping the banisters, I rushed down the stairs, regretting leaping in two bounds as pain flared in my ribs. Landing at the front door, I stepped to the left with less vigour, hoping the guy watching wouldn't think anything of my shadow.

In the living room, I looked down at the front of my jacket, watching the dark blood make its way towards my jeans. Pulling my arms from the material, I let it drop to the carpet whilst making sure none of the sticky life force touched the rest of my clothes.

With a quick wet of my hands from the kitchen tap to get the worst of the blood off, and with no time other than to wince at the pain of my left hand, I glanced down to my white top to make sure it didn't look like I worked in a butcher's shop, then saw the holster advertising my real intent.

After slipping the Glock into the rear waistband of my jeans and covering it with my t-shirt, then slinking off the holster from around my shoulders, I grabbed a fruit knife from the block which I tucked into my sock and was back though the kitchen window and over the fence, running down behind the houses a moment later.

"The parents are on the move," Clark said in my ear as I slowed at the end of the alley.

"Keep them busy," I replied, with a second glance to make sure I was clean of anything incriminating whilst I walked the short distance across the houses. Clark didn't need to reply as I crossed the road, walking as casually as I could whilst recovering my breath with shooting pains racing across my already aching chest.

The driver, a guy as young as I'd thought, perhaps early twenties, occasionally moved his mouth but didn't look in my direction once, instead peering through the rearview mirror. I held myself back from tutting at his poor field craft in letting me get right up to the glass, only turning as I gave a gentle tap on the passenger side whilst wearing an unsure smile.

The guy turned to face me through a veil of smoke, his eyes a little wide, and he seemed even more fresh-faced up close than I'd expected. Spying the bright red laptop resting on the middle seat with the screen facing the driver, I mouthed a few words with no volume. I watched as with a frown and a quick glance to the wing mirror, he placed his right hand to his side and the passenger window dropped halfway, sending smoke billowing out from the cigarette sitting in the ashtray.

"Are you going to be long?" I said, forcing a smile.

"Huh," the guy shrugged, not hiding his impatience as I leaned in closer.

"You're in our space and my husband is going to be home soon," I added with a quick glance along the quiet road.

His brow relaxed for a moment, but rose again as he spoke whilst shaking his head.

"It's not allocated parking." The window rose with his finger on the switch.

"No. Please no," I said, holding out my palms as I leaned closer to the shrinking gap and raised myself on my tiptoes. "He'll be so angry if you're here." When I saw his eyes narrow, I added, "Not with you, with me."

The window stopped about a quarter of the way closed and he looked at me with such intensity.

"You don't know what he'll do," I added, lowering myself to the flats of my feet.

The driver's brow relaxed, then turned to a frown whilst I did my best to make my eyes as wide as possible and pushed on a fake smile.

He sighed, then drew a deep breath. "I'll be gone soon.

Don't worry," he said, before glancing through the door mirror again.

I was about to step back, rethinking my next move, when he turned towards me and lowered the window to halfway. "Does he hurt you?"

Knowing from his response that I'd got him, I looked away, glancing at the door behind me, then down the road whilst again raising myself to my toes in search of the husband who didn't exist.

Eventually, I turned to the driver and shook my head.

His eyes narrowed. "Good," he said, but the words were unsure. "Go inside, Miss. I'll be gone soon," he added, as he raised his chin with the window raising again.

I looked back to the house door once more and nodded, but when I didn't move, he turned his head to the side, his eyes narrowing with a question as I bunched my cheeks.

"I'm locked out."

The window stopped moving, then lowered as he leaned towards me.

"Sorry what?" he said.

"I'm locked out. That's why my husband is coming home."

With a sigh, he nodded and looked around the cab, then watching his shoulders fall, I saw the moment he realised it would be a stupid idea to even contemplate letting me inside.

"Have you got a light?" I said, motioning with my fist and thumb as if to strike a lighter.

His eyes lit up, knowing he could help with that at least, and stretching back in his seat, he reached into his pocket as the window rolled all the way down. With the lighter in his hand, he leaned across, pushing the lighter toward me.

I took a step back, pushing my arms out and as he came almost in reach, I stepped closer, grabbing at his wrist and pulled, jumping up and using his weight to propel me forward and in through the window, scattering the laptop to the floor.

"What the..." he said, his voice pained, but before he

could finish I pushed my back into his face, forcing my weight against his mouth as he kicked out at his door. Pulling his arm to stifle his lashing out, it only took a minute before he went limp and I held him there for a couple of seconds to be sure he wasn't faking.

With a quick glance around, I moved to the passenger seat and turned to the figure slumped on his side. His pounding pulse raced as I held his wrist, then I shook my head when I couldn't see anything to tie him up with. Instead, pulling the keys from the ignition and unclipping his seatbelt, I dragged him out to the pathway, leaving him on the tarmac for a quick moment as I slid the side door across before bundling him into the empty space.

Tying his hands with his belt, and pulling his trousers to wrap around his ankles, I knew it wouldn't last long when he woke, but it would have to do.

Back in the cab I grabbed the laptop, with the screen still lit with a local map. I pulled up an internet browser, and tapped in the series of three numbers separated by full stops from memory, then pressed the pop-up to confirm to download and run the software. Within ten seconds, the process completed, and I shut the lid just as Clark spoke in my ear.

"We can't keep them much longer."

"Ten more minutes," I said as I pushed the passenger door shut. With the laptop under my arm, I rushed up the street and was back in through the missing window within a couple of minutes, holding my breath when I heard the thrash of movement above.

Leaving the laptop on the kitchen floor, I took the biggest knife from the block, then listening out, I peered up the stairs. Seeing no movement, I stepped onto the first riser, but only as my head came level with the last did I see the blood-red whites of the woman's eyes greeting me.

Drawing her lips back, she bared her teeth, but with her hands still bound behind her, she seemed drowsy as if waking from a sleep.

Not wanting to give her any time to rouse, I leapt up

the last of the stairs. Expecting to see the man come around the corner in the same state, I jumped on her, straddling her chest then using all my weight to push the knife into her eye and twisting the metal as best I could until her body stopped bucking.

About to jump up, rushing to check for threats, my gaze held on the bruised gash on her forehead, clear plasma having oozed out and run down her head. As I turned to look at the break in the skin on my hand, I felt a shiver run down my spine.

36

Pushing away the thought of what might happen to me in the coming moments, I stood and span around on the spot, suddenly aware I still hadn't checked on the guy I'd first taken care of. Finding him laying where I'd left him, the beige carpet almost completely darkened by his blood, I turned and ran down the stairs, racing to the kitchen.

Stuffing the plug into the sink's drain, I rifled through the bottles and potions in the cupboard underneath, pulling out bleach and emptying the contents. After running a little water, I plunged my hands in, scrubbing at my wounded knuckles despite the sting.

Only as Clark spoke in my ear did I pull my hands out and dry them on a towel.

"We can't keep them much longer."

"They can't come back here, not like this. It's going to need decontamination," I replied, thinking of the bodies upstairs.

"Burn it," Clark replied, and I knew it was our only choice.

Without delay and using only my right hand, I found the biggest pan stored beside the cooker and filled it with vegetable oil from a bottle in an adjacent cupboard before turning on the gas.

Grabbing a candle and a box of matches from a drawer nearby, along with a roll of clear food bags, I raced up the steps to make sure neither of the bodies could ever move again, then with my hand in a plastic bag, I sealed up the address book from the beside drawer.

Back downstairs, I placed the candle in the far part of the living room on top of magazines and papers, lighting it, then waiting a moment for it to catch before knocking it over. With the oil smoking on the hob, I killed the gas to douse the flame, then turned it back on without pressing the ignition.

From outside, I replaced the glass into the back door,

pushing the putty into place and I was over the fence, leaving the stench of gas behind with the laptop under my arm and my jacket and holster balled inside out in my hand.

With a quick call to the fire brigade to report a massive warehouse blaze the other side of the town, I slowed at the sight of a black BMW X5 parked across the alley ahead. The passenger window rolled down and revealed a woman in dark glasses who was a little older than me, with long brunette hair in a plaited ponytail. Grey men, the type most people wouldn't look twice at unless you were in my line of business, occupied each of the front seats.

Ready to drop everything in favour of the Glock in my waistband in case I'd read the situation wrong, I stepped up to the open window just as an explosion boomed out from the street behind.

Not looking over my shoulder, the woman pulled off her shades and raised her brow.

"Red?"

"Unicorn," I replied, and her hand went to the handle as I completed the challenge.

Moving in beside her as she shuffled along the seat, I pulled the Glock from my waistband, leaving it to rest on top of the bagged address book and computer sitting on my lap. She didn't bat an eyelid as I dropped the coat and holster into the footwell, then as I checked my hands for any blood before answering the call ringing in my ear.

"Are you okay?" Clark asked.

"All went to plan," I replied, catching the heavy scent of bleach in the air as I tried not to look at my knuckles, or wince as I rested my hand on top of the bundle.

"The reading was twenty, so he couldn't have been there too long ago," I said, just as a vision of the woman's bloodshot eyes filled my thoughts. "We had guests, so I guess the cat is out of the bag," I added, leaning down to grab the larger of the two pouches from the coat whilst taking care not to cover myself in mess.

"Were they still in the house?" Clark said.

"Affirmative. Both neutralised. One of them confirmed

infected."

Clark stayed silent as if not sure what to say, and I know I should have mentioned my knuckles, but as he spoke, the thought moved away.

"We have units on the way to meet with the fire brigade and sanitise the place once the fire is out. I think they'll let it burn for a bit," he said.

I nodded, even though he couldn't see the gesture as I pulled out a swab, clenching my teeth at the sting as I ran it over the wounds.

"I recovered an address book, but it's going to need decontaminating. Plus a laptop which is clean, and I installed the utility software," I said, then placed the swab against the reader.

"Great."

"What do you want to do about the guy I left in the van? He'll be waking up soon," I said, looking out from the window but not taking any notice of what I saw.

"Is that where the laptop came from?"

"Yes," I said, then with the beep I glanced down to the zero reading and told myself I'd be more careful next time.

"Leave him there," he replied. "There's nothing we can do. At least the laptop should show who he's working for."

"I recognised some of their kit," I said, and the pause told me he understood what it could mean, but like me, didn't want to give his thoughts voice, at least this early on. I reeled off a list of other things I needed, including a box of disposable gloves.

I closed my eyes for a moment, relaxing to let my mind clear, then turned to look out the window again when I heard the woman rustling for something in the passenger seat.

"No sign of the t-shirt, but I didn't go through the bins," I said.

"We'll look. I can have a portable UV decontamination unit to you within the hour. We've confirmed UV to be effective. I'll have it delivered to the barracks."

"No," I said. "I want us away from there. Find me a

place on an industrial estate. Some sort of unit. Slough's just one enormous set of warehouses. You must be able to find us something suitable."

"Roger that," he said, then I looked back into the car when I felt a touch on my left hand. I raised a brow as the woman gestured to the open first aid kit on her lap.

"Let me," she said, and I relaxed my hand, giving a shallow nod, then turned again out of the window as she placed my hand on her lap. Feeling the warmth of her touch, I closed my eyes and realised Clark had gone from the line.

"How does that feel?" she said after a few moments, her voice soft as she smoothed the plasters around the edges. I turned to look and then peered down at my hand still on her lap, which felt as if it had been there for too long, and pulled away. "Not too tight?"

"No. It's fine. Thank you," I replied, shaking my head. "So you're the liaison?"

She nodded.

"What do I call you?"

"Mother Bird," she said, and I couldn't help but laugh as I shook my head.

"I'm not calling you that," I said. "Choose another."

"I didn't choose it," she said, and out of the corner of my eye I watched as the two men in front swapped a look, then glanced back to the road when they realised I was watching.

"Pick something else."

She glanced over as if confused, and I turned away, shaking my head, wondering if I could choose another liaison.

On the edge of Windsor and heading towards Slough on the dual carriageway, I heard the first sirens and soon watched as a fire engine loomed into view before whizzing past on the other side of the road.

"What have they briefed you on?" I asked.

"Not much. Just the basics. Not run of the mill. You're going to fill the blanks in and provide training."

Clark's voice on the line interrupted my thoughts.

"There's been a sighting. We need you and your team."

"Who? Where?" I replied, looking away from the woman.

"There's a soldier running rampage at Victoria barracks."

Turning back into the car, I said, "I hope you've all got strong stomachs."

BERSERK

37

"Turn around," I said, motioning my finger in a circle and watching as the driver, without slamming on the brakes, pulled the wheel of the X5 to the right, ignoring the car horns from behind and bouncing us over the central reservation. "Get us to Victoria Barracks quick time," I added, already feeling our speed rising.

"Now listen up," I said, and didn't need to wait for the trooper in the passenger seat, a white guy with mousey brown hair that was at least four weeks over regulation length for a conventional unit, to turn, and for the driver, who I hadn't had a good look at yet, to glance through the rearview mirror just as the female liaison twisted toward me in her seat.

"I don't care about your tour count, or how many people you've killed. I guarantee you've seen nothing like what we're dealing with."

Whilst the liaison continued to look on dutifully as the car twisted and turned through the streets, the trooper in the passenger seat who looked like he'd be more at home in board shorts with no top, glanced with a raised brow to the driver, only turning back when I spoke again.

"What I'm about to say is fact, no matter how it sounds." I watched as the passenger's eyes narrowed. "The target has a condition they'll never come back from which has attacked everything that makes them human, shutting down most brain function and leaving behind just a simple will to kill. I'll warn you now, if you pause, you're dead."

Each pair of eyes narrowed, then glanced to one another just as a change in direction threw us left in our seats, then quickly right before I could look out of the window at the overweight driver of a white Transit van shaking his fist.

"This is neither a training exercise or a prank, and you're lucky. I didn't have the luxury of a warning and I nearly didn't live to tell the tale. I've worked with the Regiment many times before, and you're the best of the best at what you do, and you've seen more action than most in the military ever would, but put that macho bullshit away and listen up or you'll end up dead like your colleagues."

The trooper in the passenger seat narrowed his eyes as he lifted his head.

"You better take this in. Forget what you know about human physiology. That won't help you now. If I give the order, you aim for the head. This is a shoot to kill mission," I said, tapping my temple.

The trooper shared another look with the driver before turning in my direction.

"There's a rumour," he said, his eyes narrowing further. "About an operation in Wiltshire," he added, after glancing to the seat beside me.

I nodded, having no doubt that those who'd died storming Copper Flail were in the Regiment.

The passenger straightened up, then closed his eyes for a moment, before eventually nodding.

"Thirty seconds," said the driver, and soon rounding a corner, the tall walls of the barracks came into view, the metal gates opening wide whilst three rifle carrying soldiers glared over as we stopped.

I lowered the window.

"Parade ground, ma'am," the closest of the soldiers shouted with the other two already preparing to close the gates behind us as we shot forward, then headed through the first tight corner at speed.

"Call signs?" I said as I scoured the deserted view between the buildings.

"Moses," the front seat passenger replied without turning around.

"Hollywood," the driver added in a deep voice, and I

turned to the woman at my side as I spoke.

"Pick a new call sign, or I will."

Her eyes sprang wide before she quickly regained control, and for a moment I was thankful she was just the liaison and not someone I'd have to trust with my life.

"Look, it's easy. Just pick another bird," I said, softening my voice as the X5 jolted right, turning through the next corner.

Raising her head, a smile rose on her lips. "A duck," she said. The smile fell as she regretted what she'd said.

"Daisy Duck, it is then," I replied, glancing at Moses as he laughed. "Daisy will do," I corrected, then turned away to look out of the windows, expecting to come out into the parade ground at any moment. "ETA on the rest of the team?"

"Thirty minutes," she said, her tone assured and business-like again.

"Fuck," I replied, my heart sinking that there'd only be three of us. "We'll go in as a unit. They can back us up if the shit hits the fan, or at least retrieve our bodies."

Leaving no time for them to react, we drew to a halt a few spaces down from the converted shipping container. Other than the small groups of men armed with pistols and SA80 rifles and dressed in a mixture of military and civilian clothes, the place looked much as it had before.

Shouts echoed from a distance as we pulled open our doors just as a man's voice cut through the noise. Stepping to the ground, I glanced over my shoulder, getting my first look at the driver.

Hollywood was a tall black guy with close cropped hair and an average build. Other than the dark acne scars around his jawline, there was nothing to make him stand out.

Turning back to the buildings, I glanced to a man in fatigues striding over and soon the light crowns of his rank on the dark coloured epaulets came into view as he looked between the two troopers in jeans and t-shirts.

"What's the situation, Major?" I said, watching his head jerk in my direction as he straightened up.

"Sorry, ma'am," he said, as I finished reading the surname above his breast pocket. "We have him isolated in a section of the administration building." His eyes narrowed as he spoke, looking each of us up and down in turn. "We were all set to deal with this in-house, but I was told to hold off for specialists and secure the building with an armed guard. What exactly is your specialism?"

"That's classified," I replied, watching as he raised his chin before nodding over to the building beside the decontamination unit.

"He's on the first floor."

"You've done a good job, Major Jones," I said. "Now keep your men on the doors and I'd be grateful if you can find someone to show us the internal route."

"I'll do it myself, ma'am," he replied without delay, his brow raising as I pulled the Glock from under my arm, knowing the other two would do the same. "I'm not sure that will be necessary," he added, scowling.

"Let me be the judge of that," I said, then motioned for him to lead the way. With a glance over my shoulder as he moved off, I stopped when I saw Daisy following, then turned right around as she drew a Desert Eagle, the most powerful pistol in existence, from under her jacket.

"Is that a fifty?" I said, gawking at the silver finish.

"Yup," Daisy replied with a beaming smile. "She's chambered for the point five oh Action Express centre fire."

I couldn't help but raise my brow, but then with a curt cough from behind, I remember what we were about to do and moved off. Walking beside her, I realised it was the perfect handgun for the job and looked so large in her small hands.

"I thought you were liaison," I said.

"I am," she replied, holding the gun two handed toward the ground, her trigger finger resting in parallel to the gleaming barrel. "And I thought you were the brains?"

For a moment, I wished I could see her expression, not able to stop myself smiling as I increased my pace to catch up with the major.

As we neared the building, the soldier's huddle spread either side of the door, each man standing stiff to attention as I rushed past the major and placed my hand on the handle. I turned around to my new team, looking each of them in the eye with a hope their first reaction would be so much better than mine.

"Remember your briefing."

38

A short corridor lay ahead, and with no bloody footprints or bodies discarded with their insides spilling out, the only features were a door at the end on either wall. No death and decay assaulted my senses, only the tang of army issue cleaner hung in the air, bringing with it memories of a lifetime ago as an officer cadet scrubbing floor tiles alongside the rest of the new intake.

"Around to the left," the major's voice sounded from behind as I stepped over the threshold with my Glock held out. Without instruction, each of the two troopers moved past my shoulder to cover each of the doors, Moses to the left and Hollywood to the right, both ready to pull the handle at my command.

With a glance behind me, I saw Daisy standing beside the major with the hand cannon angled down along the corridor.

Nodding to Moses, he snatched at the handle, pulling the door wide as I pointed my aim through its length, only to find a corridor lined with office doors, the top half of the spaces between them made of glass.

I stepped in.

With an unobstructed view into every unoccupied room, I peered through to each as I made my way at a steady pace.

"Up the stairs, then it's behind the door at the end," the major said, sounding as if from somewhere towards the back of the group.

I nodded a reply before stepping to the side for Hollywood to take the lead. Doing so, he soon took his place ready to open the door at the far end.

I gestured ahead with a flat palm pushed out and with no delay, he pulled the door open as I scanned the narrow view. Seeing nothing out of place, I stepped across the threshold, turning left and pointing my weapon to the landing halfway up to the next floor as the others came past to cover each of the remaining arcs.

With everyone through, I took my first step up and then another, turning to track the rise in the opposite direction, not slowing when my aim settled on a pair of soldiers to the left who seemed more than relieved, if not surprised, at our arrival. One soldier kept his foot pressed against the base of a door as he glanced sidelong with his eyes narrowing when he saw who was following.

A second door stood behind them, but they paid it no interest.

Only as they spotted the major did they straighten up, their heads raising as if asking for confirmation when without speaking I ushered them away from the door, levelling my gun to where they'd been guarding.

With the echo of the soldier's footsteps soon disappearing after rushing down the stairs, I looked at Hollywood, pointing two fingers toward my eyes and then at the door on the right-hand side.

Without question, he stepped over to where I'd gestured, taking the handle and pulling it wide, then pointing his Glock through before closing it with care and giving a thumbs up.

Putting one foot in front of the other, I took a silent deep breath, knowing this was the moment I'd dreaded since leaving Brass Pike, but there was no time to collect myself, not the place to show any fear. I put the flat of my hand on my head and listened to the group tighten up on my position.

At my command, Hollywood pulled the door open and I stepped into the wide classroom filled with desks and chairs, my finger already tightening on the trigger as my aim settled on a man in black shorts and khaki t-shirt in the corner, holding a broken chair leg at the throat of a woman in a white smock.

With his arm wrapped around her chest and tears streaming down her face, I realised it was the nurse who'd watched me undress only hours earlier. Despite the unexpected sight and still poised to shout a command, readying to concentrate our fire, I paused on his pained, red face, staring into his eyes which were also red, but not dark like I'd seen in the others.

When he'd still not discarded her to the side and leapt over the desks, I kept the pressure on the trigger as I looked him over.

Although his arms and legs were pale, I'd smelt no decay, and had seen no scattered blood, in my first look over the room at least.

With my shoulders falling, my aim followed as I tried to push away the surprise at my disappointment. Raising my left palm in the air, I felt those behind me release their tension.

"Clear the room," I said, but before I heard the shuffle of feet, a voice cut through the silence.

"Are you sure?"

It was the major, followed by Daisy repeating the question.

I turned.

"This isn't for us," I said. "Someone up top has fucked up."

Heads turned as I stepped back, faces peering at me as if I'd just told them to dance on the spot.

"What do we do now?" the major said. "You can't just leave them like this? I thought you were the specialists?"

I sighed, then remembering the nurse, I turned back around to see her brown eyes wide with expectation. Biting my bottom lip, I glanced over my shoulder.

"I'm not a shrink," I said with a shrug. "But I can give it a go," I added, pushing the Glock into the waistband at my back as I heard steps behind me move away.

Taking a step forward, I raised my hands in the air, stopping only as the nurse winced with pain when the soldier pressed the jagged edge of the wood harder against her skin.

"Okay," I said, shaking my head, knowing this probably wouldn't end so well. "I guess you've gone through some shit."

His eyes narrowed as I spoke.

"I imagine all the business going on outside is unsettling," I said, raising my brow as I nodded.

He lifted his chin, his shoulders straightening with defiance.

"Look. I'll level with you. In some ways, we're the same. I've seen some crap myself, but I'm not about to unload my baggage on you. Your problems are personal," I said, pointing to his chest. "But it's not a competition and I'm sure they seem like they're a big deal to you," I added as I tried to ignore the nurse's eyes bulging wider with each word. "But the difference between you and me is that I deal with my demons and don't lock them away.

"In fact," I said, nodding to myself, "I think I deal with them a little too much." Then, watching his frown, I stopped as I realised he didn't know I was talking about Dr Devlin.

"What I'm trying to say is that now you've had your little cry for help," I said, waving my hand in circles, "you can start getting it sorted. And there's so many things they can do for you. Even if you end up going to prison for this little stunt."

By the collective sharp intake of breath, the sound mirrored from the corridor behind, I couldn't help but smile.

"I'm kidding," I said with a laugh. "You'll probably just get community service. I mean, that's what everyone seems to get these days. Am I right?"

His expression didn't change.

"Look. Let's get this done. Put the wood down and stop passing your problems on to the pretty nurse. I'm sure Major Jones has an entire set of pamphlets that will get you pointed in the right direction. You want to get better, don't you?"

Rather than let his arm drop, he tilted his head back in defiance.

"Okay. Fuck this," I said, and snatched the Glock from my waistband, aiming it at his head. "Ask anyone I've worked with and they'll tell you I'm a bloody excellent shot. There's zero chance you'd be alive to even hear the bang."

Fresh tears streamed from the nurse's eyes and the guy's mouth fell wide. Twitching my finger on the trigger, I didn't move my aim and within a second he'd relaxed his arms, the wood clattering to the floor as the nurse pulled free and ran towards me.

The soldier's shoulders slumped and I let my aim drop.

As he turned around, I snapped the Glock back high, shouting at the top of my voice, "get on the floor," when I spotted the dark blood stain through his T-shirt high on the back of his shoulder.

39

He was clean. No trace of the bad stuff. With his hands zip-tied at his back and Daisy pointing her cannon at his head, the boys and I had him swabbed within five minutes and handed over to the military police who'd arrived just after the rest of our team.

The male nurse who'd plunged the syringe into my arm checked the soldier's wound, self-inflicted, as he smashed the chair up to use as a weapon.

The pretty blonde nurse who'd stood out of the way whilst we checked him over arrived at my side the second I'd confirmed no threat, surprising me with a bear hug I thought lasted at least half a minute too long. When she asked me not to do that again if the situation came up, I couldn't help but laugh.

Feeling her push a scrap of paper into my hand as she pulled away, instinct told me to put it in my trouser pocket without looking at what it contained.

I turned to Daisy and the guys as they walked back out of the room, following them to the X5 where the half of the team I'd yet to meet had joined them.

In a convoy of two, we'd barely begun the route we'd started earlier that day.

"At least you've ruled out one career path if this all goes to the wall," Daisy said with the slightest of smiles.

"I don't know what the fuss is all about. It worked out, didn't it?" I replied, glancing between her and Moses in the passenger seat as he flashed me a wry smile.

"Only because you threatened to blow his head off," he replied, just as Hollywood belly-laughed.

As the laughter subsided, my thoughts turned to where Brown could be, but a tone signalling a call from Clark cleared my mind.

"I hear you're after Devlin's job," he said as I answered.

"Don't you start," I replied. "You're lucky I didn't just blow him away. Listen, we need to get better at analysing the intel. We can't have too many of those distractions."

"Agreed," he replied, then told me about a business unit on the Slough Trading Estate, which we arrived at in under ten minutes, just as a skinny man in a suit unfolded himself out of a bright yellow Fiat 500.

The last in a row of anonymous buildings, a large black number five on the side was the only thing to differentiate it from the rest. Immature, waist-high bushes marked the line between the lots, whilst a small car park wrapped around the front and sides and led to an access road linking the other buildings before heading off in either direction toward the rest of the estate.

Leaving the Glock on the car seat, and after Daisy poked her head inside the unit before giving the thumbs up, the ginger-haired agent who introduced himself with a double-barrelled name I instantly forgot, handed over a stack of paperwork which I passed straight on to Daisy, only wondering for a moment if she'd planned on becoming my assistant.

We had the unit for a week, but I knew that would be too long and for a moment I couldn't help but wonder if the crater that was once Windsor would stretch out this far if we couldn't deal with the situation more quickly.

"Where do you want everything?" Daisy said as the Fiat drove away. The guys were already unloading the car boots just as two plain white vans filled the adjacent parking spaces.

"I'll leave that with you," I said, shaking my head, then turned away, wondering for a fleeting moment if I'd been a little abrupt.

If she'd noticed, or cared, she hid it well, instead calling instructions to the team, her voice echoing as she followed them inside.

The white vans soon drove away with their former

contents piled in the warehouse. After a minute I followed the team in, watching as they busied themselves, moving or opening different sized crates under Daisy's instructions.

Much of the building was a large metal shed with a half glass partition wall at the far end, sectioning off an office with four desks where Daisy and Moses were already setting up computers. A trio of washroom doors huddled to the side next to a small kitchen with a set of domestic appliances.

With the main double doors closed, the team unloaded camp beds, dressing them with sheets tucked tight in each corner, then unpacked equipment and weapons of all sorts, laying rifles, handguns and grenades on the floor.

With a quick glance and seeing there was nothing of more use than the Glock back in my trouser waistband, I headed to the office to find out if Daisy was aware of my weapons request.

"Wait!" I called as I crossed the threshold and she froze, holding the red laptop in one hand, about to push a bright yellow network cable into the side.

"Not that one," I said, striding over and taking it from her. "It's from an x-ray. I'd bet any money they'll trip a remote kill switch if it connects to the internet."

She raised her brow and glanced at Moses as he left the room.

"Who does it belong to?" she said, placing the network cable back into a clear plastic box at her feet.

"We should know soon," I said, raising my brow as I turned away, stepping over to a spare table in the corner before examining the computer. Although a popular brand, I'd never seen the model before, and wrapped in what looked to be a proprietary shell, it wasn't easy to get more detail.

"Have you got a power cable that might fit, and an empty high-capacity memory stick?" I asked, then after fishing through a plastic box, Daisy arrived at my side with both.

"Thanks," I said as I fed the power plug into a nearby

socket and the other end into the machine, then opened it up and inserted the USB stick in the side. After reminding myself of the process, I tapped in the administrator username and the password I'd long ago memorised from training, then watched as the sand timer appeared.

When the screen changed to show an empty desktop with the sleek blue default background, I knew the software I'd installed earlier in the day had done its job and with a click of the mouse, I set about typing commands to copy its contents to the memory stick.

As the screen went blank apart from an empty progress bar in the centre, I turned my attention to the team still busy in the warehouse, looking at each of them, knowing there was only one way I would find out if they were up to the job.

Within half an hour, all six men formed a loose line, almost standing to attention, a stance that made me want to smile, knowing the Regimental Sergeant Major at Sandhurst would burst with rage if these were regular troops.

"This is not some grand speech, but there are a few things you need to hear from me before we continue," I said, watching as they each raised their heads, or otherwise showed their interest.

"Despite what you might have heard, I'm not in the military, but I am in charge. I've been told I don't play well with others, but if you follow my command, we'll get on fine and maybe you'll stay alive. Daisy here is my number two. Do we have a squad leader?" I said, although I'd already sized them up.

Hollywood raised a hand. "Sergeant Dan Heatherwood," he said, and then pointed along the line to a stocky man about my height with thin blond hair on top of a round face. I wondered if he thanked his lucky stars every day that his ears didn't stick out. "Corporal Andrew Bathhouse."

"Tubbs. Ma'am," the guy replied with a nod.

"I'm sure I'll get to know the rest of you before the week is out, because that's all the time we have." I looked along the group who, despite the well drilled discipline, couldn't hide their need to ask questions. There was a lot to tell them before we went on the hunt again.

"I'm sure Moses and Hollywood have filled you in on what happened at the barracks. It was a false alarm. Our primary focus is to hunt down a fugitive, but this assignment is different from anything you've dealt with before."

A few of the guys in the line looked at each other and smiled.

"You two, listen up," I said, watching as they snapped their heads up, the smiles falling from their lips.

I left a silence as I thought about what I should say, and how I could relay the information without sounding like I'd lost the plot.

Finding no magic words, I said, "The fugitive is infected with a pathogen that makes him superior to every one of us, in physical terms, at least. He has speed, boundless agility and the ability to take punishment that you wouldn't think possible. To add to that, he's infectious and is desperate to kill you."

One of the guys I'd only just spoken to laughed. A square jawed guy who stood around six feet tall, and seeming to be the youngest, he wasn't overly muscular in his grey t-shirt, but well enough built.

"Step forward, trooper," I said, beckoning him with a curl of my finger.

Without looking at any of the others, he did as I said, snapping to attention once he'd placed his feet.

"Do you think you're on top of the tree?"

The guy paused a little too long, and I punched him in the right of his abdomen. Although it wouldn't have hurt much, the shock bent him over and whilst he went down, I pushed the flat of my hand under his chin, pushing up and to the side. As he over-balanced, landing on the concrete floor, I stepped back, turning to the others. None of them were smiling.

"What's your name?" I said, looking down at the trooper as he scrambled up. "Stay down," I added, and he relaxed to his butt.

"Trooper Ray Donovan," He said, with no trace of dissent in his voice.

"Latenight, ma'am," Hollywood added, and I turned, raising a brow before looking back at the man I'd floored.

"You're barely on the second branch and you'd all do well to remember that," I said, then motioned for him to get up, watching as he rejoined the line and brushed himself off.

"When the time comes, and you'll know when that is, shoot for the head and don't stop until they're down. Do you understand?"

Nods carried along the line.

"And it's hand weapons only for the moment. This is a covert operation and we need to keep it that way for as long as possible. There are interfering parties, and they're armed and dangerous. The rules of engagement are clear. You may only use deadly force to protect yourself and the public. Do you understand?"

"Yes, ma'am," each said in unison.

"And one other thing, the next person to call me ma'am is going on the floor. Call me Red," I said, and after a tentative moment, they spoke as a group again.

"Yes, Red."

About to dismiss them back to their duties, Clark's tone called into my ear.

"There's been a sighting and this time it's confirmed."

40

Letting Hollywood decide who to bring, he chose Moses and Latenight and, for a fleeting moment, I wondered if he felt sorry for the guy, or perhaps he just wanted to show me he was a legitimate part of the team.

With Daisy staying behind to run the control room, and with newly minted Security Service IDs, we headed towards The Keep Hotel and the place where the team back at the Brecons had intercepted the triple nine call of a man matching Brown's description, barging his way out of the hotel covered in blood. They confirmed the sighting on the CCTV from the street seconds later.

The front desk didn't question our identity and the manager soon stepped from his office, ready with a master key along with the number of a room scrawled on a slip of paper showing where a member of staff had spotted Brown leaving earlier. Despite this, none of the staff had been up to the room, he told us in his French accent.

As the name suggested, the hotel looked out onto the high street, facing the tall castle walls, but despite the view, the faded décor of the interior was unremarkable.

Racing up the deserted stairs to the third floor, we drew our pistols only as I slipped in the master key, having warned the team that just because the fugitive wasn't here, it didn't mean he hadn't left behind trouble.

The stench of shit and blood hit me like a punch in the face the moment the door slipped open. Still, I kept my eyes from closing as I tracked my aim through the short corridor, passing over the closed door to the right and then across the length of the window as I stepped over the threshold.

Rounding the corner, the body spread out on the bed came as no surprise, but the arrangement of their arms and legs spread out like a star did more than raise an eyebrow. The cavity in the middle-aged man's torso gave me hope he wouldn't be causing any trouble, but I only tore my gaze away just as three voices behind me announced in short order the room and the adjoining bathroom were clear.

"Hollywood," I said in a firm voice, "don't take your aim from the body," I added, pointing to the bed. Without descent, he did as I ordered. "Moses, cover the door."

With my aim pointed where I looked, I repeated the search. Checking the bathroom I found nothing other than diluted blood splashed across the mirror and almost every area of white porcelain. With the wardrobe door pulled wide, I'd soon confirmed their assessment was correct and I turned my attention back to the sheets soaked a deep red, the surface potted with clots and sinew and scattered with organs discarded across the mattress.

The victim's jaw hung slack, with deep scratches running down his face. A wide gash across his forehead had little time for bleeding before his heart had stopped. I hoped the police would spare his loved ones the need to identify the body.

Despite my lack of medical training, I'd accounted for most of the major organs, and with no great swathes of flesh missing, or obvious bite marks, my first thought was that the wide open cavity was nothing more than a statement, or a warning.

With a quick glance to Hollywood still pointing his Glock where I'd asked, I beckoned Latenight over as I looked at the body once again.

"Is the threat neutralised?" I said, turning to the young trooper.

"No," he said after a moment.

"Correct," I replied. "Give me your blade."

He knelt and pulled up his trouser leg. In one sweeping motion, he slipped a dark-bladed combat knife from an ankle holster whilst I put away my Glock and drew black latex gloves from my pocket, slipping on a second pair for good measure.

Hollywood watched, his brow up as he looked over.

Taking the knife, I stepped over to the bed. After motioning for them both to resume their aim, I moved the pillow from under his head, placing it beside instead and resting my knees on top, in a hope to avoid the mess.

I didn't check, but sensed both the guys turning away as I took the jagged edge of the knife to the neck.

As the head rolled to the side, I stood and offered the bloodied blade back to Latenight, but just as he tentatively raised his hand, I pulled back.

"Probably best not to," I said, then flung it onto the bed.

Satisfied the immediate threat had passed, with care I peeled off the top glove from each hand and threw them alongside the knife as my gaze caught on a sports bag on the table in the corner, its contents scattered across the surrounding carpet.

Pulling on a second set of gloves, I stepped to the table, but finding nothing of interest as I picked through what had once been inside. Ignoring Latenight's pale expression, I walked around the room a second time.

With nothing in the room giving any clue to where Brown would have gone, we left as the police arrived to secure the scene, following the route Brown had taken through the hotel, then out into the street where CCTV lost him. Despite having nothing more to go on, we walked for the rest of the hour, peering along alleys and opening up industrial bins in a vain hope of any sign, despite knowing the trail had gone cold.

Back at the warehouse, the sun had almost set and the heavy scent of spiced meat greeted us as we opened the doors to find Tubbs laying on his camp bed reading a book, whilst the other two did press-ups in the far corner. The men made a beeline for the kitchen whilst I glanced over to the office and the eerie glow from the screens and desk lights.

With no sign of Daisy, I looked around, soon spotting a table set up in the main warehouse, its surface covered in an array of equipment, only some of which I recognised at a distance.

There were radios of all types, a line of sat phones, tracking devices, and more. Intrigued, I wandered over and picked up a khaki green box the size of a cigarette packet. It looked much like an old fashioned radio with a hollow metal antenna attached to the side and a large green dial on the centre face, which had several positions marked with acronyms I couldn't place.

"It might look like an archaic radio," said Hollywood with his mouth full of food as he arrived at my side. "But it's a disguised version of the latest RF jammer. Even works to disrupt Bowman."

Raising an eyebrow, I turned and found him with a bowl piled high with what could have been chilli.

"Flick the switch on the side and choose a setting. It works up to ten metres, or you can raise the antenna to triple that distance."

"Why have you got kit that can jam UK military comms?"

Hollywood shrugged. "It's only one function, but you never know," he said, then raised his brow before he turned away and headed back to the kitchen, his bowl already nearing empty.

Out of the corner of my eye I saw a glimmer of hair above the screen in the office for just a moment, and after replacing the box where I'd found it, I headed over.

Pushing open the door, Daisy's head popped up from behind the set of three screens, her face illuminated a gentle white.

"There's food in the kitchen," she said. "It should still be warm. Dropped off half an hour ago courtesy of Victoria's adjutant."

About to say something about what it meant to keep the operation under the radar, I glanced at the laptop in the corner, the progress bar only half filled. The words left me when Daisy spoke.

"And the UV decon equipment arrived. The address book is cooking as we speak. It should be ready in another half an hour," she said, motioning with her hand toward the warehouse.

I twisted around, squinting to the far corner of the large

room where on a small table stood a box which looked much like a microwave with a red LED display I couldn't read at the distance.

"Do we know who he was?" I said, as I took a seat. "The guy from the hotel room?"

Daisy nodded, tapping at keys on the laptop as I moved around the desk and pulled up a swivel chair to see a mugshot of a man appearing on the screen, his face impassive as if from a passport or driving licence. Concentrating on his brow before looking down to his cheeks, and despite using a little imagination to scour out the scratches on the face I'd seen, I couldn't be sure they were the same person.

"Jimmy Plimpton," she said. "From the hotel's register. Confirmed by DVLA. Your office is pulling details from his tax records to build the rest of the picture. They're fast," she added, her eyes going wide.

"Thanks," I replied, watching as for the first time she moved her gaze from the screen and looked over. "You should try to get some sleep. It'll be another busy day tomorrow. I'm taking the team out first thing."

"Where?" she said, her brow narrowing.

"I'll figure something out. We can't stay holed up in this place waiting for him to strike again."

Daisy nodded, then logged out of the computer before standing.

"Do you mind?" I said, taking my place in the warmth of her seat and opening the laptop as she stepped to the side.

"No problem," she replied, even though I was already tapping in my username. "But you've had a busier day than me. I don't mind if you want to get some shut eye?"

A rest would have been welcome, but I knew what waited for me when I closed my eyes. Shaking my head, I listened to her wander out of the door where the others were already climbing into their camp beds. Just as the lights in the main space went out, I got up and closed the office door and pulled the blinds across.

Opening a browser window, I typed the memorised

four sets of three numbers forming the IP address of the portal, then tapped in another username and password, soon clicking the link which was anonymous amongst the long line of four-digit case numbers.

As the screen showed a list of files, each one a photo taken at one of the day's three scenes, I clicked on the first, displaying a tight shot of the guy who'd attacked Christian after being bitten.

Opening each of the photos, I leaned toward the screen, scouring every angle for anything I'd missed. About three quarters of the way through the files, with an overwhelming need to rest, I leaned back in my seat, lifting my legs to the desk and closed my eyes.

No sooner than I'd let go of a long breath, the door burst open and Brown rushed in, glaring at me as he dropped to his haunches, ready to leap over the desk.

41

"Are you okay?" came a woman's hushed voice, but despite the familiar tone, it took a moment for the panic to calm and to realise it was Daisy and not the monster we were hunting.

Despite the fear subsiding, my heart continued to race as an anger built that I'd once again frozen, even though I knew the alternative would have meant emptying my Glock into Daisy.

As I tried to regain my bearings, I forced myself to speak.

"What time is it?"

"Two am," she said, her expression unsure as she squinted.

"Shit," I replied, dropping my feet from the desk and sitting up straight as I stared at the blank screen.

"Are you sure you're okay?"

I nodded, trying not to imagine the terror she'd seen in my face as she'd come through the door.

"I'll take over," she said. "Get some proper sleep, although there are a couple of snorers out there," she added, her cheeks bunching.

"No," I snapped, shaking my head, never again wanting to be paralysed by terror as I closed my eyes. Knocking the mouse with my hand, the screen came to life and requested my password. "You rest up. I'll stay awake, it's fine."

Daisy shook her head and walked around the desk. "I can't sleep. Do you mind if I sit with you?"

I thought for a moment, not trusting my brain, which was still coming down from the rude awakening.

"Sure," I said. "I was reviewing the scenes, but they're pretty grim. Are you sure you want to see?" I added, spotting the glint in her eye as she took the seat beside me.

With my fingers a blur, and safe in the thought that only a high-speed camera could capture my passwords, my index finger hovered over the return key. As I glanced at Daisy with a raised brow, she nodded.

I didn't take my eyes off her as I pressed the button, sending colours reflecting from her face. With only a subtle twitch of her eyes, she leaned closer to the screen and looking back, I confirmed it was the gruesome image of the man's empty chest cavity, a sight that would send most people reaching for the sick bucket.

"So, what's your background?" I said, using the cursor keys to switch to a closeup of the guy's severed neck.

"A civilian investigator for the MET. Five years."

"But they chucked you out?" I said, raising a brow as I turned to face her.

Her jaw dropped and her eyes went wide as she shook her head, only relaxing when she realised I was smiling.

"Most days it was just dealing with domestic abuse, petty crime and burglary. That kind of thing. I was on a conveyor belt, facing nothing but the bleak side of human nature. There was of course the occasional murder to break up the soul-destroying drudgery. Don't get me wrong."

I nodded, not able to stop myself from laughing.

"Which led you to join the army so you could see the world and now here you are in a warehouse on an industrial estate in the middle of Slough. Is it living up to the promotional videos?"

Daisy snorted a laugh. Mortified, her hand rushed to cover her mouth, and she quickly looked away.

"I'm sorry about that," she said, removing her hand when she finally turned back. "But it is. I've been in for four years, although this is my first tour with the Regiment," she added, nodding in the partition's direction. "And I have to say it's been eye opening."

"Captain?" I said.

Daisy nodded again, her eyes narrowing as if with a question.

"I know what you're going to say," I said before she could. "What rank is it up to now?"

Daisy turned her head to the side, her eyebrows lowering.

"Lieutenant Colonel," she said, but somehow kept the same expression as I laughed.

"Wow. That is a fast track," I added after a moment.

The confusion magnified on Daisy's expression. "I don't get it. They briefed us about your rank but told everyone not to use it in your presence, and when you spoke to the boys, you said you weren't in the military."

"I'm not, but the people who give your orders can't bring themselves to come to terms with that. Let's just say the army was where I started my career, but I was only in for a year, which was just enough time to pass out of Sandhurst before my current employer swept me up."

I watched as if I could see the question form on her lips.

"Don't ask, because I won't be telling you."

She smiled and nodded, touching her finger to her lips before looking at the screen. "Have the details of the rest of the victims come through, and do we have any idea how they're connected?"

"Victims?" I said, and she raised a brow.

"All this for one incident? I don't think so."

I nodded, my confidence in her ability growing with each moment.

"The details are still sketchy, but we suspect they're just in the wrong place at the wrong time," I said, looking her in the eye.

"Why?" she replied with no delay.

I narrowed my eyes.

"Sorry," she said, shaking her head. "The MET taught us to question everything."

"That's fine, and you're right to, but remember, we're dealing with little more than a monster here."

"That may well be the case, but he's not some lion attacking people on the street," she added, raising her chin.

I nodded again, pleased we shared the same line of thinking.

"Okay. You're right. We don't know, and I agree there is likely to be a link somewhere. We know he has at least got some idea of an objective in what is left of his mind."

"Which is?" she said, turning her head to the side.

I chuckled and nodded, weighing up what I could tell her, but before I could, she spoke again.

"So I guess you can't tell me everything?"

"You're right on that too," I said, looking back at the screen.

"Okay. I understand. So what *can* we talk about?" she said, leaning back towards the screen, just as I took the phone from my pocket and sent a message to Clark. His number flashed onto the screen almost immediately, despite the early hour.

"The CCTV from the hotel should be with us soon," I said to Daisy as I hung up the call.

Within a few minutes of examining the rest of the photos, my phone vibrated on the desk and, navigating back to the menu, I found a new video file.

With a glance at Daisy, she nodded, and I pressed play.

A grainy view of the hotel's front desk and a young blonde woman at reception opened on the screen. Within a few moments, Brown came from behind the camera and stood in front of the desk. The seconds on a timestamp across the bottom of the screen ticked on as we watched. The receptionist smiled as he approached, showing no sign of anything covering the white t-shirt to make her recoil.

Even though I knew much of what had happened already, I still half expected him to grab her, pulling her over the counter before ripping her in half. Instead, she picked up a phone hidden out of sight and spoke for less than ten seconds before she nodded to Brown, pointing over his shoulder.

After the exchange, he turned around, oblivious to the camera, confirming a clean t-shirt as he walked out of shot in no hurry.

The image changed to inside the lift, where he stared at the metal doors. The pictures were just as poor quality, or perhaps even worse, but I could tell he was a little grey and perhaps more drawn than when I'd seen him in the flesh.

As he left the lift, the image showed the corridor just as

he walked under the camera and along the hall, where he slowed about halfway along and knocked at a door. With a sudden light signifying the door opening, he stepped out of shot.

The video sped up without having to adjust the controls, then it slowed as Brown reappeared, the time stamp showing he'd been in the room for less than five minutes.

He paused at the door with the seconds still heading in the right direction and I watched his chest heaving, his t-shirt darkened, and he held something rectangular by a handle in his right hand down by his side. Before I could identify what it was, he turned and walked away from the camera, with the screen turning black a moment later.

"He knew what he was doing when he entered the room," Daisy said.

I nodded. "He looked very much in control," I added as I dragged the video slider back to the start and pressed play.

"And he took something from the room," she said, as the image arrived at the point where he reappeared.

I nodded and stood. "But what?"

Daisy shook her head. With a glance toward the main warehouse space, my eyes widened as I remembered the decontamination unit. "The address book should be ready now."

Daisy stood, following me around the desk, but I stopped as I came level with the red laptop in the corner and moved the mouse to check progress. The screen stayed blank.

Nothing happened as I pressed the space bar, then lifting the machine from the desk, I listened for the fans, but there was no whir of the small motors.

Pressing the power button, I watched lines of text scroll through the boot-up sequence, then it stopped, leaving just a flashing message.

Ready to install operating system.

I froze, but for less than a second, then turned the

machine around, half closing the lid to look at the ports. There was nothing plugged in other than the power and the USB stick, which I snatched from the side and turned to Daisy.

"It's wiped, but it's not connected to the internet," I said. "The only way that could happen…"

"Was if the guy you took it from was in Bluetooth range," Daisy said.

"And it connected to his phone," I added with a nod as I reached for my Glock and rushed from the office. "They're outside."

RED DOT

42

Hurrying across the darkened warehouse, the men's snores spluttered to a stop and cooled air rushed over my face as I opened the door, before bounding into the night with Daisy following.

Hiding the Glock under my jacket as I ran, I peered out across the dimly lit but deserted access road, only slowing as I arrived at the front of the building, staring at a compact white van in the next door unit's carpark.

Certain I'd seen the faintest of movements in the cab, I ran past the crisp white lines marking the spaces whilst Daisy kept pace, then with the narrow patch of grass under my feet, I vaulted high, the soles of my trainers catching the leaves of the bordering plants before I landed on the other side.

Regaining traction as the van's engine screamed to life, its lights shone so brightly I had to push my arm in front of my eyes. With the roar of the engine getting so close, and about to leap to the right and out of its path, the tyres squealed, my view clearing enough that I could watch it speed away along the access road.

I thought for a moment about raising the Glock, or grabbing the cannon from Daisy's holster and blasting a hole in the side, but it was already too far away, and the paperwork would have tied me up for hours.

"Shit," I said, surprising myself I'd managed not to scream the word. Hearing footsteps from behind, I turned to three figures rushing around the corner of the warehouse.

"Get another squad down here," I said, at first looking to Hollywood but soon turning to Daisy. "We need to beef up our operational security. No more deliveries of food from the base!"

"Yes, Red," Daisy replied, as we arrived back at the double doors and I ushered everyone back inside.

"Hollywood. Assign two on the exterior to keep overwatch. Keep them out of view and rotate every two hours," I said, motioning to the door.

He nodded before pointing at the two troopers who'd followed him out, neither of which he'd introduced me to. Together, they headed over to the table covered in equipment.

As my gaze caught the UV decontamination machine in the corner with its lights off, I walked over and pressed the door release button. Inside, a small white ceramic dish sat in the centre with the address book resting in the same plastic bag I'd placed it in.

Surprised when it was cold to the touch, I thumbed through the pages as I strolled to the office. Some entries shared Brown's last name, others shared theirs with other entries, which was to be expected. There were quite a few for people at the University of Cardiff, his alma mater, or otherwise had academic titles, but none of the entries popped out, or triggered any recognition.

"Get some rest people," I called out over my shoulder, just as the door closed behind the pair sent to hide themselves in the darkness.

Taking a seat beside Daisy who tapped away at the laptop, I felt a glimmer of thanks that the adrenaline had pushed away much of my tiredness.

"Once you've finished doing whatever that is," I said, offering out the address book, "can you cross reference these names against the database?"

Despite looking unsure, she took the book. "I'm happy to help, but I don't think I have the access."

"Yes," I said, realising she was right as soon as she spoke. I took the book back. "You have your own work to do."

"I'd help if I could," she replied, leaning forward.

Shaking my head, I stood and walked to the table where

the empty laptop sat. Using my phone, I took pictures of each page, then emailed them to Clark before calling him.

"I've just sent you the pages from the address book," I said, then glanced at Daisy watching me from over the top of the screen, but she turned away as our eyes met. "Can you cross reference them…?" I said, but stopped myself, knowing Clark would already have started the work before I'd finished speaking. "Let me know what you find," I added instead. "And I'll get you the disk image from the laptop, but it's going to take some time to upload."

Listening to the tapping of keys on the other end of the line pause, Clark spoke, as if remembering something. "I've sent you Dylan O'Connor's file. There's still a decent amount of black marker, but let me know if there's something specific you might need and I'll see what I can do."

"Thanks," I said. About to hang up, I remembered what had just happened. "We've had visitors," I quickly added.

"Understood," he replied, then as he cleared the call, I passed over the USB stick to Daisy's waiting palm reaching over the screens. I didn't have to scroll through the messages on my phone for long to find what Clark had mentioned, and started reading as I took a seat.

"Get some sleep, Daisy," I said, then looked up from the phone a moment later when she hadn't already left. With a raise of my brow, she closed her mouth, logged out of the laptop and closed the door behind her.

Sitting in the warmth of her chair, I transferred the personnel file to the laptop and called Clark again.

"Have you got some time?" I said as he answered. Even though he wouldn't have looked at the clock, it took him a moment before he replied.

"Sure," he said, his voice relaxing as I pushed in the earpiece. "And I'm sorry for what you went through."

"Was it your fault?" I said, but spoke again before he could reply. "Were you the one who sent me into that place without telling me what I was up against?"

"No," he replied. "I would never…"

"Then there's nothing to be sorry about. Okay?" Without giving him time to reply, I added, "Where was I…? He was in the service for twenty years before handing in his retirement request aged fifty. There was the usual investigation and vetting, but they found no external influence involved in the decision. He was to be monitored for a year, standard practice, but he just vanished. What would the investigation and vetting have covered?"

"They'd review the same factors covered in standard vetting. Family. Associates. Finances etc," Clark replied. "But they would have also trawled through his last few projects, making sure there were no unusual contacts or aggravating factors."

"Such as?" I said, linking my fingers together.

"I would imagine contact with enemy states or organisations. Incidents that occurred whilst operational that could have caused a changed in mindset. Any notes of concern or interest from colleagues. That kind of thing."

"Checking to see if he turned against us?" I asked.

"I would imagine so," Clark replied.

Neither of us spoke as we read through lists of names and codes, summaries of actions described in short abrupt sentences with lines of marker pen obscuring much of the detail. The visible text was just about enough to give me a flavour of his career and a highlight of his more recent operations. The hunt for a mole. Special advisor on security. A man hunt and providing a specialised escort. Most assignments were for months at a time and produced the highest rated results and praise from those above him.

Nearing the end of the file with my frustration at the lack of detail growing, I heard Clark's breathing change, as did mine, when I read the next section.

Five years ago, almost to the day, and attached to investigate a group of scientists, his assignment was stopped short of a natural conclusion, and more interestingly, his supervisor felt the need to comment that he'd witnessed a change in his behaviour.

"We're trained to monitor our operatives that way,"

Clark said.

About to comment, I changed my mind as I read on.

"After only six months, four operations later, declining his next assignment, he hands in his resignation," I said. "Shouldn't the vetting team have picked up on that?"

"Yes," Clark added. "They would have interviewed the supervisor, if possible, but there doesn't seem to have been any concern raised. After a short gardening leave, he's released and the rest we know."

"Or don't," I said, as I slid the cursor back up the page and re-read it all again, but with over three quarters of the words blacked out, there was nothing else I could get from it. "We need more on the assignment that warranted the supervisor's comment."

"I'll see what I can do."

I thanked Clark, then almost as an afterthought, read the complete file for a third time. But just before reaching where O'Connor had resigned, I paid more attention to where he'd performed his security consultancy tasking, a small village in Scotland. Tapping the name into a search engine and clicking to view the map, I held my breath when I saw the edge of the forest I'd been at only a few days early.

"Brass Pike," I said, the words slipping out almost silently from my lips.

43

"Daisy," I said, kneeling in the near darkness at the side of her camp bed. She turned from her right-hand side, breath huffing from her lungs with her eyes almost bulging out of her sockets as she sat up on her elbows. "There's nothing wrong," I added, and leaned a little closer. "I have to follow up a lead. You're in charge. I might be out of comms for a little while, but I'll come back as soon as I can. Should be tomorrow."

Flopping back down to the bed as she rubbed her eyes, Daisy leaned on her side again as I picked up the small rucksack containing a few supplies I'd grabbed from around the warehouse.

Standing, my gaze fell on the Desert Eagle holstered on the floor.

"What? Where?" she said, and I looked away from the gun, which I wanted to at least see how it felt in my hands.

"I can't say. If anything comes up, you'll have to deal with it. Send Hollywood, Latenight and Tubbs. They've had the most training. You can pick up the X5 from Slough Station later this morning," I said, glancing one last time to the weapon before turning and heading through the door before she could say anything coherent.

Taking a circuitous route whilst able to keep it short with no traffic to speak of, and with it only just getting light, I left the X5 in the station carpark before walking to the entrance. With the place deserted and the monitors overhead showing the first train wasn't for another half an hour, I thought back over the brief conversation I'd had with Dylan.

Despite my desperation to speak with him again, I owed it to him to make sure no one followed me and so took the train to London and then out west, stopping at Bristol before heading back the way I'd come until Swindon, where I was already sure no one could have survived my double backs. With no other clothes to change into, I had to hope they didn't have access to the CCTV.

Getting off the train one stop before my destination, I took the bus and headed past where I'd last stepped off before walking back from the opposite direction.

Treading new ground, the route made it a little more tricky to find the place, but eventually I came across the dirt road and took the route I'd memorised, leading me right to where I'd stepped before, but this time the bushes didn't move to the side as I closed up.

Glancing around whilst knowing he might be watching, I pushed my hands through the spiny foliage, hauling branches to the side. After several sharp stabs drawing blood, I caught the first glint of metal with a gap at the side, hinting it could be ajar.

Ignoring the digs under my nails and the sharp stings, I soon had the offensive vegetation out and confirmed I'd been right. The heavily weathered door was open.

Determined to know what lay beyond, but without drawing my weapon, I pushed through the remaining plant life. Gripping the long corroded handle, I leaned back, easing it open as I peered into darkness.

With my phone's built in torch, I scoured the rows of empty metal shelves on the right-hand wall, and with the light just powerful enough to hit the rear, my shoulders dropped as I confirmed the place was empty.

Shaking my head, I realised that not only was the place devoid of any life, but O'Connor had been living in such bleak conditions all this time, which only compounded my need to know if I was right about why he'd hidden away in this prison.

Coming to terms that I'd never get to ask having scared him off, I switched off the torch and turned to stare out between the tall trees.

I must have stood there for less than a second before I looked down at the ground surrounding the door and soon came to realise I'd seen no sign of how he'd moved his worldly goods. There was no trace of heavy steps or wheel tracks. Nothing.

Peering back between the trees, my thoughts turned to where he might go, hoping he had a back-up plan; another somewhere he could call his own that was more than a tent under the leaves to protect himself from the winter months already on the horizon.

About to turn to take another look in the empty bunker, a distant rustle caused me to pause just as something made me look down at a glowing red dot in the centre of my chest.

44

"I'm back for that cup of tea," I called out at the top of my voice as I looked through the trees with hope I was right about who aimed the weapon at my chest.

Despite no reply, I took confidence that I was still standing without a hole between my breasts to replace the red dot from the laser I guessed was attached to a sniper or other high-powered rifle.

After a long moment, I looked back down as the glowing point trembled before it drifted down my body and disappeared altogether.

Controlling my urge to run for cover, I slowly looked up and peered into the distance, whilst remaining poised to dodge to the side, depending on what I saw.

With the distant but classic double click I recognised as the de-cocking of a rifle, my gaze landed on a section of bush shuffling to the side before moving toward me. Squinting for a better view, I was sure I saw an L115 sniper rifle amongst the leaves, pointing toward the forest floor.

I held my ground with the cluster of foliage closing the distance between us.

As the rustle of the leaves grew in volume, I called out. "A laser sight?" I said, then smiled. "You must be getting old."

The bush stopped moving as a green cloaked arm appeared as if from nowhere, raising toward the top of the mound before pulling a matted clump of leaves high. Dropping the dark tangle to the side, it left O'Connor's frown obvious despite the earthy camouflage paint smudged across his face.

"I only meant it to scare," he said in a monotone voice as he walked.

"You don't want to know what it takes to scare me," I replied, as I forced myself to concentrate on the sweat tracking down his face and smearing the dark paint.

Rather than slowing, he breezed right past without

turning to face me.

"I guess you better come in then," he said, and I turned, watching as he headed into the abandoned bunker. "But you can make your own tea."

Squinting into the darkness, I followed, watching his every move with interest as to what he was doing in the deserted place. As he came alongside the empty shelves to his right, he placed the long rifle on the middle surface with care before he reached around his body, searching for hidden clips before snapping several open. The bottom half of the ghillie suite separated from the top and landed on the concrete at his feet. Raising the top half over his head, he let it fall to join the rest.

In black shorts and a dark green tee, O'Connor stepped out of what looked like a pile of leaves, picked up the rifle, then walked toward the far wall where I peered at the floor for any sign of a trapdoor I'd not spotted before.

Seeing nothing new, I looked up only to find him not slowing, but reaching out and pushing a hanging fabric out of his way before letting it drop back behind him to leave the wall swaying from side to side.

The canvas felt heavy as I swept it away with darkness and a cocktail of earthy smells greeting me beyond, but as I planted my feet, not able to see where else to walk, a low orange glow rose from the side of a wide room and bounced off a low concrete ceiling.

As O'Connor fussed around plastic crates stacked along the righthand wall, I spotted a small kitchen at the far end with cupboards covering the wall I faced, along with a small cooker and extractor hood sandwiched between wooden units that seemed as if he'd cobbled them together from different brochures.

To the right sat a three seater sofa, and after seeing nowhere else he could sleep, I guessed it doubled as a bed. Much of the remaining walls were stacked with boxes, or shelves piled high with containers, bottles, and tubs. Turning to my left, I looked with interest at the only other wall space not turned to storage.

Three shotguns hung on hooks, with a neighbouring space I guessed was for the L115, which he soon confirmed by resting the rifle in its place. More shelves waited above and below the weapons, each stacked with metal tins full of ammunition, if the stencilled writing on the side was to be believed. There was perhaps enough to hold off a company of men, especially if the containers below the pistols on the next shelf held the grenades reported by the markings.

"Where's your kettle?" I said, striding toward the end of the room, but as I spotted it on top of the hob, I raised my hand to dismiss the question. "Never mind."

With the water on to heat to the sound of O'Connor moving around, I found tea bags in the near cupboard, then searched the neighbour for cups.

"Third on the left," he said, and I nodded, finding two amongst stacks of different glasses. One bore the logo of a well-known insurance company, whilst the other I pulled out and held in front of me as I turned around.

"I heart pugs?" I said, watching as he pulled on a fresh t-shirt. Then he stared at me for a moment before shrugging his shoulders and turning his attention back to the container at his feet.

Smiling, I placed tea bags in each mug. "You should let the windows open for a bit. Get some air," I said, glancing over my shoulder.

His eyebrows rose, but he didn't catch my eye.

"Funny," he replied, just as the kettle whistled.

I didn't ask how he took his tea and handed him the pug mug, unable to drop the smirk.

"I wasn't expecting them to send *you* back?" he said, giving the tea only a casual glance as he offered his hand in the sofa's direction, then pulled a wooden box from the other side of the room before using it as a seat opposite me.

"You were expecting the goon squad?" I replied, watching as he lifted his head, then nodded. "I didn't tell anyone where I found you," I added, shrugging. "Anyway, like I said, they aren't interested."

"As long as I'm being a good boy," he replied before I

could. His eyes narrowed and he concentrated on my face, much like he had the last time we'd met. "So why would you do that?"

I held his gaze for a moment then watched as he took a hearty slurp from the mug before I took a tentative sip from mine, my tastebuds searching for anything out of place, even though I'd made it myself.

When it tasted just as it should, not too sweet or too bitter, even though there were plenty of harmful substances I wouldn't be able to detect, I swallowed. Remembering his question, I placed the cup on the concrete floor.

"I used to think you were a version of me, but now I know that's bollocks. You're a version of me that could have been." I shook my head. "I'm not you and although there are some things no one should have to deal with, someone has to, so the rest don't. I'm that someone, and you used to be."

I watched for his reaction, ready at any moment for him to stand and ask me to leave, or worse, but he just held my gaze.

"Although there are some people in our world who are doing wrong, but most people aren't, and I'll stay and fight from the inside rather than sit on my ass underground."

He closed his eyes for a second and then spoke as he opened them. "I started off like you. I was keeping the world safe but when I saw…" he said, but before he could finish, his eyebrows rose and his expression lit up. "We have met before," he said, his face full of delight.

I turned to the side and shook my head.

"Second of March, nineteen ninety nine," he said, nodding.

That was a date I would never forget; the day I took my first step into a world I'd made my career.

I continued to shake my head, still unable to place him.

"The National Portrait Museum? I was wearing a balaclava."

"Ah," I said, my eyes going wide as my mind went back in time to the moment the cops rushed in. Nothing that day was as it seemed.

Only those who'd been there, plus a select few, would have known any part of what was going on.

"So now you can be sure we're on the same side," I said. "We belong to the same family."

"And I can tell you what made me leave?" he said, raising a brow.

"Yes. What made you surround yourself with this prepper's wet dream?"

O'Connor smiled, looking away as he stifled a laugh, but his expression flattened as he turned towards the rack of weapons and ammo.

"For years I loved what I did," he said, staring at the shotguns hanging against the concrete. I nodded. "Chasing down bad guys to keep the worst from the news. I made a difference."

"And then?" I said when he seemed to get lost in his thoughts.

The faraway look remained. "Let's just say the future I saw for the planet wasn't a place I wanted to live in."

I stood, shaking my head, but he turned away as if no longer able to look me in the eye.

Turning to leave, I twisted back around.

"What did you see in Brass Pike? Just spit it out."

He looked over, his eyes blinking so quickly I thought for a moment he was having a fit, but still he said nothing.

About to turn away again, he closed his eyes then shook his head, only speaking as I arrived at the cloth covering the entrance.

"I did my best."

With a glance back, he held his head in his hands and I knew I wouldn't get anything else out of him. Reaching out to the row of weapons, I took the middle shotgun before grabbing a handful of red cartridges from the box below, stuffing a second fistful into my jacket pocket when he did nothing to stop me.

"It's the least you owe me," I said, then left. When he didn't try to follow and with the shotgun crammed into the rucksack, I called Clark as I arrived back at the dirt road.

"I've been trying to get hold of you," he said, answering the call.

"What's wrong?" I replied, as I raised my hand to the bus heading towards me, watching as its indicator blinked on my side of the road.

"There's been another incident."

"The team will have to deal with it," I replied. "They're the muscle, remember?" I added, but didn't wait for him to reply. "I've been following a lead, but it's a dead end and I need you to get me the GPS coordinates for Copper Flail immediately, no questions asked."

45

Grateful for the breeze across my face as I stepped from the bus, the rush in my veins only grew as the phone vibrated in my pocket, rising higher when I saw the set of numbers in the message and further still as I clicked the link to plot my destination.

Pushing away all thoughts of heading in the opposite direction and whilst silently repeating the lecture I'd given O'Connor, the rest of the world seemed to slow as if stuck in treacle as I walked, not speeding up as I fed the ticket into the turnstile and pushed through. Bass voices came from all around, people chattering whilst paying me no attention, but with every casual look my way, it was as if they were imploring me not to go back to where I feared. A place much like the one I'd only just walked unscathed from.

Knowing I had no other choice than to see it through, I climbed on board the train.

The second was the hardest to join. With the sights, sounds and smells of Brass Pike rolling around in my head, I knew I'd soon be within ten miles of Clark's coordinates. The taxi ride was much worse, but with five miles to go, the sight of the almost constant stream of army trucks and Land Rovers along the main road reminded me I had a job to do.

At three miles out, the driver dropped me at a quaint little pub on the edge of a village encircled by a forest. The view from Google maps told me the dual carriageway was the only way in and out, and showed how close to my destination the search engine's car with the array of cameras could reach.

I slipped from the cab, and once it was out of sight, I walked as casually as I dared along a path between the trees, heading toward the dot on the screen which from above showed nothing more than the green canopy.

Despite the season, a chill hung in the air, and with my senses on high alert, and within a mile of the spot, I stopped, pulling the shotgun from the bag and slipping four twelve gauge magnum slugs into the chamber. After pumping the slide I slipped another then added to each of the four slots underneath the stock and with the rest of the cartridges distributed amongst my jean pockets, I drew off my coat and slipped the shotgun's strap over my head before replacing the coat on top.

With a last check of my Glock still under my arm, despite all but discounting the seventeen rounds, I took a slow, deep breath and walked towards the hint of a fence line in the distance.

Taking each step, I wanted to pull the shotgun from my back, bringing it to bear toward every noise. Each crack of a twig or rustle of a leaf raised a fear they'd already lost control, leaving no one behind to report it. Somehow I held back, slowing my pace only as I neared touching distance of the tall galvanised steel fence, its angled top covered in razor wire and likely fitted with motion sensors.

Peering between the grey slats, I saw nothing but trees and shrubs along the ground, and I stepped back into the cover, treading with care along the perimeter.

The going was slow through the thick foliage, and it took another half an hour to spot the first signs of activity on the perimeter ahead. Based on the number of vigilant troops facing out, I knew it had to be an entrance. A small convoy of trucks arrived moments later, confirming my guess and showing I had no chance of getting through on foot.

I backed up, taking care as I retraced my steps, then when at least five car lengths away, I crept in parallel with the dirt track.

Within half an hour and close to the dual carriageway, I found a junction guarded by a small contingent in civilian clothes, each wearing hi-vis jackets with security written in black across their backs. But their stance and focus left me under no illusion who they really were.

Counting five men, I peered between the safety of the trees, watching another convoy of three Land Rovers pull up along the slip road where they waited, whilst the guards checked their documentation before waving them through.

Staring between the branches, it hit me that as I focused on the challenge, I wasn't thinking about where I was trying to get into.

As the last vehicle drove out of sight towards the military guard, and with none of the yellow tabards paying any attention in my direction, I ran across the dirt and into the trees on the opposite side.

Within five minutes, I crouched at the edge of the slip road, a little way down from the entrance hidden in the bushes, watching cars and lorries zip by. Every so often, more trucks and cars and Land Rovers came and went via the entrance, but unable to read any pattern to their arrival, I readied myself when I saw an olive drab truck's indicator flash orange in the distance.

The signal gave me plenty of time to prepare, and in those few seconds I crept forward, counting four blinking lights in a line. With the contents of the trucks hidden by green canvas, I waited for the first to pass by for any hint of whether I could get inside.

As the air brakes hissed and one after the other each truck came to a stop, I crept in line with the back of the last, which I knew would be my only shot. With a glance to the left, I took a second to make sure the men in bright yellow were doing what they had done each time before, then leapt across the short gap, darting for cover behind the vehicle and looking up to the open back filled with evenly spaced crates and the top half of a young soldier sitting down, staring wide-eyed as he peered up from his phone.

46

Locking eyes with the clueless soldier, I grabbed the highest point of the tailgate, then springing up on my feet, I hauled myself high before vaulting over the metal side and barrelling into his chest, giving him no time to move from his wooden box.

His pause was enough for me to control my punch to the side of his head, stunning him for a split second longer than it took to kick away the SA80 rifle at his feet, then slipping a hand to the back of his head, the other over his mouth as I pushed hard.

He toppled over, falling to the truck bed and landing between the crates towering up to the canvas roof. As his head hit the metal, his struggle began, lashing out, but only until he felt the muzzle of my Glock under his chin. Going limp, he closed his mouth, holding back whatever he was about to shout as the truck moved off.

Gripping him tight, I glanced around whilst knowing it wouldn't be long before we were the next in line for inspection. With an idea forming, I kept the Glock against his skin, his eyes going wider still as, one-handed, I pulled apart the Velcro along the front of his jacket, then slid the zip down. He followed my instructions to take out each of his arms and then lean forward so I could whip it from underneath him.

Thankful he was much bigger than me, I struggled the jacket on over everything I wore, and with the zip up to my neck and holding his glare for a just second, I raised my eyebrows and pulled away the Glock, leaving it to rest on the floor. He remained still as I reached forward, then ripped apart his green t-shirt at the hem, pulling a long tear up through the middle, before re-gripping the Glock.

The remains of the t-shirt came free with a sharp tug, slipping down his arms before I pushed the ragged remains into a ball and motioned for him to open his mouth wide.

The truck moved forward with the soldier breathing

hard against the gag, but with a raise of my eyebrows, he controlled himself when we stopped for the second time.

Knowing he'd be easy to spot if the security guard climbed even a little up the back, still pointing the gun in his vague direction I dragged him by his feet, manhandling him into the space between the first of the crates and the tailgate, then taking his place on the box. Resting the pistol on my lap, I quickly made sure the jacket was straight, leaving only a moment to spare before a man I suspected to be a soldier in disguise appeared from around the side.

Pushing a stray stand of hair from my face, the mid-twenties security guard, his skin tanned, double took, raising a brow as our gazes locked. That's when I knew I was in no danger.

"Everything okay back here, soldier?" he said, and I nodded whilst trying to look as bored as possible.

"Yes, thank you," I said with a renewed eagerness, whilst holding myself from glancing at the guy on the floor who I could just about see was staring up at me.

With a nod, the security man smiled before taking his eyes off me for the first time, then reached out and raised himself up with the edge of the tailgate. He would only need to lift a little more to see the gun resting on my jeans and I'd be done for.

"What's going on here?" I said.

He looked over and drew a slow breath, holding there for a moment before dropping back to the road.

"You'd do best to keep to your briefing, soldier," he said, looking up as I nodded and drew back. He continued to hold my gaze for a long moment, but then, with a call from further down the line, his eyes narrowed and he stepped out of view.

We soon rolled forward and didn't stop.

On the other side of the outer cordon, I glanced down, watching as the soldier looked back from the floor, his gaze locked to mine with snot trailing down the side of his face. Tearing myself away, I kept my expression as neutral as I could until the men in the fluorescent jackets turned away, their forms soon receding out of sight as we buffeted from side to side.

It wasn't long before we were slowing for the main entrance, but rather than stopping, we headed straight through and I watched the soldiers from behind as they kept their aims pointed in the opposite of my direction. The relative ease of how I'd got this far gave me no consolation when the thoughts I'd tried to push away flooded back.

Not able to rid my head of the images from the raiding party's helmet camera, I felt dizzy, a nausea rising and I couldn't quite seem to catch my breath. Only as I looked down at the soldier at my feet did I take back control and turn my attention to what I was going to do next.

Perhaps I could strip the guy right down and masquerade as a grunt, but realising I'd look like a ten-year-old kid dressed in his father's uniform, and even if I could pull it off, they'd discover the soldier in the back as soon as they went to unload.

Whatever I was about to do, he'd have to come with me.

Having decided in an instant, I stood and turned, tugging at the strapping of the nearest crate before steadying myself as a wheel hit a pothole. With the truck settling, and with a fresh idea, I rushed into the darkness between the three long rows of crates, each stacked two high and held down with thick straps tight with metal ratchets. Finding the furthest away, I pulled the release to relieve its tension.

With hope the rest of the journey was flat enough not to unsettle the load, I worked quickly to pull the length of heavy duty fabric through the pallet underneath. I soon had it coiled and held under my arm, then headed back to where the soldier lay, under no doubt we were already slowing.

With no time to think the high chance of being spotted weighed heavy on my shoulders. Not only did being captured mean I'd have to give myself up along with my plan, the inevitable delay would mean so much more to the people I'd left in Windsor.

Despite the dangers, I just had to know what Brown

had seen when everything went so wrong.

"Get up," I said in a near whisper and jabbed the gun in his ribs, then helping him to stand, his eyes went wide as I pointed for him to jump over the side.

47

Giving him no chance to delay, the bare-chested soldier landed on the dirt with a heavy thud, the remains of the t-shirt spitting from his mouth with a great out-pour of air. Before he could make a stupid decision, I rolled out of my landing, and stooping over him, stuffed the fabric back into his mouth before pulling him to his feet.

With the Glock in my left hand and the strap and heavy ratchet pinned under the same arm, I ran, dragging him along with all I could give whilst hoping the silence remained unbroken by a klaxon calling an alarm as we passed into the treeline.

I didn't stop running and pulled him against his protests as I listened out for any sign someone had spotted us, or for the squeal of the truck's brakes or the loose crate toppling. When I could no longer hear the grunt of the engines, I slowed, giving the soldier a moment to recover his breath through his nose as he hugged his red-marked chest with the arm I wasn't gripping.

Pushing away a glint of guilt, I forced him onward between the trees, stopping only when I saw the perfect thickness of trunk in amongst a gathering of bushes that would do the job just as I needed.

After a few moments, I walked back alone whilst listening out, but with no sign he'd spat out the gag or pulled free from the bounds wrapping him around the tree, I made a mental note to make sure I told someone where to find him when it was all over.

It didn't take much to retrace my steps and to hear the first signs of activity not far ahead. With a few steps more and peering between the foliage, I saw a line of trucks much the same as the one we'd just left, but with fat-tyred forklift trucks busy moving equipment from their backs as soldiers moved around like ants around a nest.

With a shrill call, I froze, the sharp noise striking a sudden fear they'd lost control of another assault, letting the creatures loose into the world.

When an unhurried command echoed in reply, I drew a deep breath and crept forward. The view clarified with each step and I soon caught a glimpse of a huge steel door, much like the one I'd rushed through at Brass Pike.

Forcing myself not to linger on what had happened only a few days before, my gaze settled on a row of four police vans parked between several of the trucks. The sight was enough to straighten me up as I tried to figure out what they could be for. The vehicles were much like ones I'd made my home while on a six-month deployment with the MET police, a time I'd enjoyed, but was cut short by events I didn't want to linger on.

Knowing the vans well, they were much as you would expect a minibus to be, but with a cage at the rear for transporting prisoners. I just hoped those in charge weren't under the impression the thin steel meant for drugged up yobs and drunks would stand any chance of holding what waited in the bunker.

People dressed in civilian clothes mingled between the soldiers and I imagined specialists, scientists too, but guessed the bureaucrats would stay well away. At least I could take solace that the number of people I'd seen meant those in charge were a long way from pulling the trigger on their last resort.

Looking down at my feet to check for rogue twigs before I prepared to back away, a voice from the compound caused me to look up and I caught sight of a TALON tactical robot, the type of which used to be commonplace on TV, disposing of bombs before the specialists went in. The machine rolled from behind a tree, followed by an operator walking behind as he peered down at the left-hand caterpillar track.

My attention held on the robot when mounted underneath its extended arm I saw an SA80 fitted with an underslung grenade launcher. Perhaps now they were getting the right idea.

For a fleeting moment I thought about slipping away to

let them get on with the job. Perhaps those things wouldn't take notice of the robot, which would give it a chance to take them out. But what would be left for me to examine after the grenades had finished exploding?

With a slow shake of my head, I left the view behind whilst listening to the occasional hum of an engine as I retraced my steps. When confident I was far enough away, I turned my attention to searching for any other sign that Copper Flail was similar to where I'd escaped from.

Circling around the compound, it didn't take long before I heard the rattle of distant laughter and saw in the distance five soldiers standing around a house almost identical to the one at Brass Pike. The only difference was the sheet of plywood in place of what was once the front door.

Parked to the side were a Land Rover and a police van, its cage doors open wide.

Taking cover behind a thick trunk, I pulled out my phone and dialled Clark, talking in a hushed voice before I gave him a chance to speak.

"What's inside Copper Flail is the key to finding Brown, I'm sure. Find out if they'll let me in," I said.

Expecting a barrage of questions, none came.

"Franklin's not the number one on this," Clark replied, his voice quiet, and it took me a moment before I could decide if I'd heard right.

"See what you can do anyway," I eventually said and hung up.

Shaking my head to clear away the thought and crouching, I peered around the tree as I turned my thoughts to what I'd do if Franklin realised where I already was and gave orders to hand myself in.

Listening to the soldiers brewing tea as they bantered back and forth, I made a mental note of each distinct voice whilst hoping the growing length of time without an answer meant my insane request was at least being considered.

When after five minutes the call still hadn't come, I wished I had the option of shooting my way in, if only I were in a foreign land. Shaking my head, I glanced at my watch just as the tone in my ear almost made me jump.

"It's a no go. We can't get you in until the decontamination process is completed. We've been assured they have a plan to clear the place out, but they won't give any details," Clark said, the words coming as no surprise and bringing with it a vision of the battered and bent robot. "I'm not asking what you're about to do. Just let me know when you're safe."

I chose not to complain or ask to speak with Franklin to plead my case. Instead, I thanked him, promising to do as he'd asked. As I hung up the call, my phone vibrated. The screen lit with a text message from a number I didn't know, but it didn't take long to figure out who'd sent it.

Do what you have to. A1.

I hadn't seen the designation for ten years and I closed my eyes, placing the phone back in my pocket.

Now wasn't a time for reminiscing.

Silently rifling through my rucksack, I turned the dial on the retro radio box, raised the antenna as far as it would go, then pushed down the button on the side before laying it in the dirt. With the rucksack on my back, twigs snapped under my shoes as I stepped from my hiding space.

"Who goes there?" came the volley of voices.

COPPER FLAIL

48

"Environmental sampling," I said, raising my hands into the air as the five soldiers standing in front of the house in helmets and full gear scrambled to bring their weapons to bear.

"Shit," called one of them, and I glanced at a soldier in the centre of the group just as his tin mug fell to the mud, splashing steaming brown liquid down his trousers. Still, he wrangled the SA80 around from his shoulder, hopping on one leg as he grimaced when he'd finally brought the rifle's muzzle in my direction.

In another place and time, that would have meant the end of him.

Five pairs of eyes stared back as I stood on the spot, looking over their makeshift camp a few paces away from the boarded up door of the house in the middle of the forest.

"Are you okay?" I said in the softest tone I could manage, as I leaned ever so slightly towards the soldier whilst trying not to change my expression when I spotted a camera high in the eaves. Too late to berate myself for not remembering, I just had to hope, like at Brass Pike, they linked only to the system inside the bunker.

He nodded, but realising one of his colleagues was looking his way, he went back to staring down his sight with a blank expression.

"Name?" came the curt question from my right, and I turned to a soldier who stood the closest to the open cage door of the police van and furthest out of the camp, the two chevrons on his chest telling me he was in charge.

"Clare Bradshaw. DSTL."

The corporal rolled his eyes and lowered his rifle, just as someone on the opposite side of the group grunted a question I couldn't quite make out.

"Science bod," the corporal replied, still staring over and I watched as he reached for the transmit button of the Bowman radio wired into his helmet.

By the time he'd spoken the first quiet words, each of the soldiers had lowered their weapons and the one in the centre wiped his trouser leg with a cloth, whilst unable to take his eyes off me as if he'd never seen a woman before.

The corporal pressed the button again, then shook his head.

"We're checking for any containment leakage," I said with a smile as I brought my arms down to my sides.

The two standing closest to the boarded up door looked over their shoulders at the plywood, then turned away as they stepped in the opposite direction.

"Any tea going spare?" I said, raising my voice as I took a step toward the centre of the camp, glancing at the corporal.

"Have the suits drunk the canteen truck dry?" the corporal said, looking me up and down, his eyes narrowing.

I smiled, bunching my cheeks as my fingers found my jacket's zipper just below my neck. Slowly pulling, I stepped closer to the house, then turned the opposite way to take in the rest of the camp.

The group was settling back into what they'd been doing before I'd arrived, two of them kneeling to tend to the burner of their grey metal stove with their rifles propped up against fallen tree trunks. Only the pair standing to the left of the camp held their SA80s two handed and ready, but with their backs turned as they peered out into the darkness between the trees.

The corporal's gaze met mine as I completed the turn and he held his rifle across his chest as voices took up around the group again.

"But who has somewhere to charge an electric car?" the guy who'd spilt his tea said low at my side.

"Yeah. You can't go trailing cables over the pavement. You'd have some twat crab filing a claim every day of the week," another voice replied, just a little further away.

I smiled and raised my brow whilst wetting my lips with my tongue, my gaze still locked on the corporal as I slowly parted my coat, then pushed my hand inside.

His eyes narrowed as I moved my hand, tightening further as I reached to my side. His head moved slightly, the question clear on his expression when I guessed he'd seen the shotgun strap pinning my t-shirt against my breasts as it ran in a diagonal across my chest.

"Where's your ID, luv?" he said, his voice slow, but as the last of his words came out, I pulled out the Glock and grabbed the scruff of the soldier making tea low at my side, his half of the conversation halting as he felt the muzzle pushed into the back of his neck.

"Will this do?" I said, my voice breathy as I raised my eyebrows.

The corporal didn't reply as I stepped back, dragging the soldier to his feet as the rest of the voices stopped when they saw me standing behind the tall man with the Glock pointed at his throat.

I stopped when each of the remaining four were in sight.

"If everyone stays calm and raises their hands in the air," I said, taking time to make sure each of the words were clear, "this will be over before you know it and you can go home to your families for a proper cuppa."

They'd each frozen, blood draining from their faces, but only following my instructions when the soldier I held let out a yelp as I jabbed the Glock into his neck.

"Good," I said, then using my free hand I relieved him of the pistol which matched the one I held to his skin. Despite a little difficulty unclipping the spiral cord attaching it to the holster, I dropped the gun to the floor just in front of the boarded up door.

"Lay on the ground," I said and watched as those standing around the camp obeyed first time. "You, too," I said, pulling back the gun and then pushing the soldier away from me.

He took his time dropping to the ground.

"Put your hands on your head."

Watching as they did as they were told, I stepped up to the centre of the camp and grabbed the two rifles leaning up against the logs and threw them in front of the door, before walking up to each of the soldiers and relieving them of their weapons to add to the pile.

With only the corporal left, his face full of scorn as he stared me down, it took the pistol pointed at his head to cast away any thoughts of a delay, and like the others, he soon tossed his rifle out of reach before doing the same with his pistol.

"You're each going to stand one at a time, but only when I say," I said, my voice even as I raised my eyebrows. "You," I said, pointing to the corporal.

He slowly stood, then double took as I motioned toward the back of the police van.

"Go on."

His shoulders slumped when he realised what I had in mind, his face a picture of disbelief, but despite the obvious reluctance, he climbed up the metal step mounted just above the bumper.

I'd never been to the circus, but I imagined this is what it would have been like as one by one the soldiers pushed their way into the cage designed to hold two or three people at a squeeze.

After relieving the last man of his helmet and body armour before he could fit, I thought perhaps there was still room for maybe another as I pushed the cage door shut.

Once I'd checked they could all breathe and leaving the main back door open for ventilation, I heard the whispered voice as someone tried to send a radio message I hoped wouldn't get through.

With my mood already darkening, I walked along the front of the house and as I holstered my pistol, I felt myself trying to reach out to answer the question of what waited for me beneath my feet. Rallying against the thoughts, I blinked away the building memory of the metallic stench mixed with rotten flesh and little red light across the room as I dropped into the darkness at Brass Pike.

As my foot knocked against a discarded Glock, I bent down, sweeping it up and into my empty coat pocket, wishing I had space for all the weapons as I pocketed another.

Already able to smell the dust and stale air as I pushed my forehead against the window, memories flooded back as I stared at the replica of where I'd been only a few days ago.

With my hand on the Glock in my right-hand jacket pocket, I pulled it out, sliding the frame back enough to see the empty chamber. Releasing the magazine into my other hand, I counted seventeen rounds and felt an overwhelming need to strip the weapon back and pull a rag through the parts, even though they looked pristine.

Shaking my head, I knew I was reaching for my happy place, delaying what had to happen. With a deep breath, I pushed the magazine home, cocked the slide and pushed it into the snug fit of my jeans pocket in amongst the shotgun cartridges, before allowing myself a moment to check the other weapon.

With each of my trouser pockets full, the material tight around my waist, I pulled off the coat, unslung the shotgun from my shoulder and held it between my knees as I rifled inside the rucksack.

My hand settled on the smaller of the two pouches and, knowing I couldn't rely on what waited inside the syringe, I drew a deep breath, then let it go. The weapon pinned between my knees was the only thing I could be sure of.

Pushing my hand further in, I found the torch I'd longed for the last time; the one thing that if I'd had back then might have changed the course of history, one way or another.

If I'd shone the thin beam down the long concrete tube in Brass Pike, I would have seen the rungs which led to the dark floor. I'd have seen the glint of red and I might have held back from descending. Perhaps I would have left to find a phone signal and call it in.

I shuddered at what might have happened if it were the cavalry that opened the main door.

Realising I was playing for time again, I checked the torch worked before slipping it into my back pocket, then took the punch tool from the bottom of the pack, another useful addition I'd found on the equipment table just before I left the unit in Slough. I gripped it tight in my fist.

Stuffing the coat in the bag which I then slung onto my back before tightening the straps, gripping the shotgun in my right, taking pleasure in its bulk, I held the punch tool in the other hand and stepped up to the double glazing, not looking for details in the darkness beyond.

Before the images of the failed assault I'd seen in the conference room could take hold, I pressed the tip of the pointed tool to the corner of the glass, then smacked the butt of the shotgun against the tool's flat end, watching the pane relax as I broke the vacuum in between.

49

I'd been right about the smell. That was clear even before I'd smashed out the glass with the butt of the shotgun. The same layer of dust highlighted in the cone of light from the torch. The kitchen units were a match, the wood chip on the walls too, and the same bulky TV sat in the corner above the same movies on VHS, but someone had replaced the copy of Stephen King's film I'd used to measure the drop into the darkness.

But no, that was a different place altogether.

Holding the torch and the barrel of the shotgun with my left hand, I kept a firm grip with my right whilst my finger rested on the guard above the trigger, ready to do its job. Sweeping my aim across the floor, I paused on the myriad of tracks, squinting at a thin layer of sand criss-crossing the kitchen. This was something I'd not seen at the other place, but I had a good idea where the trail led.

The door to the cupboard under the stairs stood ajar with a long length of black rope wrapped around the handle which then ran out to the nearest wooden balustrade one side and circled so many times. The other end rose tight to an eyebolt in the wall on the other side.

Glancing down and despite the dull light, I saw a small pile of brick dust on the carpet below. With a shake of my head, I pocketed the torch, unable to stop myself from wondering how proud they'd felt as they secured the knots.

After pinning the shotgun under my arm, I pushed my foot against the base of the door and unpicked the loops, watching as the tension relaxed before the rope fell to the floor. Resetting my hold of the long gun and torch, I released my foot from the door, and eased it open with the muzzle.

Sandbags piled high beyond, pushing up against what I knew was a hidden door.

With a shake of my head and setting the shotgun on the carpet within easy reach, and angling the torch next to it to give me enough light to work with, I heaved the first sandbag from the pile, placing it down to prop the door open.

The other sacks followed one by one, filling the doorway between the hall and kitchen whilst I told myself over and again that whatever roamed below couldn't climb the rungs of the ladder, or without breaking a sweat it would have already brushed aside the sandbags and burst through the door.

Still, I paused as I gripped the last hessian bag, allowing myself a moment for my heart's pace to relax, but all too soon that time was gone and I knew I had to take its weight.

Setting it to the side and wiping the loose dust from my hands down my jeans, the grip of the shotgun and torch reassured me I was doing the right thing.

Still, I held there for a moment, uncertain if I'd heard a call from outside.

When the sound didn't repeat, I took a step forward and was soon in reach of the hidden panel which I pushed with my knuckles, not letting the warmth of the wood draw away my focus as red light bathed the adjacent wall, bringing heat and a foul stench assaulting my nostrils.

Somehow I held back a gag as I dragged the door wider and watched the deepening red hue as the door moved through its angle, revealing the circular shaft I'd expected. With sweat already building on my brow as I stepped forward, I tried to breathe only through my mouth and I angled my aim down the concrete hole, staring at the far away dark floor reflecting the light back with an added scarlet glow.

I pulled back when an indistinct call came from somewhere outside and I held myself still, waiting for a response when the voice didn't continue. Knowing it could only mean they'd discovered the soldiers in the police van already, I slipped the shotgun's strap over my shoulder. Gripping the shaft of the torch between my teeth, I lowered myself to my ass and shuffled toward the red glow until my legs dangled down.

I didn't linger, instead leaning forward, holding the first rung and feeling its heat in my grip as I lowered down, stopping only when my feet touched the protruding metal below. There I froze as the realisation hit. I was in the place I'd been so afraid for my life; the one event in my career I'd never wanted to repeat.

Gripping the metal tight, a feeling that O'Connor had been right to walk away and take control nearly overwhelmed me. He'd made the sensible decision to prepare for a future that he thought was inevitable if what waited below ever got out.

I couldn't help but ask myself if I was the fool for not running to the hills, instead heading into the madness.

With my hands cramping with the tight hold, I knew I didn't know the answer to the question, but here I was and no matter what I thought, somehow my hands and feet worked in unison, lowering me down despite my skin crawling at each heaving hot breath of air.

Shaking my head, I continued the pace until my sweat-streaked hand slipped, forcing me to snatch at the metal with the other before I fell.

After rubbing each palm on my jeans, I retook hold of the metal and with my grip much tighter than before, I held position and closed my eyes, squeezing my lids tight.

A long moment later, I pulled the torch from my mouth.

Relaxing my lips, I tried my best to slow my breathing and took comfort that I hadn't gagged in the last few seconds, despite the ever-present stench of what I imagined an abattoir not cleaned in years would resemble.

Sweat rolled down my face, and feeling as if my clothes were soaked, I opened my eyes and pointed the torch downward, my gaze following to the red mess that seemed so much more vibrant than I'd remembered.

With another two steps, my legs would dangle into the space below and I'd have to let go to face whatever waited.

Regretting a deep breath, I pushed the torch back into my mouth and went to move, but neither my right foot nor hand would budge, sticking tight as if they were one with the metal.

Closing my eyes again, I tried my best to relax, thinking back to those I'd left behind in Windsor. The people of the town, the nurse who'd handed me the note I'd not thought about until now, then Daisy, which came as a surprise. Despite the discomfort of the torch pinched between my lips, a smile tried to form without my bidding.

Feeling myself relax at the thought, the fingers on my right hand unclasped, and I stepped from the rung, lowering to the next, despite the heat building as I dropped. As my foot rejoined the other and my hands were side by side once more, a clang of metal echoed from below and I knew I wouldn't be able to go any further.

I tried, but nothing could be done and, sagging against my weight, I came to realise for the first time I'd failed when it really mattered.

50

A vision of my drawn and desiccated skeleton filled my head, my corpse still clinging to the rungs with clenched fingers. The soldiers would find my body months later when they'd taken the place back. Or perhaps I'd fall once the last of my energy gave out and I'd roam the dark halls craving flesh like the others.

Despite my mood, I knew it was the heat and the dreaded memories speaking. If I couldn't bring myself to do what I needed, at least I wouldn't die with such indignity. If only I could lower myself a little further, the rest would take care of itself.

I had to find another way.

Taking back the tension in my limbs, I lifted my right foot, climbing to the next rung where my left followed. With surprising ease, I had control again now I was heading away from the danger.

The heat seemed to ease, as did the smell with each rung I climbed and soon I stepped from the shaft, hit by the relief of what felt like pure cool air at the top as I wiped the sweat from my brow with the back of my hand.

With the heat almost gone and able to breathe without fear of bringing up the contents of my stomach, I felt like a different person. Then seeing the rope I'd strewn earlier to the floor, a spark of optimism flashed across my nerves as an idea formed.

If I couldn't step down the rungs and drop to the floor to be at the mercy of whatever waited, another way might just work. Shouldering off the rucksack, I pulled out my crumpled jacket, then after laying the shotgun on the carpet, I stuffed my arms into the downy sleeves, already feeling the oppressive heat as I pulled the zip up and over my chest.

Not pausing at the many voices outside, I bent over and gathered up the rope, hurrying a search for the two ends of the cord. Finding both just as sounds of activity seemed to rise from all around, I stepped back into the cupboard and tried my best to ignore the heat. Looking up, I shook my head, pushing away the disappointment at not finding an eyelet above the shaft, only then remembering the one to the side of the door.

Stepping back into the corridor, I gripped the two ends in my hand, then threaded both into the hole in the metal before hurrying to pull the entire length through. As the last of the rope was about to run out, I pushed the two free ends into the loop and out the other end.

Within a few moments, I'd pulled the rope tight and it held, but with my success, the voices from outside began to clarify and it was clear they were coming to get me.

With no time to think about the discomfort of what I was about to do, I stepped in between the two strands of the rope, crossing them at my back, then passed them between my legs and gripped both ends in my hands in front of me.

As the rope formed a harness, I threw the slack ends into the shaft and retook the shotgun, gripping it tight in one hand as I held the two lines in my other. Despite the heavy steps on the broken glass and not ready to put my life in the hands of the eyebolt, I relaxed my legs and let the rope tighten around my ass as I rested my waist in the makeshift binds.

When the eyebolt didn't pull from the wall as it took my weight, I loosened my grip and stood, stepping towards the shaft just as a voice which seemed so close called out.

"Stay where you are."

Sure they were coming to snatch me back out, I bounded the last pace to the opening. Then with a hope my clothes would keep the worst of the friction from my skin just as my climbing instructor from my training years ago had assured me they would, for a short time at least, I leaned backwards and the rope tightened once more.

Still with the two lines in my hand and feeling the pinch digging into both shoulders and pulling tight between my legs, I loosened my grip. Pointing the shotgun down the shaft, I walked down the wall as slowly as I could manage.

Despite the frustration rising with the voice's volume, I daren't look up for fear of what I might see, or that my grip would loosen.

With my senses already overloaded with the heat, the searing pain of the rope running through my hand and my skin seemingly pinched everywhere, I was grateful the stench went by unnoticed and that I hadn't once thought about what waited for me when I reached the bottom.

At the halfway point, or thereabouts, the pain reached its peak, and I'd fallen into a rhythm of sorts as the voices decayed to nothing. I glanced up, surprised to see the muzzle of a rifle pointed down and a helmeted head behind, shaking from side to side.

"You stupid bitch," his deep voice echoed, just as the rope gave a sudden shudder, sending my thoughts flashing to the anchor at the side of the door which I soon forgot about when the tension across my body released and I dropped with nothing to hold me back.

51

With the rungs rushing by, I had no time to think, but instinct forced me to open my hands, letting go of the useless rope. I had no capacity to regret the weapon also slipping from my grip, no spare moment to care what I'd do when I hit the floor.

Despite my feet already past the end of the shaft, my arms lurched out, hands reaching into the space above me when a glimmer of hope forced its way into my head, knowing there was still a slim chance of grabbing on and saving myself from broken legs. As my fingertips stubbed on metal, nails scraping against the coarse finish, the rung went out of reach.

Buoyed at the fleeting touch, I glimpsed another rung and my only remaining hope. Hooking the fingers of my left hand, I slapped it against the last length of metal. My weight caught in an instant but slipped just as quickly from my sweaty grip, my right only just able to catch my weight, where it held in place and I felt overcome with joy that I was no longer falling.

The pleasure washed away as the shotgun clattered below, echoing out to announce my arrival with my legs and lower torso dangling and exposed in the space as my palm ran with sweat.

Despite the terror at what I should do next, something made me look up to the soldier still peering down, his eyes so wide and his lips moving to repeat the expletives even though no sound came out. Within a blink of an eye he was gone, the door slamming hard, followed by the first thump of the sandbags telling me there was no going back. There was no chance of escape without running the gauntlet below.

Bending my legs, I let go of the steel.

With no time to look down and preview my journey into the red-bathed abyss, I landed, ankles twisting on the floor made uneven by the fallen rope, but somehow I remained upright.

My eyes shot wide as I scoured the room in the dull red light, searching for the shotgun as my legs took the weight. Seeing only a bright red light shining from ahead, my legs settled into a crouch as I pulled the Glock from the holster and stood, arms stretched out as I twisted around for what could jump out.

When nothing rushed to attack and with my head pounding with the heat, I turned back to the light bathing the room red, the source so bright it blocked the sight of anything beyond. I held there for a moment, giving time for my breath to settle, but unable to concentrate I had no choice but to holster the pistol and pull off the jacket, throwing it to the floor before I took hold of my gun again and wiped at the sweat running down my face with the back of my hand.

With another glance to where I hoped the shotgun had landed, I vowed never to let fear take control of me again, knowing the last few moments could have gone so differently.

I'd been given another chance.

Mindful of the rope at my feet, I took a step back as I tried to recall the layout of Brass Pike and the room I'd first descended into. With my eyes getting used to the red glow, I made out a cage to my right which seemed the same, but although ransacked like its sister, many more crates and upturned containers still filled the space. When my back touched against the wall, I stopped and crouched, again scouring the floor for the shotgun whilst trying not to linger on the wash of blood that seemed to be everywhere I looked.

Keeping a one handed aim high towards the light, I reached for the torch, pleased to find it still in my back trouser pocket and I soon had the bright beam turning slowly around the room.

The emergency ladder which should have been sitting against the yellow silhouette on the wall behind me instead lay strewn to my side, covered in bloody handprints as I imagined the last moments of Brown's escape.

With a single rotation around the room, the torch-lit survey confirmed it was a match for Brass Pike, both in construction, size and shape, and how it was fitted out. But there were differences. Information posters on the walls, the contents of shelves, and these held my attention only until I saw the shotgun beside at least three scattered shells just to the right of the red light ahead.

Wiping my brow again and blinking in hope of clearing the sweat stinging my eyes, I pointed the torch beyond the light on the floor but soon gave up when it wasn't strong enough to penetrate out to what I knew should be a door the other side.

Taking a slow step with my feet tacky on the floor, I walked with my aim still pointed out to where I couldn't see as I tried not to take notice of the treacle like squelch with each lift of my feet. Within a single stride from the light, I paused and strained to listen when I heard the echo of muffled voices, bringing with it images of the creatures talking to one another.

After a few seconds, I realised the conversation came from above and the voices were already receding. Feeling I'd stopped for too long and with my aim unwavering, I lowered myself to my haunches, unsure whether I should put away the pistol or the torch in order to reach for the shotgun so I could check to see if it had survived the fall.

Annoyed with my indecision, I shook my head then tried to push away my disappointment with how I was performing, knowing that if I didn't buck my ideas up, it would end with my death. Gritting my teeth, I pushed the Glock back into the holster, then angled the torch down to where I'd last seen the long gun. Still crouching as the beam swept across the floor, I flinched, staggering back, which forced me to drop the torch as my hands went out to the concrete at my sides, hoping to prevent the fall.

My fingers slipped in the sticky blood, doing nothing to slow my backwards momentum, and as my legs went from under me, I landed on my butt.

Despite the low grip, I jumped up on my feet just as the torch beam settled to highlight the right-hand wall. After franticly wiping my hands down my jeans, I drew a deep breath, the stench the least of my concerns.

Gritting my teeth, I stepped forward, scooping up the torch before adding its muck to my trousers.

"Fucking hell, Carrie," I said to myself in a low voice, then leaned down, pointing the torch to the shotgun, which I quickly grabbed just as I caught another glimpse of a hand severed in a ragged mess at the wrist.

Taking a step back, I wiped the shotgun down my jeans, despite feeling the moisture soaking against my legs. With the lit torch in my back pocket, I felt along the length of the gun barrel. Finding everything in the right place, the muzzle seeming as round as it should be, I struggled to pull three cartridges from my pocket, not wanting to put my life in the hands of those that had scattered to the filthy floor.

After filling the spaces in the stock and with the long gun's grip in my right hand, my left resumed its hold on both the torch and underneath the barrel. I revelled in its bulk.

Stepping forward whilst taking care where I placed my feet, I eased the bright light on the floor to the side with my trainer so I could finally get a look beyond.

It wasn't long before I wished I hadn't.

52

From just beyond the doorway was the pale, severed head of a man, his eyes wide and glassy as he stared back. With his neck resting on the concrete floor, it looked as if his body were set in the concrete. Purple bruises covered the right side of his face, and he wore a black combat helmet with a camera mounted on top, the LED not lit.

Expecting at any moment for him to blink, I stared with the shotgun pointed low until I saw the bloody stump of a wrist a little further down the corridor, the black sleeve of his arm disappearing into the darkness.

Looking away and following the torch's beam beyond, the mass of blood wasn't unexpected. Knowing I'd end up much the same if all I did was linger, recoiling every other moment from the horror in this place, I stepped tentatively forward, taking solace that each dead body I came across meant one less creature to go up against.

About to sweep my hand across my face to brush away the sweat, I stopped, remembering the blood and grime I'd slipped in only moments earlier. Instead, I angled my head to meet my right shoulder, raising my arm to soak up the worst of the moisture, then repeated on the other side.

Stepping over the door's ledge after flashing the torch to check my footing, the beam broke through the darkness to reach along the corridor, before hitting the wall ahead, illuminating the same kink I'd seen in each passageway at Brass Pike.

The cone of light flowed across the doors lining the walls as I drew it back. Finding most ajar, I felt a need to search for secrets, but knew I had to finish the toughest of jobs before I could start exploring.

Putting one foot in front of the other with care, I concentrated, listening past the clinging stickiness at my feet, but heard nothing other than my heart pounding in my ears.

Rounding the first bend, I left those rooms behind. In

the torch's narrow beam, I spotted another full of glass vials and scientific contraptions containing all colours of liquid, recognising it as where in Scotland I'd found the crate which I now knew came from the Brazilian rainforest.

Forcing myself from the distraction, I instead took in the detail of the round room ahead, which formed the centre of the complex and the place I knew I'd be the most vulnerable.

In the torchlight, I confirmed the other two corridors were where I'd expected them to be. With both doors wide, the one ahead should lead to the main entrance I could still picture in my mind, and the place I'd need to run to if I'd underestimated the task at hand.

To the left, I hoped for the labs with the half glass walls, and I listened for some clue as to where my biggest threats would come from. With the silence giving nothing away, I felt a tug of guilt in my chest when I remembered the lone survivor I'd found in a cupboard much like the one I stared at.

That day, without realising, I'd signed his death warrant.

Looking away from the cupboard door smeared with bloody prints, I peered back to the middle room as I stepped slowly through the debris at my feet, sweeping the torch and shotgun left and right. Just like Brass Pike, furniture lay scattered around, busted and broken across the floor, mixed with the seemingly endless supply of blood coating almost every section of the concrete.

Lifting my leg over the door frame highlighted with yellow and black tape, my foot came to rest on the other side and I stepped back in sudden fear of a hoard of the creatures rushing from both angles despite the lack of evidence.

Realising my breathing had sped, and still with no sign of an assault as I looked between the two doorways, I slowly stood tall and took a deep breath.

With the silence weighing heavy on my thoughts, I turned, grabbed the handle of the heavy metal door hanging at the side and tugged, hoping it wouldn't make a noise.

When its weight swung with ease through the angle, I guessed at some hidden mechanical help.

Not letting it close all the way in case I had to run back, I could at least know if something was headed this way as I explored the remaining two corridors.

The CCTV screens to my right were blank, and with no red LEDs along the bottom edge, I settled on the power to the whole place being out, the light from the first room perhaps battery powered. The radio lights were off too, and I found the words Copper Flail on a printed sign just above, then next to it a map confirming the bunker was a match for its sister in all the ways that mattered.

An indistinct noise caused me to turn, but as its echo faded to nothing, I held my breath and pushed all my concentration into listening for the source as I swung my aim through the darkness.

I imagined the grinding of teeth, or the crack of a bone as the picture in my mind clarified to a tall rabid figure crouching over a pile of flesh as it looked up from taking his fill. I knew if I didn't act, I would be the next meal.

A shower of thoughts sparked through my mind as the sound came again, none of which helped my motivation to do anything but rush back the way I'd come, scrambling up the ladder to bang on the door and offering myself up to the military's mercy.

Shaking my head, I knew that wasn't a choice I would make and the only thing I could do was to walk through the corridor leading to the main entrance and where I was pretty sure the sound came from. If I didn't find what I needed, then countless other people would feel the same terror and I wouldn't wish that on any other living creature.

The sound continued like a beacon. The crunch and crack of something I didn't want to think about at least told me what to expect as it guided my slow steps through the corridor. Sweeping my aim from left to right, I had no trouble ignoring the ajar doors, instead feeling that at any moment I was walking into an ambush beyond the gap, whilst knowing if there was nothing inside, they would at least be a place of safety. Or a place I could starve to death if no rescuers came in time.

Despite the background chatter in my head, I kept up the slow progress as I rounded the corridor's kink, forcing one foot in front of the next and wishing I'd taken the earlier chance to give the shotgun a more thorough check.

With each placement of my feet, the sound grew more distinct, the crunching joined by the tearing of flesh along with the slap of something wet. My legs felt heavier with each movement, bringing with it a fear I might seize up; a reminder of how I might still have been in the shaft if I hadn't pulled myself together.

The thought didn't help to lessen my weight, but somehow I lifted my pace as I came around the corner, sweeping the narrow beam from side to side, then slowing as it found steep steps rising with a short ramp alongside.

Pausing at the significant difference to the last place, I forced away the first glimmer of panic. Not giving it time to settle, I moved the torch to the right, and it came to rest, shining back from the metallic skeletal remains of a TALON robot shattered into pieces on the concrete.

After realising the wretched sounds had stopped, I spun on the spot and lit the empty corridor behind. Taking a breath, I turned slowly back around, my eyes widening when the beam fell on a naked figure, his skin smeared with a dark mess and a putrid liquor dripping from his hands as he crouched on his haunches, his eyes reflecting the light right back at me.

This was it, I told myself, and with energy rushing into my muscles, I felt my strength bulge under my clothes as if my body had waited for the right time and it wouldn't let me down.

Settling my finger on the trigger, I strode forward, holding the figure in my sights as I marvelled, knowing that no matter how quickly it reacted, the shell would get there first.

Still, I held my finger back, stepping closer in order that there was no chance I'd miss, despite the desperation for the cartridge to blast its head clean off.

Lifting the gun a little higher, I stopped when I heard a heavy click echoing as if from all around me, quickly followed by the same sound again just as the lights came on, forcing my eyes closed.

I had them open quick enough, my lids blinking fast when to my right I saw two new figures streaked with blood, both staring at me as their mouths fell open and a high pitched, glass shattering chorus of screams cut through the silence.

"Oh fuck," I said as my breath ran out.

RICOCHET

53

Gritting my teeth, somehow my grip on the shotgun held firm as I resisted my body's need to recoil and force my hands to my ears to stop the piercing squeal ripping through my head.

My feet seemed fixed to the spot, despite an almost overwhelming need to turn so I could give in to my fears and run from the two naked figures covered in blood on the other side of the room, revealed by the fluorescent lights.

Taking a breath, my mood lifted when I realised I'd remained in control and the constant doubt plaguing me since Brass Pike had been for naught. I dropped the torch and re-centred my aim as I took another step closer to the creature I'd first picked out in the dark. Then, gripping the barrel tight, I pulled the trigger.

Even before I'd seen the mess left behind by the head shot, I pumped the sliding hand guard back and adjusted my aim, just as the creature's reach came to nothing with the first shell's momentum forcing it backwards. The screams halted just before I pulled the trigger a second time as I watched only long enough to see the creature who'd once been a man fall back, its body twitching as it hit the sodden concrete.

Adding to the mental count of my shots, I pumped the third into the chamber as I swung the weapon around to where I'd last seen the other pair.

Not knowing what they'd done in the time it had taken to blast away the first, with the loud echo of the gun's report only just dying, I wasn't surprised to see both had risen, dropping the stinking offal feasts from their laps, as side by side they pounced in my direction.

Not looking away from the pair, I stepped back, even though it gave me no benefit. Then I planted my feet as I levelled my aim, singling out the taller one to the right on impulse alone.

As they bounded shoulder to shoulder, my finger tightened on the trigger, but spotting a dark tattooed outline of wings on either side of a parachute on the taller one's arm, I paused just a fraction of a second before I pulled my finger all the way back.

The shot missed where I'd intended, smashing instead into its right shoulder rather than its head, sending it staggering back, but only for a moment before it caught itself and rejoined the rush with its fellow demon.

With no time to replace the three missing shells, I swung the gun around through the short angle. Knowing I had little time left to settle my aim, I pulled the trigger, hoping that with its bloody torso almost in arm's reach, the shell would do the job I needed it to wherever it hit.

I needn't have worried when I saw the implosion between its eyes sending it reeling backwards, the force sweeping it from its feet and crashing to the ground. Not lingering to see what happened next, I turned again to find the other naked figure's muscles tight as it made to leap towards me.

Well aware of the single remaining round in the chamber as I pumped the slide, and not knowing if I could bring my aim up and make a shot to its face in time, I fired at the base of its hip.

The round hit where the leg joined its body. Its gnarled expression didn't change as it pushed off the ground with the limb hanging limp at its side as it toppled over, landing in the mess and leaving it to scrape its fingernails across the concrete in search of traction.

Slipping the four shells stowed under the stock into the breach without thought and forcing another from my pocket, my ears ringing and sweat pouring down my face, I surveyed the room with a quick glance, then turned again, this time taking a little extra time when I realised the screams echoing in the background weren't just in my head.

The two I'd hit in the face were motionless, if I ignored the occasional twitch, leaving only the third who gurgled deep from its gut as it slowly dragged itself towards me. With a quick glance to the left and down the corridor bathed in white and red light to confirm nothing else rushed toward me, I slipped the strap of the shotgun over my shoulder and drew the Glock from my right trouser pocket. Feeling the tension around my waist lessen, I stepped toward the struggling creature with my aim outstretched.

Spotting the pair of Roman numerals under the Parachute Regiment tattoo on the upper arm, I glanced away, my gaze landing on the other shoulder where dark ink covered the skin in a continuous sleeve. My study lingered when in the centre of the art stood the silhouette of a man with another figure carried over his shoulder and the vibrant red of a poppy underneath. I had to turn away as I saw the words below, not able to acknowledge that I'd already processed their solemn meaning.

Telling myself that the ink-marked hero had long gone from the flesh before me, I looked back, but soon regretted again as I spotted the white lines of a scar, a long laceration from nipple to shoulder on his left and a knot of tissue I recognised all too well as a healed gunshot wound from many years ago.

He'd been a lucky man in life, and I owed it to him to put him out of his misery if any part of the rotting flesh was still human.

None of the five shots missed as I fired the Glock point-blank at its forehead, my aim tracking down as the creature crumbled in a heap.

The screams had stopped as the last shot's echo died and I peered around the room, taking my time to calm my breath with my finger still tight on the trigger. Catching sight of black body armour and an MP5 assault rifle scattered amongst torn dark clothes, I closed my eyes for a long moment, only opening them again when a squeal echoed, reminding me I wasn't out of the woods yet.

Pushing the pistol back into my trouser pocket and retaking my grip of the shotgun, I stared up the short ramp. For a moment I couldn't push away the thought that safety waited on the other side of the large steel door, but then if I opened it, all I'd gone through so far would have been for nothing.

Taking the torch from the ground, I turned it off and wiped the worst of the gunk on my trousers, regretting a look down at the awful dark sickly mess across the fabric. After looking away, I forced the cylinder underneath my belt and turned to face down the corridor, listening out for the vague sounds echoing from that direction.

I'd stopped three creatures, and the man who'd lost his head was out of action. Three at least were part of the assault party I'd witnessed on the video stream. Four of the Regiment had lost their lives that I knew of, which meant they were back down to the numbers who'd started off in this place. How many there were I didn't know, but now wasn't the time to question why I'd not sought this basic information before.

Doing my best to shake away the thought, I listened with care as I stared into the bright corridor, hoping I wouldn't live to regret not taking more time to prepare.

54

After convincing myself those outside had turned the lights on to give me the best chance of survival, with the place so much brighter than Brass Pike had ever been, the glare of the fluorescent strips fixed to the ceiling brought the full extent of the mess and destruction into focus in its glorious foul rainbow of colour.

The blood splashed across almost every surface, and covering much of the concrete floor was a patchwork of sickly hues. A dark, almost mahogany depth where it had dried ran all the way through to a maroon and then, where my feet were slipping in the centre of the corridor, was a bright scarlet shimmering with the overhead lights.

Amongst the different burgundy shades were dark earthly colours and shapes, whose odour and origin I didn't want to think about.

Stepping into the corridor, I peered past each door standing ajar on either side, a task which gave me more confidence now the rooms were lit up bright. They were much like those in the other place and most held a promise that urged me to come back to explore when the time was right.

With the corridor's kink just ahead, I took more care not only in placing my feet but in trying my best not to let the mess bring my spirits down. My eyes wide, I reminded myself to stay focused on what might jump out at any moment.

Nearly at the bend and about halfway along the corridor, I glanced to the right and in through another door open. I spotted a room with a wall stacked up to the low ceiling with the rugged red equipment containers I'd first seen in Brass Pike, each with the edges marked with yellow and black tape and dotted with hazard warning triangles across each face.

Fighting against my need to take a closer look, whilst managing to keep my feet from slipping, I didn't stop myself from easing the door open a little further with the nose of the shotgun. Despite the squeal of the hinges making me suddenly so conscious of the silence I'd broken, I stared into the room, my focus catching on the transit labels facing out on some of the boxes, showing off the bold black letters of the same Brazilian airport I'd seen on the same container I'd found in the other place.

Holding my breath, I listened out, but hearing nothing, I looked back in the room, somehow knowing that this was a place that might hold the answers I'd come for.

Before long, I realised I'd taken a step over the threshold, but the thought soon fell away as instead I busied myself taking in the room. Stainless steel tables stood on either side of the door, with a red container resting on the one to the right, its lid open as plastic bags plump with something green and white I couldn't quite make out lay strewn around it. Similar bags had fallen to the floor, where I noticed the only bloody marks were those I'd traipsed in.

Glancing around the room for a second time, I held back and stared at the row of red boxes, my head tilting to the side when it looked like they could be more than one layer deep. Feeling a change in air pressure followed by a sudden sense I was being watched, I turned around, but despite there being no one there, I was suddenly wary of what might be just out of sight a little further down the corridor.

It was enough to convince me it still wasn't time to start my search, but that this would be the first place I'd come back to when it was.

Stepping into the corridor, I crept around the kink with the raised shotgun still leading the way. I let it droop when I saw, in the centre room just ahead, all but one of the CCTV monitors were lit with crystal clear colour images, which kept switching back and forth, after a short delay, between the views of the bunker's rooms and corridors.

I recognised many of the places. The entrance room with the big steel door where the three fresh dead bodies lay. The place with the cage where I'd dropped down through the shaft in the ceiling. Long runs of anonymous corridors, including the one with the headless body.

The central monitor showed the room where I stood and a figure looking off to the right with blood smeared down her face and streaking her white t-shirt.

I was more than a little surprised I didn't look worse.

My interest in the image waned as each of the screens changed all at once, and I focused instead on three figures, naked or in various states of undress. Two were feeding whilst the other stood and faced down the corridor, its chin raised as if it were sniffing the air.

I couldn't have been more delighted at the find, understanding all at once the advantage it gave me. Buoyed with confidence that I knew their number and position, and that I'd already taken three of them down with near clinical precision, I checked the shotgun one last time and turned toward the remaining corridor, striding along with the weapon pointed out, not missing a breath when I saw the first creature through the laboratory's half glass wall.

As it lifted its head, still chewing, it raised to its feet, sending a carcass from its lap to the floor. I already had the long gun aimed by the time I'd passed through the glass door, releasing two shots in quick succession and sending its brain to decorate the far wall.

I'd turned away before the body hit the floor and had two new rounds from the stock filling the spaces in the chamber. Then I turned left, not letting my stride falter when the other pair were only just moving from the far end of the room where I'd expected them.

Confident enough to empty the chamber, the five shots soon sent their bodies crumpling to the concrete.

As my gaze lingered on the gnawed bones scattered at my feet, for a moment I wished they hadn't gone down so easily and had held my attention for a little longer.

The sight of blood-sodden clothes scattered by the walls almost tipped me over the edge and I quickly turned, covering my mouth as I stood there for a moment.

"Job done," I said under my breath, filling the shotgun's

chamber with the last of the cartridges from my pocket as the sense of satisfaction gave way to the need to start the task I'd come to this place to complete. I just had to hope it had been worth it.

Still with the shotgun raised, even though I was confident enough the danger had passed, I couldn't help thinking for the first time in what form the secrets I searched for might take.

Paperwork, perhaps, or another trail of some sort. Maybe notes from the experiments, or anything like an entry in a notebook that might lead me to Brown, or give me an idea at least as to what he was trying to achieve.

With the thoughts cascading through my head, I glanced to the CCTV screens as I stepped back into the central room, but seeing nothing that I hadn't expected, I turned toward the corridor leading to the exit, keen to search the room I'd promised myself I'd explore first.

At the time, I didn't know what it was, but something caused me to stop and I twisted slowly back around, looking over my shoulder at a monitor in the far corner. I saw nothing other than an empty corridor, and about to turn back, the images switched and there stood a figure in full black body armour and a helmet.

My thoughts turned to a second attempt by the Regiment to gain control, but it didn't take long for the idea to melt away when I realised the figure had no skin on its face and was running towards me.

55

With my feet slipping in the ever-present mess, I turned and ran from the faceless creature, only twisting back around as I reached the corridor's opening. After levelling my aim, I pulled the trigger, holding my glare long enough to watch the round dent the helmet. The creature's step barely faltered as his head went back and within less time than it took for a breath, it was upright again with the pale white of its jawbone hanging wide.

Despite indecision at first turning me away, I changed my mind and twisted back around, soon pulling the trigger again, but the shell ricocheted from the far wall before blackening a CCTV screen to my left, sending smoke rising from the housing.

Bounding with long strides, it was already so close, and I moved my right foot to get a better stance, but as I pulled the trigger, my foot slipped. The muzzle dropped as my finger clenched and the round thumped against the hard plate in the centre of its chest, tearing apart the dark fabric as the energy dissipated without harm.

The two remaining rounds gave me a simple choice; to turn and run, hoping to reach the exit with enough time to spare, or hold my ground whilst knowing the gap gave me only enough time for a single shot. Anything less than a hit square to its face would mean my terrible ending.

I did both.

Letting the muzzle drop, I took the shot, aiming for the black trouser leg just above the combat boot, but I had no time to see if I'd neutralised the threat before I spun, pushing down my feet in search of grip as I tried to run.

I'd made it around the corridor's bend before I looked over my shoulder where it was still running, albeit with a slight limp, and closing the gap. Whirling back around, I knew the main entrance was too far away and the floor too covered in slippery mess waiting to foul my speed. I wouldn't make it in time, but perhaps I could reach the next side room.

Hearing the snapping of teeth in my wake, I lengthened my stride and reached out for the lip of the door already ajar, my fingertips touching the hot steel and I pulled the heavy metal wider, then gripping the outer handle, I gave everything I could to speed up. Soon at the opening and with the door now wide, I let go of the metal and latched onto the inner handle, using my hold to slow myself down and swing in towards the room whilst pulling the door up behind me.

I'd made it, my feet holding firm on the floor as the door glided towards me in my wake. Panting hard, I gripped the handle tight, unsure if I should drop the shotgun, just as I realised I'd ended up in the room with all the bright red containers and the place I'd longed to search.

Choosing to keep hold of the shotgun, I revelled in the relief that as I pulled and the gap between the door continued to shrink, the foul animal hadn't yet appeared. With a last burst of energy, I tugged at its weight using all of my reserves, just as ten black gloved fingers showed themselves between the jamb and the door.

Despite feeling spent, still I held on, clinging to the hope the heavy door's momentum would shear the fingers clean at the bone with a satisfying clink.

The sound didn't come.

Instead, the door flung wide, the handle ripping from my grip and sending me stumbling backwards to my ass with the dark, featureless creature already charging forward, its bulk filling the doorway.

Air pushed from my lungs as I landed with a thump, sending boxes scattering to the floor and down over my head. Somehow, I'd kept a grip on the shotgun and raised it, aiming square at its face until a falling box clattered on top of my hand.

My finger slipped from the trigger with the impact. Despite the ache of effort pulsing in my muscles, I lifted the gun a little higher at the beast almost in my face as the boxes seemed to settle. With the bones and teeth exposed, it seemed to wear a permanent smile.

Knowing it was the final round in the chamber, and that it might be my last ever, its gloved hands reached out towards my face, readying to pull me close and bite down hard.

I pulled the trigger just as another box fell from above, this time hitting the top of the gun, taking with it all hope that I'd get out of this place alive.

56

The shell clanged off the creature's helmet, knocking its head to the side before pinging against the door's steel surround, then ricocheting out into the corridor where it resounded like a bell.

Still sitting on my butt, I grabbed the empty weapon by the stock with both hands and pulled it back, then after a quick swing, I hit away a gloved hand as it loomed up to my face. With the other arm already reaching out, I knew I had no time to swat it away as instinct forced my eyes shut.

When its firm touch hit against my face, I felt no pain and it left behind a warmth that made my skin crawl as I batted it away. Forcing my eyes open, the stubby end of a wrist leaked a dark liquor as it went out of view.

Not giving the rising nausea time to take hold, I took joy in the minor victory that one of my earlier shots had saved me from having my face ripped off.

Not wanting to give it time to attack again, I kicked out at the red boxes at my feet, pushing them forward and into its path, adding more as it floundered unsteady on its feet until I scrabbled up to stand, just as it lunged across the gap between us.

Its mouth opened wide, and I saw the stubby end of a tongue as I threw the empty shotgun in its face, which it knocked to the side and stood up tall before taking a step back and dropping to it haunches where, from experience, I knew it was preparing to leap over the obstacles between us.

The delay was long enough for me to snatch the Glock from the holster, pulling at the trigger before it came level with the creature's head, then shooting again as I grabbed the second pistol from my left pocket.

So many of the shots missed, pinging against the wall or from the helmet, some embedding in the armour plate across its chest as the constant wall of noise rattled my brain as if my skull were made of paper. Still, my fingers tightened over and again on the triggers, a few rounds ripping through flesh and shattering bone, enough at least to keep it at bay.

Not able to keep count of both sets of shots, I guessed there were only two rounds left in each, and although a dark liquid leaked through a crack in its left cheek and its jaw hung slack, held by sinew alone, as the faceless beast glared, I paused and leaned as close as I dared, aiming both guns at its eye sockets.

The right-hand hole doubled in size as the eye disintegrated, the recoil knocking my right hand back whilst the gun in my left did nothing. Realising it was empty without the need to glance over, I pulled the right-hand trigger for a final time and watched the weight of the helmet collapse on the skull as in the propellant-laden air filled with a thin mist, the figure slumped in a heap at my feet.

I closed my eyes and controlled my breath. With the muscles in my arms aching, I bent over, letting both the guns clatter to the concrete to add to the cocktail of shell casings, blood and flesh that covered it.

At least a minute must have passed before I stood tall, and despite the pain, I took the last remaining Glock from my right pocket and secured it in the holster to rest under my arm before I peered around the room.

Blood flecked across the disordered scattering of containers, igniting my need to search the place. I shook my head, knowing I'd already made that mistake once. I had to check the whole site was clear first.

About to step around the slumped corpse and head into the corridor, against the wall I'd been standing close to I saw a series of wooden crates that were previously obscured by the piles of red boxes.

Walking over, I pulled the closest bare box up from the floor, my fingers leaving sticky red prints on the wood as I drew it closer. Examining the tacky remains which I guessed were where someone had peeled off a shipping label, I lifted the lid, levering it open on its simple metal hinge, but I found the box empty.

Moving to the neighbouring wooden crate with the

same tacky area, I picked up the nearest red box and straight away saw the shipping label, which was almost identical to the one I'd seen at Brass Pike.

Glancing across the red boxes scattered across the room, I saw shipping labels on many of them.

Pushing the rest of the red boxes from the wall, I found another four wooden crates, each with their labels removed, but out of the corner of my eye I found another which had scattered to the other side of the room. My heart sank when, picking it up, I felt the tacky remains, before my spirits lifted when I saw the corner of a label with a ragged torn edge, the paper no bigger than a match box. In faded black ink was the address of the travel agent I'd tracked Brown to.

This was what I'd been looking for all along; a link between what we'd witnessed on the outside and evidence someone was bringing in material not tracked by the officials. It opened up so many possibilities of what they were doing unsupervised at this place, and that Brown was right in the middle of it.

Feeling as if the temperature had risen, my head swam with the heat as sweat rolled down my face. Despite knowing all too well what covered my hands, I couldn't stop from wiping away the moisture with the back of my hand.

After drying my palms on my jeans and seeing the pink of my fingertips for the first time in a while, I peeled the remains of the label from the box, then did the same with the label on the nearest red container, pausing part way through before pushing them both into my pocket when I heard a sound; perhaps the grinding of a heavy door followed by silence, broken by faint whispers and rushing steps filling the void.

They were in.

With the slow drip of sweat rolling down my face, I placed the container on the floor, shaking my head when I realised what I mess I was in, looking so much like the creatures I'd destroyed. I thought for a moment about checking how many rounds remained in the Glock, but as a burst of gunfire rattled through the bunker, I steeled myself as through the open door red laser dots bounced up and down along the opposite wall.

Raising my arms in the air, I waited as a figure, their dark clothes and protective gear matching those of the mess of a creature at my feet, came into sight, with only their wide eyes and pinched lips visible through the balaclava. Their assault rifle turned toward me in an instant as their finger tightened on the trigger of the weapon pointed at my chest, as the deep voice uttered the word I dreaded the most.

"Contact."

57

When the masked man hadn't already riddled me with bullets, a second figure, who was almost a match for the first, rounded the door frame to join his colleague. Both breathed hard with their fingers on their triggers.

Unsure of what had caused the first man's delay, I held my breath, fearing the second man might come to a different decision.

Keeping my hands high in the air when in that split second I still wasn't on the floor bleeding to death, another joined at their backs as many more blurred in the corridor behind and headed deeper inside the bunker.

None of them spoke to issue commands or ask questions into their radios, and I felt a sudden need to scratch at the bloody mess drying on my face, but I daren't chance my luck.

Behind their balaclavas, helmets and dark tactical dress, they were indistinguishable from each other apart from their height and the colour of their eyes. That said, and despite the fleeting moment I looked over the third soldier's covered face, there was something about his narrowed eyes as he towered over the first man's shoulder.

His glance turned to a stare with each rushed beat of my heart and he tilted his head to the side, looking me up and down before he drew back just a little when he caught sight of the limp body of their fallen colleague at my feet.

"Carrie?" he said, looking up, the rise of his brow obvious despite the face covering.

It wasn't his northern drawl that pulled the memory from my brain, but the smile through the mouth hole showing off the bottom row of crooked, yellowed teeth below the shining whites of his straight top set that gave him away.

"Tommy?" I replied, the word slow. "Tommy fucking Barton," I said with growing confidence. "I thought you'd be scattered across the moors by now," I added, as the corners of my mouth rose to a weak smile in reference to where he'd once said he'd wanted his ashes buried if he died in the line of duty.

Only twelve months ago, if that, I'd spent a week with Tommy on the tail end of a two-month mission collecting evidence deep undercover with an organised crime group I wasn't allowed to write the details of. For the last seven days I'd slip away to meet with Tommy in bars and cafes across Manchester, talking for hours as I relayed the intel and formed a plan for the takedown over neat vodka with no ice.

When the time came for the ten-man team led by Tommy to raid the group, all went to our plan, apart from a kid who'd just joined the group and thought it a good idea to take aim at Tommy with a pistol.

The eighteen-year-old was the only casualty, and once I'd knocked him to the ground with two shots in his centre mass, then held my hands against the wounds to stem the blood, Tommy confirmed the gun had been loaded with the safety off.

I'd saved his life, Tommy declared, but I laughed it off, reminding him the kid was probably a terrible shot.

I never found out if the kid survived and I hadn't spoken to Tommy since, instead having to leave the scene before the police's arrival complicated things.

"Lower your guns, you stupid cunts, or she'll have you for fucking breakfast," Tommy said, as roaring laughter followed from the bottom of his lungs.

Despite the near constant flow of more people at their backs, the other two did as Tommy said, their eyes narrow until Tommy barged past, stepping with care as he rolled up his balaclava to the brim of his helmet and looked as if he was about to lean in for a hug if it weren't for the rotting flesh between us.

As he looked me up and down again whilst shaking his head and laughing, I dropped my arms to the side and glanced down at the shotgun beside the body.

"Nice. Yours?" he said, having followed my gaze.

"It saved my life a few times," I replied, and watched as he bent over and, after taking a moment to pick out a clean spot on the black metal, he picked it from the floor and handed it over.

I nodded and took it from him, surprised at its weight and the tiredness in my arms. Just about able to sling the strap over my shoulder, he gave a sympathetic smile as he leaned forward and gently touched at my elbow to guide me towards the door.

"Come on. Let's get you the fuck out of here. I don't know if you've seen yourself, but you need a bloody shower," he said, motioning for the two still at the door to move to the side before glancing back to check I was following.

The calls of 'all clear' echoed out as we walked, but the words sounded far away as I carefully placed my feet, stepping over uncoiled guts, great bloody clots and scattered body parts.

Eventually reaching the ramp rising to the exit, I looked up, unsurprised to find four muzzles pointed in my direction with the men behind straightening up as their eyes locked to mine.

58

"Fucking move," Tommy barked as he motioned his arm from side to side as if to brush the four men out of the way. Each were dressed just like him and shared a question in their sideways glances. Their answer came after Tommy repeated the order, louder this time, with the first one peeling to the side of the ramp, soon followed by the others as light came through the space they'd left behind.

"I better look after those," Tommy said as he turned toward me, motioning for me to hand over the weapons.

With fresh air breezing through the doorway, I released my tight grip, giving him the two guns and my rucksack, then let Tommy guide me forward by the elbow and into the daylight where cool air chilled against my sweat, leaving warm patches highlighting where the sickly gloop had dried.

They'd fortified the entrance since I'd last seen the door through the trees and sandbag positions stood set back a little on either side, each manned by a soldier staring down the length of a general purpose machine gun with their sights tracking my every move.

Back further still, men in hazmat suits peered through transparent plastic domes encapsulating their heads, none of them hiding their fascination as they pointed metal instruments with long trailing cables in my direction.

Behind another short wall of sandbags, a soldier in green dress uniform stood, his face expressionless; a brigadier based on the three stars underneath a crown on his epaulets. Next to him were two men in tailored suits. The man to the right, stout and red-faced, looked over with a growing disbelief as we locked eyes.

After a moment, he turned, his face scrunched up and arm raised as his finger outstretched in my direction. He looked up to his companion, who was thin with drawn skin pronouncing his skull and appeared to be in his late sixties.

"I want her put down for what she's done. This is beyond the pale," he said, spraying the tall guy's suit with spit.

Before he turned back, Tommy had me by the elbow again, guiding me to the left and a row of trailer boxes parked a short distance away, each with a door open at the rear and a figure in a yellow hazmat suit waiting inside.

As I stepped away, surrounded by disbelief that I was still alive, I felt the sudden need to call Clark, but my earpiece had long gone and knowing I still wasn't in a place of safety, now wasn't the right time to pull out my phone.

On autopilot, I stepped up the three steps, feeling the pressure changing in my ear as the door sealed behind me. Locking eyes with the man through his clear plastic visor, he stepped away, stopping only when his back hit the far wall where he looked me up and down, his eyes wide open.

He still hadn't spoken as I began to shake, the tremors gentle at first, but becoming more violent as the silence continued. I closed my eyes, telling myself it was just the comedown.

"I'm sorry," the guy said, his nondescript accent startling my eyes open as he shook his head. The tremors calmed.

"There are no women officers available," he added. "We didn't…"

"Expect me to come out alive?" I said and watched his face rise with an awkward smile. "Don't worry. I know the drill," I added as I pushed my hand into my pocket, bringing out my phone and the two packaging labels, going back in when I realised there was another. The number from the nurse.

"I need these," I said, my voice reverberating along my dry throat, then watched as he turned and tore a small yellow biohazard bag from a roll and held it open at arm's reach with his hands covered in thick yellow gloves. I dropped my things inside and he zip-tied it closed before placing it on the floor by his feet.

Blood flaked from my trainers as I kicked them off, then I peeled down my white socks patched with red where the mess had soaked through. Not glancing over at the man,

I didn't turn my back as I pulled my t-shirt over my head where I felt my hair matted together. Enjoying the relief of unclipping my bra, I threw everything into a large yellow bag in the corner I hadn't needed the guy to point out, but he did anyway, whilst doing his best to avoid catching my eye.

Dried blood ripped at the thin hairs on my legs as I pulled off my jeans, and I tried not to grimace as the fabric clung, leaving behind what looked like war wounds that weren't mine.

Picking the plasters from my knuckles, the guy leaned in at my side, but with relief the skin underneath seemed clean and uncontaminated.

"Step forward," he said, his words soft as I shook again, even though the space felt warm enough. Putting one foot in front of the other, I stopped as I reached the drain in the centre of the floor before revelling in the scalding hot water soon raining over me.

After what felt like a long time soaking up the heat, the shakes calmed and my mind cleared enough to remind myself I'd done the job I'd needed to do, and all that was left was to hold it together for just a little longer.

Using my stubby nails to scrub and scrape the crud from my hands, then after looking myself up and down, I rubbed at the rest of the stubborn stains across my skin before pulling and running my fingers through my hair in search of every foreign trace.

Almost forgetting the guy watched, I ran my hands over my body, tracing the texture of my scars and dark bruises covering my torso. Feeling a little relief, I turned and looked the man in the eye, watching as he rapidly blinked and pulled a lever to the side to stop the flow.

Holding his palm up to stop me from stepping away, he pulled another lever, which sent another flow from above whose caustic stench forced me to close my eyes.

Rinsed with cold water, he produced a white towel and once I'd dried, he handed over a paper overall, which I slipped into. Then he took a pair of standard service issue boots from a cupboard, before looking at my feet and raising a brow as he handed them over.

They were only one size too large and after I'd laced them up, pulling them as tight as I could, I took hold of the small yellow bag and opened the door, already hearing the shouts of the round man calling for my head on a stick with the brightness of the day flooding in.

59

Despite being in the trailer for what I thought to be at least fifteen minutes, the same raised voice from when I'd entered still dominated my senses as my feet landed on the hard-packed mud of the forest floor.

All eyes were no longer on me; instead, it seemed that only those of the two military police officers wearing high vis jackets over their fatigues took any notice. They followed my every step, shadowing me on either side, and it wasn't long after I rounded the side of the trailer that the plump man in the suit looked over with the vitriol in his voice rising.

The brigadier was nowhere to be seen.

The MPs didn't try to clutch at my arms and didn't force me into cuffs, but even if they did, I felt no will to resist anything they attempted. It was all I could do to glance around, my gaze settling on the area around the front of the bunker's entrance, finding a metal-framed archway which someone had erected since I'd gone into the trailer.

The arch held sheets of white plastic to obscure the view through the door as every few moments a black clad member of the Regiment emerged from around the side to be greeted by a figure in a bio-hazard suit, who escorted them to one of the waiting trailers, many of which had their doors closed with the sound of rushing water coming from within.

With a lull in the expletive laden tirade, I turned back towards the suits, locking eyes with the fat man and watched as his face grew the colour of beetroot. As his bluster exploded, his arm raising and finger wagging toward me, over his shoulder I saw the brigadier walking from the opposite direction, followed by four soldiers in temperate fatigues, pistols holstered on their thighs as they marched at his side. The lack of visible rank and name tags, along with their beards and longer than regulation hair, told me they weren't regular soldiers.

"Where the fuck have you been?" the rotund suit called out as he turned then quickly looked back to me.

The corner of my mouth raised in a thin smile whilst I watched the high-ranking officer's reaction. Despite being one of only twelve of the same rank in the British Army, and therefore unaccustomed to such a level of disrespect, he simply raised his brow and offered a slight nod in my direction.

"Organising the arrest team," he said. "Sir," he added, almost as an afterthought, then walked straight past the pair of suits, striding up to me.

I'd already stopped walking and looked him in the eye, as with a swish of his hand, he dismissed the two guards and they melted away from my sides.

"Lieutenant Colonel Harris," he said, lifting his chin. With surprise, I almost felt a comfort in the address.

"Arrested! You should shoot her for what she's done," the fat man called out, only lowering his voice when the man at his side leaned in and spoke in his ear.

"Don't worry, sir," the brigadier said without turning. "She'll get what she deserves," he added with a raise of his brow.

I stood impassive as a silence fell all around, as if everyone waited to see how I reacted.

He'd called me by a rank he would have known I didn't recognise, and although I was well known in the special forces' community, my views on where I belonged were equally understood.

This was a test. I was under no illusion. For the sake of my liberty, he wanted this minor victory as I stood unarmed and naked under the paper suit. Could I put the needs of all those people I was trying to protect before my pig-headedness?

In that three word greeting, he'd asked if I could put away my stubborn belief and acknowledge my roots and what they had done to get me to where I am, but for what? More lenient treatment perhaps?

With a glance at the grin on the fat man's face and still

looking like he could have a heart attack at any moment, I locked eyes with the brigadier and hoped I'd read his expression right.

Standing up straight, I snapped my right hand to my forehead and stood to attention.

"Yes, sir," I said, lowering my hand from the salute.

A thin smile slipped onto the brigadier's lips, but fell almost as it formed.

"You are under arrest for unauthorised entry into a class A secure facility and for committing numerous offences yet to be determined. You are to be transferred to a holding cell whilst we work out what to do with you."

The men who'd been waiting patiently behind him stepped around, none of them making eye contact, but still I knew straightaway I'd never worked with any of them before.

"Take her away," the brigadier said in a stiff tone, as he looked me in the eye before stepping to the side.

"Yes, sir," came the smart reply.

I didn't wait for instructions, instead following in step as they formed around me. Flanked by the soldiers, we marched along the dirt track between the trees, re-tracing the journey they'd just made.

Leaving the bustle that seemed to rise as soon as we'd started moving, I wondered for a fleeting moment what they'd do if I ran. Even in the poor excuse for clothes, I could probably outrun each of them, unless they were under orders to shoot me down if I tried anything.

Perhaps I could snatch a pistol from one of their holsters, but vastly outnumbered, maybe I'd be better off leaving this to Franklin to bail me out. Even though it would be the first time.

The options raged around in my head as we marched, but when instead of taking the well-trodden trail around to the left and toward a group of military vehicles, we stepped in between the trees and my thoughts turned to more sinister concerns.

With every step off the beaten track, I couldn't help

thinking that perhaps I wasn't meant to arrive in the garrison after all. Maybe I was to fall foul of an accident, or the result of an escape attempt with the earlier charade meant to put me at ease. After all, I knew none of these men and had no idea who they ultimately took their orders from. I'd come across enough traitors in my time for nothing to surprise me.

At the rustle of leaves beyond, I tensed, but not ready to make my move, I continued following in step, until a figure dressed the same as my guards stepped out from a tree directly in our path.

BANISHED

60

Each of the guards halted in front of the tree, their stiff presentations melting away as they turned around on the spot. My gaze flitted to each one in quick succession, then back to the soldier who'd come around from the tree in our path as I tried to figure out, with none of them yet drawing a weapon, who I should go for to stand the best chance of survival.

Outnumbered, there was no real hope, but I wouldn't go down without a fight and despite the sudden need to do anything other than stand on the spot, I watched as each man turned their backs as if trying to look anywhere but in my direction.

Decision made, I focused on the soldier who'd appeared from around the tree, expecting to peer down the muzzle of a pistol, but he'd also turned away and, like the others, searched out towards the trees as if keeping a lookout.

About to call out in desperation to know what was going on, a man in a paper suit matching the one I wore stepped around the tree with a rucksack over his shoulder and my shotgun held by the barrel, the muzzle pointing to the sky. It appeared someone had cleaned it since I'd handed it over.

It was Tommy.

Still, with fear of betrayal in the forefront of my mind, it was only when his smile beamed from ear to ear that I began to relax.

"Debt paid," he said as he shook the bag from his shoulder and held it out by the strap.

Tilting my head to the side, I glanced at each of the men

again as they continued to peer between the trees.

"You helped yourself a lot with that salute," Tommy said, stepping forward when I still hadn't moved, and motioned for me to take the bag, which I'd only just seen wasn't the rucksack I'd carried around the bunker.

"Brig Green was happy enough to put one over that fat twat in the suit, but only if you gave him what he wanted. Otherwise, I think he might have thrown you in a cell for a couple of hours before letting anyone know where you were."

I nodded as I stepped forward and took the bag, gingerly pulling open the zip and peering inside to what looked like a bundle of clothes.

"Thank you," I said, still a little unsure of what was going on, but took the shotgun as he held it out.

"Like I said, it was my turn. Now leg it that way until you reach the road," he said, pointing through the trees to my left. "There's someone waiting for you."

I nodded, knowing I'd be a fool not to grab the opportunity with both hands. About to turn and run, I held back.

"Northwest from the house, about half a click, there's a squaddie tied to a tree with a ratchet strap."

Tommy laughed.

"Grab him and his section a case of beers each, for you lot, too, and bill me. I'll weigh you in when I'm next at Sterling Lines."

Tommy didn't stop laughing as he nodded.

"Okay. Now fuck off or we'll all be in the shit," he said, still laughing even after I turned and ran, with no thought of keeping the sound from my steps as I jumped over fallen logs and hurried around wide tree trunks. It was only as his laughter receded after a few minutes more, that I stopped and peered around.

Finding nothing of concern between the foliage, I unzipped the bag and upended the contents in amongst the leaves.

A white t-shirt, black boxer shorts and combat trousers

fell to the ground, followed by the two dark pouches and everything else I'd had in my backpack. The only thing I was missing was the torch and my earpiece.

Ripping off the paper suit which had done a surprisingly good job of keeping out the breeze, I slipped on the black boxer shorts, followed by black trousers which were a little big, but the canvas belt did well enough to nip them up around my waist. About to pull on the t-shirt, I paused, my heart sinking when I saw words scrawled in black marker across the front, then turned it around to see the matching bold letters along the back.

Lt Col Princess.

"Bastard," I said out loud, but I couldn't help but laugh as I pulled it on, then swore again when I realised it was at least a size too small as it hugged my curves.

Shaking my head, I stood up straight, looking at the crumpled and ripped paper suit, wishing I hadn't destroyed it as I took it off. Drawing a deep breath, I realised the laughter was exactly what I'd needed, the heavy fog that had clouded my head having already cleared.

"I'll get you for this," I said to myself, and smiled as I stuffed everything, including the remains of the paper suit, into the sack, then slung the shotgun over my shoulder and rushed between the trees again.

The driver of the black BMW had made no effort to hide, instead parking on the verge at the edge of the forest. Daisy sat upright in the front seat, spotting me only moments after I'd seen her, and reached over to open the passenger door.

I threw the bag and shotgun on the empty back seat before climbing into the welcome warmth.

"Do I salute?" she said as she stared wide-eyed and stifling a smile.

"Don't," I said, raising my palm.

Turning away with a guilty look, she swallowed hard.

"Just give me your jacket and let's get the fuck out of here."

Smiling, she leaned forward and did as I'd asked and I

soon savoured the warmth of the black denim zipped up to my neck as we rolled off the curb and onto the road.

We'd driven in silence for what seemed like an age, but when I glanced at the clock on the dash, it had only been five minutes.

"Did you find what you wanted?" Daisy eventually said, her tone business-like again.

Not able to stop myself from rapidly blinking as memories of the past hours flashed through my mind, I couldn't answer.

The rush to get to Copper Flail. The fall into the unknown. The red light so bright. The scattered body parts and the sense of the impending battle I didn't know I could win.

"Are you okay?" she said, her voice soft.

I raised my chin and looked over. It was all in the past now. That's what I kept telling myself. I'd done what I'd needed to do, the fear of failure gone, and I'd found what I'd been searching for.

The rest didn't matter. For now at least, but I knew I wouldn't know if I'd banished my demons until I tried to sleep.

61

"Red?" Daisy said. Blinking quickly, I realised I was still staring at her as the world came into focus again.

"I'm okay," I said. "At least I think so," I added, turning back to the windscreen.

"You smell like my childhood," she added, and I glanced back with a lowered brow. "TCP. The antiseptic. I think my mum went through a bottle of that stuff every month patching up my knees and elbows. I was such a tomboy."

I turned away smiling, my thoughts flashing to my teenage years climbing mountains and following trails with the cadets, but then merged to images of a young Daisy playing in the woods with her friends. My smile dropped as the vision shattered and I thought back to the partial label in the yellow hazmat bag.

"They had a side project," I said, still staring through the windscreen. "And we have no idea what they were working on. All we know is it was under the radar. It could have been anything."

Daisy kept quiet, and I realised she didn't know what I was talking about. She knew nothing of the conversation I'd had with Franklin, Clark and the professor.

"I guess it doesn't matter what they were doing," she eventually said. "Only what Brown has become. The rest we can deal with in slow time."

I nodded; she was probably right, and at least we had a lead.

"The travel agent is the key. The place I first tracked Brown to. I've confirmed they were helping smuggle additional raw material into the bunkers."

"But this doesn't tell us where we can find Brown," Daisy replied.

"No, it doesn't. At least not yet. I've got to make a call," I said, glancing at Daisy who didn't even try to hide her confusion.

After a couple of minutes, I pointed to a long lay-by in the distance. "Pull over there."

Turning in my seat as we slowed, I stretched my arm out to grab the rucksack from the back.

"There's a McDonalds up ahead if you don't want to chance the food poisoning," she said, which caused me to look up and notice the burger van at the far end of the lay-by.

I winced at the thought of food, not able to remember back to when I'd last eaten.

"Grab some coffees, please. Do you have a first aid kit?" I said, and watched as she looked at me with concern, her brow raised.

"In the boot. Are you injured?"

I shook my head and as we came to a stop, I pulled the door open and jumped from the car. Bringing the rucksack with me, I headed around to the rear as Daisy walked away with some reluctance, heading toward the food van.

With the yellow plastic bag from the rucksack laid on the curb, I grabbed the first-aid kit from a pull-out side panel in the back of the car.

Wearing two sets of disposable gloves and after picking out half a dozen alcohol swabs, I pulled a bandage from its plastic, wrapping it over my mouth before circling it around my neck and tying it off at the back. Using the bulk of the car to shield the bizarre view from the passing traffic, I pulled off the tie wrap holding the bag closed and took the phone out before wiping it with each of the swabs, their sharp tang reminding me of the shower.

Changing the top layer of gloves to a fresh set, I used the last wipe to go over each of the phone's surfaces again. Then after giving it a few moments to dry, I pulled the test kit from the rucksack, glancing over to Daisy where she smiled at the server through the hatch in the van's side.

When the high tone sounded out, I read the zero on the small screen.

Still with the gloves on, I pulled out the two label fragments before using the phone to take pictures of each, then replaced them in the yellow bag followed by the gloves and rubbish before sealing it with a thick double knot.

Removing the bandage from around my mouth, I revelled in the air's chill as I threw everything into the rucksack and retook the passenger seat, just as Daisy arrived with two white Styrofoam cups and a bulging paper bag in each hand.

I was already on the phone to Clark by the time she retook the driver's seat, pushing the cups into holders between us. Then she held out a bag in each hand and whispered, "Brown or red?"

I shrugged, then turned away, already hearing the relief in Clark's greeting.

"You're okay!"

"They're bringing in extra material," I said, not waiting for him to catch up. "The travel agent I tracked Brown to. They were smuggling it in. We need access to their computer system."

"Okay. Okay. Let me think. Um. Right. We're tapped into their network, but their records are vast. There's nothing we've found so far that seems to be of any interest. To be honest, we don't know where to start, other than the obvious names, but they've brought back nothing."

"I have a partial label from one of the packages," I said, putting the phone on speaker before finding the photo I'd taken only moments before. About to call out a number printed along the bottom, the smell of warm salty bacon sent my stomach into a spasm, filling my mouth with saliva.

After a pause I recited the numbers, then turned to Daisy who was halfway through her roll with a circle of ketchup in the corner of her mouth, beaming as she chewed.

"We'll see what we can find, but I don't know how long it will take," he replied. "But we've got an id on the poor bugger in the hotel."

"Great," I said, turning away from Daisy and out of the side window to look between the trees.

"Timothy Grant. A former major in the Royal Engineers, now working for a company based in Windsor.

Bennet Williams. They're listed as an unclassified industry on Companies House and they have zero public information."

"A front?" Daisy said, still with food in her mouth.

I glanced over as she stuffed the last of the roll in. "Shit, sorry. I have call sign Daisy with me and you're on speaker."

"Acknowledged," he replied, his tone stiffer when he spoke again. "It looks that way."

"Where does he live?" I said.

"South West London. Hammersmith," he replied.

"Only a short train journey away," I said.

"Yeah. That's not far enough away to stay in a hotel," Daisy added.

"My thoughts too," I said.

"Perhaps he didn't feel safe at home," Clark said and I looked along the road, wondering if Timothy Grant had known what was coming for him.

"What's the address of the company he works for? Let's pay them a visit," I said.

After a moment, Clark said, "St Leonards Road. Almost in the centre of the town."

Daisy looked over, her eyes wide. "Is that near the old fire station we were at this morning?" she said, but before Clark could reply, she made eye contact with me and carried on speaking. "We had a shout shortly after you left. A possible sighting of Brown called in by a police officer. He only had a fleeting glance before losing sight. When we got there, there was no sign, and no evidence he'd ever been there."

"Yes," Clark said, his tone sharp. "It's just around the corner."

62

The four-man team was already on site long before the hour it took for us to arrive on St Leonards Road, but I only knew this from Hollywood's voice over the speaker of the radio Daisy pulled from the car door's side pocket.

Tubbs and Moses waited in a car somewhere along the street, but not another X5. Despite searching as we approached the only remaining parking spot a few doors down from the target, I couldn't tell which vehicle they were in. From back at the warehouse in Slough, Hollywood assured us they had eyes on the front of the building from a little way down the road, whilst Philips and Scotch, neither of which I'd met, were milling around down a side street, having confirmed there was no rear access to the property.

Our parking space gave us a clear view of the frosted plate-glass window covering the building's front, but not of the single door standing at the side described by Hollywood as made of the same opaque glass.

Once upon a time it had been a shop, but with just a sign about the door, Bennett Williams in a cursive font, the frontage did nothing to entice people off the street or indicate what went on inside.

About to step from the car, I spotted a traffic warden in the driver's wing mirror in a black peaked cap with a yellow band around the edge as he ambled along the path, glancing across the windscreens of the cars in our line.

"Take care of him," I said without looking away from the mirror, only turning to Daisy when she didn't react straight away. A question hung on her lips as she frowned back.

"What?" I said when she hadn't spoken.

"Warn him off?" she said, her brow bunching as the words came out.

"Get a ticket," I said, scowling, then watched her eyes light up and her shoulders relax. "Did you think I wanted you to rough him up?" I asked, then pulled the door open, not waiting for an answer.

Daisy left the car as I headed towards the front of the target building.

Walking out in the open reminded me I wasn't wearing a bra, bringing with it a renewed sense of frustration about the t-shirt, even though Daisy's jacket hid it from view. The thoughts soon fell away as I stepped up to the glass door, tapping my knuckles on the wooden frame.

With no immediate answer or signs of activity inside, whilst I waited a little longer I glanced at the standard Yale lock and the mortice keyhole at around chest height. When still no one answered, I pulled the handle just below the locks, pushing it down hard, not surprised when it didn't move.

Feeling someone arrive at my back, I glanced over my shoulder at Moses and Tubbs, who carried a rucksack over his shoulder and tucked themselves quickly into the recess alongside me.

"We need to get in," I said, and watched a sly smile bloom on Tubbs' face just as Moses turned around to survey the street.

Shrugging the rucksack from his back, he silently drew down the zip, then rather than handing me what I'd expected to be a thin glass cutter blade, from inside the bag he pulled a bright yellow battery-powered angle grinder fitted with a disc that sparkled in the sunlight.

Despite my surprise, I took its weight and confirmed from the disc's label the industrial diamond coating as I knelt down. Tubbs leaned in at my side and pressed the handle of a double suction cup firm to the same surface in the middle of the bottom half. Pushing down a black lever on each cup, he nodded from above.

Needing no further prompt, I angled the blade close to the glass where it met the frame along the lowest edge and pressed the switch, surprised to barely hear the growl of the electric motor which was soon drowned out as the diamonds shrieked against the glass.

After drawing the blade halfway up the door and

manoeuvring around Tubbs as he continued to hold the suction cups, I cut across the middle then down again before, with a slight click, the panel came free, drawn away by Tubbs as I moved out of the way.

Glad of the respite from the high noise as Tubbs rested the panel against the wall, I peered in at the space for a moment before I crawled through the opening and swept a small stack of post to the side and across the dusty wooden floor.

Stale air hung in the space as I made way for Moses to follow in behind.

Empty of furniture, there was no place for anyone to hide other than behind a door marked 'Staff Only' at the far end, which Moses, with his hand poised to reach under his jacket, strode off towards.

As I followed, he waited until I stepped to the side of the door, grabbing the handle as he pulled out his pistol, pointing it down to the floor. With a nod, I pulled open the door, watching as Moses barely paused before surging forward.

With the dark corridor cleared, three closed doors waited, one at the end and then two along the right-hand side. A toilet, a kitchen and an office, if the black writing on the silver signs were to be believed.

They hadn't lied, Moses clearing each in quick succession.

Light streamed down from a skylight grotty with patches of moss in the ceilings of the kitchen and office, both only just big enough for two people to stand in at the same time. As Moses lowered his gun and backed out of the office which someone had squeezed a table and chair into, I peered into a mug and a layer of green mould, then to a wastepaper bin filled with unopened letters addressed with a multitude of names and companies.

By the time I'd dropped the junk mail back into the bin, it was clear the address was a glorified post box.

The mail I'd brushed aside at the front was much the same, but the bulk was for the company with the name above the door and addressed to four different people. The oldest was postmarked eight days ago.

Pulling out the phone ringing in my pocket, I answered Clark's call.

"It's empty," I said, turning to look around the space again. Clark made a noise on the other end of the line as if it was what he'd expected. "And I think they're due to collect the post. I've got some names."

"So have I. From a search of the directors," he replied.

"So who are they?" I asked when he didn't list them off.

"It's not who they are, it's who they were," Clark said, but not waiting for me to ask the obvious question, he continued. "They're all in Brown's address book. Three people listed as professors at Cardiff University, and each had worked on the project, stationed at one or other of the bunkers."

"You said it's who they were?" I replied when Clark paused, as if distracted.

"Yes," he finally said. "They each resigned as director, one at a time, over six months. I did a little more digging, and they were all for the same reason."

"They'd died," I said.

"Yes," he replied. "How did you know?"

"A hunch. Is the remaining director a Peter Lonsdale?"

"Yes," Clark replied. "But he never worked on the project and only became a director after the first two professors resigned."

"And he's not one of the bunker's…" I said, pausing in search of the right word. "Victims?"

"No. We've seen nothing official on him in connection to either of those places," Clark replied.

"There's mail for him here, along with the dead guys. What's his address on Companies House?"

"You're standing in it."

"Who is he to them?" I said, staring at the blank beige walls.

"No idea yet, but I'll see what I can find. What else is in the building?" he said.

"Nothing, but if we had enough time we could wait to see who collects the post, but we'll need to fix the front door. Otherwise it's a dead end."

Back in the car, Daisy and I watched the front of the shop with the missing part of the door's glass hidden from our angle, but easy to spot from the other direction. With the rest of the team remaining hidden, there was nothing else to do but wait.

"Three professors working on an ultra-secret project set up a side-line supply of the raw material they're researching," I said in a causal tone, then glanced over to Daisy in the driver's seat before looking down at the phone and reminding myself Clark was still on the call.

"Why?" she replied, staring out along the street.

"We don't know, but it's for their own agenda. Everyone expected the outcome of the project to be far reaching. We're talking mammoth. Life changing, and not in the ways we've seen."

She turned towards me with her brow lowered, not hiding the question from her expression.

"Think about the dawn of antibiotics. Their development extended life expectancy by twenty years," I said.

She raised her brow, then lowered it again and tilted her head to the side. "But antibiotics can't end a life in an instant and turn them into whatever Brown is now."

I nodded. "I'm guessing that's not what they were looking to achieve. At least at the beginning, but who knows where they were thinking of taking it?"

"Were the professors killed on duty? Were they testing on themselves?" Daisy asked as her face scrunched up.

"Clark. Do we know what happened to them?" I said as I turned to look at the phone on my lap.

"Heart attacks," he said without a pause. "And not at the facilities. That would have been a red flag."

"All three?" Daisy replied before I could.

"Yes," Clark said as I raised my brow and looked over to Daisy and her matching expression.

"That would be enough of a warning for me," I said. "Did anyone investigate it?"

"All I can tell is they put it down as a coincidence. A product of their advanced years and the stress of the task at hand."

"A coincidence?" Daisy said, huffing air with a mock laugh.

"For Peter Lonsdale anyway," I replied, nodding as I felt a prickle of excitement across my body. "I think we've now got a good idea who Brown is searching for."

63

"But why is Brown searching for the head of the company who's importing the raw material the scientists were working on?" Daisy said, looking at me and then back at the phone on my lap.

I shuffled for comfort in the X5's passenger seat and stared out along the road as my thoughts lingered on what we knew.

"The scientists, including Brown, are working on sanctioned projects," I said as Daisy nodded in my peripheral vision. "But on the side, some, or all of them, are pursuing their own unsanctioned research, which means smuggling in additional raw material, all organised by the professors."

"And we have no real idea what they were working on," Clark added as I paused for thought.

"We mustn't forget they're scientists still," Daisy chipped in. "And they would have been making meticulous recordings. It's part of the scientific method, otherwise how do they know what works and what doesn't. There's no point finding the cure for cancer then realising you can't repeat the results."

Daisy held her palms open as I looked over. "I'm a geek, shoot me," she said with a shrug and I tapped under my arm where my Glock usually sat, then tilted my head to the side as I raised a brow.

"Not today, sadly," I said as we both laughed, but then our expressions fell as I continued. "But you're right. Despite all I've seen, the bunkers weren't some mad scientist's labs. They were staffed by top academics."

"Still," Clark said. "Without access to their computer systems, or going back in," he added, not able to see my eyes flaring wide at the thought, "there's no hope of getting hold of their records, and how else would we know what they were working on?"

"Can we get a list of project proposals the management

team didn't approve?" Daisy said, looking down at the phone.

"Maybe they would have considered it yesterday," I said. "But not after what I just did, and even if we had all the access, we don't have time. Brown could be infecting new people right now."

Daisy shook her head and looked me in the eye. "It doesn't bear thinking about."

I slowly nodded. "If only we had a choice not to. Anyway, like I was saying. They're busying away doing all this research and everything seems to be contained, but then one by one the professors die of what they recorded as natural causes. Peter Lonsdale steps in to fill the void in their front company, but where did he come from? How did he get involved? Is he on anyone's radar?"

"I'm working on it," Clark said, and I nodded even though he wouldn't see it.

"Still, it's been a year, and it's all ticking along again with no one raising any official concerns, that we've heard of, until something happens at Brass Pike and we lose it along with Copper Flail. Amid the turmoil, an infected Brown flees, heading straight to the travel agent importing the extra material, before following the trail to Timothy Grant of Bennett Williams, stealing what we think is a briefcase."

"So where is Brown now?" Daisy asked, tapping the top of the steering wheel.

"I think that depends on what he found in the briefcase," Clark said.

"And if he's part of this or a victim?" I said, looking out along the street again, half expecting Brown to appear at the front of a crowd of creatures baying at his back.

My pulse raced as I thought about their senseless need to feed and their unerring instinct to end human life. As a vision of the soldier's faceless skeleton loomed into view, I realised I'd closed my eyes and opened them, turning towards the passenger window when I saw Daisy look over. After drawing a deep breath as quietly as I could manage, I hoped my voice remained steady.

"Based on what I've seen, I know Brown was involved in the experiments. His reaction to the infection was nothing like the rest. Thank goodness," I said, as I turned my head to the side once more and closed my eyes, opening them only as I felt Daisy's hand on my leg, the surprise of her touch banishing the terrifying reminders already creeping in.

"Are you okay?" she mouthed silently.

I nodded, looking down at her hand as she withdrew it.

Gently coughing into my fist, I opened my mouth to speak, despite the dryness of my throat. "We still don't know why he's following this trail."

"Maybe he's looking for a cure?" Clark said.

"Isn't he too far gone for that? He must realise by now?" Daisy said. "There's no denying he's a clever man."

"For profit then, selling to the highest bidder?" Clark added.

"That's one explanation why our friends keep turning up," I replied.

"Or just plain old revenge," Daisy said. "Maybe he wasn't a willing participant and I've seen it too many times in the MET to rule out one of the most base motives."

"We just don't know," I replied. "How do we find out what was in that briefcase?"

Daisy twisted in her seat and I turned to see her looking back, wide-eyed with her palm raised a little.

"What if he find's Lonsdale's name in there?" she said, raising her brow.

I nodded slowly at first, but its magnitude soon grew.

"Clark, we need everything you can find on Lonsdale asap," I said, but already heard his furious tapping at the keyboard.

We stared at the front of the shop, listening to the clatter of keys and the occasional soft breathy noise coming through the speaker. When the tempo slowed, then paused after a few minutes, Daisy and I turned to each other, only looking away when the taps grew more furious than ever.

"What have you got?" I said, but only the hurried clicks

replied and I knew better than to interrupt again.

"Peter Lonsdale was co-author on academic papers with each of the professors," he said, rushing out the words. "They go back many years, right to the time…" he said, his voice slowing. "… They were all at the same university."

"No surprise there," Daisy said.

"But wait a minute. Brown's listed too," he added with a slight uncertainty in his voice, as if he was checking what he saw. "Yes. He's listed on many as well. Hang on a second," he said, as the key presses stopped and silence followed.

I thought perhaps I heard a tiny click in the background, perhaps of his mouse.

"Yes," he eventually said with triumph in his voice. "There it is. Peter Lonsdale is in Brown's address book. Shit. I should have checked that first, and he lives ten minutes away."

64

Lonsdale's street was on the other side of town. With school pickup traffic adding another ten minutes to our journey, we were the first to arrive in the street that was much like where we'd just come from, but with houses either side, each standing up to the pavement with no front gardens.

Daisy chose a space ten cars down from the bright orange front door, just as the call came in that Latenight and Hollywood had arrived, Tubbs and Moses only moments behind, leaving the other two to watch the address we'd just left.

After handing over a spare radio, I dispatched Daisy and Latenight to an office building a few streets away that towered over where we watched.

Sliding over to the driver's seat, unsure if I was glad to be alone with my thoughts, I had Hollywood, Moses and Tubbs wait on an adjacent street as I watched the traffic slowly building. Cars soon filled the rest of the empty spaces, disgorging mums and packs of kids in scruffy uniforms with their school bags hanging from their shoulders to disappear behind more brightly coloured doors. None went into number ten, the house I wouldn't look right at.

Fifteen minutes after she left, the radio squawked to life, and I twisted the volume to the left as I listened to Daisy report they were in position on the top floor, and had a clear view of the target house, but couldn't see the cars parked on the side of the road, including my position.

"Received," was my simple reply as I dialled Clark's number, speaking as he answered. "Have you checked Brown's finances for any other source of income?"

"Yes. There's nothing other than his official salary deposited for the last two years," he replied.

"But they've known each other for over ten years. Go back further," I said.

"Will do," he replied and hung up, just as Daisy's voice

came over the radio.

"IC 2 male heading from the south on foot. Do we have a description of the target?"

"Brown or Lonsdale?" I said.

"Lonsdale. I've seen Brown's photo. It's not him," she replied, and I tapped a message to Clark on my phone.

As I looked up, I saw the person Daisy had seen first. Wearing black trousers and a white shirt, the average height male looked like an off duty copper, but still I watched as he came up to the target house, only losing interest as he strolled past the front door.

"That's a negative," Daisy said at the same moment.

"Received."

It was ten minutes more before Clark called with a glimmer of excitement in his voice.

"We've traced every transfer and direct debit. Three years ago, he transferred a pound to a different bank. It was a numbered account so not traceable to an individual, but we got in and each year for the last three there's been a deposit of just over six thousand pounds every month from Bennett Williams. No withdrawals. The balance is almost two hundred and twenty grand."

"So Brown's on the payroll and it looks like he's turned on them," I said. "It's useful to know, but it doesn't help us much."

"No," Clark said.

"Do you know how they smuggle the extra material into the bunkers?" I said.

"What do you mean?"

"The security at those places wasn't to be sniffed at, so how do they get an unauthorised package in?"

"I got you," Clark said. "Let me see what I can find out. I should be able to track the route of the packages from the travel agent's records. That number you gave me should help."

Clark hung up, and I looked back along the road, leaning to the side and along the line of cars, but despite the four by four's height, I couldn't see much other than the car in front.

Settling back into the seat, my thoughts turned to Lonsdale, wondering if he realised Brown was after him, or that we were on his trail. But then I remembered our friends, too. There was a high chance our competitors would figure this out soon enough, if they hadn't already, even though I didn't know where they were getting their information from.

Picking up the radio, I moved it near my mouth.

"Hollywood, this is Red."

"Go ahead," he replied, the commanding tone of his voice easily recognisable.

"Send someone for a stroll along the road."

"Will do. Are you looking for anything specific?"

"No," I said and put the radio back down to rest in the centre console.

"Received and understood," he said without delay, and I barely heard his voice cut from the speaker before Daisy's high tone replaced it.

"Another IC 2 male heading from the south end of the street. He matches nothing we've seen and is wearing a grey tracksuit top and jeans."

"Received," I replied as I waited the few seconds it took for the man to come into view, unsurprised when he matched her description.

Watching him closely, I only looked away when, to my left, Tubbs strolled past the car on the pavement on my right-hand side. Soon glancing back at the man, I narrowed my eyes just a little as he reached a couple of doors down from the target address. My phone rang quietly in the centre console and I answered it whilst still focusing out of the windscreen.

"Someone's screwed up," he said. "We've figured out loads of tracking numbers from the travel agent's computer system and they go back further than three years."

"Shit," I replied, taking my eyes off the man. "They've been working outside of the system for that long?"

"Yes, but that's not what I was getting at," he said, as I looked back down the street and thought perhaps the man

I'd been watching had slowed as he reached for something in his pocket.

"The last package was delivered two days ago, but the bunkers have been out of operation for four now," he replied.

Still watching the man, he seemed to speed up again when he put a phone to his ear. I didn't speak until he walked past the target address and I relaxed, settling into the seat, not realising how much I'd tensed.

"Hang on," I said, more so I could go back over the conversation I'd only half been listening to. "But we already know it's not likely the packages would go straight to the bunkers. It's not as if there's a letter box they can just pop the mail through. Check the delivery address."

"Shit. Yes," Clark replied, and the flurry of keystrokes were back just as the radio came alive.

"Red. This is Tubbs."

"Go ahead," I said, pulling the radio up to my mouth.

"Ten cars down from your position there's a man and a woman, both IC 2 sitting in a blue Renault SUV, glancing over to the target address. Rear windows are tinted, so there may be others inside."

"Received," I replied. "Clark. Did you get anything from the laptop image yet?" When only the incessant key taps came down the line, I tried again. "Clark?"

"Sorry," he said, not hiding the distraction in his voice. "We haven't cracked it yet. It's top level security."

"It's them again. Isn't it?" I said, referring to the organisation I constantly came up against. The organisation that was much like ours that worked in the same realm but for the highest bidder. The organisation I'd almost taken down on my first operation so many years ago, and those who'd been a constant in my career.

My thoughts turned to how the hell they were keeping up with our pace. There had been no sign any of their operatives had got to any of the key leads before us.

Lifting my chin, my expression hardened as I thought back to their recruitment techniques and the group I busted at what felt like the beginning of time. No one was beyond their reach, at least then.

My thoughts went to Daisy, then to Hollywood. They were the only people who knew anywhere near as much as I did about the operation. Clark, of course, knew everything too, but I quickly dismissed him, chiding myself at the thought as his voice came back on the line.

"The packages were delivered about once a month. Sent to RAF Brize Norton, they probably have a consolidation centre there for the bunkers."

"So that's the answer," I said. "Can we get more people on the laptop?"

"Oh shit," he said, and I looked down at the phone.

"What is it?" I replied.

"It's a different delivery address on the latest one," he said.

"You're kidding me," I said. "Where?"

"A warehouse in Slough."

65

"Are you sure?" I said, my gaze darting around the car as I tried to figure out what the revelation could mean.

"Yes. It's here in black and white. A unit on the trading estate about ten minutes from where you've set the team up," Clark replied.

"Let's hope it's just some kind of storage facility and they're not taking what they were working on in the self-contained bunkers and doing the same thing in a tin box in the middle of a hundred and fifty thousand people."

Adrenaline raced through my veins as I thought about the implications, my mind scurrying to figure out how this fit with me sitting in a car on a street in Windsor, only a few miles away from what could be the start of a whole new nightmare.

Regret pulled at my stomach that I'd not gone straight to our home station to grab a new firearm as my mind flitted between what I should do next. I had people covering Bennett Williams whilst, along with myself, most of the team were at this address looking for some guy. But maybe we should all suit up and go straight to the place that might change the world if I didn't make the right decision.

However, Brown was still on the loose following his unknown agenda and he was as much of a risk, if not more, than what we might find in that unit. As I held my breath, another thought sprang into my head, pushing the rest of my concerns to the side.

"What time and date did we lose Copper Flail?" I said.

Clark didn't reply straight away, as if I'd caught him off guard.

"I'll check," he said as I tried to stop my thoughts from racing away before he answered. I hoped I was wrong.

"Fourth of September and the last comms were at the ten am check in," he said. "What are…"

"And Brass Pike," I said, not giving him time to speak. The following silence seemed to go on forever.

"Fourth of September. Last comms…" he said, then paused as if double checking what he saw. "Ten am check in."

"Shit," I said, not able to hold back my racing thoughts any longer. "They went down at the same time."

"You mean…" Clark said, but wasn't able to finish the words as if they'd become solid in his mouth.

"This was a planned attack to shut the official programme down," I said, rushing out the words as so many questions filled my head.

"So they could take it elsewhere while we were all distracted," Clark said, his words mirroring my thoughts.

"I think Brown is trying to stop them," I added, then pulled open the door, leaning on the car as I stood and savoured the cool air whilst I tried to think.

Daisy's voice came over the radio before I'd rushed a breath, her words giving me enough cause to look up and along the road to a man wearing light grey trousers and a white shirt in the far distance. I didn't recognise him but saw another figure followed him and despite the distance, he had at least a passing resemblance to Brown.

There was no need for Daisy to confirm the positive ID on one of our targets, but her hurried words came anyway, bringing with it the reality that I was unarmed and unprepared, and all I had were three troopers on foot, one at each end of the street, along with Daisy and Latenight in the tall office building a ten minute run away.

I'd fucked up big style.

I should have called for every member of the Regiment. Along with the SBS and Royal Marines, I should have asked for the Paras. I should have called for everyone.

Instead, all I could do was grab the radio handset.

"Get everyone here now," I said, gripping the radio tight even though I knew it would take them too much time, leaving three of us, and me just with my wits, to take down the crazed man hell bent on revenge who could turn at any moment into something too scary even for my nightmares.

Dropping back into the car seat and leaving the door

open, I watched Brown come close enough to see the concentration in his expression, his eyes burrowing into the back of the head of the guy he was following.

Closing the door, I started the engine, but uncertain what to do, my foot hovered over the accelerator with my hand gripping the gear lever. Fearing the man Brown followed was already doomed, and knowing Brown would destroy me in a moment if I got in his way, perhaps I could at least snatch the person I hoped was Lonsdale so that I might get away too quickly for Brown to follow.

With an indecision alien to my everyday life, the blue Renault SUV described by Tubbs pulled out from the curb and headed towards me, just as a small white van sped around the far corner and onto the same road. They'd decided for me, leaving nothing else I could do, so I pushed the clutch pedal hard to the floor and jammed the stick into gear as I twisted the steering wheel to the left and jabbed the accelerator hard, sending the wheels spinning.

In the moment it took for the rubber to catch on the tarmac, I watched the SUV get so close to the stranger before mounting the curb and cutting across his path. I was moving but not quickly enough and watched the rear passenger door on the pedestrian's side open and a figure leap out, grabbing the stranger at the back of his neck before pushing a dark pistol to his temple.

My speed built as I jockeyed with the wheel to correct my course, the radio lighting up in the corner of my vision as rushed voices went back and forth over the airwaves. I had no capacity to listen; instead my stare switched to the van rushing up behind the SUV which also mounted the curb without slowing.

Before I knew what had happened, the van slammed into Brown, sending him out from my view with the tyres squealing against the pavement and careering towards the blue Renault.

Only just slowing in time before the two vehicles touched, three men jumped from the van, but I knew I couldn't let them take my concentration as they forced what looked like a limp Brown around to the back. I would be with them all in a moment and I had to choose what the hell I should do next.

I lined up my wheels and headed towards the Renault which was already bumping down the curb as the van raced backwards, its engine whining away down the street, all the while not able to understand how they'd subdued Brown enough not to be ripped to shreds.

Reaching out for the seatbelt, despite knowing I was already too late, we hit square on, the airbags bursting open and slapping me hard back into my seat.

I was out cold, but for what I hoped was only a moment as I came to with only the blur of a memory of what had happened in the seconds before.

Pain stabbed in my chest, igniting the earlier injuries I'd all but forgotten about as I stared out through the meandering airbag dust floating in front of my face. It took me a few moments more to notice the flames licking at the bonnet.

Over the ringing in my ears I heard a voice from the radio I could no longer see. The words shouted from what sounded like the footwell as oranges and yellows grew bright in my vision, soon followed by acrid smoke.

Opening the door, I fell to the road, feeling a sudden surprise at how much more comfortable the seat had been. A loud bang I recognised straight away rang out, the gunshot bringing the world back into focus and I watched the rear passenger door of the car I'd collided with open, feet stepping unsteadily to the road. The door slammed closed to reveal a man with a cut above his eye and blood dripping down his cheek as he brought a Smith and Wesson 442 revolver to bear in my direction.

I watched, almost disconnected from the reality as he blinked hard, and although his hand shook, he seemed to steady himself with each moment before he pulled the trigger.

I was already moving, rolling along the road and away from the car as I glanced to the hole in the X5's side that hadn't been there moments earlier. Stopping the roll as I lay on my back, I knew the gun was tracking my direction, but the only chance I had was if he wasn't quick enough for me to reach inside the jacket.

That's when I remembered the writing on my t-shirt and the missing holster that should have been weighed down by the only thing that gave me a chance of staying alive.

66

Laying with my back against the cold hard road, my empty hand retreating from under my jacket, the helplessness of the moment stuck in my throat as I tracked the shaking 442 revolver in the guy's grip. He stood beside the Renault, pointing to where I'd rolled, his aim quivering less with each split second that passed.

Still, I wasn't ready to give in, and even though I thought it in vain, I forced myself forward onto my butt, willing myself to push up from the road and stand.

When a gunshot flashed through the air, I realised I was too late, despite feeling no pain.

On hearing the high-pitched twang of a metal reply, I was on my feet, barely standing before I raced forward, aiming my right shoulder for the man's ribs, even though he was already staggering back with one hand to his chest and the gun in the other, still pointed right at my head.

Invigorated with a new strength when my body kept telling me no bullets had hit, I pushed on, dropping my shoulders low just before I made contact.

We both went down and as the air forced from his lungs, I twisted around, ignoring his agonising squeal when I reached out for the gun, just as another loud shot's recoil snapped his arm back, sending metal clanging against the side of the car.

Hitting at his wrist with one hand and then dragging the revolver from his grip with the other, intense heat flared from my side. Not letting my weight settle on top of him, I was already scrabbling to my left side, the heat growing as I swung the gun around and raised to my knees, aiming at the growing bloody mark darkening the chest of his pale grey hoody.

Another shot rang off, and I thought better of lifting myself to my feet. Instead, I kept my head below the window of the blue SUV. With one eye on the injured man, I edged backwards on my knees.

Unable to take the heat intensifying with every movement, I glanced over my shoulder at the flames licking from under the bonnet of the BMW. Fearing the fuel tank could go up at any moment, I stood, stooping against the pounding ache in my head and the sharp stabs around my ribs preventing me from taking a deep breath.

Just about able to raise the 442 level, it followed my search for faces in the Renault.

I saw the muzzle first, pulling the trigger before I'd spotted the figure in the passenger seat holding the weapon. The window shattered as I veered out of her angle of attack and I watched the gun fall from the blonde woman's grip as her hands rushed to hold back the blood spurting from a hole in her neck.

Her threat neutralised, but with no time to help stem the flow and give her half a chance at life, I rushed along the side of the car, aiming at the blacked-out windows behind her that could have hidden anything. Grabbing at the handle, I pointed the gun into the space beyond, my finger already halfway through pulling the trigger.

The tension in my finger relaxed when I saw the man they'd pulled from the street with his hands raised, palms on show, his eyes wide and cheeks streaming with tears.

Footsteps rushed from behind, and I turned, bringing the gun to bear, despite already guessing it would be Hollywood, his pistol outstretched, with Moses not far behind. From his shallow nod I knew he'd been the one to save my life, but with no time to linger on what could have been, I span back around and pointed the 442 to the driver's seat and the man slumped over the steering wheel.

With sirens already calling in the distance, and a crowd gathering, I grabbed the stranger who Brown had followed, yanking him from the car by his wrist and dragging him whimpering to the ground, just as Hollywood and Moses pulled the unconscious driver from his seat.

Pushing the revolver into my waistband, I rushed my hands over his pockets, moving my palms around his body as he flinched against my touch. Finding only a phone, which I relieved him of, I rested his back against the Renault's rear bumper and crouched in front of him as I looked into his eyes.

"You'll be okay," I said, finding his only injury to be a slight bruise on his left cheek. Perhaps it was my rushed tone, but my voice had the opposite effect of what I'd intended, instead renewing the stream of tears running down his face.

"Thanks," I said, standing when Hollywood came around the side of the car holding a Sig Sauer; I couldn't quite see enough of it to confirm the model. He nodded away the greeting whilst I tried not to let his actions colour who I thought the traitor was.

I turned my attention to the crowd, and despite my head still a little cloudy from the crash, everything told me they were out of place. In my experience, a fire fight in the middle of the street would send people screaming for cover, not forming groups around open front doors, or peering out from behind curtains.

As Hollywood confirmed the blonde's time was up, along with the man he'd saved me from, Daisy appeared through a line of people standing around the entrance to the street, scowling as she jogged with Latenight not far behind; the relief in her expression not hidden as we made eye contact. She slowed to a fast walk and spoke into her radio, but she was too far away to hear her words.

"Are you okay?" she said, a little out of breath as she arrived at my side.

"Fine. Nothing a few pain killers won't sort out," I said, stretching out my arms and relieved the discomfort was already easing. With one eye on the stranger, I explained what had happened and watched as Daisy's scowl grew more intense as I spoke.

"What's up?" I said when I'd finished, seeing she was desperate to speak.

"I'm sorry I wasn't there," she said, and I shook my head.

"It was all over in a heartbeat," I replied, but I could tell she had more to say.

"Latenight went for a piss just before it all kicked off," she said. "And I had to search for the fucker because he'd not brought a radio."

We glanced over to where he stood beside Moses, each directing small fire extinguishers spraying white clouds of carbon dioxide at the bonnet of my car.

"He's just green," I suggested as I shook my head. "Like I said, there was nothing you could have done."

Daisy shook her head, my words seeming to have done nothing to ease her annoyance, but then we both glanced over to the crowd moving either side of the road to make way for two black X5s, followed by an ambulance with its blue lights strobing across the street.

I pulled the stranger up by the arm and he got to his feet, just as I felt the vibration and heard the trill of his phone ringing in my jacket pocket.

Pulling him along, I headed towards the approaching cars, walking past two women standing at the open door of a house. Despite their hushed tones, I heard their words.

"Doesn't it look realistic," the first said, and I couldn't help but smile as I realised the rumours had done their job just as another voice replied.

"Yeah. But where are the cameras?"

67

"I'm going to ask you a question, and I urge you to take a moment and think with some care before you answer," I said, keeping my voice low as I sat in front of the hooded guy we'd rescued from outside Lonsdale's house.

I'd wanted to use the small kitchen for this purpose, but with our number now over twelve strong, the men had made their feelings about limiting access to their food very clear.

Contrary to many people's belief, I could be a team player, so instead I sat him in a chair with his arms tied with paracord behind the seat back and his legs bound to the office chair's central pillar, all in the space between the cubicles and the sinks, facing away from the door in the ladies' toilets.

Hearing the distant trill of his phone, I stared at the hessian hood as the rough material pulled in and out with each laboured breath. Waiting a moment, I dragged his chair forward by the arms, rolling its wheels across the tiles. Despite his attempts to draw back, I pushed the hem of the musty canvas up to rest on the bridge of his nose, then untied the knotted t-shirt from around his mouth before letting the sopping wet mess fall.

Staring at his blotched red cheeks, I rolled his chair back into place as his breathing calmed.

"I hope you've taken my advice," I said, and he nodded, sending beads of sweat racing down the length of his nose before dripping from the end. "What's your name?"

"Harry," he replied, the low words rasping against a dry throat, but still I could hear the lack of any strong accent.

Keeping my expression neutral, I glanced over his shoulder at first to Hollywood leaning against the far tiled wall, and then to Daisy standing beside him, who looked back with her brow raised.

"Harry what?" I asked.

"Woodridge. Harry Woodridge," he said without delay,

259

the words seeming to come more easily this time. Daisy tapped at her phone as he spoke. "I don't have money. We're not a rich family, but I can give you a little and I won't say anything to the police."

Fresh tears had formed on his cheeks and rolled to the corners of his mouth.

"I don't want your money," I said, softening my tone. "Just answer my questions and you can be on your way."

"What questions?" Woodridge said, the well-formed words coming quickly, but then he shook his head. "I don't know anything important. I can't imagine what information you might want from me."

"Harry," I said, stopping him from speaking. I then leaned a little closer, lowering my voice. "You need to relax and calm yourself. This can be over quickly. All you need to do is listen to the sound of my voice. Do you understand?"

He nodded, his head tipping back and forth with speed.

"Take a deep breath, and then another," I said, watching as eventually he followed my instructions, his chest rising and falling a few times before I spoke again.

"Thank you," I replied. "That feels better, doesn't it?"

He nodded, but much more slowly this time.

"Now tell me who you work for?" I said after a long moment.

His head twitched to the left and then to the right and I imagined his eyes wide as he realised what this was all about. When after a long moment he still hadn't replied, I rolled my seat slowly toward him. Sure he would have heard the hard wheels across the tiles, I leaned right up to his face, ignoring the humid, musty air around the hood.

"It's a very simple question," I said, watching him flinch as I spoke. "Who... do... you... work... for?"

Drawing away from the smell, I gave him more time, despite my fears of what they were doing to Brown or the mess he was making of his captives.

My patience lasted just over five minutes before I could no longer contain my questions.

"This is my fault," I said, staring at the point on the bag

where his eyes would have been. "Let's start with introductions. How does that sound?"

The hooded man lifted his head and slowly nodded.

"Good. My name isn't Claire, but you can call me that if it makes you feel better. Right now we're in a building about a twenty minute drive from where we rescued you. And although it might not feel like it now, I can assure you it was a rescue."

Sitting completely still, he didn't react.

"I work for an organisation you won't know exists, so I'm not going to bore you with their name, but believe me when I say we have your best interests at heart, but only as long as you make the right choices."

Woodridge lowered his head.

"I won't beat around the bush. We know everything that's going on and our job is to put an end to it with as little mess as possible. I'm sure you can understand, we have a limited time to achieve this." After giving him a moment for the words to sink in, I paused. "You're a lucky man, Harry Woodridge. You were moments from being decorated across the pavement, and if Brown hadn't got to you first..." I paused for a moment at the slight twitch of his head.

"... And we weren't watching, then you'd be in some other building in another part of this fair town, but perhaps with fewer fingernails. I guarantee you'd be singing like a canary. I know that because I've been there too."

He remained silent.

"I was in my early twenties and brand new to this job. Packet fresh, having not even deployed on my first assignment, when people from the same organisation that targeted you, drugged me and snatched me from a coffee shop, of all places. I woke to find myself in very much the same situation as you. The only difference was that I wasn't in over my head."

"Uh?" the sound came from his mouth hanging open but he soon sealed his lips together as if regretting what he'd betrayed.

About to speak, I glanced at Daisy, who stared over with an intensity written across her brow and I looked back at the man with the coarse hood on his head.

"Sorry, did you want to say something?" I said and when he didn't reply, I continued to speak. "They questioned me for hours. Made threats. Made offers. But when I wouldn't break, they stripped me naked and doused me in water."

Even without looking up, I knew Daisy's mouth gaped open.

"Now if you're imagining this as a great opening scene to your favourite alone-time fantasy, then think again, Mr Harry Woodridge, because this didn't have a happy ending.

"But we don't need to go into that here. I think you're bright enough to get the picture and you'll be pleased to hear we won't be doing any of that today," I said, and watched his shoulders relax as he blew out a slow deep breath.

Pulling the revolver from the waistband at my back and with the barrel pointed to the floor, I span the cylinder, savouring the unmistakable clicks as it rolled around in my hand.

"That process takes time, which is a luxury we can't afford. Instead, I have something much quicker in mind," I said, bringing my hand down on his knee and sending his whole body flinching as he yelped before a dark patch formed across the crotch of his grey trousers.

Grimacing, I pushed myself backwards, gliding on the wheels to put distance between me and the mess already dripping to the tiles.

The phone rang again.

"So tell me, Harry, and please make this good because the tiles are wipe clean and I have plenty of cleaning materials. Who do you work for?"

68

"Peter Lonsdale," Woodridge said, unable to hold back a quiver in his voice as he sobbed.

"Thank you," I replied. "Now tell me everything you know about what the hell he's up to."

Before he could answer, the phone in my pocket buzzed, and I pulled it out to find a message from Clark telling me to answer the call just as it started ringing in my hand.

I stood and walked around Woodridge's seat, being careful to avoid the puddle, then motioned to Daisy to come close as I leaned in, before whispering into her ear. "Get the PIN for his phone. It won't stop ringing," I said, then as I headed through the toilet door, I couldn't help but linger on the memory of Daisy's sweet, almost musk-like perfume.

Stepping into the wide space of the warehouse, and despite the momentary distraction, I noticed a few unfamiliar faces glancing over before they went back to pulling on their assault gear and readying their kit.

Laughter rose from a group of three men standing around an equipment table at the side of the space. Looking over, I saw two men I'd yet to meet laughing at something Latenight had perhaps just said.

Pushing the phone to my ear, I turned away.

"Is it Lonsdale?" Clark said.

"No," I replied. "But it looks like the guy works for him and he's just started talking. Any idea where they've taken Brown?"

"No," Clark said. "No trace on either of the two vehicle's plates."

"And I don't think our guy is going to know, but we'll see," I replied. "We'll find out pretty soon if he's a long-term prospect, but if he's no good to me, we'll hit the address where you said they made the last delivery. Two seconds," I said, then drawing the phone away from my mouth I shouted over to Tubbs, who was sitting and cleaning a pistol on his lap. "What's the ETA on the recon of that address I gave you?"

"They left two minutes ago," Tubbs called back.

I nodded, then just as I was about to turn away, I spotted a small stack of green crates in the warehouse's corner that hadn't been there last time I'd looked.

"Sorry. Carry on," I said, pushing the phone back to my ear.

"Like I said, both vehicles are a dead end, but facial recognition of the bodies confirms they're known associates with our friends, with confirmed sightings on a least two operations. Partial matches for many more."

"And now they have Brown," I said, a little too loud. "Shit," I added, lowering my voice as I headed through the main double doors, the chill in the air reminding me of what little I was wearing under Daisy's jacket.

"Shit indeed, which means he's on the inside eviscerating them one by one and doing what we've been trying to for so long…"

"I'd give him one of my medals for that," I said.

"… Or somehow they've kept him under control and he's selling his secrets," Clark said.

"No," I replied, shaking my head as I walked around to the front of the building, watching the sun painting the horizon orange as it drifted down. "I'm pretty sure we have common aims and he's trying to end all this."

"But he's infecting people," Clark said.

"One person," I replied. "I think the guy he turned was an accident, perhaps because I disturbed him. He killed all the other victims outright and in such a way they wouldn't come back."

Clark didn't speak, but the constant background sounds of activity in my ear confirmed the line hadn't dropped out.

"It's fucked up. Isn't it?" Clark said.

"Yeah," I replied, still staring at the setting sun. "And we've seen fucked up things before."

"This has to be the worst," he said, his voice low and solemn.

"And like always, you won't even be able to tell the grandkids," I said, raising a smile as the faint sounds of a laugh came from the other end of the line.

"Stop ageing me, Carrie," he replied with a renewed spark to his voice.

"Right," I said, standing up a little straighter. "I'm going back in. We'll deal with these problems one by one. First shut down the psycho scientists and then we'll get Brown back, hopefully taking out a few of our friends whilst we're there."

"You have to neutralise him, Carrie. No matter what his plans are," he said, his voice low again.

"I understand that," I replied. As I turned and headed back to the building, I peered at the narrow view of a group of the men still preparing. "We have another problem," I said, but didn't elaborate as I walked across the wide space.

When in through the office door, my foot connected with something unseen, sending an almighty clatter echoing across the room, and I looked down to find the metal bin rolling across the floor, scattering its contents in my path.

"What was that?" Clark said as I turned around to faces from the main room, only just looking away as I raised my hand to confirm I was okay.

"Nothing. Just not watching where I was going," I said, leaning down, the phone pinned to my ear with my shoulder as I ushered the waste paper back to where it came from.

"You were going to tell me about your new issue?" Clark said, as I closed the office door whilst leaving the blinds open.

"We have a mole," I said in a low voice. "Someone's leaking to our friends."

"How certain are you?" Clark said, but I knew it was just a reflex when he didn't give any space for a reply. "Suspects?"

"A few," I replied as I stood facing the blank office wall, not turning because I knew many of the men were skilled lip-readers. "I've locked down external comms and we've taken the trooper's phones away."

"I'll get their personnel files pulled," he replied, and I imagined him nodding. "Do you need anything else?"

"More boots on the ground. I know we want a small footprint, but Lonsdale's place was a close-run thing," I said, reminding myself.

"Leave it with me," he replied. "Carrie," he then said, causing me to halt my slow walk to the corner of the room.

"What is it?" I said, an edge of uncertainty in my voice.

"Remember the standing order," he replied. "If you find the traitor, you know what you have to do."

I nodded, even though there was no one to see. "I remember," I replied and ended the call as my gaze fell on the rucksack I'd left in the room's corner.

With my back to the inner window, I pulled Daisy's jacket over my head along with the t-shirt, then slipped on a bra and a better fitting plain white tee. About to leave the office, a vibration rattled against the desk and I turned just as Woodridge's phone rang again as it rested face up in front of the keyboard.

An unknown number. I watched the screen, not looking away when it rang out and showed it was the tenth missed call from someone not wanting to let on who they were.

"Be ready at short notice to move out," I called as I strode back into the warehouse toward Tubbs, catching the eye of as many of the men as I could, who by now looked alike apart from their height and subtle differences in their build.

"Tubbs," I said, standing beside him as with a long metal rod he pushed a rag through the barrel of a Glock, the remaining dissembled components scattered on a table beside him. When he looked up, I slipped the 442 from my waistband and presented it barrel first.

"Yes m…" he said, and I raised my eyebrow just as he caught himself. "… Red?"

"You got a spare?" I said.

With a nod, he pieced together the weapon's parts, snapping everything into place in a matter of seconds before handing it over, along with three full magazines of ammunition.

"Thank you," I replied, raising a brow, but he was already motioning over to the green crates in the warehouse's corner.

"You had a delivery."

I nodded, remembering the request I'd made in what felt like such a lifetime ago, and did my best not to give in to the desire to head straight over. "Crack them open and make sure everything is in order. I think we're going to need what's inside real soon," I replied, then turned and strode back toward the washroom.

With the background activity of the men and their low murmured talk and resting my palm on the metal hand plate, I heard Daisy's muffled voice and I paused with the outer door only part way open.

Her words were gentle, and she sounded so relaxed I couldn't quite hear the detail. Pushing the first door fully open, I stepped into the square lobby, then eased it closed at my back as I waited in front of the second door where her voice had clarified.

Despite feeling a pang of guilt at not showing myself, I listened.

"She'll be back in a minute, expecting a lot more than you've given me," Daisy said. "And I think you know by now she gets what she wants."

When I hadn't heard a reply for a long moment, Daisy spoke again. "I know she scares you, Harry, but she scares everyone. She scares me, so I wouldn't push her buttons if I were you. Why don't you just give me something so I can say you've been helpful?"

A silence hung in the airless space before she spoke again.

"I'll level with you, Harry, because I think you're a good guy, and from what I've seen, I think all you've done wrong is to be in the wrong place at the wrong time."

I eased the door open, hoping Woodridge wouldn't be able to tell.

"All you need to do is answer her questions and

267

everything will be fine, but do you want a bit more advice?"

The sack nodded back and forth quick enough for the raised front to fall from around his nose and cover his mouth.

"If for whatever reason she takes the hood off, you better pray you don't look her in the eye."

"Why?" he said, his voice high.

"It means there's no going back. It'll be game over and you won't get home to your family."

I watched the colour drain from the skin on the back of his neck as with a wide grin I caught Daisy's eye. Then I swung the door open behind me, letting it hit hard against the jamb.

"Right," I said, taking the seat Daisy stood from. "Has he been a good boy?"

69

"He wanted to wait until you came back, boss," Hollywood said. The captive's head twitched at the sound of the sergeant's deep voice.

"Great," I replied, tapping the bound man on the knee after choosing a point well away from the damp dark material which had overtaken most of the upper half of his trousers. "Are you comfortable? Do you want a change of clothes, or perhaps it's time to take the hood off?"

In one sharp movement, his head lifted before shaking from side to side. "I'm fine as I am," he said, hurrying out the words.

"Okay," I replied. "So what was it you were waiting to tell me? Shall we start with the PIN for your phone? Then maybe you can tell me what you do for Mr Lonsdale?"

He couldn't get the four numbers out any quicker if he'd tried, whilst out of the corner of my eye Daisy took notes. After repeating the code twice more, he told us that despite having the same PHD in neurochemistry, graduating as classmates, Lonsdale employed him as his assistant, but he was quick to point out he did little more than admin, barely getting involved with Lonsdale's academic work.

The smell of piss strengthened as he continued to talk, and needing only to provide the occasional prompt to keep him on track, I rolled my seat back, hoping to escape the stench.

With his head raised, his voice only slightly muffled by the hood, he said he'd never himself been involved in the official programme, whereas Lonsdale had worked on the side lines, assisting the professors and other researchers.

I tapped out a message to Clark, letting him know what he'd missed.

"They were like a family. Working and living in such close confines. They didn't have a choice but to get along, I guess. Their only exposure to the outside world was travelling between the facilities. I didn't see Peter the whole time he worked there, but he got back in touch after he left."

"What was he like when he came out?" I said, leaning in closer, then moving back when the smell urged me to draw away.

"Distraught," he replied. "They'd got rid of him."

"Why?" I asked, keeping my voice light as I raised my brow and made eye contact with Daisy.

"Budget cuts. The higher ups wanted the greatest achievement of the twenty-first century but on a shoestring. The results were there, but only in Petri dishes. Despite this, Peter was still so excited."

"Excited about what, in particular?" I said, but he didn't reply, shaking his head instead as he sniffed, sucking up snot.

I nodded to Daisy, and she walked slowly around from behind him, Woodridge's head twitching with each footstep until she stood at his side, raising her hands to the bottom of the hood.

"No," he cried, shaking his head whilst pulling his arms and legs against his bonds.

"I'm just lifting the bottom half," Daisy said, and he flinched at her voice, then relaxed a little as the hood stopped at his nose, revealing a string of clear snot hanging from the end then falling against his upper lip.

After stepping back out from the toilet cubicle, Daisy wiped his mouth with toilet paper.

"Thank you," Woodridge said.

"Just keep talking," Daisy replied, her voice soft and motherly. "We want to report back that you've been helpful."

He nodded.

"Why was he so excited?" I asked, leaning back in the seat as Daisy retreated to the wall.

Woodridge's head tilted to the side, and I imagined his brow narrowed at the question.

"He'd seen all that it could be. He'd seen the greatest of gifts anyone could give to mankind," he replied, awe clear in his voice.

"Specifics, please," I said when he paused.

He shook his head, then seemed to think better of it.

"The end of suffering. The end of watching your body decay year after year. The end of having to say goodbye to those you love."

I looked up at Hollywood as I listened and his expression barely changed, other than a raise of a brow. Daisy, on the other hand, stood up from leaning against the wall, her eyes growing wider with each word as she stared at the back of Woodridge's head, not noticing me.

"What could be a greater discovery?" he added. "And it was his moment."

"But they'd sacked him?" I replied.

"At first, that didn't matter. He thought his name was already written into the history of the project. His part had already been immortalised, and not just in the scientific world. He talked of a shared Nobel prize, more than one perhaps."

"What changed?" I asked.

"It only took a few weeks for him to sink into a depression, but when the professors running the project said they'd get him reinstated, his mood lifted and it was as if he were re-energised. And they followed through, in part at least. They gave him an unofficial role doing research in the university labs, but soon that wasn't enough. He saw it as scraps just to keep him happy. It made him so angry."

Filled with emotion, he stopped talking and I gave him a little time as I listened to his breathing.

"And then the professors start dying," I said, watching his head twitch to the side. "Did Lonsdale have anything to do with that?"

"No," Woodridge replied without delay, his body tensing as his voice went high and he shook his head.

"I'm not accusing him, but it's our job to ask tough questions," I said, watching his shoulders relax. "Look. We don't give a shit what Lonsdale did. We're not the police," I added when he hadn't spoken for a little while.

"He didn't do anything, but after Professor Rogers died,

the other two engaged with Peter a little more. They started giving him what he saw as more useful work."

"But it still wasn't enough?" I said, and Woodridge nodded.

"They said they'd try again to get his job back, perhaps along with a professorship."

"How long was it before the other two professors died?" Daisy said, moving away from the wall.

Harry twitched his head to where she was standing. "A few months. They advertised the role they'd promised to Peter without letting him know. They didn't even ask him to apply. When he found out, he was enraged."

"Enraged enough to kill them?" I said softly.

Woodridge kept quiet and held his head still.

I tutted. "We were doing so well."

"I know nothing about the deaths," he said, rushing out the words. "But shortly afterwards, things changed. People from the inside began feeding us information on the project and soon reams of research were flooding in."

"From who? Isaac Brown?" Daisy asked.

Woodridge shook his head. "Not just him. Peter had so many more contacts. About ten days after the last funeral, Peter brought me to his house and within half an hour I was frantically typing as someone I didn't know dictated reams of research over the phone. He was talking so much Peter and I had to take it in shifts to type. All the while we were taking in the results. They were beyond belief.

"By then, each of the researchers were running their own side projects on different aspects that piqued their interest. With new management inbound, they feared a crackdown and they'd lose all of their hard work whilst being forced to work on official projects only.

"We listened to the details of trials of a compound that sped up healing, drugs that cured common afflictions through the regeneration of cells, fixing burns and replacing damaged organs. And, of course, those that caused, you know."

I glanced at Daisy and we shared a look, her eyes wide,

not hiding her astonishment.

"They were doing so much research that they had to bring in extra material, but they still struggled and were desperate for more. That's when Peter offered them an alternative approach."

"To take the research private?" I said.

He nodded. "Pretty much all of them loved the idea of freedom to follow their own path. When anyone mentioned worries about breaking away from the company, Peter reminded them of the many scientists who'd become household names because they were mavericks, only able to achieve greatness by breaking the rules and releasing themselves of the shackles of governance."

I looked between Daisy and Hollywood, raising my brow. Hollywood shrugged, and I turned back to the captive.

"He sounds like an inspiration," I said and watched the sack nod. "But was everyone on board with his plan?"

Woodridge shook his head. "There were a few that didn't agree."

"What about Brown?" I said, leaning closer despite the smell.

"He was on our side at first, but something changed. With all the scientists locked together in such close quarters, all it needed was one firm opinion to sway them all. Peter spent so much time on the phone trying to sell his case, but Brown became a loud dissenting voice and eventually he won out and convinced many of them to change their mind."

"But Lonsdale went ahead despite this?"

He nodded, lowering his voice. "I think when he realised there was no turning them around, he liked the thought that there was a way he wouldn't have to share the credit."

I looked up at Daisy, then caught Hollywood's eye, not hiding my intrigue.

"So what happened?" I said slowly.

"We had a vast array of their research and knew the

bunker's operation so well by then, Peter came up with a plan to plant a small explosive charge into a specific room which would set off an inevitable chain of events."

Swapping glances with the others, I took a moment to process his words.

"You planted a bomb to release the pathogens," I said, being careful to keep the rising emotion from my voice, still unsure, having seen no evidence of an explosion at either of the bunkers.

"Peter did," he said as he nodded. "We had the device delivered with the rest of the material we were already shipping in."

"Lonsdale weaponised the research?" Daisy replied, standing at my side.

Woodbridge nodded. "He theorised that even a tiny explosion would be sufficient to aerosolize enough of the cultures they'd been developing. He just needed to infect one person, then what happened after would do the rest."

"And shut down the operation," I said. He nodded. "But Brown?"

Woodridge turned his head towards me as if he could see through the hood. "I guess he survived?"

"You could say that," Daisy replied, and Woodridge lifted his head, then nodded as he turned towards her voice.

"You mentioned him earlier, but I wasn't sure I heard right. I guess he'd been experimenting on himself. There was nothing mentioned like that in the research he passed over," he said. "How is he presenting?"

I reached forward and ripped the hood from Woodridge's head, sending his lank, sweaty hair falling around his face as I pointed the Glock at his forehead.

"You better tell me where the fuck Lonsdale is."

70

Squinting, Woodridge's eyes darted left and right, furiously blinking as his breathing raced. Before he could bow and hide, I jabbed the Glock's muzzle against his forehead and pushed.

"No. No. No," he squealed, forcing his head against the gun as he screwed his eyes closed.

I didn't reply or withdraw the pressure. Instead, I watched the tears roll down his face, dripping to his already sodden lap whilst I waited for his breathing to slow.

"Where the fuck is Lonsdale?" I said, keeping my tone even when the space between his breaths lengthened.

"I don't know. He doesn't tell me where he goes. He's fucking paranoid and says I don't need to know," he replied, rushing out the words.

Pulling the gun away, his head dropped and he pulled against his bonds as if trying to reach the floor.

"I promise you I don't know. He thinks everyone is out to get him because of what he's done," he sobbed, the muscles in his neck tightening as he grappled with the paracord.

"He's not paranoid. We're after him," Daisy said, and I couldn't help but smile as I slipped the Glock into the waistband at my back.

"What about Berwick Avenue? The place down the road?" I said, reeling off the address where they'd delivered the latest package.

He nodded, but thought better of lifting his head. Based on what he'd said about not knowing anything of use, it wasn't the answer I'd hoped for.

"It's a forwarding address," he replied. "For deliveries. I don't know where they go after that. I told you, he doesn't trust anyone. Not even the postal service."

I looked up at Daisy and then to Hollywood. "What does Brown know about this setup?" I said, turning back to Woodridge, his arms still tight against his bonds.

"Nothing," he replied, rushing his bowed head from side to side. "There's no way he'd speak to Brown about anything he wouldn't tell me. Only the people working at the facility have any chance of knowing where it is, and I wouldn't put it past him to blindfold them all when they travel. He doesn't even let them go home. He makes them live there, just as if they were at the bunkers."

I glanced at Daisy again and then across to Hollywood as I narrowed my eyes. Both looked back with the same steely concentration.

With a shake of my head, I slipped the hood back on, then motioned for the pair to follow as I left, speaking quietly when the second door closed at Daisy's back.

"I think he's telling the truth, but we better check out Berwick Avenue in case he's bluffing. Be prepared," I said. "For anything. Someone put him in a change of trousers and package him up. He can come with us in case we need more answers."

Hollywood nodded and stepped away into the warehouse, where I watched him scour the room before his head settled in the direction of Philips and Scotch.

"Rolling in five, everyone," I called out as Hollywood strode over to the pair.

The reaction to my words was instant, each of the faces turning in my direction and as I finished talking, activity rippled through the group with the men donning helmets and the last of their tactical gear.

I walked to the green crates which, after Tubbs had set them up in the centre of the room, he'd laid out the array of shotguns alongside case after case of brown ammo tins.

Only two men remained in their civilian clothes and helped their colleagues prepare. I guessed they were two of the four singled out by Hollywood to stay back and protect where we stood, which we'd earlier designated as Alpha base.

Moses, already dressed head to foot in black protective gear, strode toward me from the side of the room carrying a pair of ballistic vests and helmets, which he handed over to Daisy and me in turn.

"Brains," she said, catching my eye as I slipped the heavy body armour over my head. "Remember," she added as I set the helmet on the floor, crouching down to inspect the array of shotguns.

Despite wishing I had more time to examine each weapon and run my fingers along their sleek lines, I stood without looking up.

"Take your pick, then fill your pockets with shells," I called out, soon forgetting what else I was going to say when my gaze fell on a bright red equipment case about the size of a briefcase.

Pleased to find no one had yet opened it, I moved along the stack of ammo crates and knelt at its front. Flipping the lid, then pulling away the foam protection, I found a row of shells that looked much like the standard cartridge, but with a bright yellow body instead of the usual red.

Taking the first from the row and pushing it into my pocket, I counted ten rounds in total. Picking at the foam edging, I was more than a little disappointed when I couldn't reveal another layer.

"Explosive rounds," I said, looking up to Hollywood who'd strolled over from the washroom. "Distribute as you see fit. But this is all we've got and there's no time to check their effect."

"I'll brief the team," he said, pulling a cartridge from the foam before examining it.

"Daisy and I are supposed to stay away from the action," I said, then crouched at the nearest of the ammo tins, grabbing two handfuls of the red cartridges before stuffing them into the pockets at the front of the protective vest.

Standing and holding the helmet in my hand, Hollywood smiled, nodded, then turned away, striding toward the equipment laid out on the tables along the wall just as the washroom door opened. Two troopers dressed in dark assault gear came through, leading Woodridge, still hooded, his arms bound behind him and in black combat trousers.

"Don't forget the child locks," I called out. Both troopers nodded before I turned to head toward the office via the equipment table, where I grabbed a thigh holster for my Glock.

Tipping the contents of the rucksack onto the nearest desk, my eyes were drawn to the phone number on the scrap of paper the nurse had pushed into my hand, reminding me of her smile and the feel of her arms wrapped around my neck.

Grateful for the distraction, if only for a second, I couldn't help but wonder what it would be like when I wasn't in constant fear of the next encounter with those terrible creatures.

Stuffing the bio-bag back into the rucksack, I grabbed the pouches containing the antidote and the swabs, pushing them into the last of the pockets of my body armour. Glancing out through the office window as I loaded three cartridges into the side of the shotgun, slipping the yellow jacketed shell into the final space in the stock, I watched Hollywood talking to his men who'd formed a neat line in the centre of the warehouse.

I closed my eyes, hit by a sudden guilt that someone out there might need the round more than I did. Pulling the shell from the stock and clutching it in my fist, I promised myself I'd learn each of their names as soon as I could.

71

"Today you will do great things," I said, standing in front of the men still lined up in loose formation in the middle of the warehouse. "Once again, you're putting yourself in the worst danger to protect the public, and if all goes to plan, no one will ever know what you've been through."

Holding the shotgun one handed across my chest, I couldn't help but wonder how many of those in front of me would still be alive at the end of the day.

"We don't know as much about where we're going as we'd like, but your colleagues report a business unit devoid of activity. That could well be the case. If it's deserted, we'll think again, but equally, behind those doors could be so much more than you've experienced in your worst nightmares."

A few in the line raised their heads, and I took a moment to look each of them in the eye, knowing I didn't need their names to be sure they were all warriors who would go beyond to execute the mission. Except for the traitor, and for them, I had to trust their team would keep them in check on the battlefield.

"You need to be quick and precise. Be ready for anything, but above all, be decisive. Do you understand?"

"Yes, Red," they called out in unison.

"Aim for the head. I won't be there to hold your hand, but you'll know I'm right when the time comes," I said. "Do you understand?"

"Yes, Red," they repeated as one.

"Let's go save the world," I called out, watching as energetic nods carried along the line before Hollywood and Tubbs broke off from the rest as I beckoned them over.

"I want the four staying behind ready to join us at a moment's notice," I said. Both men nodded, then Tubbs turned before calling out.

"Nate. Silver. Gear up. You need to be ready to move," he said, heading over to the pair that hadn't yet changed into their combat gear.

Finding the sun had set and with light pouring down from the high mounted units on the side of our building, Daisy and I took the first X5 with Woodridge's hood twitching from side to side as we relieved the two operators of their vigil. He didn't speak or struggle against the belt pinning him into the rear seat with his hands tied behind his back as we waited for the rest of the team to pile into their cars.

Google maps confirmed the eight-minute drive, and Daisy got us through the trading estate's quiet, street-lit roads in seven.

After realising I still held the yellow cartridge in my fist, I slipped it into the front pocket of my vest before plucking one of the two radios from the centre console and pushing the talk button on the side.

"Strike," I called as we approached the anonymous stretch of tarmac, then watched as the other two cars steamed past us one at a time with their engines roaring, soon followed by another as the advanced party came out from where they'd been hiding.

Without needing further orders, Daisy stopped our vehicle in the car park's entrance, blocking the route as we looked over the tall one-storey building clad in grey metal sheeting. With the parking spaces empty and windows dark, it seemed just as deserted as the scouts had described.

Veering to the right, the first four by four soon mounted the curb, its fat tyres leaving churned grass in its wake as it disappeared around the building's near corner, just as the other two vehicles slammed to a stop either side of the main entrance double doors.

The troopers were out, boots dropping to the road in unison before they rocked to a stop, their shoulders hunched over and weapons aimed ahead with underslung torches shining brightly as they formed up, pressing themselves against the walls either side of the entrance.

Glancing in the rearview mirror, then looking back from Woodridge shivering, the radio in my hand lit up as a whispered voice came from the speaker.

"South entrance primed."

By the time I'd looked up, two troopers stepped back from the double doors, having left a square black frame I could barely make out in the low light stuck to the middle of the doors.

"North entrance primed," another voice sounded off as each of the men tucked tight against the wall.

"Ready." Hollywood's deep voice came from the speaker and I brought the radio up to my mouth.

"Breach," I said, being sure to keep the word crisp, and with barely a delay the explosives detonated as one, creating a sound no louder than a muffled firework. After a flash of bright light at the door, the figures didn't wait for the smoke to clear before being swallowed by the building's darkness.

I closed my eyes, listening for the first report, which came quicker than I'd expected, the radio's screen staying lit as a medley of voices came one after the other as if on a beat.

"Front hallway clear."

"Rear hallway clear."

"Front right office clear."

"Rear left office clear."

"Front toilet clear."

"Rear large office clear."

"Front second office clear."

"Code green," a deep voice said, breaking the flow, warning the other team they were about to meet in the middle.

"One last door. We're going in," Hollywood said, and we heard the thump of metal echoing from the building as I held my breath, my hand itching to reach for the shotgun I'd stuffed between the seat and the centre console.

Willing for another voice from the radio, I strained to listen, hoping to catch something from the speaker before I heard any screams from the building.

"It's empty, Red," Hollywood said. "There's nothing here. It's a bust."

I looked at Daisy, unsure if what I felt was relief, but the feeling soon fell away, replaced with a rising anger. Twisting in my seat, I stared at Woodridge and lifted the radio up to my mouth.

"Are you sure? Look for hidden spaces, false floors. You know the drill."

"Red, there's nothing. Come and look. It's empty," Hollywood replied with no delay.

Still with the radio in my hand, I turned to Daisy, her brow scrunched up, mirroring just how I felt.

"It looks like you were telling the truth," I said, turning back to Woodridge. "You better not be fucking with us or you'll live to regret it."

Before he had a chance to reply, a hurried voice came from the radio.

"Hollywood. It's Scotch."

As I looked down at my hand, the radio was still dark, then I spotted the lit screen of the handset in the centre console as the tone grew more frantic.

"A van just careered backwards into Alpha Base. We're under attack."

Pulling the first radio up to my mouth, I grabbed at the door handle and stepped to the road. "Hollywood. You getting this?"

"They're in through the doors," the voice from the other handset said before Hollywood could speak. "Shit. They've seen us. They know where we…"

The transmission ended, replaced with distant automatic gunfire echoing out across the night.

RECOIL

72

Daisy's mouth hanging open and her wide-eyed gaze switching between me and the radio in my hand was enough to confirm I'd heard right that a van had reversed into the warehouse we were using as our base of operations.

When our repeated radio calls to Alpha Base found no reply, our convoy's tyres screeched across the tarmac only seconds after I'd given the command to return.

By now, the distant gunshots had fallen silent, replaced with a storm of questions whirling inside my head as I searched for what had happened back at the place we'd only left behind less than half an hour before.

Daisy gave the other three cars no chance to overtake, racing through the streets as we retraced our route, slowing only as we arrived at the approach to our building before rocking to a stop at the entrance to the car park. Two black Range Rovers, lit by the building's tall floodlights, had parked side on at the far boundary of the tarmac.

The rush of Woodridge's fast breath filled my ears as I looked over to the two luxury cars parked nose to tail, the front seats empty and the rear windows blacked out. Despite the unease at the lack of obvious activity, I peered at the shadows beyond the reach of the building's powerful lights, scouring as best as I could along the hedge-line to the silhouetted trees in the near distance.

With no sign of our men, or any remains of what had caused the abrupt end to their radio message, I turned to the left, spotting the nose of a white Mercedes Sprinter van just visible past the corner of our building.

Despite the bulk of the building obscuring most of the white metal, a pit inside my stomach opened up, filling me with dread as the words from the radio message raced through my head.

Glancing at Daisy, she stared back with an unasked question hanging on her lips. As I nodded in reply, she edged the car forward. We'd barely moved before a blood-curdling scream echoed out from the warehouse.

Turning toward the sound, I saw the rest of the van, its buckled rear pushed up against the distorted metal siding around the warehouse's entrance.

I didn't linger long, my body lurching forward as we came to a stop. Seeing feet down low the other side of the Range Rovers, within a blink of an eye a group of dark figures, their faces covered, rose from behind the vehicles, lifting assault rifles in our direction.

"Get down," I screamed, only just able to drop before the windscreen smashed in time to the first loud beats of an orchestra of gunfire. Glass and hot metal rushed over my head as I squeezed down into the dark footwell. Feeling each round slam against the bodywork, every impact's tone a little different to the last, I forced my head low until suddenly the chaos stopped.

Not knowing how long the pause would last before the rain of lead started again, I lifted my head, peering through little light coming from outside. I turned to the place where I'd been sitting only seconds earlier and the shredded leather potted with orange foam showing through a peppering of ragged holes.

Despite fearing what I might find, I looked across to the driver's side, relieved to see Daisy peering back, her neck crooked at an angle, contorted into the space underneath the steering wheel.

With narrowed eyes and clenched jaw, I saw her anger and determination as she stared back, poised for what I might say. Pleased to find her composed, I nodded, guessing it wasn't the first time she'd been under fire.

Pointing my flattened hand between the seats, she replied with an uncomfortable nod but didn't delay before twisting around, moving her arm out of sight before I heard our tail gate rising, bringing with it a renewed barrage of gunfire. With lead clattering against our metal shell, I motioned once more between the seats.

More gunfire added to the wall of noise, the sound urging me on at the thought of our guys returning fire. Daisy was soon out from her safe space with her head low and body flat, wriggling between the remains of the leather.

As she turned to the side, angling her hips to squeeze out, the rear left seat fell forward and Tubb's face appeared, fixed with concentration and quelling my panic.

As he reached a hand out, Daisy grabbed hold.

She was out of sight within a few seconds, pulled through to the rear, leaving me alone to lift my head as high as I dared, before dropping low when a rush of air seemed to scatter my hair.

Peering back up, Moses had reappeared at the space and I grabbed the shotgun which had fallen to the carpet, shook off the glass, then crawled between the front seats, pausing only when in the rear I saw Woodridge slumped against the side window, the front of his hood soaked a deep red.

Not wanting to linger despite the flash of guilt, I edged through the gap, pressing myself into the leather with each metallic clash that seemed closer than the last, before taking the offered hand, gripping tight as Moses pulled me into the boot space and out onto the tarmac.

Crouching at Moses' side, with Daisy tucked in against the bumper next to me, her cheeks rosy and glass peppering her hair, I nodded a furious thank you.

By now, the gunfire had slowed, leaving only the occasional short salvo every few moments, often followed by a loud staccato reply from the other side. Looking over my shoulder and back to our other three cars, even in the light thrown from the side of our building, the holes peppering much of the bodywork were more than obvious, along with the missing glass.

With no sign of how the stalemate could resolve, other than by those who were the most economical with their ammunition, keeping tight to the car's bounds I looked around for inspiration.

My gaze lingered on the back of the van jammed against the warehouse door where a darkness flashed against the bright lights leaking out from under the doorway.

Turned away by a single shot ringing out near my head and feeling the bullet's impact through the metal I leaned against, with it came an idea which meant undoing all the help Moses had given.

73

Wishing I could dismiss the plan, but without a rifle or the belt of grenades I longed for, the only inspiration I'd so far received was the best I could do.

I turned to Moses. "Watch my back. I'll ram them, then you lot give everything you've got," I shouted over the din, ducking as a volley of shots peppered the car as if they'd heard what I'd said.

When the echo died away, I lifted my head. "Use the car for cover."

Moses' brow fell, looking certain he'd come up with another plan, one perhaps that wasn't such a risk, but soon, raising his arm as if to climb into the boot, he nodded.

"I'll do it," he said, but held himself back as I grabbed his arm and shook my head.

"No disrespect, but compared to me, you're a fat fuck. You'll get stuck in between the seats," I said, and he paused as if unsure what to say before bursting into laughter and dropping back down.

Leaving no delay in case he changed his mind, keeping my head low and the shotgun gripped tight in my right hand, I slithered into the boot and with a quick glance over my shoulder, saw Moses beckoning others over as covering fire rattled through the air.

Sliding on my body armour across the glass-covered carpet, dipping my head low as each renewed shot rang out overhead, about halfway through and onto the back seats I raised my head as high as I dared, my heart sinking when I saw the windscreen had caved in, the sheet of shattered glass having spilt in two great sections to cover the front seats, taking with it any hope of getting to the controls.

Reaching forward, I gripped the handbrake and pushed the button to let it down, but adding insult, the engine spluttered, then died. With no other option, I rolled onto my side and shouted out of the back.

"You have to push!"

Not able to see if the pair behind had heard, it was only as the heavy car rolled forward that I knew they'd taken notice. A volley of shots from all around replied to our motion, and it sounded as if I was about to crash through a wall of explosions which had overtaken my senses with lead beating against the metal all around me.

It didn't take long for us to slow to a stop.

"Shit," I called out, but before I could worry about being stranded in no-man's-land, or if we'd stopped moving with Moses taken out, the car moved again with a jolt.

Twisting from my front as our speed built again, I could just about see a red-faced Hollywood squeezed in beside Moses as he pushed at the bumper, whilst others crouched in our wake with their weapons levelled.

Despite the genuine fear that at any moment the hot lead could find its way around the engine block and end me, I readied myself for what would happen as we closed the rest of the distance. With no time for the thoughts to expand, metal crunched against metal and we came to an abrupt stop.

The volley of gunfire seemed to take a breath as I lurched forward, my helmet hitting against the soft back of the driver's seat and I soon ended up halfway into the footwell, joined by a heavy weight landing on my back and forcing the air from my chest.

Under the crush of what I guessed was Woodridge's lifeless body, I didn't pause. Instead, struggling against the pressure, my fingers somehow found the door handle, and I pulled with hope that the metal would open, despite the damage from the firefight.

Relieved when the door gave as I forced it away, I launched the shotgun through the opening, wincing as it landed on the road with a clatter before I pushed with my feet, whilst trying not to think of what I was forcing myself away from.

The wall of sound felt so much louder than before, but the volume was the least of my concerns as I raced out from the car headfirst with my arms reaching out to slow my fall.

With the darkness of the road looming towards my face, I tipped my head down, letting my momentum carry me into a forward roll. Realising I was heading away from my gun after one revolution, I jumped to my feet where my gaze locked with the white eyes of a figure's silhouette, his face hidden by a dark balaclava as he glared in my direction, his hands working at a frantic pace to unclip the magazine of an MP5 assault rifle.

Regretting my empty hands, I turned away; not waiting to find where my weapon lay, stooping low I dove back towards the car, catching sight of the shotgun's barrel.

After landing on my arm which pinned at my side, I grabbed the barrel with the other hand, pushing the stock into my shoulder and swinging it around, just as I heard the click of the MP5's new magazine.

With a pull of the trigger, I added my instrument to the booming score, already forcing myself to my feet before the dark figure fell backwards against the road, just as our troopers swarmed from my side with the beams of their underslung torches bouncing up and down as they fired.

Who was who in the melee I couldn't be sure, but with round after round resounding from their weapons, I brought my shotgun around to cover the remains of the assault. The roar of an engine followed by the clash of metal to my left caused me to stand tall, bringing my aim around as I followed the pained calls when, one after the other, each of the hole-potted X5s smashed into the Range Rovers our ambushers had been using for cover.

It took a little longer for the gunshots to calm, replaced instead by voices hurling commands.

With the shotgun held out as I caught my breath, I looked over the five smoking cars destined for the scrap heap and the car park sprinkled with shattered glass glinting in the floodlights, whilst men dragged crumpled dark figures onto the grass verge.

Although the apparent threat had passed, the team fanned out, directed by Hollywood, taking knelt defensive positions to scan their surroundings whilst levelling rifles taken from the bodies.

Out of the corner of my eye, I watched two figures rush towards the copse where I guessed they'd hope their worst fears wouldn't come true.

Pained moans percolated through the new calm and my hand rushed to grab a replacement cartridge from my pocket as I turned through a half circle, but finding only gloved hands pressing dressings against the wounds of those who'd survived, I forced a deep breath, reminding myself how the infection spread.

About to offer aid, it wasn't long before the figures reappeared at the treeline, both Moses and Tubbs shaking their heads with Hollywood striding towards them, leaving no doubt what they'd found.

"We have a traitor," Hollywood said, arriving at my side and I turned, looking him in the eye as every fibre of his body seemed to bristle with anger. "Fucking cowards."

Nodding slowly and about to tell him what I knew, I held back when the drum of something heavy banged against the metal skin of the warehouse, drawing my gaze to a silhouette passing through the light from under the van.

"Have you had any contact with Silver and Nate?" I said, despite already guessing the answer.

74

"No," Hollywood replied, following as I took a couple of slow steps toward the van pressed into the mangled warehouse opening. Both of us stopped when, for a second time, a dark shape blocked the light coming from underneath the vehicle.

I turned to Hollywood, then looked around, pausing on Daisy kneeling beside one of our team as she wrapped a bandage around his arm, his face pinched and teeth gritted.

Looking away, I counted those standing guard and watching their arcs.

There were four missing.

"Your radio," I said, gesturing to the handset clipped to Hollywood's belt.

Without question, he reached down, yanking the earpiece cable from the side before pulling the handset from its home and handing it over.

"Silver. Nate. This is Red. Are you receiving?"

With no reply, despite repeating the message twice more, I took slow steps toward the warehouse. At the sound of footsteps from behind, I raised my fist in the air when the light once more disappeared from under the van.

"Keep everyone back," I said, not turning around when the footsteps stopped.

"Red?" It was Daisy.

Not taking my eyes from the light, I shook my head and stepped further forward.

Peering at the gap, I squinted tighter the closer I got when my high angle meant I saw less of the space under the van, but still I carried forward, clipping the radio to the front of my body armour then taking the shotgun in a two handed grip, pointing at the ground in front of me.

Unable to stop myself from imagining what was happening out of sight beyond the wall, I continued the slow walk, stopping only when another weighty metallic boom echoed out into the night, sending the van lurching forward before it rocked on its suspension and back in to place, tight against the wall.

When after a moment only silence followed and the van hadn't moved, I took another couple of steps before calling out, "Who's there?"

The boom of hollow metal resounded again, much louder than before, sending the van rocking forward with a screech of the tyres. As it came to rest, a thin sliver of light shining around the van's edge looked like a halo until something blocked it at the side.

Despite the gap of only perhaps a finger's width, I knew without doubt it was one of our troopers.

"Soldier," I called, the word sharp and high, but a moment later the light had returned, the figure moving away.

Now certain the attackers had rammed the doors to insert Brown to overpower those we'd left behind, I took another step closer.

The sound came again, as loud as before, forcing the gap between the van and the warehouse as wide as a balled fist. Holding my ground, having closed half of the distance to the building, I peered across the space and raised the shotgun.

Within a blink of an eye, a trooper stood in the gap, this time plain to see, half his face recognisable, but the other side of his features gone, exposing the bare bloody muscle so even his mother wouldn't have recognised him from that angle.

His dark gaze locked onto mine, but before I could fire, he'd gone again.

If I'd held any uncertainty of what had happened whilst we were away, all doubts had now vanished with another thump against the back doors, sending the vehicle lurching forward.

"On me," I said, keeping my voice low as I took a tentative step backward whilst staring at the space wide enough for someone to walk through.

Voices spoke softly from behind as Daisy and others I

didn't recognise tried their best to settle the moans of the injured.

Daring not to turn away, I repeated my instruction a little louder. "On me."

Before I heard footsteps following my instructions, two figures, both dressed head to foot in the same black body armour we wore, surged from the gap.

"Contact," I shouted at the top of my voice, as one after the other the figures dropped to their haunches, leaping high in the air before I could get a shot off.

Tracking the long barrel of the gun high, they were out of my arc all too soon.

About to turn to pick them up as they landed, I held back as a high-screeched call came from the warehouse. Realising the pair were going too fast and weren't dropping on my position, it was clear they were aiming for those behind me instead.

Gripped with a rush of fear I'd lost control, it felt as if a cavern had opened in the pit of my stomach as the pair landed at my back.

The worst had happened. The nightmarish creatures were out in the open and all that stood between the end of civilisation as we knew it were the men I had no choice but to trust had taken on board everything I'd told them.

About to twist around in hope I could pull the trigger before they attacked, I held firm, my gaze locking to the light at the warehouse door, blocked by another figure who was once a man. Black veins spidered across its face, tracking down its pale, naked skin to trace its muscular, blood-streaked torso as its reddened teeth bared in my direction.

Before I could blink, it rushed toward me.

As I tried to bring my aim around, my gaze landed on the wide missing patch of skin at its left shoulder, a gruesome window to muscle and bone gleaming with a sickly wet reflection against the high lights. The muscles tightened, then relaxed as it swung its arm with every stride.

In the blink of an eye, and before I could bring the gun to bear, it ate up the space between us in a blur.

About to pull the trigger, I realised it wasn't Brown who'd already slapped away the barrel, sending the shot and my only chance of survival slamming into the side of the van.

75

Just as the realisation I was losing control took hold, the unmistakable report of the Desert Eagle electrified my eardrums. Sounding as if it were right by my ear, the noise jolted me from the sinking feeling threatening to send me cowering from the creature that was on me with a speed I'd not seen before.

Instead of falling apart, I feinted to the right, and although its movement was too quick for me to change course, I knew at least it hadn't taken hold and sunk its teeth.

I dropped to the ground, letting myself fall without control as blasts of gunfire went off behind me.

Twisting around on to my back, I lifted the shotgun, pumped the slide and fired at the shadowy arm rushing towards me.

Seeming to hit just under the ribs, its pale body lurched away, staggering back as I scrabbled to my feet whilst pumping the slide once, my gaze fixed on its red eyes.

I'd barely stood tall before it had already gathered itself, watching with dismay when it charged forward, its hands grasping at the air as if the action would speed its pace even more.

I shot again, regretting I'd not had a chance to consider my aim and instead giving into the panic at how quickly it was so close again. The round smashed into its already damaged shoulder, leaving a tangle of split muscles on display.

As it steadied itself, I shook my head, riddled with shock at its speed whilst rushing to convince myself it wasn't a sign of things to come and it was perhaps just unburdened, not fat and lethargic from feeding on its former colleagues.

Knowing the reason wouldn't matter if I had no time to consider it at a later time, I pumped the slide again as it rushed forward for another charge.

My mind sped, unable to stop processing all I'd seen despite my utter terror at the unstoppable creature lunging toward me. Adjusting my aim, I corrected to the left, pointing the gun toward its shock of jet black hair on the top of its head, which matched the thick covering around the lower half of its face and groin. With the distance closing too soon to comprehend, another blast boomed at what sounded so near to my head, just as I pulled the trigger, the round careering off into the side of the warehouse.

Its dark stained hands came into reach and I swung the butt of the gun, the wooden handle slapping against the raw flesh of its cheek and I looked into its wide eyes, bringing with it a realisation that rather than this thing being the empty husk of a man overtaken by a foul organism, having pushed the van from out of their way they must have teamed up and worked together to achieve their goal.

When its head barely deflected from the blow, I wrenched the gun back to take another swing and pulled the slide back, cocking another round into the chamber. But with its mouth lurching towards my face, all I could do was grab the barrel in my other hand and push the gun out like a bar to hold back its head, whilst its hands reached to claw at my arms.

Despite its press against the shotgun and giving everything I could, I somehow resisted and even though I knew my muscles couldn't hold much longer before I collapsed, I couldn't help but ask myself why those that had once been members of the regiment had attacked the others, leaping over me so the naked one could take me on instead.

The thought chilled my every nerve. It was clear they were collaborating, the revelation bringing with it a new urgency to stop the creatures at this very moment.

Feeling my strength drain to almost nothing, I dropped to the ground, pulling back the shotgun from where I'd held it out, then rolled away to the right before looking up to find it was already turning my way, covering the short space, its teeth snapping together and its clawed hands reaching.

Aiming at its head, I pulled the trigger, but watched as if in slow motion as it jerked to the side long before the round hit.

About to pump the slide again, a sudden panic gripped my every thought when I couldn't remember if I'd already taken three or four shots. Forcing myself to hold it together, knowing to do anything else would sign my death warrant, I pumped the slide once again, hoping I'd packed one more in the chamber.

With filthy fingers curled in a fist to the sound of shots going off all around me, I pulled the trigger. Relieved at the sound and the recoil, with my fingers working as fast as they could to push another round blind into the chamber, I ducked out of the swing of its hand, moving just in time for the swipe to miss my face.

Before I could move, a loud explosion close by sent my ears ringing as it blotted all other noise. With no time to consider the others locked in their own battles, with a shake of my head I lifted my chin to find the foul creature so close and about to grab me around my upper body.

In no time at all, its arms reached around my back, squeezing the gun between us and pushed its head forward with its mouth wide open. All I could do was bring my forehead down, smashing the rim of my helmet against its nose.

Its grip tightened with the impact, pinning my hands still holding the shotgun angled to the sky with my finger still pressed against the trigger.

I thought of pulling my finger down, despite knowing it would blow both of our heads from our shoulders.

Not able to get the notion from my mind, as I pushed my head to keep its mouth at bay, I couldn't think of any alternative that wouldn't end with me losing my life.

In spite of its grip and constant struggle, I felt a calm descend, clarity settling and with no other choice apparent, I leaned back, forcing my head as far away as I could before closing my eyes and pulling the trigger.

76

The pressure wave flashed across my face, forcing bright light through my closed lids, its deafening wall of sound overtaking every other sense as I clung to the hot metal barrel pressed between us.

I'd survived.

The thought dawned as my senses calmed, but with my ears ringing and face numb, I didn't know if I was about to be mauled to death only to come back as some other form of life.

Only when the weighted grip around my upper body fell away did I open my eyes to find darkness all around. Slowly, out-of-focus light emerged, first as pin pricks before it clarified, gaining a crisp focus after a few moments.

With sensation slowly returning to my face and the ringing in my ears dulling, bringing with it the sounds of struggle and a feeling as if I'd been out in the sun too long, I turned to the sky as what felt like heavy rain fell over me.

The downpour soon ceased as I touched my face, my fingers coming back with a black sticky tar that I realised wasn't the water I'd expected. Looking down to my feet, I saw the headless naked form slumped, its missing flesh and bone scattered across the tarmac.

I quelled the elation I'd lived through another ordeal when, turning to my left, I saw dark figures everywhere, bodies discarded around the perimeter. Remembering many of those were from the firefight only a few moments earlier, I concentrated on those standing and locked in furious combat.

Daisy took a swipe to the head from a figure dressed as everyone else, sending her to the ground where she landed hard with an outrush of air.

Anger flared from my core just as Hollywood punched at another figure with its back to me, the effort of barely keeping it at bay written across the lines on his face.

Moses, Tubbs and Scotch rushed from where they'd

been at the edge of the car park, but despite their expressions lit with determination, disbelief showed itself as they waved their weapons, angling their aims this way and that, continually frustrated they couldn't get a clean shot.

Only just realising I'd slipped another round into the chamber, I pulled back the slide, levelling the weapon at first to the back of the creature on Hollywood, then to the foul thing in body armour pouncing to where Daisy raised up from the ground, lifting her gun.

The Desert Eagle's recoil snapped her arm high, the point-blank shot sending muscle and blood splattering out from the unseen point of impact, but the thing didn't falter, landing on top of her, pushing her back whilst pinning her arms against the road, the powerful handgun scattering towards me as it fell.

Knowing any shot I could make at this range could equally take her life as well as ending the foul creature's existence, all I could do was rush toward her, watching the seconds tick by as she pushed herself up, using the lip of the helmet to keep the thing's mouth from her soft flesh, just as I had done.

To the out-poured breath of effort from Hollywood as he fought just as hard for his life, and with the rest of the squad shouting as they rushed, bounding over and almost in reach, a knot in my stomach tightened as Daisy's head went back, forced with a heavy hit from the side. The creature lunged, its mouth diving towards her neck and I spotted its body armour riding up to expose the bare small of its back.

Without hesitation, I pulled the trigger.

The shot hit just as if I'd aimed at a round circle on a range and slammed its body forward, collapsing on top of Daisy.

She squealed, sending fear spiking that I'd done the opposite of what I'd intended. But rather than sink its teeth, after a moment's pause its muscles tensed and lifted on all fours, its head turning to peer over its shoulder, glaring into my eyes as it jumped up.

I backed away as it stood tall, its right shoulder tipping

to the side. Then, taking a slow step it almost fell, but caught itself, correcting the other way.

As we each took another move in the same direction, I watched as if the thing with only half a face were figuring out how to walk again despite the damage I'd caused. My finger felt for the space where I'd pushed the special yellow round, but a shiver of ice ran down my spine when I found the slot empty.

Frantic thoughts rushed through my head as it took another step. I followed but in reverse, watching as with each new movement it gained confidence and I knew it wouldn't be long before I'd have to turn, pretending to myself I'd have any chance of outrunning it.

The front pocket! The memory of where I'd pushed what I hoped would be a life saver crashed into thought and I dashed my hand to the material bulging with red shells that would do little to help me now.

Ripping up the Velcro, I had no time to look down, too afraid to take my gaze from its bulging red eyes and instead putting my faith in my memory.

After slipping the round into the chamber whilst still backing away, with its shoulders tipping forward I knew I had little time left and pumped the slide.

Giving no thought as to how the shell might work, but knowing that to miss would do the creature's job for it, I aimed as it pounced, but about to pull the trigger, my heel caught on something behind me.

I fell backwards.

To say time slowed would be incorrect, but I felt a calmness descend and somehow I fought against the instinct to drop the gun and wheel my arms in the air, instead tilting my head up so I could correct my aim and pull the trigger.

The recoil hurried my fall, forcing me against an uneven surface both hard and soft in places, but as the back of my head slammed into the hard road, giving thanks for the Kevlar helmet, the boom of the detonation sent a shockwave rushing over me.

Not waiting for my body to recover, I scrabbled to the

side, climbing over the lumpy mess I realised was the naked body of the headless man. On my back again, I opened my eyes, pleased not to see the figure looming and about to bite down on my face.

Standing, I didn't know what to expect as I turned to where I'd taken the shot. Desperate to know what damage the shell had done, I sought out the figure but saw nothing obvious. The creature had vanished, and with Daisy flat on her back, her face ashen and peering around as if in a state of shock, I turned to the last remaining creature still locked in battle, the desperation smeared across Hollywood's face, his hands empty of any weapons.

Despite his arms still lashing out and somehow finding the will to swerve left and right as the creature swung its arms like a crazed beast, I shouted at the top of my voice.

"Drop," I screamed, my fingers finding my armour's pocket and feeding shells one after the other into the chamber.

He'd heard me and didn't delay, his legs collapsing from under him as if he'd taken a fatal blow.

I fired, my aim square on the back of the attacker's helmet.

The glancing shot did its job, not blowing away its head or sending it reeling forward, but instead causing it to halt its assault and turn towards me. But when it looked away, my blood ran cold as I watched it jump over Hollywood then sprint with such speed, scattering the three soldiers still trying to get a clear shot.

The worst had happened, and there was little I could do to stop it escaping to the trees and out into the big wide world.

77

"No," I screamed, but as the uncharacteristic call echoed into the night, I felt a sudden urge to slap myself around the face, realising the surge of emotion had done nothing to solve the terrible problem.

Knowing I had to do something, at least giving everything I had left, I forced the butt of the shotgun against my shoulder, but with my aim blocked by Moses, Tubbs and Scotch gathering back together, the creature raced away with lightning speed, almost reaching the metal fence at the edge of the railway track.

Racked with despair that nothing could be done, still I charged forward. Waving my hand from side to side, I urged the trio to clear a path, but rather than following my frantic instructions, almost in unison the three turned their backs then racked the slides of their shotguns, sending unspent cartridges flying from the ejection ports before reaching for their yellow jacketed shells.

As the combined light from their underslung torches illuminated the speeding creature, the sight felt like a shot of adrenaline direct to my heart, bringing with it a surge of optimism and the sudden need to grab the nearest weapon so I could be the one to blow it off the face of the earth.

Scotch fired first, the recoil forcing him back, the shell bursting against the fence with the tangled metal doing nothing to impede its escape.

Tubbs was the next to fire, pulling the trigger no sooner than he'd charged the chamber. I winced, already shaking my head, knowing he'd missed as the explosion shattered the top half of the tree to the left, sending leaves and splinters raining down from above as a cloud of dust and smoke caught in the torchlight.

I closed my eyes, almost ready to give in when the final loud boom from Moses' weapon signalled our last chance had gone.

Still shaking my head, I opened my eyes just as the

explosion flashed bright, then holding my head still, I blinked over and again as if it would help to clear the smoke and falling leaves still obscuring the view.

"Did it hit?" I said, rushing past the three men when I still couldn't get a clear view. But when the sound of their following footsteps was the only reply, their beams of light bouncing up and down across the haze, my gaze darted all around for any sign.

With the smoke only just clearing as I covered half the distance to the fence, having left the tarmac for the grass surrounding the car park, I held back when a red mist caught in the combined beams of light.

As the trio joined at my side, I swapped my shotgun with Scotch and used his underslung light to scan from left to right, quickly at first but then much more slowly when I hadn't found what I'd sought.

Only on the second review did I find remains scattered over a wide arc, the helmet resting the furthest away, surrounded by scraps of black fabric. Chunks of Kevlar lay beside what I guessed were scraps of flesh, but having seen all I needed to, I didn't linger.

That's when I heard the first sirens in the distance and for a moment, I wondered how long they'd been there whilst too preoccupied to notice. Dismissing the thought, I turned away from the perimeter and tried to think what I could say to the cops to explain away everything that had happened.

"Clark," I said, pinning the phone to my ear with my shoulder as I swapped my gun back with Scotch. My voice sounded dulled to my ears as if stuffed with cotton wool as I slung the weapon over my shoulder. "Do what you can to hold back the cops. If they see what's gone on here, I don't think we can keep them from taking over."

"What's happened?" he said. "Are you okay?" he added before I replied.

"Tell them it's a quarantine zone. We need ambulances too, but we'll have to bring the injured out once we've made sure there's no infection."

"Are you okay?" he repeated as I was about to hang up, but I didn't know how I could answer.

"We need reinforcements," I said after a pause.

As I killed the call, I spotted each of the three men stood in front of me staring back, their faces pale in the moonlight.

Without speaking I walked between them, heading towards the building where Hollywood stood over Daisy, helping her to her feet where she cricked her neck to the side then dusted herself off.

Drawing a slow, deep breath of relief, I covered the rest of the distance between us.

"Injuries?" I said, watching their eyes widen as they turned towards me.

Hollywood shook his head, Daisy repeating the gesture, but spotting a dark mark on her hand, I pointed it out, ignoring my gloves glinting in the floodlights.

"Check that," I said, pulling my hand back. "Then get everything squared away. We need to clean up as much as you can before the cops get here. Do a roll call. Hide the damage on the cars as best as you can and get everyone swabbed, especially the injured."

"Are you okay?" Daisy said, looking up from her hand.

I pulled the swab pouch from the pocket in my vest and threw it to Hollywood.

"Check everyone," I said before walking towards the warehouse.

Under my feet the ground felt uneven and I wished I hadn't looked down when I saw the scattered red and white flesh almost everywhere, even down the front of my armour.

The skin on my face felt tight and dry, but I dared not lick my lips, knowing the disgusting sheen that covered everywhere I'd seen so far. With the thought, the vest seemed to tighten around my torso, the helmet sitting so heavily on my head. The gloves too tight on my hands.

After setting the shotgun on the ground, with growing frustration I fumbled at the catch underneath my chin, eventually pulling off the helmet along with what felt like half of my hair before letting it drop, then struggling with the tacky Velcro down my front.

Pulling the zip free, I shouldered the weight of the vest down to the floor and as my gloves soon fell after, I stretched out with my eyes closed, my head turned to the stars as I revelled in the cool night air swirling around my body.

Within a few moments footsteps arrived at my back and I said the first thought that came into my head.

"It wasn't Brown."

When whoever it was didn't walk away or arrive at my side, I twisted around to find Hollywood staring down at the remains of the naked man. The sergeant held a shotgun by the barrel in his right hand with the black pouch in the other.

My gaze soon joined his before following the dark veins against the pale body like a map.

"Two walking wounded," Hollywood said, looking up, his voice gaining definition as he caught my eye. "And two unaccounted for."

"Who?" I eventually said as his words filtered through my brain.

"Philips and Latenight are missing."

"The injured. Where are they?" I said, glancing over his shoulder.

When he didn't reply straight away, I grabbed the pouch he'd held down by his side, then strode toward the edge of the car park beside the clutter of luxury cars potted with more holes than a cheese grater.

Enjoying the freedom without the stifling weight, I arrived at the two men sat next to each other on the edge of the car park.

Not quite hearing the name of the topless and shivering soldier, despite Moses' volume, I watched Tubbs follow my instructions with the swab whilst knowing everyone else in the group that had formed were looking at the Glock I'd pulled from my leg holster.

My gaze held firm, following Tubbs' hands as he eased the first of the field dressings from the bloody graze at the top of the soldier's arm before touching the fabric around the gash, the patient doing his best not to react.

All attention then turned to the LED readout.

The relief came as low, slow breaths and thin smiles appearing on lips, but they soon fell away as the group moved to the next man resting his bandaged hand on his lap. Without being asked, he pulled down his own dressing, tensing, ready for the pain as the swab touched the edge of the through and through wound.

The reader's beep was enough to turn me away, pushing the pistol back into the holster, and bringing with it the realisation the sirens had died away, replaced by low chatter from those in the car park.

About to call for the injured to be led along the road to where I anticipated there were ambulances waiting, a hollow clang of metal echoed from the warehouse.

The voices quietened, heads turning to the sound I recognised.

"What was that?" Daisy said.

Not looking towards her, I narrowed my eyes, peering towards the building.

"The missing men. Or what's left of them," I said, striding towards the building and picking up my shotgun as I passed.

78

"Hold position," I said, peering over my shoulder, taking comfort that each of those that were able raised their weapons. Despite the fatigue obvious in their eyes and their dishevelled battle-hardened stares, their focus was fixed firm on the jagged gap between the warehouse and van. "Shred anything that tries to get out," I called, before I turned and strode forward.

Dismissing the thought of going back to pull on the tainted protective gear, even though it might save my life, I was soon at the entrance, straining for any sound as I peered into the bright space where the overhead lights made the floor glow a bright patchwork of red.

Even ignoring the bloody mess across the floor, the cots laying upside down and a table standing on its side, the thousands of pounds of equipment it had held scattered across the stained concrete, it was enough to paint the scene of the ferocious fight before the infection overtook them.

Despite the still air and empty space, I couldn't help but fear that the missing Latenight and Philips had somehow found their way inside and we'd lost them forever too, transformed to add to our nightmare.

Edging sideways into the space with my shotgun levelled, my legs grew heavier with each step, reminding me of the paralysing fear I'd felt clinging to the ladder at Copper Flail. As the sensation grew, bringing with it an anxiety that it might overwhelm me at any moment, I felt a sudden need to make a call for the RAF to rain bombs from above.

But no, already pushing the boundaries of what we could explain away with our rumours, it was only a matter of time before the wrong people joined the dots, only needing to scrape at the surface of our charade to blow our cover with a thin breath of wind.

Peering around the bright room, the rainbow of sickly colour streaked across the floor dragged me back into the terrible place where it had all started.

Realising my downward spiral, I drew a deep breath, but it did little to wipe away the knowledge that despite all we'd gone through, we had nothing to show for it. No Brown. No Lonsdale, and no clue as to where the new facility stood and what terrible tasks they were performing.

But this was not me. Self-pity was not something I did. Never had I let a mission, no matter how serious the consequences, defeat me, and now was not the time I was going to fail.

Raising the shotgun a little higher, I swung my aim across the view and took another step forward. With a look towards the far left, I hoped to catch a glimpse inside the kitchen, toilets and office, but found each door closed.

The ring of the phone in the far room filled me with a sudden dread that if the PIN Woodridge had recited was no good, my opportunity to get the right code lay still hooded and dead in the back of the X5.

Forcing my eyes wide and with a quick shake of my head, I reminded myself of the danger in the present, but when none of the doors had yet flung wide, forcing me to stand my ground against a horrific charge, I looked over to the office, noticing the closed blinds I'd left open.

Taking care where I stepped, I walked toward the narrow slit beside its door, the leading edge streaked with blood as my boots echoed against the concrete.

When the door hadn't moved before I'd arrived and the phone now silent, I pushed against the wood with the shotgun's muzzle, then reached over the threshold and pressed on the light switch. In the brightness, I peered around the edge of the door, scanning every corner then bending to peer under the desks, soon spotting the metal wastepaper bin on its side and not where I'd left it.

Crossing the threshold with a tentative step, I examined

the room as I moved around the desks, but with no one leaping out or found hiding in the corners, I turned to leave when my gaze fell on Woodridge's phone and the smear of blood across the screen, leading to a trickle of red circles along the floor.

The trail led nowhere.

After setting the shotgun on the desk beside the phone, and pulling on a pair of purple disposable gloves from the dispenser, I tore a sheet of paper defaced with a doodle in the corner and wiped it across the screen, but with the blood almost dry it left behind a smeared mess. Despite the disgusting mark, the screen was clean enough to show the twenty missed calls before the message disappeared as I tapped in the PIN from memory.

Endorphins rushed as the screen lit, but the feeling fell away, replaced with a kick of adrenaline at a noise from the wide space. Slipping the Glock from its holster but keeping it aimed at the floor, I listened, soon letting myself calm when the sound didn't repeat. Hearing only the orders voiced to the men outside, I reminded myself I'd yet to witness the monsters sneak around.

When no one showed themselves at the doorway, I dismissed the sound, turning instead to scroll through the list of missed calls, each from an unknown number.

Walking to the door, my gaze landed on the battered main entrance, the wood folded in on itself much further than they were ever meant to.

Finding no one had disobeyed my order and followed me inside, I headed back to the desk as my fingers worked the screen to find the contacts list empty, the messages and outgoing calls the same.

With no apps that weren't already on the phone from new, I tapped in a number. Thinking better of pushing the soiled screen to my ear, I activated the speaker.

"Ming's Dry Cleaners," the strong accented Chinese voice said, answering after three rings. Lowering the volume with the buttons on the side, I leaned towards the phone.

"Jo Ming," I said, then listened to the line click with no

other reply.

"Ming," came another male voice after a couple of seconds of dead air. Despite having only spoken a single word, I could tell he had a thick Welsh accent.

"Get me a reverse trace on the last call to this number," I said.

"Wait one," the man on the other end replied before the line went quiet for a few seconds. "Have you got a pen?"

"No need. Just give me a trace of the originating number's location."

"It's a mobile," he said without delay, and I prepared myself for the disappointment.

"Triangulate on its current location, stating the error tolerance in metres."

As I waited in the silence, I prepared for his likely words describing a wide location scattered with towers, serving thousands of handsets, or if it was out of a town, perhaps he'd report just one that covered miles of sprawling properties we'd need to rule out.

"Five masts," the voice said, but his tone, which was a little higher than before, caused a flicker of optimism I tried to push down. "Slough Trading Estate," he added, the words not coming as a complete surprise as I pictured him leaning into the screen to read the finer detail. "There's a twenty metre error distance predicted for Plymouth and Yeovil Road. Mapping shows only three units in the zone. If I had to put money on it, based on the signal strength, I'd say it came from forty nine Plymouth."

"Shit," I said, letting the surprise slip from my lips. "Thank you," I added, then hung up, shaking my head as I deleted the number from the log, only looking up towards the doorway with the sound of footsteps.

"Red?" It was Hollywood's deep voice echoing out in the space and I felt myself relax, but about to exit the room to find out why he was calling, I held firm as he spoke again. "There you are."

Unsure who he'd just spoken to, and leaving the gloves on, I walked from the office, my gaze falling to Hollywood standing halfway between me and the entrance, then turning his head to catch my eye.

Daisy stepped out from his shadow, but rather than looking at me, she peered to the right where Hollywood's gaze had returned.

Turning to where they looked, all I saw was the open door of the gent's toilet.

Tensing, I took a step to get a better look.

"Reinforcements are on their way," Daisy said, but paying her little attention I stepped further into the wide space to improve my view. "Thirty minutes, I'm told."

I took no notice of her words when I saw a dark figure waiting just back from the washroom doorway, the bulk of his helmet covering his face, his head turned low. My gaze followed to where he looked and the blood spotted around the concrete at his feet.

"It's you, isn't it?" I said, as the man slowly lifted his right hand from behind his back, revealing a red sodden field dressing gripped in his fist.

As I took a step closer, the trooper raised his head, his eyes narrowing as he glared in my direction.

79

"He's what?" Daisy said, but I didn't need to look over to know she was glancing between me and Latenight, who stood in the doorway.

"Red, what do you mean?" Hollywood said, his stern tone echoing across the wide space with his steps matching mine as I took a few towards the washroom door.

"You find Philips?" I said not looking away.

"He was tending to the wounded," Hollywood replied and Latenight's expression turned to a grimace as he adjusted the red, sodden field dressing covering his right hand.

As I stared, I saw his clothes looked pristine, not covered in decaying flesh, nor scuffed with the trials of combat, or splashed with foul blood like the rest of the team. Tight, pressed lines remained running up the front of his combat trousers and past the Glock holstered around his right thigh.

"We have a traitor," I said, unsurprised when Latenight's expression didn't change, then glanced to Hollywood at my side, who unclipped the strap from under his chin before drawing off his helmet as he eyed Latenight.

"What?" Daisy said as she stepped beside the sergeant.

Turning back to the man in the toilet's doorway, I linked my purple surgical gloved fingers together and rested my arms at my front.

"I respect you, Red," Hollywood said, keeping his voice even. I raised a brow whilst my gaze remained locked to Latenight's, watching his cheeks bunch in a subtle motion. "But you know I'm going to need plenty of evidence to back that up."

I nodded, taking another step towards the man I'd accused, who glanced over to his superior before looking back to me, drawing his head back a little when I hadn't spoken again.

Hollywood was right, of course. He should protect his

man. It was how the army worked and I would do the same in his position, especially if someone like me had made the accusation.

"They tipped the people working against us off," I said. "You know this already, of course. Someone must have given them Lonsdale's address. How else would they get there before us?"

"That's a wide pool of people," Hollywood said as he matched my step.

"It had to be someone who was on that tasking," I replied.

"That's still a of lot of suspects," he said.

I nodded, still staring at Latenight, who gave the same response.

"Latenight left his overwatch post. Isn't that right, Daisy?" I said, not turning to find if she was following our slow forward progress.

"He went for a piss," Hollywood said. Out of the corner of my eye, I saw Daisy arrive to stand at his side.

"Before you say any more," I replied in a low voice, "remember, I've been on selection. I've trained alongside many of your brothers. I've laid in bushes next to your colleagues in monsoons. Likewise, I've crapped in bags and shoved them into my Bergen rather than compromise the objective. In all this time I've never heard of a member of the Special Air Service leaving their post. Especially not just before a contact."

When Hollywood said nothing, I took another step forward. His feet matched my move.

"I couldn't have picked out your men on the perimeter. No one could, even if they knew they were there. Still, somehow, our friends surprised them."

"This place was compromised from the beginning. We were well aware of that," Hollywood said, no emotion in his voice.

"They could still be watching us," Daisy added.

I glanced over my shoulder to find she now stood a few steps behind Hollywood, her eyes narrow and uncertain.

"Please tell me there's more," Hollywood added after a moment.

I nodded, taking another step, having covered all but the final few paces between us.

"What's he doing in here?" I said, but continued before anyone had a chance to answer. "I found blood on Woodridge's phone. Barely dry," I added, watching the incessant drip of blood from the red bandage wrapped around Latenight's hand. "Did you find him standing in the doorway?" I asked, glancing at Hollywood, who raised his chin and gave a single dip of his head.

"It's still not enough," he replied, his head turning from side to side.

"Agreed," I said, knowing it was right to keep the bar high because of what my orders compelled me to do. "Show him the phone," I said, for the first time speaking to Latenight.

He didn't react, his head remaining still, not blinking as I spoke.

Hollywood didn't match my latest step as I came within arm's reach of the trooper.

"He handed it in," Hollywood replied. "I took everyone's handsets from them. Just as you requested," he said, and although his voice was flat, I heard the question in his tone. "Do you have a phone, trooper?" he asked as another drop of blood fell from Latenight's fist. "That's a nasty injury."

"Stray bullet. It took the tip right off," Latenight replied, his voice quiet.

"But it doesn't stop you answering my question," Hollywood said as he stepped past me, pushing his face right into the trooper's personal space.

Latenight yelped as Hollywood took the bandaged fist in his huge hand.

I turned away, strolling to the remaining upright equipment table. To the sound of laboured breath, I looked over a line of four identical holstered combat knives with blades as long as my palm. Picking up the closest before slipping it from the sheath, I held it up to the light.

Latenight hadn't spoken as I slowly turned around, but his high bunched cheeks told of his pain as the drips from his fist quickened down to the concrete.

Daisy watched my slow footsteps as they echoed across the wide space, her eyes going wide as she saw what I held.

A sharp rush of breath pulled my attention back to Hollywood as he dropped the soaked bandage onto the floor, grabbing Latenight's wrist with the other hand.

"Give me the phone," I said, arriving close with the knife held out in front of my face as I ran my gloved finger along the flat of the blade.

Latenight glanced over.

"Fuck you both," he shouted, his eyes flickering wide then forcing his lids closed as Hollywood's grip tightened before leaning down, pulling the Glock from Latenight's leg holster and pushing it into the waistband at his back.

"Do you have any idea who you're dealing with, Trooper?" Hollywood asked in a low voice, standing tall and leaning into the soldier's face.

"I'll take that as a no," I said when Latenight didn't reply. Then I stepped forward, barely hearing Daisy gasp as I slashed out low towards the trooper's pocket.

80

With a final slash of the knife, I caught a black handset falling from the remains of Latenight's trouser pocket as Hollywood's grip tightened around his wrist, stopping him from drawing back.

"Ooops," I said, stepping back as Latenight gritted his teeth, his face scrunching up with an effort as if trying not to react.

"You stupid cunt," Hollywood spat, releasing his hold and drawing his hand back, flicking the running blood from his fingers and grabbing Latenight by the risers of his protective vest.

Dragging him from the doorway, the trooper's feet slipped as Hollywood forced him against the wall to the right of the open door.

Swapping the knife and the phone between my hands, I tapped at the screen with an index finger.

"You better talk," Hollywood said, jerking Latenight away from the wall before slamming him back again, the back of his helmet thumping against the plasterboard.

"What's the code?" I said, not looking up from the numbers on the screen prompting for a PIN. When only a grunt replied, I lifted my head, staring into his narrowed eyes as he glared back.

Taking a moment, I reminded myself that much like I had, each of these men had trained to resist interrogation. He'd break, everyone did, but the fate of civilisation had no time to wait. And I had an order to follow through with.

Forcing a wide smile, I watched Latenight's eyes widen as Hollywood glanced over his shoulder at me, his brow low and eyes like slits when he saw the screen prompting for a fingerprint.

Latenight had seen it too, but as Hollywood turned back, he let go of the vest with one hand, instead grabbing at Latenight's hand once again, pushing his finger onto the wound.

"Don't struggle," I said, stepping close as Hollywood pressed his shoulder into Latenight's chest to top him from moving. "It works just as well if there's no blood pumping through the finger. Trust me."

In his personal space, with his warm breath rushing over my face, Latenight tensed, testing Hollywood's hold, but soon realised he could do nothing to stop me from angling his finger against the small round touchpad.

I found the call log empty after taking a step back, and much like the other phone, had no additional apps other than those already installed when pulled from its packaging. A single conversation waited in the messages, a back and forth along with a couple of sentences not yet sent.

I'd got the right man.

"They know where Lonsdale is now," I said with a sigh, not looking up from the screen as I read the conversation.

"Where?" Daisy said, reminding me she was still in the room. With a glance, I saw she'd stepped closer to the exit, her face paler than I remembered.

"Not far," I replied. "Perhaps you should supervise what's going on outside."

Her eyes narrowed but when she didn't step away, I looked back down at the phone, reading again the word-for-word dictation from the operative in the Brecon Beacons, then moving down to the message not sent, outlining his plans for me. A service he would not charge extra for because he proposed I would pay for it myself.

Slipping the phone into a pocket of my combats, I stepped back up to Latenight's face.

"How were you going to do it?" I said, swapping the knife into my right hand and holding it down at my side. "A bullet in the back of the head in the heat of it all, or something slower and more drawn out? Perhaps you and me in a quiet spot," I added with a raise of my eyebrows. "Then a knife to the heart when you'd had your fun?"

Hollywood lifted his head, increasing the press of his shoulder against the soldier's chest.

"Here's your chance to explain," I said, watching his lips

grey as he pushed them together. "Tell me I've got the wrong idea. Tell me you're not the one who's betrayed every member of the team. Tell me you're not the person who sold out humanity."

His eyes narrowed and his head raised, tilting to the side as the pained expression fell away.

"How much did they pay you for the end of the world?" I added when he remained silent.

"This is your chance, Trooper," Hollywood said, pushing his face right up to Latenight's.

"He's not worthy of that name. Never has been," I said. Hollywood nodded, but still Latenight didn't react. "And I'm afraid we don't have time for being nice anymore."

"You can't say I've not warned you," Hollywood said after what seemed like a long silence filled only with Daisy's slow footsteps.

"I don't think he's going to say anything," she said, her voice higher than I'd heard before. "I'll call the RMP. They can take it from here."

"Police?" I said, not turning towards her. "I'm afraid that's not how things work in my world."

"What?" she said, the word shrill but filled with uncertainty. "Hollywood?" she called out, her tone rising higher still when he didn't reply. "Sergeant Heatherwood? Dan?"

Not turning to look at Daisy, I leaned closer to the soldier.

"The problem is a standing order I can't ignore, and it states there is only one way to deal with a traitor." Bending my knees, I stooped low, ignoring Latenight's renewed struggle against Hollywood's unmoving press.

"No. No. You're bluffing." Daisy's shrill voice called through the air.

Ignoring her words, I slipped the knife between Latenight's legs.

"You can't... This is Britain, for God's sake... You're bluffing. She's bluffing. Dan!"

Latenight's eyes widened, but he kept his mouth shut as

the flat of the blade ran along his inner thigh, flinching only as I turned it through ninety degrees, separating the fabric with a single motion.

"What the hell? No. No. No," Daisy called out, her voice right at my ear.

The thrashing began as his flesh split, but with the rush of warmth flowing over my gloved hand as I delved deeper, I withdrew, knowing I'd found the femoral artery.

After sending the knife skittering across the concrete behind me, I stepped away.

"What…" Daisy said, the words muffled as if covering her mouth. "What have you done?"

I stared at Latenight as his lips parted, watching the colour draining when all that came was a rasp of breath.

"It's too late to say anything now, I'm afraid," I said with a shake of my head.

"Oh my God. Oh my God," Daisy repeated, her breath rushing faster as bright red blood spread across the floor. Hollywood stepped back and Latenight dropped into the mess, collapsing as if he were a puppet and someone had cut his strings.

81

Trusting Hollywood to deal with Daisy's emotions, the high pitch of her voice receded as the washroom door closed at my back before the sound went altogether, my breath halting when I caught my reflection in the mirror.

Dark clots clung across my face, with each disgusting island of decay joined by smeared blood. Having dried almost everywhere I looked, scabs flaked, falling like putrid dandruff from around my eyes and mouth.

Not for the first time, I looked like the she-devil herself.

Glancing down at the sink, blood from my purple gloves spotted the porcelain, reminding me of the order I'd just carried out. The act came with no regret. The death of the young man was on him alone, he being the only one to blame if he couldn't comprehend the consequences of taking money to betray his friends. His colleagues. The whole of civilisation.

After pulling off the gloves, I filled the sink, lathering hand soap from the dispenser across my face to form a sickly red foam, then dowsing water across my skin before pulling off my t-shirt, emptying the sink and repeating.

In my bra, I angled my head many ways, turning left and right as I sought anything foreign on my pink scrubbed skin. Drying my face with hand towels, I'd just about finished up as the outer door opened, followed by the second, Daisy's voice screeching before it shut behind her.

"You're going to prison for this, you…" she said, but paused, stuttering as she saw me. She'd taken off her helmet since I'd last seen her. "You're a monster," she added in a softer voice once she'd regained control.

The door soon opened with Hollywood's giant hands grabbing onto the armour at her shoulders.

"Get your hands off me, Sergeant," she called out, her volume returning.

"It's okay, Dan," I said, looking over. As he caught my eye, I nodded and he let go of her upper arm, raising his hands high as she swapped glances between the pair of us.

"Give us a minute," I said, then with a flare of his eyes, he retreated, the doors swishing closed behind him.

Turning back to the mirror, I leaned toward the reflective glass, again twisting my neck to each side as I studied my pink skin before pushing my hand into the water to flip the rotating plug, releasing the dam.

During the time it took to wash my hands, Daisy still hadn't spoken, almost as if expecting a defence against her accusations, but she was right, in part at least. They'd trained me to be a monster, if that was what the situation demanded.

I'd made peace with myself many years ago, the process starting when I felled the towering chimney on top of the woman I loved. That act had made the world a better place, a fact I'd come to terms with and would repeat to protect the innocent, no matter how much of my humanity it took away.

There was no getting away from the fact that a traitor could never be trusted again. We set robust examples for that reason, and although the operational call was mine to make, I'd dealt with the situation in the most humane way possible at the time. I wouldn't be going to prison any time soon, no matter who she threatened to tell.

Her face screwed up as I turned back toward her.

"You didn't need to do that. He was so young," she said, her voice a little high, but calming as she continued. "You've got the evidence you needed to put him away for a very long time."

Taking a step towards her, she moistened her lips as if about to speak, but didn't when I leaned in close.

"You and I live in different worlds," I said, almost in a whisper. She raised her chin and swallowed hard as my breath washed across her face. "You have no other choice but to handle that," I added, and leaned back.

Before she could reply, the door swung wide and Hollywood appeared, his gaze locking onto mine.

"The cops are approaching," he said, his words rushed.

"Kill the flood lights. Is everything out of the way?" I said, keeping my voice low.

"As much as possible," he replied, and with a nod, disappeared back through the lobby.

Turning to Daisy, she held her breath with her head tilting to the side, just as she raised her right brow. "Tell them you were just following orders," she said, her voice almost back to normal. "See how that works out for you."

My cheeks bunched as I forced a calm smile, her eyes widening as if uncertain what I was going to do. Her expression fell as I shook my head.

"If you'd lived my life, then you'd know it was the right thing to do," I replied, but I gave her no chance to say anything else as I turned away and headed out into the warehouse, where strobing blue lights flashed through the gap between the double doors and the van.

82

With light no longer pouring down from the side of the building, the darkness between the moments of blue seemed so much deeper than when I'd last looked. Cursing under my breath, I took a wide route to avoid the blood around the other washroom door, where someone had moved Latenight's body. The streaks in the liquid that should have been inside him marked where he'd been dragged the short distance before disappearing behind the washroom door.

After changing into a clean white t-shirt and bomber jacket from my bag in the office, I found Daisy standing at the other washroom door, looking up from the blood as I emerged. I didn't meet her gaze, instead navigating between the mess and out into the cold night air where three cop cars parked in parallel across the entrance to the car park, with our men standing like a wall of players on a football pitch waiting to hold back the ball from a free kick.

From what I could see, their obstruction did a reasonable job at blocking the path of the police car's headlights and the views of the six armed officers in their tactical dress, lit only by the incessant blue strobe.

With a glance to the left, I saw the men had hustled the cars into two lines, somehow hiding all but a scattering of holes in the metal seen between the flashes. At first look, the surface of the car park was clear of much of the debris, but still glinted in places with each strobe of light.

Striding toward the blues, I listened to the police officers talking in loud voices at the soldiers, the cop's chests inflated and their bulk pronounced by their armour. But at least the officers of the law kept their MP5 assault rifles from their grips, with each of our team leaving their weapons hanging by straps over their shoulders.

"You were told to stay back," I called out as I arrived at the line.

"New orders. We can't ignore reports of a gun battle on the streets," the closest police officer said, peering around

Hollywood.

With the cop double taking in my direction as I stepped around him, whilst being careful to ensure only the undamaged part of the building loomed as my backdrop, I held his attention.

The furrow of his brow remained obvious, despite the rim of his helmet.

"Are you in charge? What the hell's going on?" he said.

"It's a quarantine situation," I replied, stepping closer as I held his gaze. "And we're under orders to keep all unauthorised person's back, for their own safety. I'm sure you understand."

Each of the police officer's heads twitched in my direction before looking at the guy I was speaking to.

"But the gunfire?" he said, his brow twitching.

"Armed terrorists," I replied, watching his expression cycle as he processed the information.

After a moment, he shook his head. "Division knows nothing about this?" he said, turning away for the first time since I'd arrived as he tried to look past Hollywood.

"It all happened too fast. We've been trailing them for days, but they only just entered your jurisdiction. There was no time," I said as he caught my eye again.

"What is it?"

The voice came from someone behind the cop, and I leaned around to find the other five officers craning their necks to get a look at me.

"Ebola," I replied, raising my voice. "You know, the one ravaging Africa that eats you from the inside. Get in your cars if you don't want your slow, painful deaths to become stats on the evening news."

The cops turned to each other, swapping glances as a rush of unvoiced questions tormented their expressions. Those furthest away stepped back, moving between their cars as they pushed their dark gloves up to their mouths.

The guy standing next to me didn't flinch.

"What about you lot?" he said, his voice gruff as he looked up and down at my casual clothes.

"We're vaccinated," I replied, but rather than continue to look at me, he lifted himself on to his tiptoes, his gaze catching on something of interest over Hollywood's shoulder. "It's mandatory in our line of work. Now get back in your cars and turn off the vents. Maybe reverse up a little to be sure and I'll get you some masks, unless you want to take it home and kill your families?"

The officer dropped from his toes and stared back, considering me as if not sure if he'd heard right.

Despite what I'd said, he pulled on the strap of his rifle, moving it around to under his arm and made to head between the sergeant and myself, stopping only as I stepped into his path and pushed my palm out, with Hollywood closing the remaining gap.

"One step further, then it's a month for you and your team in a quarantine hotel eating microwave meals and watching shit TV," I said as I held his gaze.

His right eye twitched, and he glanced back to his colleagues who, although three of them still held the line, seemed unconvinced by his actions.

After a moment, he shook his head. "I'm sorry, ma'am, but our instructions are to secure the scene," he replied, rising again to his tip toes and pushing his chest against my palm.

"How are you going to get out of this, ma'am?" It was Daisy's voice that came from over my shoulder and I tried not to react, despite being uncertain of what she'd say next.

83

The cop's eyes narrowed as he glanced to my right where Daisy had appeared, but I didn't look over, instead keeping my palm out and pressed against the chest of his body armour. Whilst he looked away, I sought the clip holding the strap which kept the MP5 slung under his arm.

Meeting his gaze again as he turned back, my mind raced over what I'd do if Daisy said anything more. Not able to let her jeopardise our task, and with a rehearsal rushing through inside my head, I visualised grabbing the strap and releasing the clip so the gun would drop, whilst certain the rest of the team would do their best to disarm those who stood in front of them.

"Stand down, Captain," I replied, whilst maintaining the cop's stare when she hadn't added to her question. "I'm afraid the captain is under a lot of stress with all we have to deal with."

Out of the corner of my eye, I saw Daisy turn her head to the side and forced myself to relax, despite anticipating what she might say next. With a flourish of her arms at her side, I couldn't help but stiffen when she opened her mouth.

"I've just found out this career isn't for me," she said, and I readied myself, watching as the cop's eyes narrowed a little further. "I just can't stomach the needless death."

The cop turned to look at her, then back at me.

"It's not for everyone," I added with a shrug.

He shook his head, blowing out a frustrated breath. "I must insist you step aside so we can secure the scene," he said, standing up straighter as if it would help him look into the darkness behind.

"Officer," I said, matching his movement to block his view as best I could. "Please do me a professional courtesy and make another call to your superiors. I will call mine and if they both agree to allow you to sign a waiver relinquishing my duty of care over you, then I'll let you walk yourself into an agonising few weeks in an isolation ward. Your death will not be on my conscience."

"I bet," Daisy was quick to chip in, but her voice was quiet enough that I suspected I was the only one to hear it.

The cop raised his chin, glancing over his shoulder at his nearest colleague, who, with a furrowed brow, replied with an almost imperceptible shrug.

"I trust there are enough ambulances on standby up the road for you and your team?" I added.

Despite my words and his colleague's reluctance, the cop stepped back from the hand I'd kept pressed against his chest before he twisted the radio from the breast of his armour, pulling it from its mount before turning his back to me.

I took my phone from my pocket and looked away. Then, about to speed dial Clark, I held off from pressing the screen when the copper's voice trailed off after a single word I didn't quite catch.

Instead, hearing the guttural low tone of truck engines in the distance, I glanced back and saw he held his radio at his side as he stared off down the road, where the streetlights illuminated a line of three bulky Ridgback armoured vehicles rumbling towards us.

Each were missing the desert paint colour scheme, RPG armour cages around the exterior and top-mounted heavy machine guns I'd grown used to on my many trips to Afghanistan.

Behind them, three olive-green trucks followed, two with their rears covered with canvas, the other a flatbed loaded with the green container I recognised from Victoria barracks.

With a glance over his shoulder in my direction, I smiled at the cop when he said nothing before stepping to his car and slipping down onto the passenger seat. His colleagues followed without a word and their engines soon purred to life, but with their only way of leaving blocked by the convoy, they each reversed into the adjacent car park, tucking their four by fours into the furthest away spaces.

Whilst the three Ridgbacks continued towards our line

still blocking the entrance to our car park, soon rocking to a stop as they arrived, the two canvas trucks veered to the left and into the one for the building next door, only just stopping before a stream of soldiers carrying SA80 rifles jumped from the rear, with many of them spreading across the view and holding their weapons to attention, whilst the rest joined the flatbed as it lowered the container to the tarmac.

Major Jones jumped from the cab of the closest truck, walking over as he peered into the darkness behind us before glancing sideways to get a look at the building's battered entrance.

"Ma'am," he said. "We're ready for your orders."

I held my response just long enough for Daisy to show her hand, but when her shrill voice didn't fill the space I'd left, I spoke.

"Secure the perimeter for the decontamination crew," I said, and he nodded, but about to walk away, he stopped himself.

"The facility will be ready for you in five minutes."

I shook my head as the container landed on the road with a heavy thump.

"Where we're going, there's no point in us scrubbing down," I said. Then, after looking along the line of our men, he nodded and walked away, calling out for a subordinate whose name I didn't catch.

With the Ridgback's doors opening, and the figures dressed head to foot in the same tactical gear walking from behind the vehicle, it took me a little longer than it should to recognise the first man who stepped up toward me.

"I said no gifts," I shouted over as Tommy beamed, surprising myself when I realised how good it was to see him.

"Someone told me you needed professionals," he said before his hearty laugh boomed across the night. "I hope you found a change of clothes," he added with a renewed bloom of laugher as I raised an eyebrow.

Hollywood pushed out his hand for Tommy to take, but

Tommy shoved it to the side, instead stepping in close for a vigorous hug.

As they locked in their embrace, I turned to Daisy, corralling her away from the forming group.

"You have a choice," I said in a low, soft voice as I watched her eyes pinch together. "Leave your contempt behind and do the job you're paid for, or walk away now and do whatever it is you need to. There is no in-between. No compromise. Everyone's, and I mean everyone's, lives depend on it."

Her expression didn't soften, and she held my gaze without reply, but after a few moments she nodded, then turned and walked over to where Moses was talking to those who had just arrived.

Clapping my hands together several times, I stood tall.

"Get your shit together. Briefing in five minutes and then let's get this finished once and for all."

84

Fresh from the harsh fluorescent light bouncing around the inside of the warehouse still smeared with the remains of the two soldier's battle for their lives, with my rucksack over my shoulder, the shotgun fitted with an underslung torch on the other, and labouring with a fresh armoured vest pinned under my arm, I welcomed the waft of fumes as Tommy pulled open the back of the Ridgback.

Although I'd deployed in many of the vehicles before, they'd either been in the stifling heat of the desert, where diesel fumes, dust, sand and the haze from sweating men who'd been gassing their way through ration packs for weeks would fill my nostrils, or on the windy plains of Salisbury where the odour of wet dog, unburnt fuel and sweat prevailed.

The stench of exhaust was still apparent, but with the rest absent, it seemed as if the vehicle had been in storage for a while.

Designed for reconfiguration to each theatre of operation, gone from the inside of the truck was the bulky air conditioner that had taken up so much space in the baking battlefield. The stretcher bay I'd seen run along the left bulkhead wall was no longer there either, replaced by a narrow desk with two ruggedised laptops open on the top and a pair of seats bolted to the floor just in front. A pair of radios with thin spiralling cables sat between the two computers.

The other wall filled with electrical cabinets and squeezed in between were a rack of four SA80 rifles. Stacked along the floor against each wall and under the desk, ammunition cases filled much of the remaining space.

Just as a trooper slid into the driver's seat on the left, with the passenger's side obscured with a cabinet housing fire extinguishers and medical equipment covering a third of the truck's width, both front doors slammed shut.

Laden in her tactical gear and ducking her head, Daisy

climbed into the back. I followed once she'd taken her seat. After stowing the shotgun in a nook, and sliding the armour behind the seat, with the rucksack on my lap I sat down in front of the computer just as my phone vibrated in my pocket. It was Clark.

"How sure are you that it's the right place?" he asked.

The call with the analyst in Wales ran through my head.

"I'm confident enough that you'll need to explain away three armoured vehicles travelling through the middle of Slough Trading Estate."

"Okay," he replied as his tone made it clear no one had told him about the details of our plan.

"I've just taken my seat in the back of a Ridgback," I said, unsure how he'd receive the news.

"Good," he said, much to my surprise. "Based on the conversation going on with the Joint Chiefs, it's not the worst place to be."

"How long have I got?" I replied, knowing his words could only mean technicians were already securing high explosives underneath the wings of Tornados as we spoke.

"I'm afraid we don't know," he replied, then lowered his voice. "You'll be under surveillance, and they'll call in the strike should things get out of hand again."

I glanced out of the corner of my eye, watching as Daisy tapped at her laptop before turning as if she knew I was looking. Her eyes narrowed with a question. Keeping quiet, I looked away when Franklin's voice took me by surprise.

"Just get the boys in and account for all targets. Let us know as soon as you can that it's the place we're looking for. You'll get one shot at shutting them down, but if anything…" he said, pausing as if searching for the word, "… gets loose, the RAF will take care of a wide radius. Stay in that Ridgback."

The line cut just as the truck's engine rumbled to life and I didn't speak, instead staring through the laptop's screen as his words rolled around my head. Even though they'd come as no surprise, I couldn't help but think back to when we'd almost lost control. And what would have happened if things had been different.

Unsure if the firepower waiting above to do our job if we failed was comfort or not, the thought disappeared as with a jolt to the side, we moved off. Letting the rucksack from my lap down to the floor, I slid the zip open, then moving the yellow hazmat bag out of the way, I took out the pouch.

Resting it on the desk, I slipped the bag behind the seat as I stared at the black material, not for the first time, wondering if it was just a placebo, a ruse designed so I didn't lose all hope.

85

Closing my eyes, I pulled in a deep breath before leaning forward from the seat bolted to the floor, where I took the closest radio resting on the desk and pushed the earpiece into my ear. After checking the channel, I pressed the button on the side.

"It's Red. Listen in. By now you should all realise the monumental task we have ahead of us. You've seen it first hand. I have every confidence that together we can beat this, but I've been honest with you all along, and will continue to do so. The brass don't have the same faith, but that's their job, and so the RAF will soon leave their plush hotels to hover overhead, ready to pull the trigger on each of us if we fail.

"But, I must stress, this is not a suicide mission. Stay confident and be precise and you'll walk out of there alive."

I held my breath, lingering on what I should say next, but the words didn't come.

"Now let's kick their fucking asses. Red out."

I felt our speed building just as my voice decayed, and we veered to the right, then left, before straightening up. My gaze fell on Daisy's screen.

With a tap of her keyboard, the screen separated into nine squares, each of the same size and showing feeds of various cameras mounted on trooper's helmets, the men in their tactical gear indistinguishable from the next as they sat along benches against the bulkheads.

A glint flickered in every man's eye. Whether brought there by excitement or adrenaline, I didn't know, but I was sure fear wasn't the cause.

After a moment, Daisy leaned over, tapping at my keyboard and bringing to life a similar matrix of views, including those from cameras staring out from our vehicle into the night.

Bravo team followed in close formation with remains of the original team lead by Hollywood inside, and seen as we took a corner, Charlie team followed with Tommy in charge of those he'd brought to the party.

As the command vehicle, we were Alpha.

Catching sight of a car waiting at a set of red lights as we crossed the junction before heading between two tall anonymous warehouses, I couldn't help but wonder what they must have made of our procession, the likes of which they'd have only ever seen kicking up dust from desert roads on the TV.

Our team was ten strong, excluding Daisy and me, whose orders compelled us to stay inside the vehicle, the words feeling like a pair of shackles tight against my wrists.

Despite carrying enough firepower to stage a coup, my only wish was for those wonders in yellow jackets, but only a handful remained scattered between Hollywood's men.

With only a basic plan in my mind, and knowing our friends had a head start, we had no time to scope the place out. Instead, we would have to think on our feet as we arrived. We couldn't risk them arriving first. Based on what we'd already seen, they'd ignore even the most basic of quarantine protocols and send the world spiralling on a trajectory it may never recover from.

If the place was quiet, the teams would go in, storming through the doors with shock and awe. After taking control, I'd call off the warplanes, and we'd roll out the red carpet for the cavalry to take the glory and leave to pick up the search for Brown.

If our friends were already there, we couldn't avoid conflict. We'd win that battle, I was sure.

Clark had offered soldiers from the barracks to assist, or even the police for perimeter control or to boost the numbers. But no, despite knowing what we were about to do, there would be an afterwards, in some form at least, and I hoped the ending wouldn't bring with it a need to explain to an unsuspecting public what we'd been doing.

With only a minute having passed on the drive I expected to take ten more, I composed and sent a message to Clark, checking if the target's phone had made any further calls we could triangulate.

His quick reply confirmed there was none.

As my gaze landed on Daisy, I turned away when her reaction to what I'd done to the traitor replayed inside my head. The thoughts brought with it the let-down that she'd not looked past the mechanics of the act, nor taken a moment to seek the bigger picture.

"What?" she said, and I realised I was looking right at her again.

Turning away, I hoped she'd do the same, but as I peered out into the darkness, I could feel her still staring.

"What about the research?" she said, and I looked back, lifting my chin when her question took me by surprise. For a moment the disappointment washed away, leaving me lost for words.

"What about it?" I eventually managed.

"What are the orders about retrieving the research?" she said, shaking her head as if her question was obvious.

"There are none," I replied. "This is a containment mission. Our orders are to halt the infection risk. They're not interested in saving the data." As I spoke, I already knew that if they hadn't asked for the data, it meant they already had it.

Her eyes grew wide, not coming to the same conclusion.

"But… But… But there's so much promise," she said, her tone rising with each faltering word. "There's so much potential for good, I mean."

"It won't be lost on them. Don't think they know any less than we do," I replied, and turned away when a deep voice came over the radio.

"Sixty seconds."

I sat up higher in my seat, watching as Daisy twisted back around and tapped at her keyboard with a confidence that she'd do her job and protect the men, be a professional, until the objective was complete at the very least. What would happen after would be someone else's problem.

"Eyes on," she said, and I turned to the laptop, focusing on a vast dark warehouse looming through the front-facing camera. Clicking on its square, the image filled the screen, displaying the detail of the tall building, its perimeter wrapped in a tall metal fence.

"Show time," I said under my breath, as I reached for the talk button.

DEAD END

86

"Hold back," I called out, before letting go of the radio's talk button as we arrived around ten car lengths from the warehouse compound.

Gripping the seat's arm as the Ridgback came to an abrupt stop, I concentrated on the tall metal fence lit silver by the streetlight's glow, before leaning towards the screen to get a better look at the mammoth building beyond the boundary.

Except for the front facing wall made of glass panels forming a curve, its lines were straight and sharp, the unblemished tall metal panels rising high. But with few windows to break up the flow, it was near impossible to tell how many floors were inside.

The closest part of the building held my attention, but despite the high lights around the perimeter, I could only just make out what I thought to be a spacious reception in the centre of the glass frontage.

A small car park waited empty in front of the glass, with enough space for two long rows of vehicles. Wrapping around its nearest side were more lines marked on the tarmac, and from the Google Map view, the side I couldn't see in person was much the same.

A two-section thin metal mesh gate wide enough for two stocky Ridgbacks side by side blocked the route to the entrance road.

I called Clark, questioning again if the phone had made a call, but he repeated the same answer he'd given before.

"We found where our friends have been using as their base of operations," he said before I had a chance to hang up.

"Where?" I replied.

"Maidenhead. Just down the road. The place was empty, cleared out in a hurry by the looks of it," he said.

"Any sign that they were keeping Brown there?" I asked.

"Yes. Based on the state of one of the rooms. You don't want to know the details. I promise you."

"Where have they gone?" I replied.

"We're gathering CCTV as we speak."

"Let me know as soon as you have anything," I said, hanging up the call as the radio came alive.

"Are you sure we have the right place?" It was Hollywood and I turned to Daisy's screen, scanning the images until I saw a face looking right into his colleague's camera.

"There's only one way to find out," I said, recognising the determination in his eyes. "Brace yourself," I added, turning to Daisy before I called out an order to the driver.

The gates flew open, clattering to either side, but with no sound or vibration from the impact felt inside the steel shell, I wouldn't have known if I hadn't seen it for myself.

We didn't slow, surging down the left-hand side, and I watched the rear camera as the two behind peeled off before the building blocked their view, knowing Hollywood raced to our opposite side whilst Tommy would rock to a stop in front of the reception's glass wall.

Gripping the handhold above my head just in time, the Ridgback lurched to a stop as I scanned the cameras before concentrating on the pair of anonymous panels we'd parked next to.

As the suspension settled, the front doors opened, with boots hitting the ground before the metal slammed back into place, leaving us alone in the back to watch the pair arrive at the side of the building, only to be joined with another two troopers from Tommy's team to form the Delta callsign.

The radio remained silent as we watched two of the group fix a long, thin frame packed with plastic explosive to the right-hand panel, before they peeled either side, pressing their backs against the wall and holding their thumbs up for the cameras.

Within the time it took me to scan the view, I confirmed each trooper gave the same sign as I lifted the radio to my mouth.

"Breach," I said, keeping my voice low, the word soon followed by a puff of smoke then what sounded like the popping of a cork through our thick protective shell, whose main purpose was to shield us from bullets and roadside explosions.

By the time the smoke cleared, the men had already disappeared, stepping over the fallen fire exit door and following the brightness of their underslung torches.

With too many feeds to take in at once, and with nothing on screen to show which men the images belonged to, I picked one of the three taking the lead and followed their slow journey down a corridor, whose only feature was a CCTV camera in the furthest corner.

As they made considered progress, I couldn't help but look away, scanning the outdoor feeds for anything out of place, returning to the view when I found no evidence of uninvited guests.

Back glaring through the camera I'd only just picked out, I leaned a little closer when I saw the men had stopped, each of them focusing on a door.

With only the number thirty nine labelled along the high edge, there was nothing to show what waited beyond as a dark, gloved hand reached out for the handle with an integrated lock. But before it twisted, the view swept to the left as the trooper glanced over his shoulder to his colleagues. Finding each pointing their weapon in a different direction, ready to cover what could happen next, the view turned back to the door, with the end of his shotgun raising up as the hand came back into the shot.

I leaned a little closer to the screen as he grabbed at the metal, then withdrew when it wouldn't twist in either direction.

Realising I'd held my breath, with a nod the view swept back down the corridor as they continued along its path.

Within a short few steps, they'd found another door, repeating the process. This time, as the handle twisted, a view opened up to reveal a small, darkened room, which was empty except for a few high stools.

The door soon closed and they continued on the route.

I chose another feed, soon switching again when it became clear they were all having much the same experience. With a glance at the outdoor views, I shook my head when, despite having only been inside the building for three minutes, they were yet to find any sign of life.

"Something's not right," I said, reacting to an unease rising inside my chest. With my fingers on the laptop's touch pad, I minimised the camera feeds and pulled up Google Maps. Navigating the static satellite image to where we waited, with a shake of my head I looked around at the top-down view of the building's neighbours. A dumpy business unit sat to the left, with a much smaller warehouse on the right.

"Could they have fucked up the triangulation?" I said, not looking up.

Daisy said something which I didn't quite catch as I tried to understand how we hadn't yet found anything of interest, when the margin for error was only twenty metres. Someone had to have made the call from this building.

About to take my phone from my pocket, I looked up from the screen with my breath held.

"Unless," I said, looking Daisy in the eye, "he's played us, and hidden a phone somewhere close to redirect the call."

87

I'd executed the technique myself in the past; hide a phone where you're happy for someone to find it. With a simple setting change and a little help from the network provider, any calls made to that handset would redirect to another, masking the original sender's location.

Simple but effective.

When Daisy's expression didn't tighten to the scowl I'd expected, I kicked myself for letting Lonsdale disappear down another blind path.

Sitting back in the seat, I racked my brain as Daisy leaned over and switched the laptop screen back to the cameras.

When we'd arrived to find the place undisturbed, I'd congratulated myself that we were the first to mobilise, despite being an hour behind our friends. The thought of a diversion hadn't even crossed my mind.

With a shake of my head, knowing there were no more threads to pick at in order to find where the scientists were working at changing the world forever, I reminded myself that at least our friends should have fallen for the same trap, led here by Latenight.

Or had they perhaps decided Brown was all they needed? Surely not.

Looking back at the video feeds, no longer surprised to see the empty corridors and locked doors repeating on all the views, perhaps it was time to call the team back out and set up positions to snare those who I expected wouldn't be able to keep away.

"I fucked up," I finally said, not looking up from the view of three troopers with their weapons raised high as they climbed a staircase.

"Really?" Daisy said, meeting my gaze. I was surprised to find her features had softened, barely showing any signs of the earlier contempt.

I nodded and a thin smile bunched her cheeks as she

reached her hand across the gap.

"Where the fuck are they?" I said, shaking my head, my words sending her brow bunching into a scowl as she pulled her hand back.

"I thought you meant..." she said, then looked away, twisting back toward her screen.

Not paying attention to her words, I looked beyond her head, leaning a little to the left to get a better view out of the windscreen and the grassy embankment beyond the far perimeter.

Narrowing my eyes as a thought crossed my mind, I turned back to the laptop and, much to Daisy's annoyance, minimised the camera feeds again before pulling up Google Maps and tapping in the postcode of our position.

Soon finding the large grey rectangle and the vast roof of the building we parked next to, I pinched my fingers across the trackpad, zooming in as far as I could. Everything was in the same place as I'd expected and already viewed on my phone just before I'd given the briefing.

The car parks stretched down on either side of the building. The fence tracked the perimeter. With no vehicle access to the rear, the narrow gap between the building and the fence was blocked by two small compounds loaded with equipment.

Beyond the far fence and over a short mound of earth covered in grass I could also see through the windscreen, there was another much larger car park serving a building about twice the size of the one we were beside. The sight brought with it a question.

Were they hiding in plain view?

The thread fell away as the radio came alive.

"Red." It was Tommy, his voice hurried. "What was that?"

I looked sideways, swapping a glance with Daisy, her brow furrowed as she shook her head.

"This is Red. Clarify," I said into the radio, before listening to a moment of dead air.

"The building shook," he added, "after what sounded

like a clash of metal."

"Wait one," I said, as I switched the view back to the cameras to scour the feeds. When an explanation for what he'd said wasn't obvious, I leaned across Daisy and looked at each of hers.

When neither of our screens showed the cause, I went back to mine to pick over the detail from the three external cameras.

"Nothing," Daisy said, pointing to her laptop where a handful of images were replaced with those from the other two vehicles.

It only left one place to check.

Pulling off my seat belt, I hunched over, pressing my hand on Daisy's knee for balance as I clambered into the front compartment and landed in the driver's seat.

Scanning the controls, I was pleased to see they were much like the other armoured vehicles I'd driven and not dissimilar to that of a car. Finding the ignition button, the engine jumped to life as I pushed at the round of metal.

"What are you doing?" Daisy said, joining me in the passenger seat with her computer resting on her lap.

"I need to check," I replied, and with a lurch, we rolled forward as I released the parking brake and pressed my foot on the accelerator, whilst glaring at the gap between the fence and the metal siding I'd seen for the first time in person.

"You can't drive this," Daisy said, her voice hurried and gripping the seat as we sped towards the fence.

Hoping I hadn't left it too late, I stomped on the brakes, pushing harder when we didn't slow as quickly as I'd expected. Then, holding the wheel tight, I forced my foot down with all my strength.

The fence moved, bowing out as we rocked to a stop. I looked to the right, waving my hands for Daisy to get out of the way, then reached out and eased her to the side.

After pushing with a little more force, I saw the fence had fallen a short way beyond the edge of the building. Squinting for better focus, I drew back when I caught sight of a transit van with its bonnet buried in the building's panels as either steam or smoke billowed out.

Clambering to the back, I grabbed the radio and pushed it to my mouth. "All units. We have a breach at the rear. I repeat, a breach at the rear. Prepare for contact."

With the last of the three acknowledgments coming over the air, and about to call Clark, a tap on my shoulder caused me to turn to Daisy who, with a furrowed brow, stared at the laptop screen.

"Red," she said, before turning it around.

My gaze fell on the slightest movement on the rear camera.

Leaning in, a figure with the bulk of a man was dressed in black and carried what I thought was a shotgun over his shoulder as he rushed between the gates we'd smashed through, heading towards the door our team had blown off its hinges only minutes earlier.

88

Scrambling back between the front seats, I grabbed an SA80 rifle from the rack and released the magazine. After confirming the thirty five-five-six NATO standard rounds filled the space, I pulled the cocking handle back and let it return.

"What are you doing?" Daisy screeched, chasing after me despite the confines.

Rather than reply, I pushed the rear doors open and jumped to the road, soon framing the figure through the scope.

He froze as his balaclava-masked head turned towards me.

With just enough pressure on the trigger, I held the view, waiting for him to react whilst my brain raced to understand why his form looked so familiar. Was he another member of the squadron sent by the higher ups to observe, who had instead decided to lend a hand? Or was he perhaps one of our friends caught out by misplaced confidence?

When none of my answers seemed to fit and with my earlier radio message warning of an imminent attack having raised the chatter in my ear, I forced myself to focus on the figure's dark tactical clothing, which appeared much like ours but with subtle differences.

About to take a step, the rear floodlights from the back of the Ridgback burst on, bathing the figure in bright light and forcing him to squint, despite the distance.

Still eyeing him through the scope, I pressed a little more tension against the trigger as I stepped forward.

"Raise your hands in the air or I'll put a round through your eye," I shouted, watching as he complied. "Now identify yourself. Delay and you're a dead man."

With obvious and slow movements, the man raised both his hands. His right went to his face and pulled down the dark covering.

Realising I'd stooped, I stood up straight, taking my eye

from the sight when I could hardly believe what I saw.

With a sideways smile, Dylan O'Connor lowered his hands to his sides but kept his palms out flat and facing to the ground as I shouldered the rifle.

Still not quite ready to believe what I saw, I watched his every step as I matched his movement to close the gap between us. The radio chatter continued to intensify and for a moment, I thought about pulling out the earpiece to give room for my thoughts.

"What the hell are you doing here?" I said, arriving within arm's reach.

"I'm here to do what I should have done five years ago," he said, raising his chin.

Still confused, I shook my head. "But why?" I asked, watching his cheeks bunching with a thin smile.

"Not long after your second visit, I realised you were wrong," he said, my eyes squinting ever so slightly. His hands raised as he spoke again. "I realised I *was* once you, but I'd forgotten what that meant. Now I'm here to put things right. If you'll let me."

Impatient to understand how I felt about his arrival, I couldn't help but narrow my eyes. What he'd said made some sense, but with all that had gone on, could I trust him?

A shiver of doubt ran up my spine.

"How did you find us?" I asked, taking a step back.

"I also came to understand," he said, nodding, his words softening as he raised his brow, "that you never retire from our job. Once you're in, you're part of the family for life."

I tried my best to take his words in, but so many questions kept rolling around in my head. About to give them a voice, a muffled succession of three gunshots cut off my train of thought and I turned towards the open doorway next to me, just as Hollywood's voice cut through the others in my ear.

"Contact."

89

"Fuck," I said under my breath, as I turned to the doorway and took a step, stopping when I felt a touch at my upper arm. Spinning around to glare at O'Connor, he pulled his hand away as he shook his head.

"Don't be stupid," he said, looking at me as if over a pair of glasses he wasn't wearing. "If you charge in full of fear for your men, and with just that pea shooter, you'll be no good to anyone. You know they're more than capable of taking care of themselves."

He was right, of course. With no sign of what the scientists were creating, they were the best fighting force the world had to offer for dealing with other men.

I turned away, jogging back to the Ridgback with O'Connor following.

No more gunshots had spiked my fears by the time we arrived at the open back doors of the armoured vehicle.

"Sit rep," I said in between breaths. The vehicle's bulk didn't move as I rushed up the steps whilst Daisy lowered the Desert Eagle and made way for me to take my seat so I could scan the matrix of camera feeds.

"False alarm," she replied, not taking her narrow-eyed stare from O'Connor.

After setting the SA80 down on the table, I looked toward her heavy gun and shook my head.

"A manikin," she said, pushing the gun back into its holster at her thigh. "Who the hell?" she soon added, still looking at O'Connor standing in the doorway.

"A manikin?" I said with a shake of my head, before I followed Daisy's finger, pointing out a square on the screen where I glimpsed the washed-out white of a naked figure with a tight formation of three holes in the centre of its deformed forehead.

Narrowing my eyes, I tried my best to push away concern at the uncharacteristic lack of discipline.

"Red." It was Hollywood's voice. "We're turning on the

lights. It's too much of a risk."

"Roger that," I replied, touching at my radio, then focused on the laptop screen as a dark arm reached out to the wall and pressed at a light switch. Four screens flashed bright, but as a loud, distant bang filled the air, the sound crystal clear through the open doors, the images darkened.

"Lights failed. Do you hear that?" Hollywood said, his voice fighting with the whine of a high-pitched siren in the background.

"Received," I replied, just as a plume of smoke rose along the centre of the external camera's view down the back of the building. "With me," I said to O'Connor as I jumped from the seat, the rifle back in my grip. "We need to check that out," I added, pointing to the screen when Daisy looked over, her brow furrowed with uncertainty before her gaze latched back onto the man standing next to me.

"Who is he?" she said.

"An old friend," I replied, turning to leave.

"Are people just turning up now? Should I expect any more guests?" she said, and I could tell she was doing her best to keep the whine from her voice.

I shook my head and turned to leave.

"Red. Remember your orders."

I looked her in the eye. "Things have changed," I replied, handing my rifle to O'Connor. "On the ground, I call the shots. Now hand me my body armour."

Daisy didn't move, other than to fold her arms across her chest.

"And if I don't?" she replied, her brow lowered. "I won't be an accessory to your crimes."

"Don't be a fucking child," I said. "Your men's lives are on the line."

Daisy raised her chin. "Will you treat me like a traitor if I don't do as you say?"

Letting out a breath, I scrambled up the steps, thankful she leaned to the side and let me bend to pull up the heavy vest, before lifting it up from behind my seat. As I stooped over, I leaned so close to her face I could feel her breath.

"Don't make this into something it's not," I said, almost in a whisper as I held her stare. "And don't get in the way of those men's lives."

She was the first to turn away and I dropped back down to the road, pulling the vest over my shoulders before drawing up the zip and taking the rifle back from O'Connor.

"I'm going to check out that noise," I said, not looking at Daisy before I turned away.

"Red," she said, and I glanced back, ready to shut her down. But rather than speaking, she held out my helmet, which I took and placed on my head.

"Thank you," I said, before pushing the doors shut.

Peering toward the transit van as we jogged, by the time we'd covered the short distance to the alley behind the building, the white steam rising from the crumpled metal of the engine compartment had almost stopped, leaving grey smoke billowing to the sky from beyond.

"What's going on between you two?" O'Connor said, slowing as we stepped into the building's shadow.

I sighed.

"I mean, what was that all about?" he said.

"I found one of the team passing information to our friends."

"Ah," he replied. "And she doesn't agree with the standing orders?"

"No," I said, feeling a weight, some of it at least, lift from my shoulders at being able to talk to someone who knew I'd had no choice.

By now, strict radio discipline had returned and neither of us spoke as we stepped with care along the building before clambering over the metal struts of the fallen fence, drawing closer to the van embedded in the building's metal panelling. As the distance shrunk, it soon became clear that the low thrum of an engine wasn't coming from the vehicle we'd reached.

Checking the ground before I placed my feet, with O'Connor following, his shotgun drawn, I moved around the back of the van and its open doors. With the rifle leading the way, we found the rear empty of all but a lingering smell I hoped was due to the nerves of those who'd been inside and not the alternative I didn't want to think about.

Remembering I'd meant to call Clark to check to see if they'd had any luck with the CCTV, when a change in the wind's direction washed acrid smoke across my face, I instead turned in search of the smoke's source. Only a short distance away was another vehicle, a minibus, but with no sign it had crashed, the smoke seemed to come from further along.

Deep gouges trailing in the mound's mud and thick clods of dirt collected in the wheel wells told of the minibus's journey before it came to rest. The sliding side door stood open, as did both at the front. At almost an equal distance between the two vehicles were a set of double doors, leading into the building with darkness beyond.

A loud snap of a small explosion made me crouch, but finding myself not peppered in shrapnel, I stood, rushing around the rear of the minibus where my gaze was drawn to flames licking up the side of a large grey metal cabinet which, despite the mangled metal of its door and the surrounding scorch marks showing the fire hadn't started by itself, I spotted yellow electrical hazard signs.

They were right. There was indeed a danger of death.

Thin smoke rose from a chimney set in the top of a smaller red cabinet at the damaged box's side and what I guessed was the source of the low rumbling sound.

"All teams, this is Red," I said, holding the talk button down. "The power's out. No chance of…"

My words cut short as the muffled boom of an explosion came from inside the building.

90

"What do you see?" Daisy's voice came through the radio as I let go of the button.

"Captain. Clear the air," I said, not needing to wait long for Hollywood's voice to take over.

"Confirmed contact."

"I see smoke. Is the building on fire?" Daisy said, not hiding her concern.

Stalking side by side with O'Connor, I walked back around the minibus, shaking my head when I saw her standing halfway out of the top hatch in the Ridgback's roof.

"Negative," I said, her arm raised high above her head, beckoning me over just as a subdued clap of a shotgun round caused me to turn. The darkness beyond the double doors felt as if it were drawing me in, leaving me desperate to know what headed toward our men.

"You're needed here," Daisy said, her voice sharp as if she'd read my mind.

"I'll go," O'Connor said at my side.

Glancing over, I caught sight of something through the minibus windows.

"Give me your radio and I'll report back."

Not acknowledging his words, I stepped closer to the van, cupping my hands on either side of the rear window as I pushed the front of my helmet up to the glass and peered in at the empty ammunition tins strewn across the interior.

With my heart beating hard in my chest, I turned to O'Connor and then to Daisy back at the armoured vehicle, torn between whether to deny my nature and walk away from the danger, or to step back to the safety of the metal shell and take command like I was supposed to.

"Argh," I growled, soon lowering my noise despite being desperate to scream at the top of my voice. With a look up, the blinking anti-collision lights high in the sky reminded me of the many reasons I had to get this right.

"Thank you," I said, then with a nod toward O'Connor,

I pulled out the earpiece, snatching the handset from my belt. After securing the radio in place, he slid a switch on the torch under the shotgun before rushing between the open doors without a glance back.

Disoriented by the lack of voices in my ear, I forced away the growing regret as I jogged back to the Ridgback, watching Daisy lower herself down and pull the hatch closed.

Sealing the rear doors behind me, I scanned the images next to which Daisy had already rested her radio as voices clambered for time on the air.

"What's happening?" I said, as I tried to pick out what was going on from the camera feeds.

"Multiple contacts," she replied, distracted by her own search across the images.

Flashes of light brightened the cameras scattered across the screen, with many of the squares a chaos of light and dark and different shades in between; none of which satisfied my urgent need for information.

With regret ballooning in my chest, my skin crawling to push the doors open and find out for myself, I instead closed my eyes, drawing a slow deep breath. As the need to pick up the weapons and charge in guns blazing ebbed just enough, I opened my eyes when a distinct voice called on the radio.

"We're pinned down."

Despite not recognising the owner, I didn't linger in my attempt to place it as another voice soon filled the void.

"We can't move."

I looked at the images again, leaning towards the screen in hope I would see what they were facing, but before I could get the handle I needed, Daisy's outstretched finger pointed at the screen.

The square I locked onto was completely black.

"Is it broken?" I said, glancing over.

With her eyes wide, she shook her head. As if to confirm her diagnosis, the square image brightened just a little before fading to black again. Her finger moved and I saw another three shared the same view.

"Bravo, this is Red. Report," I said into the front of the radio.

Hollywood's voice came over the line. "Multiple contacts. Some kind of armed resistance. We're pinned down."

"How many contacts and what's your position?" I replied, as I tried to figure which of the cameras belonged to the sergeant.

"Impossible to count. We're on the first floor and have covered about a quarter of our search area, but other than these mercenaries throwing lead at us, it's just offices and empty space."

Kicking myself when the report added weight to my fears that Lonsdale had drawn both of our organisations to this place to knock the stuffing out of each other, I clenched my grip around the radio.

"Received," I replied. "Charlie. Report."

Tommy's voice came without delay. "Same situation. We're pinned down. They have assault rifles."

"Received, Charlie. Delta. Report."

Dead air was the only reply to my first call and continued when I repeated it twice more, staring into a square of darkness.

"All callsigns. Delta is down and you have a new single callsign in theatre. His designation is Echo."

Two acknowledgements followed in quick succession.

"Echo. Report."

"This is Echo," O'Connor replied. "No contact yet, but I don't like what I'm seeing. The place looks like someone's just moved in. There are half empty boxes around what look like labs with multiple signs of a struggle."

"Any signs of the occupants?" I replied, his words the first to suggest I might have come to the wrong conclusion.

"Nega…" O'Connor said, but his voice was drowned out by a gunshot. "Contact. Contact. What the hell?"

The transmission cut off and I waited a moment, listening out for another report, but I soon had the radio back up to my mouth when I could wait no longer.

"Echo. Report. What do you see?"

After a few seconds, a rushed and garbled voice came over the air, then cut off before I could hear anything meaningful.

Glancing at Daisy, I shook my head. We had one team down and the other two pinned and ineffective. With O'Connor not replying, I had to fear the worst.

Despite the weight of the unseen aircraft overhead feeling as if it could force me into the ground at any moment, I reminded myself I'd rather die than let myself crumble.

Standing, I pulled the shotgun from where it rested on the floor.

"Red?" Daisy snapped, her tone high, but not giving her a chance to follow up, I swung the muzzle toward her.

"I will not let my men die like this. If you try to stop me, you'll find out how much of a monster I really am."

91

Daisy kept quiet as her mouth fell open. I dropped the shotgun's aim and knelt, filling the pockets of my armoured vest from an ammunition tin behind my seat. With just enough space to slip the antidote pouch into the last pocket, whilst keeping my eyes on Daisy, I reached behind me to open the door before jumping down to the road.

When Daisy stayed silent and made no move to hold me back, I felt for the Glock in my leg holster and then to the pocket in my combat trousers to confirm I still had the spare magazines. Pushing the steel up, I jogged toward the two double doors through which Delta had disappeared, all the while trying not to envision the four men laying dead somewhere inside.

My mind cleared as I stepped over the threshold, focusing instead on the wide circle of light projected along the corridor from under the shotgun and the sight I'd already seen through the cameras.

Not letting the surrounding muffled gunshots ruin my stride, my aim swept from side to side, but despite the floors and walls not stained with blood or potted with fresh holes, I forced down the frustration of not being able to communicate.

It wasn't long before the corridor split, leaving me with a choice either side. But after peering down each and finding both as plain as the next, the same cameras in their far corners, I chose the left, hoping Delta had delved deeper into the massive space.

I ignored the doors I found either side, knowing the team had already searched those they could access, choosing speed instead in hope I might change the immediate course of history.

The corridor soon split again, and hugging the left-hand wall, I peered around before repeating the same to the right, where a scattering of dark marks on the floor ahead tugged at my interest.

Directing the torch toward the stains, I squinted at the marks in the distance as I took cautious steps. Soon realising I hadn't heard the exchange of gunfire for a short while, hope and fear in equal proportion battled to win over my concern that one side or the other were victorious, but without a radio, I had no way of knowing.

The sound of faint footsteps pushed the thought to the side.

Pausing my step, I span the torch around, but reassured with the sound gone, I headed back in my original direction.

The sound came again, but this time out in front and was almost a mirror image of the noise my boots made on the polished concrete floor. I halted once more, raising the torch a little higher, but found nothing ahead other than the slight bend in the corridor.

When the noise didn't repeat, I shook my head, telling myself the sound was an irregular echo, perhaps an artefact of the corridor's design. With the concern pushed to the back of my mind, I forced my focus to the blood and the smeared prints of military boots beside the litter of strewn brass casings and the occasional spent red shotgun cartridge.

Visions of the conflict that had caused the mess filled my mind. Lifting the shotgun, I could just about see the faint streaks along the corridor guiding me along the same route they appeared to have dragged their fallen.

About to pick out a path to follow, another sound pulled my thoughts away. Not those of the battle, which were still in a lull, but soft footsteps I couldn't at first decide from which direction they were coming.

Still unclear if they were from behind or ahead, when I saw no other sign as I scanned the light all around and despite feeling they could just be in my head, I pushed my back against the wall and turned off the torch.

Peering into the pitch black, I waited, glancing to the left, then the other way, all whilst aware of every second that passed. Despite knowing I should retrace my steps to make sure I wasn't being stalked, with no evidence other than the steps, which each time I concentrated, I concluded were coming from a different direction, I had no other choice but to move.

Covering the head of the torch with my left hand, I pushed the gun's weight against my armour and slid the switch. As my hand glowed red, I retook the gun in my right, then spread my fingers apart to give just enough light for me to navigate the mess.

Cursing the sounds playing through my head, I followed around the kink in the corridor whilst adjusting my fingers to give a little more glow, finding the haphazard trail led to a door on the right of the corridor.

With a glance back to reassure myself nothing had changed, I pulled my hand away from the torch and squeezed my eyelids closed just enough for them to settle as I pushed the stock into my shoulder and stepped towards the door.

Pausing long enough to confirm no sound came from beyond, and pleased to hear the footsteps had gone, I grabbed the handle, twisted and pushed the door open.

Four bodies lay face down just beyond the threshold, each dressed like those I searched for.

The bloody trail led to the figure on the far right. The white and red of the field dressings against the dark of his combat attire singled out the wounds on his arm and leg. Stepping over the threshold, I didn't linger, instead swinging my aim in a full arc, confirming the small space was clear except for a scattering of small cardboard boxes.

Dropping to my knees, I placed the shotgun against the wall for the light to bounce off the ceiling and brighten the space, before manhandling the first trooper to the left, rolling him onto his back.

The driver of our Ridgback had a slow, feint pulse at his neck, but not able to find any injuries to account for his lack of response after manipulating him into the recovery position, I moved to the next. Each of the first three were the same, their pulses a little higher or lower than the one before, their hair and exposed skin soaked with sweat, but with nothing to explain the reason for their state.

I sniffed the air, despite knowing it would be too late if I found what I'd sought, but when the smell of lingering propellent and the metallics of the wound were all I found, I shuffled to the far right of the line.

The trooper moaned as I tugged him onto his back whilst keeping clear of the hastily applied field dressings, each soaked a deep red. Despite his pale expression, the pulse in his neck throbbed against my finger.

With nothing more that I could do for them in the moment, taking the shotgun back in hand, I stepped into the corridor where it took me more than a breath to realise a bright light glowed from the direction I'd arrived from.

As the light dropped, I brought my aim to bear, only to find Daisy pointing the Desert Eagle in my direction, the muzzle flaring as she pulled the trigger.

92

Only as the immense echo decayed did I realise my body hadn't split wide, but a clatter of metal from behind me caused the relief to subside. Turning on the spot, the light from my underslung torch found a figure crumpled in a heap with another bright beam bathing the plain wall at their side.

Spinning back around, my aim found Daisy with her weapon still raised, and for a moment I couldn't tell if she still pointed it down the corridor for cover or directly at my head.

"What are you doing here?" I whispered when our gaze's locked, but instead of replying, we held there for a long breath, until with a twitch of her head, in unison, we lowered our aims.

"Come see," I said when she still hadn't replied, turning away as I beckoned her over. Her footsteps and torch brightening the corridor told me she'd jumped into motion. "They're okay. For now, at least," I said in a whisper, pointing out the four men curled in the recovery position.

"What happened?" Daisy whispered, as she stepped into the side room and crouched at their feet.

"I don't know. It must be some sort of drug," I replied, watching as she repeated my tentative sniff before shaking her head.

"Why didn't we put them in NBC suits?" she asked with less volume than before.

"Keep the ass-kicking for the debrief," I said. Leaning over, I placed my hand on her shoulder and she stood, backing out of my reach. "We need to get this place cleared so we can get them the help they need."

"I couldn't leave you on…" she said, before I cut her off with a raise of my hand as I focused on the fallen figure just before the next junction in the corridor.

Raising the light, I glanced away from the bloodied chunks of flesh and bone sliding down the far wall as I stepped closer, reminding myself that by ignoring what I'd heard, the figure with a hole in his head could have been me.

Only hearing our collective breath as I arrived, I peered down at the man dressed in jeans and a scruffy grey jumper. The bullet had punched a neat hole just above his right eye, but other than deforming the socket, the wound gave no tell of the empty ragged mess I knew I'd find on the other side. Not that I had any intention of looking.

Pushing away the urge to congratulate Daisy on the shot, my attention instead fell to his side and an odd shaped pistol-sized weapon discarded close by.

Crouching, I took another look. I knew weapons more than most, but the compact metal looked like something out of a science fiction film, its details not recorded in any of the reference books I'd studied.

"What's he doing with a tranquilliser gun?" Daisy said, peering over my shoulder.

I stood squinting at the realisation, but before I could come up with an answer, Daisy stepped to the body and pulled at the man's shoulder.

You're not so squeamish now, I thought, as she manhandled the body onto its front to reveal the gory cavity at the back of his head and a small leather bag I hadn't spotted with the strap crossing his chest. Relieved I'd not given the words voice, I watched her pull the satchel open; it wasn't the place or time to ramp up friction between us.

With an echo in the distance I'd already promised myself I wouldn't ignore, I lifted my head and my aim, but finding nothing I hadn't expected, Daisy raised a plastic syringe up at my face, my focus drawn to the feathers at the end.

"Drugged. You were right," she said, her brow low.

Much investigation had taken place around the world into the use of tranquillisers as a non-lethal method of incapacitation for law enforcement, but it was almost universally agreed that the chances of overdosing the target were too great, and at a safe dose the drugs were too slow to nullify the threat at a useful speed.

I shook my head, not able to understand how they'd taken out our four men who were at the pinnacle of the elite.

"Get on the radio and tell the teams what we know," I said in a low voice.

"Which is?" Daisy said without delay.

I thought for a moment. She was right, of course; we knew little they could use.

"Okay. Tell them if they can't clear their positions, at least keep the enemy busy. I'm going in."

After relaying the message and nodding confirmation they'd all replied, pinching her torch between her lips, she pulled a thick round from her pocket, slipped the magazine from her gun, and filled the space before sliding it back home.

"I'm coming with you," she whispered, the torch back in her hand.

My immediate reaction was to shake my head, but knowing now wasn't the time to argue, and welcoming the power of the Desert Eagle, I motioned along the corridor before covering the end of my torch to dull the brightness.

Following suit, she turned her light off and together we crept along the corridor. But with a raise of my clenched fist, we stopped when a muffled panicked call came from ahead, its volume rising as dull light filled the empty corridor.

Killing my light, we pushed ourselves against the wall. With the continuous loud click I recognised from a taser, the cry's tone rushed higher, soon turning to a shriek of pain before ending with a heavy thud as the sounds halted, replaced with laboured breath.

I froze, struck with a sudden fear I'd hoped I'd left at the bunkers. Unable to move my feet or speak at the sounds of wet flesh I didn't want to linger on, it was all I could do to pull breath.

"Please," a voice whined, the tone giving no sign of the owner's gender.

"Come on," a man snapped in reply. "This way. There are plenty more to find before you're done."

93

A whimper followed the harsh command and with it, control of my muscles returned just as the light that had glowed from somewhere out of sight faded. Switching the torch back on, I rushed toward the junction, using my shoulder against the opposite wall to stop myself so I could make the turn.

With a huff of breath as I hit the plaster, my torch's beam brightened a double set of doors which had just settled closed, but rather than rushing after what had gone through them, my gaze fell on a figure in jeans and a white t-shirt convulsing on the floor in what I guessed was a slick of his own blood.

Arriving at the prone man's side as he thrashed his head this way and that, foam forming at his mouth, I couldn't help linger on the skin and muscle that had once allowed him to talk but now hung loose down his chin.

He threw up, turning his head to the side before spewing vomit across the floor as I jumped out of the way. Then as his stomach stopped emptying, he caught my eye as if seeing me for the first time, mumbling something I could only guess was a cry for help.

I knew what I had to do.

"Close your eyes. We're here to help," I said, and he did as he was told as I dropped my aim to his forehead. With my finger tightening on the trigger, I glanced over my shoulder, only just able to see Daisy staring at the man wide-eyed before catching me looking right at her.

She swallowed hard as she saw my raised brow and the angle of my weapon, then tipped her head before stepping back and turning.

I pulled the trigger, then slipped in a replacement round.

"We should call it in," she said quietly at my side, and I turned toward her. "Now we know what we're dealing with, I mean."

I shook my head. "It's nothing they weren't expecting,"

I said, then twisted away, heading towards the double doors.

My gratitude to leave the vomit's stench behind was short-lived when it was soon replaced with another I knew so well, the foul odour of sewerage intensifying with every step. Pushing away the concern as we neared the pair of double doors blocking the corridor, my gaze fell onto a smear of blood on the right-hand side.

Not glancing back to Daisy, I instead forged on, knowing indecision would get me killed. But still I slowed as I saw an access keypad at the side of the door with the rectangular magnetic locks protruding from the ceiling.

If this door no longer remained locked, then what would happen to the others we might find that were supposed to hold back the dangers they were engineering in this place?

Covering my light again, I gestured for Daisy to do the same just before I shouldered the door open enough to find it dark on the other side. Pushing a little further in, I swung the gun around, removing my hand from the end of the torch to reveal the full force of the light.

The beam swung fast around the wide room, highlighting scattered tables and chairs filling the space at regular intervals. But rather than like a canteen, besides the tall stools were sofas and tables of different heights, the place seeming more like a breakout space of a high-tech company than anything else.

As the cone of light found another double door at the far end, I couldn't be sure if it too had just settled from moving.

Having paid little attention to the detail of the room on the first turn with the torch, I repeated the gesture more slowly the second time, swinging the gun through the arc and picking out doors along both of the side walls. Each had no name, just numbers up high, much as we'd seen before.

Distant gunfire came from a direction I couldn't determine, the first I'd heard in a little while, causing me to pause and move again only when Daisy spoke somewhere from behind in a low voice.

"All clear?"

When nothing new revealed itself, no bodies on the floor or signs of someone hidden behind the furniture, I walked into the space, doing my best to avoid the drops of blood around my first few steps.

Daisy followed. Staying silent, I plotted a course through the centre between the spilt furniture. As the door closed behind us, Daisy's light scoured the room.

Sporadic muffled shots somewhere in the building kept my senses keen, but meant I had no chance of listening too hard for signs of activity nearby. Having reached the midpoint of the room after guiding the way around the clutter of chairs laying on their side, I felt a tap on my shoulder.

Glancing backwards when she'd not spoken, Daisy gestured with her head to the left and I turned to follow, at first confused when I saw her bright beam highlighting a blank wall off to the right. It was only as I felt her guiding me to turn to the left, that I looked a little more closely, concentrating on the darkness.

Before I could bring my gun around to follow, I felt her other hand hold it back, just as I saw a thin strip of light, the first we'd seen in the whole place, coming from under the door to the left.

The light was so dull it was no wonder I hadn't seen it before.

HELLFIRE

94

Staring at the dull light under the door to the left where Daisy had guided me in the otherwise dark and spacious hall, I swept the shotgun and its underslung torch across the walls for the third time.

Finding it much as I'd already seen, I turned to Daisy with obvious movements, turned off my light and motioned for her to do the same.

Despite the question hanging on her expression, she did as I asked before I took a gentle hold of her jacket cuff and guided her with soft steps around the toppled tables and chairs I'd plotted only moments before.

Nearing the door and hearing nothing from the other side, I grabbed the handle, wrenching it down before pushing against it as hard as I could.

The door opened to just over a finger width before hitting on something hidden behind. Pushing all my weight into my shoulder, I shoved, only opening the door a little wider as what sounded like chairs scraped against the floor on the other side.

Daisy soon joined, adding her weight, and together we forced a space wide enough to fit through.

Swinging the shotgun through the opening, my aim swept to the first corner and into a room lit with an eerie white glow. With the corner free of concern, I scoured around to the right and a black painted wall, then directed myself the opposite way, finding a bank of tv monitors arranged in two rows hanging on the adjacent side.

Still with no threat in sight, I bounded in through the opening, sending my aim to the extreme left whilst paying little attention to the ghostly images on the screens.

The dark walls formed a room just a little smaller than a domestic garage. Behind the door stood the motley collection of office chairs, stools and short tables I'd expected, but all with no sign of who had set up the barricade.

With a glance back to my right, I scanned the array of screens, half of which were blank. Suspecting what I'd seen were at least two figures slumped in otherwise empty corridors, and despite seeing the occasional person walking with their hands against the walls as a guide, I tore myself away and swept my aim across the room once more, knowing there had to be someone hiding.

A hum of computer fans came into focus as Daisy stared at each screen, in front of which were built-in desks cluttered only with keyboards and mice, the space underneath seeming empty.

Trying my best to ignore the renewed muffled gunfire, I crouched, then slid the torch's switch before running the beam along the underside of the desks in search of what I could have missed.

About to shake my head when I'd revealed nothing new, the light caught the far left end of the row of monitors and the desk in front, and realised there was a dark opening rather than a continuation of the wall.

Sliding the switch to kill the torch, I stood, pointing two fingers toward the space and waited the moment it took for Daisy's aim to join mine in the same direction.

"It's clear," I said whilst shaking my head.

She nodded, seeming to understand as she took a step away and shoved the door closed.

With the lightest steps I could manage, and with the shotgun leading the way, the hum of computer fans intensified as I crossed the threshold. To the right, I found a compact dark room lit with a sea of LEDs blinking a rainbow of colour.

"Don't move," I screamed, tightening my finger on the trigger as my torch beam highlighted a man in a t-shirt and jeans cowering at the base of a server cabinet.

95

With my words still echoing around the small space, I took a step forward as Daisy's light sprang on at my side to highlight a dart gun clattering to the guy's feet. With a sharp crack, a thin clear liquid spilled from the loaded syringe.

"Don't shoot," he screamed, pressing his hands against his face.

"Get your hands in the air," I shouted at the top of my voice, with Daisy repeating the same call.

Flinching with every word of our verbal assault, he forced his hands high but succeeded only in banging against the computer equipment above his head.

Taking another step and holding the shotgun steady in one hand, I grabbed at his t-shirt, yanking him forward whilst ignoring the yelp as he fell, his arms springing out to catch his fall.

"Hands in the air," Daisy screeched as I pulled him up to his feet.

His quivering arms raised high.

In the low light from Daisy's torch, I took a step back and slung the shotgun over my shoulder. Then, reaching up, I grabbed his arm, pulling it low, before taking hold of his wrist and twisting him around so I could grip the other.

I ignored the huff of air as I pushed his face against the black plasterboard, blanking out his squeals as I pulled his wrists as high as his joints would allow without breaking, then looked around the room, following Daisy's light as it glanced across the view.

Finding no new threats in the cramped confines, my gaze landed on a container overflowing with bright coloured cables.

"Can you?" I said, nodding to the box. The light went with her as she stepped to my side, plucking the first cable from the top. As I angled my hands out of the way, Daisy wrapped the pink cable in a figure of eight around the guy's wrists before tying it off with a double knot.

After a quick test of the bounds, I felt him relax as I released his wrists, instead taking hold of his arm and turning him around to face us. Padding his pockets and feeling nothing that could do me any harm, I pushed the flat of my palm against his solar plexus, pinning him to the wall.

With his face blotched red and eyes bloodshot, it looked as if tears had not long evaporated.

"What's your name?" I said, keeping my voice calm, but when he stayed silent and stared back, I pushed a little harder against his chest. "I said, what's your name?"

When he didn't reply, I delved into his pockets. Turning my nose up, I discarded a handkerchief before pulling out a brown leather wallet and handing it behind me.

"Mr Lonsdale. Nice to meet you," Daisy said over my shoulder.

I smiled, tipping my head to the side as I raised a brow. "You're not what I expected."

His gaze darted between us.

"Are you sure we've got the right man?" Daisy said. "He doesn't look like a murderer."

I turned back, tilting my head to the side. "What do they look like, exactly?" I said.

Daisy lifted her chin and stood a little straighter. Then, as if about to say something, she shook her head.

I looked forward and leaned in close, pushing my face right up to Lonsdale's. "There's no mould for their kind of sickness," I said, pressing harder on his chest as his eyes looked like they could bulge out from the sockets at any minute.

"Why's there power in here and not everywhere else?" Daisy said, and his head twitched to the side as he seemed relieved to look elsewhere.

"There's an emergency generator," he replied and I nodded, remembering the hum from the red cabinet beside the smoking substation.

"Get your people to lay down their arms," I said, keeping my voice calm. But when his blank expression stared back, I grabbed him by the front of his shirt, manhandling him along the wall and into the other room.

Paying no attention to the screens, I pushed against Lonsdale's chest, forcing him to stumble backwards towards the far wall. Before he could reach it, I swept his legs out from under him. Once his squeals had stopped and he'd tried his best to sit up, despite the improvised handcuffs, I looked away and glanced across the images, working from left to right.

The first was of a long room filled with two rows of beds and reminded me of an old school barracks; but with disordered and unmade sheets, that's where the similarities ended.

The second showed the room beyond where we stood and seemed much like we'd left it.

The third was an equal size but with rows of benches with inbuilt sinks and glass-fronted fume cabinets lining each wall.

The fourth and fifth were long, anonymous corridors. The sixth showed what was perhaps an office with a couple of desks. Movement soon drew me closer to four heads cowering in the far corner as they stared at what I could only guess was the door, each of them dropping back for cover with every round of echoing gunfire.

The seventh showed the end of a corridor with a jumble of tables and chairs lining one side, and every so often an assault rifle appeared from around the corner, followed by the echo of gunfire, the muzzle flash coming a split second later.

Movement on the last screen drew my attention, my gaze skipping those in between when I found nothing of note. But as I settled on the screen, all I saw was an empty corridor.

"Talk," I said, turning to look down at Lonsdale staring at Daisy by my side. When he didn't reply, I stooped, slapping the back of my hand across his face.

"We're just doing research," he said, his voice high and quick as he looked up. "We're doing good things."

"I'm sure that's what you believe," I replied, raising a

brow. "Now tell me where you keep your abominations."

Lonsdale's cheeks bunched as he squinted. "What?" he said with a shake of his head. "I don't understand."

With a glance over my shoulder to Daisy who looked up from Lonsdale, I turned back and crouched, leaning my face right up to his.

"You know what I'm talking about. You knew full well what you did to those people in Brass Pike and Copper Flail," I said, poised for his denial. But instead, he lifted his chin as his expression hardened.

"That was a mistake," he said, his voice low and words considered. "That's not what I meant to happen, and it's got nothing to do with our work here."

Holding his gaze, my eyes narrowed as I stood. "You're telling me you have no human test subjects?" I said, lifting my chin.

He nodded and swallowed hard. "We're researchers. There won't be human testing until the stage five trials, and that won't be until we've provided sufficient evidence to the authorities that it's safe," he replied, his words charged with a renewed confidence.

"Safe?" I scoffed. "I've seen the aftermath too many times already, and I know what caused the injuries we saw in the corridor."

"I don't know what you're talking about. All I know is you lot came in your big trucks all dressed in black, blowing the doors off before creeping down the corridors," he said, looking at me with his face bunched up. "Then the gunshots and explosions started."

His words seemed accurate enough, and I turned to Daisy before glancing at the monitors. How was he to know it wasn't just us attacking?

"Where are your people?" I said, after finding nothing useful on the screens.

He shook his head. "By the time I got the cameras back online, they'd scattered. The building's big and there's not many of us," he said, looking between the pair of us.

"How many?" Daisy asked.

"About fifty. Give or take," he replied without delay.

I glanced over at Daisy. "Where do you keep your guns?" I said, looking back.

"Guns?" he replied, shaking his head. "We're scientists, not cowboys."

After striding back to the computer room, I picked up the tranquilliser gun by the handle whilst taking care not to touch the clear liquid dripping from the muzzle.

Arriving back, he flinched as it clattered against the floor at his side.

"Oh, that," he said, shaking his head. "They're for the chimpanzees. You can't blame my people for defending themselves," he added with a shrug, but I'd barely noticed, my mind instead filling with visions of blood-thirsty apes, who were naturally strong, now gripped with an overwhelming need to feed on whatever they could get their hands on.

96

"Monkeys?" I said, glancing past Daisy toward the door.

"Apes. They don't have tails, and they're not due until tomorrow," he said, nodding.

Despite my best effort to keep the relief from my face, Lonsdale burst out laughing when I turned back.

"We're not making zombie primates," he said with a final chuckle before his expression dropped. "We're here to find the cure for old age and you're going to ruin everything."

Stepping forward, I brought the mouth of the gun up to his forehead, watching as his expression fell and his eyes went wide as I pushed against it.

"If I find out you're lying," I said, leaning down toward him, "nothing would give me more pleasure."

"I'd believe her if I were you," Daisy's voice came from behind me.

"I swear. I swear," he replied without delay, shaking his head as much as the gun's pressure would allow. "We're not experimenting on people. We're not."

Pulling the gun away revealed a red O on his forehead. I glanced back over at the screens.

"If it's not one of yours..." I said, almost under my breath, my gaze darting to the far left screen when movement caught my eye.

Edging closer to the screen, I watched what looked like the back of one man as they led another. The one behind held his right hand up. Expecting to glimpse a gun, or perhaps a taser ahead of him based on what I'd heard in the corridor, they disappeared out of shot too soon and didn't reappear on any of the other screens.

"Why are half the cameras not working?" I said, glancing back at Lonsdale.

"The generator doesn't give enough power," he replied, distracted, as if the image had raised the same question.

"I don't see many of your people," I said. "If we're right

about what I saw, then under no circumstances can we let that thing find them."

"If they all turn, we might as well turn the lights off," Daisy said.

"They have to be hiding. But where?" I said, glaring at Lonsdale. "We're not here to hurt people. We're just here to mop up the mess you started at Brass Pike. Where are your people?" I said, doing my best to take the urgency out of my voice.

His brow twitched, then he moved his head in a slow nod.

"We're doing good things here. I assure you. The data we're collecting will be world changing," he said, his tone rising again.

"That's not our concern," I replied. "But listen up. If we don't get this place secure, then your precious data and your people, including us, will be wiped from the face of the planet."

He swallowed hard as he glanced between us and then at the images.

"There's a basement," he said, rushing out the words. "It's the main plant room and storage area and where I told them to evacuate to in the event…"

"Get them on camera," I butted in, motioning to the screens with the shotgun.

He shook his head, swallowing hard. "There's none down there."

"Get up," I said, stepping forward and grabbing him by his collar. "In which case, you'll have to show me yourself."

His legs gave way as he shook his head, but after swinging the shotgun onto my shoulder, I grabbed him with my other hand and he got to his feet.

"No. No. No. If what you're implying is out there, then what if it finds us? The basement entrance is just the other side of the door. Not far at all," he added, gesturing his head to the side.

"We want to find it. That's the whole point," I replied, pushing him back and pinning him against the wall with my forearm as he tried to twist around to show me his hands.

"At least take these off," he said.

About to blurt out a reply, the sudden change of the fan's tone caused me to turn to find Daisy out of sight.

Dragging Lonsdale by the upper arm, I pulled him around the corner where I found Daisy standing at the front of the computer rack, unclipping disks from their mounts and stuffing the thin drives into her pockets.

"No. Stop that. What are you doing?" Lonsdale said, taking the words right out of my mouth.

"Captain?" I snapped when she'd taken no notice.

"The research," she blurted out.

"What…?" Lonsdale replied before glancing over, my expression stopping him from saying any more.

"We have bigger problems to deal with. You said yourself what will happen if it gets in amongst those people," I said.

She paused, turning to look me in the eye, and held there for a long moment as we stood in silence.

"Okay. Let's fast forward a year," I said, taking care with my words as I tilted my head to the side and fixed her with a stare. "Am I coming after you?"

97

Letting out a nervous laugh, Daisy's cheeks bunched as she shook her head.

"Of course not," she said, standing tall and stepping back from the tall computer rack.

"Good," I replied, nodding with an exaggerated smile. The corners of my mouth dropped as I turned around. "We've got no time to waste," I said, pushing Lonsdale into the centre of the space, where I glanced over at the CCTV camera feed of the room on the other side of the door.

Finding the way clear and still with the shotgun hanging on my back, I gripped Lonsdale by the upper arm and eased past the jumble of furniture to open the door, before peering out into the darkness, poised to slam it closed if the need arose.

With nothing jumping out of the darkness, I pulled Lonsdale past me, shoving him out into the open.

Despite his yelp and twisting around, about to protest, he calmed as I shrugged the shotgun into my grip with the torch's beam brightening the double doors we hadn't yet stepped through.

Daisy's light soon swept out from my side, combing across the view before returning to the same doors.

"Lead the way," I said, jabbing the muzzle against Lonsdale's back when he didn't move. He twisted toward me again, his face pale in the torchlight. "It wasn't a question," I said, prodding him harder this time.

Taking a step, he stopped as an explosion, which sounded like it came from just outside the doors behind us, sent a shockwave through my chest.

Daisy spoke into the radio.

"That's the last of your yellow specials," she said, after pausing for the reply to her request for an urgent report. "Bravo think they've broken the stalemate."

Nodding, despite being unsure how I felt about having none of the explosive cartridges remaining, and knowing they could have made such a difference to where we were heading, I prodded Lonsdale with a soft jab, forcing him to move toward the double doors.

Joining him at his side as he arrived, I pushed the barrel of the gun against the wood to ease it open where the beam cut through the darkness in the corridor, picking out doors cutting off the long space ahead and lining the walls either side of the otherwise empty area.

Shouldering the door wide, I pushed Lonsdale through first.

"Where now?" I said in a whisper.

"The stairwell is…" he cut off, just as quietly, before stopping in his tracks as I followed the motion of his head to a trail of blood from the far end of the corridor, which led to the furthest door on the left.

"You don't need me anymore," he said, shaking his head with his volume rising. "That's the one, it'll take you to the plant room. It's only one level down."

"Quiet," I replied, prodding him with the shotgun to force him on.

As he dragged his feet, I couldn't help but agree with him. If he stayed with us, he'd likely get in the way, but the only alternative was to let him run loose, and that just wasn't a sensible option. Who knew what chaos he'd cause, or how quickly he'd get himself killed? Or perhaps he'd run out into the open, sending the bombs to pull the building down over our heads.

"You're staying with us," I said, pushing him on with the end of the gun.

"Red," Daisy said, and I stopped, glancing back. "Bravo and Charlie have cleared their positions. Shall I direct them our way?"

I shook my head, not needing to think.

"Are you sure?" she said, furrowing her brow. "If it's down there, don't we need their help?"

"No," I replied, without skipping a beat. "Get them to cover the exits, but they must stay inside until I give the all clear."

After a moment's silence she whispered the order, then gave one word replies to the questions I guessed would come after.

"Anything from Echo?" I said, leaning closer before turning back and pushing Lonsdale along when I heard him step backwards.

Before Daisy could reply, I raised my fist when I heard footsteps ahead.

With our lights off in a snap and our backs against the wall, I strained to pick out detail whilst keeping my aim down the corridor on the emerging low light from under the double doors ahead.

"Get on the radio," I said, keeping my voice low.

"Echo. Report your position. We're in theatre and can see a light." Despite her whisper, the words seem to carry in the darkness.

The light ahead went off before it flashed on again with barely a pause.

"Affirmative," she said, her volume growing. "It's your mysterious friend," she added in a different tone.

Still, I kept peering along the sight as the double doors opened with light bouncing down the corridor, washing towards us before it paused to highlight the blood stains.

"What are you doing in here?" O'Connor said, after bounding over and glancing at Lonsdale in the torch light.

"Long story, and good timing," I replied, as I ran my hand to the torch to turn it back on.

"Take him," I said to Daisy, grabbing Lonsdale by the arm and dragging him towards her.

Daisy's eyes widened, almost glowing white from the light bouncing off the walls.

"Take him and find the others."

"But…" she said.

"That's an order," I interrupted.

When her eyes narrowed and her familiar scowl returned, I was ready for anything she'd say. Instead of putting up a fight, she took Lonsdale by the arm and pushed him off to walk ahead as they retraced our steps.

"What have you seen?" I said, leaning in towards O'Connor.

"A small band of armed men, but I took care of them," he replied, then shook his head. "I found a couple of guys," he added, but stopped himself as he closed his eyes.

"Did you take care of them?" I said. "We found one too, with half his face ripped off."

O'Connor nodded. "I did what I had to do."

Mirroring his gesture, I looked along the darkness and raised the shotgun to bring the light up.

"We have around fifty civilians in the basement," I said, nodding in the same direction as my aim. "But they're not alone," I added, turning to look him in the eye.

O'Connor stared at me for a long moment.

"It's what you came here to do," I said. "But now's your chance to turn away. No hard feelings. My dreams are already screwed, so I've got nothing to lose."

He held my gaze for a long moment, but as a muffled scream cut through the air, he turned to the door.

"To be honest, I don't sleep that well and retirement's not what it's cracked up to be."

With our torch beams bouncing up and down as we ran the short distance, neither of us paused at the door as O'Connor took the lead, rushing through to a renewed chorus of screams growing in volume.

Racing down the concrete steps side by side, we followed a thin scarlet trail whilst trying not to breathe in the hint of sewage hanging in the air.

Arriving at the bottom of the short flight, with no other choice but a single door, O'Connor shouldered it wide, charging into the darkness and pausing only when he found a choice of left or right on the other side. After only a brief delay, he stepped to the right as I swept my light in the opposite direction.

The screams had stopped and we'd left the bloody trail back in the stairwell.

Finding a set of double doors with a keypad at the side and magnetic contacts protruding from the ceiling, I turned back to O'Connor to find him glancing over his shoulder.

"Split up?" he said, but I shook my head. Not lingering on the decision, he turned away, already striding to where the raw concrete walls branched either side again.

Taking the left, which ended with another set of double doors, we found more lining the walls, but each were locked.

The screams were back, louder this time, and with the volume growing with every moment, we settled our aims on the double doors. When the noise grew to such a clamour, I turned side on, pushing my back to the wall. Just as O'Connor did the same, the doors flew open, and I tightened my finger on the trigger.

A crowd of people rushed out, but we kept our restraint, ignoring the panic in their eyes as I tried to look at each unfamiliar face running past, oblivious to either of us despite our bright lights.

With too many people to count, I searched for the end of the group, readying myself for whatever chased them.

98

I'd paid little attention to the shrill noise of the receding crowd, but by the time they'd disappeared out of earshot, nothing had burst through the doors we'd kept our aims levelled at.

"Tell the others. They need to know," I said, not looking away from the beige door lit by my underslung torch. "Radio all callsigns. Tell them again not to let anyone exit the building under any circumstances."

"All callsigns," O'Connor began in a whisper. "This is Echo. We have multiple civilians rushing up from the basement. Red's orders are to ensure they do not leave the building."

"And use any means to stop them," I said, listening as he added my words to the radio message.

Despite a desperation to move to a more comfortable position, I held my ground, staring ahead as I waited for O'Connor's confirmation they'd received the command.

"Nothing back from any callsign," he said after a long moment, as I imagined him shaking his head.

"Shit," I replied and for the first time I looked away, glancing at O'Connor staring ahead. Wanting to do anything but wait, I felt the almost overwhelming need to push the doors wide and hunt out what had caused the stampede. Every moment it remained loose meant another infection that would amplify our task, soon causing a devastating avalanche of monsters we'd have no way to defeat. But first we had to get that radio message to the teams, or we were dead anyway.

"There's a Tornado flying above our heads, ready at a moment's notice to rain down hellfire if anything or anyone leaves this place before I call in and say it's clear," I said, doing my best to keep my voice even, despite having heard a new rush of footsteps echoing close. "We have to go back upstairs and get that message through."

Without moving his head, O'Connor peered up to the

ceiling as if he might see the aircraft through the concrete above us.

"I'll go," he replied. "It'll take two minutes."

"I'll come with you," I said, but having already turned, he glanced back and shook his head.

"It makes sense to hold our position. I won't be long," he replied and I turned back to the door where I'd heard a male voice. Glancing over my shoulder, O'Connor was already halfway down the corridor.

Settling my breath, I kept my feet planted as I tried to think of anything but the torment of coming face to face with those things again. Instead, I concentrated on the passing time. Sixty seconds came and went. Another twenty passed before a vibration in my pocket stopped the count as I realised somehow my phone had signal, but the radio hadn't.

Dragging my gaze from the doors, I pulled out the phone to find Clark had tried calling twice and had sent a text message.

They'd tracked two vans leaving the position in Maidenhead and confirmed there were no other vehicles involved.

Before I could explore what the message could mean, the distinctive boom of a shotgun shocked the air from behind. Not thinking twice, I turned and ran towards the sound.

99

It seemed as if the corridor stretched as I ran with the beam of my torch bouncing up and down with every long stride until I slowed. Swinging around the corner, I found the single door to the stairwell closed and the pair ahead sealed shut.

With no ejected cartridge or any other sign O'Connor was in trouble, other than the smell of propellant and the call of the discharge that had faded long ago, the muffled sound of a struggle emerged through the double doors.

A chaos of flickering light greeted me as I kicked the door wide, along with a tangle of brawling figures I couldn't yet unscramble. Only with a rapid succession of clicks, followed by a pained and strangulated call did I bring my light to bear, highlighting O'Connor pushed against a wall by Brown, his bloodied face contorted in a frenzy.

For what felt like a long moment, I stared at sharpened metal claws on the end of his fingers as he grappled with the shotgun O'Connor gripped with both hands like a bar to block the attack.

Behind the man we'd been hunting all this time, stood another just out of arm's reach, holding a pole with a handle on the end and a trigger much like a litter picker. Similar to a rigid leash, the pole connected to a bright yellow collar around Brown's neck with wires spiralling out to a backpack.

The man squinted over as if unsure where to look, surprise printed on his brow as his head jerked back and forth with indecision, before eventually he dropped a torch from his other hand.

I fired.

The rapid clicks ceased and Brown calmed almost immediately as the man's body hit the floor.

Panting, Brown seemed to let O'Connor push him back, and Brown looked toward me, his bloodshot eyes wide and stained mouth hanging open as if confused at what was happening.

Feeling a sense of relief, not fear, as I held Brown's gaze, the sensation grew as I realised that having brought Brown to this place and with both the vehicles they'd travelled in accounted for, all we had to do was sanitise the building and the nightmare would be over.

With elation rising through my chest, it took me a moment to notice Brown had stepped towards me, but with my aim centred on his forehead, highlighting his slack, down-turned mouth, I wasn't concerned.

Out of the corner of my eye, O'Connor raised himself up. Too late, I saw him swinging the shotgun around and bringing his aim towards Brown's head.

"No," I called out, rushing forward, desperate to get the short word out.

I was too late. The boom of the shotgun's report enveloped my voice as the solid round clashed against the metal collar. Brown jerked to the side as sparks showered from the point of impact to the chorus of frantic clicks breaking through the echo.

Brown's expression tightened in an instant and he turned, pouncing on O'Connor and sinking his teeth into his cheek.

Flesh flew from Brown's arm as I fired at point blank range and he pulled his head away, teeth still clenched and gripping ripped flesh. He staggered sideways and swiped his arm out, the back of his hand catching my chest, knocking the wind from my lungs as I landed hard on the concrete. Pain shot up my spine, the shotgun scattering to the floor and sending us into near darkness.

Scrabbling for the weapon as my fingers found the metal, I jumped to my feet, bringing the torch up just in time to catch Brown heading through the doorway and toward the stairwell. My shot splintered the door jamb as I stepped forward, but about to run, my heart sank as I turned the light onto O'Connor and what remained of his face.

"Make it quick. You've still got a job to do," he said, my thoughts flashing to the syringe in my pocket, but only for a moment before I pulled the trigger.

"I'm sorry," I said, then took a deep breath before leaning down, unclipping the radio from the corpse and ripping the cable from the handset.

Stepping between the two battered doors, I raced toward the stairwell, hoping I could catch up before it got to those who'd run away.

Before it got to Daisy.

100

"All call signs. Do you copy?" I called into the radio as I pounded up the stairs. "Daisy. This is Red. Are you receiving?"

The radio felt misshapen in my hand and with only fragmented voices replying as I rushed, I stopped at the top of the stairs and glanced at the set. The black casing had separated along the side seam and was missing a small plastic section of the base, the rest covered in scuff marks.

Smacking the side of the radio against the wall, the two halves snapped together with a satisfying click, and I pushed the handset up to my mouth as I shouldered the door open.

"Multiple civilians rushing to the exits. Do not let them leave the building or we're all dead."

Garbled voices and static replied.

"Daisy. If you can hear this, Brown is on the rampage. Find somewhere to hide. I'll come get you."

Clipping the radio to the front of my body armour, I pushed through the first set of double doors and swung the shotgun's light around the wide space where we'd found the CCTV room and Lonsdale. With nothing out of place, I slid a new shell into the chamber to the sound of a commotion from the other side of the doors just ahead.

I didn't slow as I rushed across the room, barging the door wide to find a dull light highlighting a disappearing stampede at the far end of the corridor. But my focus soon fell to the body scattered on the floor, his remains spread across the corridor with his bloodied mess smeared and stomped into the concrete, carried along by the stampede.

A crackle of electricity echoed out, bringing with it the rapid clicking of Brown's taser collar as I peered down, hoping to swerve and avoid much of the mess. By the time I'd passed enough of the gore to lift my head, my light landed on the distant backpack with the hanging pole bouncing up and down as Brown ran.

Ahead, the corridor split and I raced to recall the way

we'd come as some of the crowd he chased veered to the right, while others headed straight on, followed by his pained calls.

Closing the gap, my heart sank when I spotted Daisy's dark body armour and her arm outstretched as she dragged Lonsdale at her side.

Dismissing the thought of taking a shot for fear of hitting the innocent, I pumped my legs harder, somehow closing in. But so it seemed was Brown, and I didn't know how long I had left to catch him before he got to Daisy.

Despite my desperation for her to let go of Lonsdale and save herself, I held my tongue, knowing she wouldn't listen. Instead, I fired a single round at the edge of the wall, but the bang did nothing to distract Brown and instead ignited a renewal of the shrill calls, just as I spotted what I hoped was another corridor leading to the right, bringing with it a recollection of our earlier route.

"Right," I screamed at the top of my voice, hoping Brown would follow those choosing to keep on the straightest path.

Daisy followed my suggestion, veering out of sight whilst pulling Lonsdale along without slowing.

As did Brown.

"Oh shit," she called, just as I pulled the trigger, taking the first chance of him alone. The round smashed into his arm before he vanished down the corridor, leaving a trail of blood smeared against the wall.

Breathing heavily, I sped up, having slowed to take the shot. About to turn the corner after what felt like an eternity on my own, a high visceral call rushed out, followed by a squeal.

Rounding the corner, my breath felt sucked from my lungs when I realised I'd directed Daisy down a dead end.

With Lonsdale only just out of Brown's reach, he fell, taking Daisy with him as she grappled in vain to keep him vertical.

101

Brown couldn't have dropped any quicker to follow if someone had swiped his legs from under him. Giving me no choice but to fire, the round smashed into his lower back but did nothing to stop the blood gushing in the torchlight as it spurted up, with Brown's face buried in the crook of Lonsdale's neck.

Still running as I pumped the slide, Brown's head rose with a sickening tear of flesh, but about to shoot again, I glanced to the right to find Daisy to ensure she was clear of the firing line.

Finding her scrabbling backward on the floor, the Desert Eagle was nowhere to be seen as she tried her best to push herself along the wall on her ass, her disgusted stare fixed on Brown's face.

Retaking my aim, I shot again, hoping the round would do so much more the closer I'd got. The dripping wound at the base of his back spread wider, scattering vertebrae and sending him flopping forward, but still he grasped out, catching hold of Daisy's ankle.

I pumped the slide again, but she was too close and I'd almost caught up, watching helpless as Daisy grabbed the disks she'd stuffed across her body armour and chucked them at his face. Each glanced off without even a flinch as he pulled her closer.

"Save the research," she shrieked, as I aimed at the backpack and pulled the trigger, point blank.

The incessant click stopped, as did the constant convulsions I'd not noticed before, only obvious once they'd stilled. Its grip on Daisy's ankle relented and, pushing herself by her feet, she moved out of his reach as the room fell silent, broken only as I pumped another round into the chamber.

Lit by my aim and with awkward movements, Brown slowly rolled onto his back and lifted his head. His bloodied lips turned down at the edges and I thought perhaps I saw the man behind his bloodshot eyes as tears streamed down his face.

"I'm sorry," I said, then pulled the trigger, but with a dull click, the round jammed in the chamber.

He didn't move, not even blinking as he stared down the barrel. With a boom I recognised as Daisy's hand cannon, the magnum round shattered his head as I waited for the shockwave to ebb.

Smoke caught in the light as I brought the shotgun around, not surprised to find her holding the Desert Eagle raised.

But as my pocket vibrated, I hadn't expected to follow her gaze to the bite on her ankle weeping blood.

102

Lifting the phone from my pocket, my hand felt wet and as I raised it up in the dull light, I found blood soaking my palm and a deep ragged scratch at the base of my thumb. Closing my eyes, I sighed, remembering back to when Brown had knocked me down and the sharp pain I'd felt but ignored.

"What's your status?" Clark said as I accepted the call, the phone sticky in my hand. Concentrating on the blood making its way down my wrist, I stayed silent.

"Agent Harris," Franklin took over. "Are you there?"

"Call off the RAF... It's under control..." I said, doing my best to put myself back in the now, rather than replaying the moment he'd knocked me to the ground. "Brown's dead... Permanently, and he was the last... The perimeter is secure," I added, turning to stare into Daisy's eyes.

Moving to lean the shotgun against the wall, I slid down to my ass.

Clark cheered in the background and a chorus of claps replied from the speaker.

"Well done, Carrie," Franklin said, the relief clear in his voice.

"It's not a well-done situation, sir," I replied. "We fucked up," I added, still staring at Daisy.

"Are you injured?" he asked, and the noise in the background lowered. "Because we found more of the antidote and all tests show it should work just fine. You've just got to be quick to administer it."

I hung up the call. "That's great news," I said, but just to the darkness.

"What now?" Daisy said. "I mean for you. My story's already written," she added, looking down at her ankle. She smiled as I shook my head. "I bet within a week you'll be out there killing bad guys and saving the world again."

I looked down at Brown's body, the mess of electrical wires exposed in the backpack and the blood-covered metal collar around his neck.

"I don't know if I can do this again," I replied, my words soft as I yanked up the Velcro pocket of my armoured vest.

Pulling out the pouch, blood dripped to the concrete floor.

"Oh shit," Daisy said, looking over as another drop joined the other. "I guess that makes two of us that are fucked," she added, looking away for the first time.

I didn't reply. Instead, without taking my eyes off her, I pulled the Glock from its holster.

"Well, I had a good run," she said, before breaking into laughter.

I couldn't help but smile as I straightened my arm and aimed the gun.

Daisy flinched as the two shots smashed into Lonsdale's skull.

"Be quick," she said. After glancing over to see his body settle, I turned back and found her looking down at her hand resting on her lap. "Fuck it. Wait a minute," she added, holding up a finger. "If I can't say it now, then what's the point?" Daisy looked down at her armour and began pulling at the Velcro to get to the zip. "We could have had fun, you and me."

I shook my head and she bit her lower lip.

"I would have enjoyed that," I said. "But you'd have soon found me out."

She stared back. "I already know you're a cold-blooded killer."

I shrugged and shook my head.

She looked away.

"You'd find out that I'm not such a great person to build a life with," I said.

Daisy laughed, turning back. "Wow," she replied, tensing as if with pain as she pulled the zip down her front. "You're getting ahead of yourself," she added. "I said we could have had some fun."

Nodding, I smiled as she looked away. I knew where it would have gone, like it had every other time I'd grown close to someone.

Daisy moved her arm out to her side and gripped the Desert Eagle by the barrel before reaching over.

"For me?" I said, raising my brow.

She shrugged then laughed. "You've been lusting after it since we first met."

I took the weapon, already enjoying its weight in my hands.

"You'll have to do yourself," she said, her voice tailing off. "I can't."

"Where did you get it?" I replied as I looked down at the shiny metal which seemed to glow despite the low light.

"Spoils of war."

"That sounds intense," I said, looking up.

"It was. I swiped it during a raid on a Taliban drug factory. Back when life was straight forward."

Taking great care, I placed the heavy gun on the floor before pulling up the pouch and opening the flap.

"What's that?" Daisy said as I pulled out the syringe.

"An antidote for his condition," I said, nodding toward Brown's remains. "A single dose, I'm afraid."

"You had it all this time."

I nodded. "I only just found out it should work."

"Well, I guess this isn't where it ends for you. At least now you won't have to worry about my report."

"That's true," I said. "But then again, I've never been a worrier."

"Can you do something for me?"

"I'll try," I replied.

"Can you give someone a message?"

"A message to whom, or is it who? I can never remember which it is," I said, gripping the cylinder of plastic in my fist and readying my thumb on the plunger.

"That nurse. The one you saved," she replied.

"What's the message?" I said, not letting my intrigue colour my tone.

"Tell her I thought she was fit and that you and her would have made a great couple."

Laughing, I shook my head and pointed to Daisy's right. "Look," I said.

As she turned her head, I leaned over, pushing the needle into her ankle and pressing the plunger. "Tell her yourself," I added, my voice echoing as she sucked air through her teeth and grabbed at her ankle.

Picking up the Desert Eagle, I stood and walked down the corridor into the darkness.

"Thanks for the gun," I said without turning.

Epilogue

Some people travel to see nice things, or perhaps nice places, or maybe to find themselves. My need for travel has always been for another reason and I've spent much of my adult life on the road. Not homeless, but certainly of no fixed abode.

I have no bills to pay. No gas meter to top up with credit. No tv to licence. No broadband subscription.

I have everything I need. A random bunk in the Brecon Beacons to call my own for a night or perhaps a week, or at any allied military base, or embassy anywhere in the world. Or a hotel from five to a single star, should the need arise. Or any number of safe houses, or properties rented in some else's name, the details taken care of by an administrator who I'll never meet, and who wouldn't know who I am, real or imagined.

I have all the money I could ever spend in five lifetimes, but I've bought nothing for myself. It just sits in a series of hidden bank accounts waiting for if I ever want to change my life and do things that other people seem to fill their days with.

I'd never travelled for myself.

I'd never travelled for pleasure, or to find my elusive self, but after the last few weeks I needed to let the bruises heal and to answer a question, and it turned out I *am* the kind of person who could laze by a private pool with nothing to do but slowly cook under the Spanish sun.

Travelling light with only a single name and address in my mind, I used contacts in France to gather the essentials, then drove for two days in a four by four with the AC turned up higher the closer I got, as I lost myself in thought on the long right-handed stretches of road.

I'd spent days in the coastal hills of Torrox, sunning by the pool, and I wasn't long away from eating tapas in the local restaurant with a few beers to the side.

I'd not drunk beer since Sandhurst, almost a lifetime

ago.

My mind switched off during the day, filling the hours with books from a small library gathered from the ghosts of the previous occupants. The cool nights were for exploring.

Admiring the near perfect view, the walks were a necessity. On the first couple of days, at least. One reason was to keep my fitness high, and boy, did they do the job. Up one side of the mountain, then across to the peak opposite, then repeating in reverse, giving me time to relax during the day.

I left my phone on, but those back where I called home knew not to trouble me, not even with life and death, because that was all I'd dealt with anyway.

The long hot days were like medicine for my mind, reminding me what normal life meant, to other people at least, helping to show that it didn't have to be about living out your nightmares.

I kept the place tidy, almost as if I wasn't there, the fridge stocked only with the essentials, none of which I'd taken from the local supermercado's brown paper bag.

As day four slipped into five, enjoying the rays whilst floating in the pool on a bright green lilo, I thought perhaps I'd seek someone to share the place with. For a day or two at least. Perhaps the waiter from where I'd lunched, or the waitress with the deep tan and skirt that hinted at her perky ass. The thoughts vanished as my phone pinged and I turned to look at the mountain range over the balustrade.

Slipping from the inflatable and into the water so much colder than the air, I pulled myself up the short ladder and dried with the towel I kept laid out at its side.

Reaching for the binoculars under the shade of the balcony above which I'd only ventured to once, I sat back in the wicker chair beside the pillar holding up the concrete above my head. Putting the optics to my eyes, I pointed the business end to the right of the column, then moved my fingers to focus on the white walls of the extravagant villa nestled in the distance.

The sensor I'd slipped into place days before had done

its job, alerting me to the fleet of three SUVs settling on the long driveway.

Taking the binoculars with me, I headed inside. Grabbing a white dress, knickers and bra from the small case, along with two white towels and the long and heavy black bag I'd picked up from my associates as I'd arrived in the continent, I climbed to the roof.

Spreading the first towel over the hot concrete, I unpacked the long bag, but having made all the preparations as I'd arrived, all I needed was the last component. With it slipped into the neat space, I laid on my front, spreading the second towel over my back before pulling the bolt back.

Within ten minutes of settling my eye on the scope, I squeezed my finger against the curved metal, then re-centring the view, I confirmed success whilst pushing away a tinge of sadness that the holiday was over.

Refreshed and ready to get back to what I did best, I grabbed my suitcase along with the food from the fridge and was out in the car before the echo had barely scattered.

With a glance at the healing cut at the base of my thumb, I knew I'd found myself again. All I'd needed was a little luck, then a break, some sun and to wipe another wicked man from the earth.

Visit my website for more details, an episode guide
and for free books!

www.gjstevens.com

All my books are available from Amazon on
Kindle, paperback & audio.

Search 'GJ Stevens'

Agent Carrie Harris Action Thriller Series

If you like high-stakes thrills, strong female heroes, and action-packed adventures, then you won't be able to put down these intriguing novels.

In The End Zombie Apocalypse Series

In The End is a fast-paced post-apocalyptic zombie thriller. If you like nightmarish settings, reluctant heroes, and action-packed adventures, then you'll love these spine-chilling novels.

Agent Carrie Harris short stories

In Harm's Way

On what seemed like an ordinary morning, Carrie finds herself in the crossfire of a violent bank robbery. As the horrible scene plays out before her experienced eyes, she must find a way survive the encounter, and save the day.

Out of the Blue

Waking in paradise with no memory of who she is, can Agent Harris piece together the true picture and retrieve her skills before it's the last thing she ever sees?